The Desk from Hoboken

A Genealogy Mystery

ML Condike

Karen M. Ford (1950 - 2019)

*A beta reader
who provided insightful feedback
while undergoing cancer treatment.
Her contributions live on in this story.*

Chapter One

"Come on, girl! It'll be fun." It was mid March and I stood in my bathing suit on the edge of our pool in Wyncote, Pennsylvania. Our corgi, Sophie, watched from ten feet away, ears flat against her head. Her look suggested she wasn't joining me. She didn't like water, never mind fifty-eight-degree water. It would be shocking.

Every year, my husband, Sam, and I vied for the title of First-In-The-Pool. Today, I was determined to swim and win regardless of the pool temperature.

"It's now or never!" I leaped in, submerged, and then in a split second, shot straight up out of the frigid water. "It's cold! It's cold! It's cold!"

Sophie circled the pool, barking as I splashed my way to the steps and climbed out.

"Phew! What a wake up call, Sophie!" I toweled my hair while she licked my wet legs.

"You win!" Sam shouted from the back door, saluting me with his steaming coffee mug.

"I'll be in as soon as I dry off."

He grinned, disappearing back inside.

Five minutes later, I grabbed the hot mug as the last fragrant squirts of Cinnabon coffee gurgled from the Keurig. Something had changed in me overnight. It could have been the promise of spring, with the leaves budding, but I had a hunch it had something to do with the phone call from late yesterday afternoon. A potential client needed a genealogist.

Whatever it was, I felt alive again. Smiling, I joined Sam in the breakfast nook.

"You look happy. Finally beat me to the first dip. How was it?"

"Bloody cold." I sipped my coffee in silence. The strong brew made my lips tingle. Or maybe it was simply rekindled optimism.

I, RaeJean O'Leary Hunter, a notorious workaholic, hadn't entered my home office since the mental fog set in six months ago. Life's current had pulled me under. Today, I'd resurfaced, gasping for a breath of fresh air.

Sam gazed at me over the rim of his mug. "Thinking about returning to work?"

"Actually, I am. I received a voicemail late yesterday about a case that could be a good segue back to work. Easy, I think." My stomach fluttered at the prospect, but I knew I had to take the plunge, not unlike diving into the frigid pool in order to feel like a winner again. I smiled to myself.

Sam grinned. "That's great. Maybe we should resume the office remodel."

"I'd like that." We'd purchased the house as is and had been remodeling for a while. Actually, it was more of a restoration, but we'd suspended our work when I got pregnant. If I took the case, I'd need a workspace other than our library.

"Great. I'll call the contractor." He kissed me and disappeared into his office.

After rinsing my cup, I scrambled upstairs with the intent of checking on my neglected office and preparing it for the work crew. I rushed past the door to the room where I'd wallowed for months. After two steps, I froze. A lingering compulsion sabotaged my plan. Instead, I stepped back and entered the unlit nursery.

Scooping up the stuffed bunny that Sam had bought the day we'd learned I was pregnant, I sat in the Boston rocker, reliving the months after our loss. The tiny bunny sprawled across my lap as I agonized over the only thing I tended to worry about since that time, the secret I'd kept from Sam.

Determined to move on, I sucked in a breath and glanced down at Sophie. "Big girls don't cry."

It worked. Today, I didn't shed a tear.

I stood, tossing the toy onto the chair. "Let's go." I followed the dog as she padded out the door.

* * *

After yesterday's call, there was a chance I'd landed a routine case that would finally stimulate me. As a forensic genealogist, I'd mined online DNA databases and mapped family clusters to locate the relatives of fugitives as potential candidates for FBI agents to interview. I'd become proficient and could undoubtedly return to high-profile cases, but I was worried that I'd lost my instincts for the job.

Better to start slow.

My older sister and only sibling, Caitlin, would be pleased. Five years my senior, she'd mothered me most of my life, especially after our dad walked out, leaving our mother to work two jobs to keep us afloat. Since Mom died, she'd been my closest and best friend, except for Sam.

Caitlin suggested I accept a kinship project, assisting in the search for someone's ancestor or lost relative to help me ease back into the rat race. My gut said she was right. It was time to rejoin the living and say goodbye to the sloth I'd become.

The case sounded simple. Professor Michael Carver, Head of the Anthropology Department at Connecticut College in New London, wanted me to confirm the identity of human remains found on campus by one of his students. According to Carver, little of the original wooden casket survived, but the body was in remarkably good condition. They suspected it had been dislodged from one of several upstream historic cemeteries during a flood. In his voice-mail, he suggested the victim might be Mary Rogers, a woman originally found floating in the Hudson River in 1841, and whose final burial location was still a mystery.

From his brief description, the case sounded simple enough. He'd need three primary sources to prove Mary's body had been buried in New London. If not online, I'd probably find them in state or local archives.

I wiped dust off the chair seat and desktop, then settled at my makeshift desk while summoning the courage to call Carver. After a half dozen rings, my call went to voicemail. "It's RaeJean Hunter regarding the human remains. Please reach out if you're still interested."

I looked at Sophie, fast asleep at my feet. "Who's Mary Rogers?"

She cracked open one eye, sighed, then rolled onto her side.

I laughed. "My thoughts exactly."

Wrapping my arms around myself, I let out a long

breath. My skin hurt. Raw nerve endings, no doubt. Noticeable signs of life returning.

I was back in the game.

* * *

Sam had already left for the weekend when my phone rang the first few notes from Beethoven's Fifth Symphony, a tune I'd selected years ago. My stomach tightened at the sound. It used to charge my batteries, but no more. I made a mental note to change it.

"RaeJean Hunter," I said by way of greeting. "How may I help you?"

"It's Mike Carver at Connecticut College, following up on my voicemail. Austin Bradley recommended you. He claims you're the best forensic genealogist he knows. I could really use your help."

Austin was a lawyer I'd met several years ago at a conference. Typically, I hated dealing with lawyers, but he'd changed my opinion on at least one of them when we worked on the same FBI case. I'd used my DNA mapping skills, and Austin did what lawyers do. Jointly, we located the suspect's family.

"Is Austin involved?" I didn't mind, but I was curious.

"No, he isn't. We just go golfing together. Bradley got tired of hearing me moan after my genealogist quit. He recommended you. Like I told you in my message, I need help confirming the identity of hundred-eighty-year-old bones found on campus. We believe it's Mary Rogers."

"If you already have an identity, I can't imagine why you would need me." I relaxed, once again sensing an easy case on my hands.

He cleared his throat. "It's a long story. One I'd prefer to discuss in person."

"Okay." I hesitated, then asked, "Should I know who Mary Rogers is?"

"If you're an Edgar Allan Poe fan, maybe. It's a famous unsolved case that inspired him to write his second whodunit, *The Mystery of Marie Roget*."

"I liked a lot of Poe's stories, but *Marie Roget* wasn't my favorite."

Carver laughed. "Mine, either. But Poe believed he'd solved the mystery of her death."

"What happened to her? Why was the case so famous?" I couldn't recall much about her from Poe's version of the story.

"She fascinated the public. Youth, beauty, charm." He went on to tell how she'd clerked at a Manhattan cigar emporium, a regular hangout for New York journalists like the *Herald's* James Gordon Bennett, the *Sun's* Benjamin Day, the *Evening Post's* William Cullen Bryant, as well as writers such as James Fenimore Cooper and Washington Irving.

"And, of course, Poe," he added after taking a moment to think. "The daily penny presses went wild over Mary. Reported her movements like today's paparazzi do with celebrities."

"So, her youth, beauty, charm, and tragic death sold newspapers." Using her to sell papers gnawed at me, but with that kind of notoriety, I'd likely find sufficient data to conclude the remains could be hers.

"That's right. Will you take the case?" Carver asked.

Unsure if I was ready for a public appearance, yet fascinated by a project with a connection to Poe, I mumbled, "Maybe."

"I have the remains in my office, if you're interested. We could meet tomorrow around, say, one o'clock. I only teach one class on Friday afternoons. It's not until three-fifteen."

His offer to meet sounded more private than public, and he seemed anxious to begin. It wouldn't hurt to hear him out. Plus, I would love to see the specimen. I'd seen human remains before, but none that old, except museum mummies. "Okay. I'll travel up in the morning."

"Fantastic." Carver's voice conveyed relief. "I'll see you after lunch tomorrow."

* * *

My hands shook as I called my sister. Realization set in. I'd moved forward. It was a baby step forward, but a step in the right direction, nonetheless.

"Hey. You up for a weekend visitor?"

"Let me check my social calendar." Caitlin hesitated, maybe two seconds. "Looks like you are in luck, Cub. The Governor canceled."

I laughed. Caitlin had been a freelance reporter in and around Philadelphia for a decade. She lived in Granby, Connecticut, a little over an hour northwest of New London, not far from the Hartford airport, and had relocated there three years ago as an editor for a small local newspaper. Since her first job, she'd always called me Cub, claiming it fit me—small and feisty.

"Great. I have a meeting in New London tomorrow about a potential case. It shouldn't take long. I could be at your place by five."

Yes! A warm feeling washed over me. I loved spending time with Caitlin.

"What about Sam? Are you deserting him?"

"No, Sam deserted me. He left this morning to meet an antique dealer at a vintage furniture show in Boston. He won't be home until late Sunday night." I missed him already.

"What's the case about?"

"It's a confirmation-of-identity issue. I'll tell you about it over a glass of wine." I looked down at Sophie. "I have to call the Canine Fitness Camp. Sophie needs a place to stay."

After we hung up, I moved to the library window, hoping to settle my nerves. Cardinals flitted in and out of the cedar copse near the edge of our property.

I'd done it. My first step back into the outside world.

My mind sputtered, then shifted into gear as I planned my trip. I'd take the early morning train on Friday to New Haven, then rent a car for the weekend. On Monday, the train would take me from Hartford back to Philadelphia and I would be home by noon. I hadn't traveled in six months. Until now, I hadn't felt ready to separate myself from Sam or leave my home library.

I texted Sam, explaining I'd be spending the weekend with Caitlin. He sent back a quick thumbs-up emoji and a big red heart. He was my rock.

There was no way to deny it, I'd begun to crave the therapeutic buzz that came from working. I'd taken on easy projects before to recover from especially gruesome cases. Like eating strawberries at a wine tasting, it cleansed the mental palate. This case would be my strawberries.

Chapter Two

I arrived on campus at twelve-thirty, remaining in the car to wolf down the peanut butter and jelly sandwich I'd packed. After checking my teeth for remnants, I ventured toward the Winthrop House. A plaque outside the entrance indicated it was constructed in 1916 to honor John Winthrop, Jr., the founder of New London. Hard to imagine founding a city.

The hall was dark, except for a beam of light where Professor Carver's door stood ajar. I peeked inside and marveled at its resemblance to Dumbledore's office at Hogwarts. An arched beadboard ceiling loomed over cherry bookcases lining three walls. A cluster of dusty furniture blocked a wall cabinet in one corner.

I cleared my throat. "Excuse me. I'm RaeJean Hunter, here about the remains."

Professor Carver looked up from a lighted specimen case. "Please, come in and join me. I am fascinated with this nearly intact cadaver after almost two centuries."

I peered into the glass-covered display containing

human remains. Empty eye sockets stared back. Dark curly hair and brownish skin clung to the skull. The skeletal frame lay prone. Scraps of floral fabric hung from the leathery tissue still attached to the joints. I'd expected bare bones.

The air around the display case smelled musty, like soil recently sprayed with glass cleaner. An index card indicated *homo sapiens, female remains, approximately 180 years old, 5' 5" tall.*

At that height, she beat me by six inches.

Not sure what to say, I remarked on the condition of the remains. "She's well preserved."

"Yes. Luckily, she was packed in a clay substrate most of the time." Carver gestured toward a couch. "Please, have a seat. Let's discuss the project in detail."

The oversized loveseat dwarfed me. My feet dangled six inches above the floor. Carver fought a smile as I perched on the edge. His reaction was nothing new. Besides being petite, I looked nineteen—well, maybe younger. I was actually thirty-two.

I'd built a career, and now I only accepted new clients based on referrals. Even so, my youthful appearance sometimes caused concerns with the new customers until I proved my worth. A college professor would likely give me the benefit of the doubt after having taught so many brilliant female students of all ages and sizes.

I took the lead. "Tell me how your student found the remains."

Carver proceeded as if delivering a lecture. "Every spring semester in my advanced archaeology class, I assign a field project. Each student selects a site and postulates what they hope to find."

He paused to flick something off his shoulder, maybe a hair. "One fellow chose the isthmus on the Thames River by the boathouse, downstream from the Rogerene Cemetery."

"What compelled him to choose that site?" Rogerene was a new term to me.

"He hoped to find missing bodies from the cemetery. He'd built a fascinating model using historical map coordinates of the river. Over decades of flooding, the model revealed a shrinking cemetery and a small isthmus forming at the Coast Guard Academy's northern boundary. He hypothesized that the river had dumped the dislodged caskets there."

"I assume you agreed with him since you approved his project." It sounded reasonable to me, but I didn't know much about limnology.

"I've suspected the same thing. Most rivers change course over time. That's why we have an ongoing project to locate bodies buried within that cemetery." He leaned back, grinning. "Forty-one so far, with records indicating forty-four more that are yet to be found. The Rogerenes complicated things by refusing to mark their graves."

"And?" Travel fatigue crept in, playing with my attention span. I blinked to keep my eyes from glazing over. My mind wandered to the Rogerenes.

"We found original documentation indicating the cemetery was twice its current size."

"Interesting. And that fact led you to believe the remains are Mary, I assume."

He adjusted his chair. "Analysis of the physical evidence. The skeletal characteristics and bits of fabric indicate a female. Plus, DNA results from three independent labs converged, suggesting she's a descendant from two prominent families—Mather and Rogers."

I had noticed sufficient skin and hair still remained for a decent DNA test. Sometimes, all a lab analyst needed was one or two cells to develop a meaningful profile. Still, after so many generations, finding matching markers would be pretty iffy.

He held up a russet-colored expandable folder. "I've made copies of the DNA reports, my research notes, and a few other items. Irrefutable evidence requires confirmation documents, which is where you come in. We need three confirmable, primary sources."

"Which means additional research." *This sounds easy.*

"Exactly. We had a top-notch genealogist working on it for two months, but she resigned."

She, the professor had said *she*. Claire Allen, a friend from graduate school and the mother of my sixteen-year-old goddaughter, Emma, was the best female genealogist around.

Before I could ask Carver if it was Claire, he added, "I'm not at liberty to reveal her name."

That confused me. "Why not?"

"Per her request." Carver shoved the expandable folder across his desk toward me.

I couldn't explain it, but my rational side pricked a warning—*refuse the case*. If Carver's files included any supporting information, I wouldn't be there.

"You don't have much research data. I'd have expected a full banker's box by now."

"True. However, the genealogist quit suddenly, without explanation, and retained her work files. We offered more money, but apparently that wasn't the issue."

If it was Claire, why would she react like that? We'd

talked a few times over the last six months, but she never mentioned this case. She'd sent me a family-sized bag of M&M's on a regular basis to let me know she was thinking of me. I owed her a call.

"Austin Bradley is pursuing the work files," the professor added. "Legally."

"Yesterday, you said he wasn't involved." This surprised me, but I was pleased to have Austin on the case. We worked well together.

"I hired him this morning after the genealogist refused my latest call."

A bad sign. The original genealogist resigned without explanation and refused to cooperate. And Carver's twitchy right eye suggested he had a secret. I bit my lip, looking toward the display case. At least the specimen hadn't moved.

He finally spoke. "If my sponsor is correct, you could reveal a long-held family secret: Mary's final resting place."

"A sponsor? You're saying that the real client wants to remain anonymous."

"Exactly. You do work with intermediaries." Carver looked uncomfortable.

"I will. But typically, I prefer to work directly with the person paying the bills." Something didn't feel right, but I waited for Carver to explain.

"I'm handling things for a man I've known for years. He has a reason for anonymity."

"I'll take your word for it, but I'm still puzzled about how he got involved in the first place, and who wants to know if the remains belong to Mary."

"He does. One night at dinner, I talked about our discovery and the DNA results." Carver paused. "He got a strange look, then suggested the remains might be Mary Rogers."

"Did he explain why?" *This is getting interesting.*

"Sort of. Due to the body's condition, city authorities quickly buried Mary in a pauper's grave in a Presbyterian cemetery on Varick Street. More than a century later, a developer relocated the cemetery to build a hotel."

"Is your friend related to Mary?" I was confused about the purpose of the project.

"I don't know, and it doesn't matter. Mary's name wasn't on the list of bodies exhumed and moved."

"Why was he researching her in the first place?"

"He wasn't." Carver went on to explain how the friend had happened upon the list of relocated bodies while searching for dirt on the hotel developer. Having recently worked on an article about Sybil's Cave in Hoboken, New Jersey, he expected to find Mary's name among those moved. "But he said a red flag went up when it wasn't there."

I surmised that Carver's sponsor was a journalist. "And someone built a hotel on the site. There must be more evidence than that."

"Of course. The fabric found with the remains fits the period. Plus, my sponsor read that Mary's aunt, a Mrs. Downing, insisted Mary was buried with family and not in a pauper's grave. He suspects when the coroner exhumed the body for further confirmation of identity by family, they relocated Mary's remains to the New London site."

"What kind of further identification? Why would they bury her without family involvement?" I couldn't fathom leaving family members out of such an important decision.

"Arthur Crommelin, a former boarder at Mary's house on Nassau Street, identified her based on clothing and the hair pattern on her arms. Bloating from the water had rendered her unrecognizable." Carver swallowed. "Crommelin claimed he knew her well. The police accepted his word and opted for a hasty burial. Later, doubts arose about it being Mary at all."

I shuddered. I'd seen what water did to a corpse. "And no family involvement."

"None. The list of moved bodies and the aunt's claim aren't conclusive, but the first genealogist's files might contain supporting documents. I believed my friend when he said the remains are Mary Rogers."

I admired Carver's conviction, but it wasn't enough. I needed Mary's background. "Tell me about Mary. The person. Who she was."

Carver's eyebrows arched. "I expected you would have researched her after we talked yesterday."

His comment stung. I regretted my slipshod preparation for the interview, but after dropping Sophie at canine camp, calling Caitlin, and packing, I had headed straight to bed. "Sorry, I ran out of steam."

Carver thought for a moment. "As I said, she was a Manhattan celebrity. Every city paper covered her death, each printing their own versions. To this day, the case remains unsolved."

"It sounds like you are asking me to identify her cause of death. I'm sorry, but unfortunately I'm a genealogist, not a coroner." I didn't want him to see that my hackles had been raised, but clearly, my diplomacy hadn't returned. Exhausted, I glanced at my watch.

Carver delivered the punchline. "Solving the mystery is not a priority. But if you do, my sponsor promised a sizable endowment to the School of Anthropology."

Cha-ching. Here we go. "Ah, an endowment."

"Plus, a bonus for you," he added.

"I solve the mystery, and we both get a bonus. Not a bad deal." The case was about money, not the poor woman. There probably wasn't a relative alive who cared if the remains belonged to Mary Rogers.

Carver straightened in his chair. "Students always need research money. We also plan to expand our archeology minor. Develop a degree program."

I wasn't convinced the case had merit. "Hearsay evidence suggests Mary's family moved her body. But you've got no evidence to indicate they did."

"True. But if they did move her, it's a strong possibility the remains are hers. All we need from you is proof she was moved here."

Even amid the self-serving intentions, he'd roused my curiosity. The pieces of the puzzle might just fit. I mulled over the facts. Eventually, lost family plots scattered across New England were discovered. The past had a way of seeping up through the soil.

I slid off the couch and wandered toward the window. Carver drummed his desk with his fingers, watching while I debated how to answer. "So, what do you think?" he finally asked.

I continued to roam, weighing the pros and cons. Not many genealogists got the chance to solve a hundred-eighty-year-old cold case. I stopped to read the identification plaque on a woman's portrait.

Isabelle Kemp, Ph.D., Professor, School of Anthropology, 1939 to 1989.

The dates on the brass plate suggested she was Carver's predecessor. I moved on.

The endowment soured me, and the previous genealogist had quit. Not to mention, the odd appearance of a sponsor, who sounded more like a shadow client. The case oozed uncertainty.

Nothing like the strawberries I'd hoped for.

When I turned to answer Carver, a light flashed beside me. A sunray had breached the clouds and entered through the office window. It reflected off a ladies antique secretary desk in the corner amid a cluster of chairs, a trunk, and an old bookcase.

The desk reminded me of my impending office remodel at home. Sam and I had bought our Victorian house eight years ago. Room by room, we'd started restoring it, beginning on the ground floor. Last year, we'd reached the second level, redid our bedroom, started on my office, and then refocused on the nursery when I became pregnant.

Waves of sadness ebbed and flowed as I studied the piece. Charmed by its simplicity and character, the secretary attracted me—a perfect fit for my 1800s decor.

"This desk is beautiful. May I take a closer look?" I gestured toward it.

"Of course. Help yourself."

A trace of fish odor hung in the air as I waded into the afternoon light. Shifting a table aside, I stepped next to the piece and swept my hand along its front. When I touched the inlaid tulip on the hutch, it felt warm. Pigeonholes and tiny drawers with green knobs revealed themselves as I rolled back the top. A desire to possess it intoxicated me. "Is it for sale? I'm restoring my office. It would be a perfect fit."

"Will you take the case?" Carver looked surprised.

Unsure of my decision, and lightheaded from discovering the desk, I didn't answer immediately.

Carver drew in a breath. "Well?"

I searched for the right words. "To be honest, my expertise is interpreting genetic groupings, or pinpointing areas of family clusters. I prefer locating the living, not the dead."

"As I said, the sponsor will compensate you well."

The longer I touched the desk, the more I wanted it. On impulse, I turned to Carver. "I'll take the case if you include the secretary."

"You're sure? I'm authorized to double your current rate."

The money tempted me, but the desk soothed me. Rather, it beckoned to me. I reached up and touched the crystal tulip. "I'd prefer the desk."

"Our offer is worth considerably more than the ladies secretary." His mouth hung open.

"It's not about the money. I want the desk." I startled myself with the decisive reply.

"Okay. It's yours. As it happens, the college asked me to dispose of it. We haven't found a historical significance other than its age, circa 1830."

As I fingered the dry leather blotter, the sunbeam reached the crystal tulip. A blurred image appeared, then vanished. I gasped.

Carver hurried toward me. "What's the matter?"

"Whew. I'm fine. Just a strange play of light through the tulip."

He returned to his desk.

"I'll take the case." Neither the doubled rate nor the bonus had convinced me. It was solely the desk. "While I'm here, I'd like to visit the discovery site and the Rogerene cemetery."

Carver collected his lecture notes. "My class starts in ten minutes, but you're free to go there yourself. You can't miss it. It's marked with yellow caution tape."

I produced the campus map I'd printed from the college website.

Carver marked an X north of the Coast Guard Academy, then circled a wooded area upriver. "The cemetery's here. A huge boulder marks its location. Again, it's hard to miss."

Chapter Three

Rain threatened as my rental car snaked down Deshon Street's steep incline. A gravel road bordered the southern end of a meadow and led toward a cove in the Thames' west bank. Strands of yellow caution tape fluttered in the breeze at the discovery site.

The entire dig was comprised of a sod pile and a patch of exposed clay. Muddied cotton grid strings drooped into the dirt. The spot didn't reveal much. After several photos, I moved on.

A breeze stirred as I strolled north along the railroad tracks parallel to the river. A granite boulder guarded the cemetery. Two students jogging along a cartroad on its west border ignored me as I stood by the rock. Typically, I loved old cemeteries, but this one possessed an unsettling sadness.

The few engraved markers leaned at odd angles or had long since fallen. Rough fieldstones marked random plots, likely Rogerene graves. A woodland musk enveloped me when I kneeled to read the inscription on a lichen-covered headstone:

In Memory of William Peck
Of Norwich who died
On board the ship Sally
Sep 1798

Skirting the perimeter, I checked for more graves. A deep gorge formed by centuries of erosion separated the burial ground from the railroad berm along the riverbank.

The remains could easily have washed downstream from this cemetery to the dig site.

Finished with my inspection, I climbed onto the boulder. A gap in the trees provided an unobstructed view of Groton on the east riverbank. The sun, still visible, reflected off the windshield of a passing boat. Dark clouds billowed just beyond the blue sky.

I planned my next steps. Read, research, report. Similar to other forensic fields, a genealogist's process tended to be iterative and empirical.

I'd review and catalog Carver's data, then test its credibility and compare it to public records—deeds, birth and death certificates, marriage licenses, church records. After that, I'd build the Rogers and Mather family trees.

I would need to study the Rogerenes. There was a chance there would be a connection to Mary if the remains were hers.

If I got lucky, I'd be done. If not, I would widen my search and try to locate a living relative. Maybe that was why the other genealogist quit—a hostile relative. It wasn't unusual in genealogy research. Hopefully, I'd find a cooperative family member.

The sun had disappeared. Water droplets spattered the

oak canopy. I slid toward the ground, legs stiff from the cold granite. Rain washed my face as I trotted across the field to the car. My gut told me this could have been Mary's final resting place. If I traced her lineage to a Rogerene, it would explain her burial here.

On my drive to Caitlin's, I contemplated the sponsor's explanation. His theory about the remains being Mary Rogers could be true. I found it strange that he'd hidden his identity, though.

I recalled the desk and smiled. I couldn't wait for Sam to see it.

Chapter Four

As I drove into Caitlin's yard, I admired her historic home. I loved the house. One of Granby's first Puritan settlers built it in 1787 on property owned by the Hayes family, ancestors of the nineteenth U.S. President, Rutherford B. Hayes. Each time I visited her, I imagined the Hayes family gathered around its four-sided central fireplace.

As their family grew, they'd expanded the original one-story Cape Cod by adding a second floor under a gambrel roof. Caitlin spent months reglazing the six-over-six, wood-framed windows to preserve the original pontil-scarred panes.

Caitlin waved as I entered her yard. Her Yorkie, Nellie, bounced around at her feet. "Hey, Cub. Just in time for wine." I grabbed my overnight bag and followed her into the house. Caitlin had a full glass already waiting, and she poured me one to match.

We retired to her patio, where I briefed her on the project, confiding how Carver had chided me for not doing my homework. "I'm still smarting from his remark. I hate not being prepared."

Caitlin grabbed her laptop. "Let's do it now. It'll be fun. I'll search for blogs and articles."

"Great. And I'll see what I can find in the city and state records in Connecticut and New York." I began with a search for Mary Rogers. It returned a long list of women, mostly from New York. Too many to easily sift through. I tried using Mary Cecelia Rogers. Nothing.

"Whoa. Look at this." Caitlin turned her screen toward me. "There are dozens of articles about Mary's unsolved death. Her story's all over the Internet."

I closed my laptop. I'd research the official records later.

"It says here nobody's found Mary's birth record." Caitlin scowled as she handed over her laptop for me to read the article. How I'd missed stories about Mary baffled me. She'd been the topic of TV shows, online blogs, and books, including one on psychology. I cringed, recalling how I'd learned about the Poe connection from Professor Carver.

"Read what it says." Caitlin leaned against me.

"Let's see. Daniel Rogers and Phebe Mather married in 1814 in Lyme, Connecticut. According to this, Mary was born six years later in 1820." I frowned. "Without a record of her birth, Phebe must have provided the police or reporters that information."

"What's wrong with her giving them the information?" Caitlin asked.

"Nothing. Except it seems like a long time after their marriage before Mary was born."

"Maybe Phebe lost babies in between." Caitlin's eyes softened when she realized what she'd said.

"Maybe." A pall settled over me while I skimmed the

next few paragraphs. Then, I found information about Daniel Rogers' death that caught my interest. "He died in a riverboat explosion in New Orleans, leaving Mary fatherless and Phebe a widow."

"Keep reading. I'm hooked." Caitlin snuggled in next to me.

The article described Phebe and Mary's struggle to run the Mather farm for a year. In 1835, they moved to New York City and lived with a man named John Anderson, a business associate of Phebe's late first husband, Ezra Mather. "Wait! Carver said the DNA indicated both Mather and Rogers ancestry."

"Ezra Mather could be the connection," Caitlin suggested.

"I don't think so. He died years before Mary was conceived. But someone in his family could be." I continued to scan, reading aloud bits that felt important. "Anderson owned a Cigar Emporium, where Mary worked. He hired her for her beauty to attract customers."

Caitlin rolled her eyes. "Figures."

"It worked. Says here that Anderson's shop became the hangout for Tammany Hall politicians and Democratic Party figures. And I already know Poe frequented it."

"She knew some famous people." Caitlin lifted an eyebrow.

"Sounds like it. They came from nearby offices for a smoke and to flirt with her."

We stayed up until midnight reviewing the information. Most articles used the same source and became repetitive, but I kept their links just the same.

Saturday and Sunday, Caitlin and I played. We visited one of our favorite parks, went to the movies, and stuffed ourselves on fish and chips. We had fun, but my mind kept drifting to Mary Rogers and the Rogerenes. I was anxious to find out more about them.

Chapter Five

When I returned home on Monday, trucks blocked the driveway. My office remodel had officially begun. I grabbed my overnight bag and hurried inside.

Sophie greeted me at the door and tagged along to Sam's study. He'd collected her from canine camp the previous evening.

"I'm home." I kissed his cheek.

He swiveled around in his office chair. "Hey, Sherlock. How was it?" Before I could answer, he added, "By the way, I moved your office things into the west bedroom."

"Thank you. I should have done that before I left." I inhaled. "I took the case. It's about a woman named Mary Rogers who died almost two centuries ago."

"Fantastic." Sam pulled me close, kissing me on the lips.

We'd been together almost ten years, and I still responded like a teenager. My heart raced as I melted into his arms. I'd never grow tired of him. Nah. Tall, dark, and handsome–the old cliché. But that's what he was. Straight teeth and round, brown eyes, with dark, curly hair that included a rogue lock that tickled his forehead whenever he moved. He smelled good, even when he was dirty. And his laugh made my world sing.

When we finally disengaged, Sam returned to his desk. "You can share the details later. I'm up to my eyeballs in an appraisal for a mahogany sideboard buffet. I'm ninety-nine percent sure it's a Romweber Chippendale. If it is, it's worth at least six grand. I promised my client I'd send over a value later today. What's your plan for the rest of the day?"

"Unpack and review the documents Professor Carver provided."

Sam kissed me again. "I'm not giving you the cold shoulder. I'm just on a roll."

I smiled, my mind already drifting to the case. "No problem. I'll see you for cocktails at five on the deck."

After unpacking, I gathered the essentials and set up a temporary workspace in a corner of our library. I tried Claire but got her voicemail. "Call me ASAP. I accepted a case in New London and wondered if you worked on it before me. It's about human remains found at Connecticut College."

My instincts had kicked in. Claire was a straight shooter. We'd collaborated on an unsolved serial killer case for the FBI that had pointed to opposite U.S. coasts. She handled Boston, and after my two trips to San Francisco, we'd managed to solve it. We also worked together on a controversial inheritance case needing rush identification of distant relatives. If she was the previous genealogist, she had a good reason to quit, which I would do well to heed. But I'd cross that bridge if, and when, needed. Until then, it was time to get to work.

* * *

By the tender age of seventeen, Mary had become a New York celebrity. According to my research with Caitlin, Mary's beauty was the stuff of legends. The newspaper articles described her as poised, witty, and full of life. One writer described her as taller than average, slender, shapely, and graceful. Reading between the lines, I added sensual, mysterious, and adventurous.

I envisioned a young woman who desperately wanted independence.

A lump formed in my throat. I rubbed my eyes to erase the memory of the remains. Empty eye sockets. A skull with matted hair. Skeletal bones draped with scraps of leathery tissue.

The body in Carver's office may have belonged to a beauty. A woman, full of life. Poised. Witty.

How sad.

So far, I'd not found Mary's second interment mentioned. Although disappointing, this inferred that the bones found in New London could be her, which is what I needed to confirm. To do that, I'd address three questions.

Was she buried in the Rogerene cemetery in Connecticut?

Did the body match Mary's description?

And was she part Mather?

If I could find answers to these questions, the remains could be hers. I gave the bonus question a lower priority. How did she die? I'd get to that later, if at all.

I began cataloging Carver's files by source and relevance to my case. He had provided no evidence linking Mary to the Rogerene cemetery. The only unique data in the file was the draft report of the ground-penetrating radar study locating the forty-one graves. He hadn't included a map of specific gravesite locations. That, along with plot numbers, would give me a starting point. If I had her plot number, I could pinpoint her grave. If it fell in the eroded area near the railroad berm, the body might be hers. Pretty iffy, but I'd follow up with Carver.

Other than the DNA results, Carver's data was limited to a copy of the original police report and hearsay from old newspaper articles. His expert opinions came from Amy Srebnick's 1995 book, *The Mysterious Death of Mary Rogers*. Carver included professional photographs of the skeletal find, including multiple headshots. Plus, I had the list of relocated bodies from the Presbyterian cemetery in Manhattan, which didn't include Mary.

Using the police report, I cataloged Mary's clothing the day she disappeared. The report indicated she wore a white dress, but the fabric on the body was definitely a floral print, possibly explained by the family reinterring her in fresh clothes.

Carver's student had identified Samuel Slater's textile mill in Pawtucket, Rhode Island, as the weaver of the rose-colored, floral stripe on a cream background. I confirmed his conclusion, finding a fabric match on the National Museum of American History's website. The material design didn't eliminate Mary.

The student had estimated the body height at five feet, five inches." According to newspapers and police reports, Mary had curly, dark hair, fair skin, was tall and slight of build. The specimen's hair matched. The brown, leathery skin wasn't dark brown. It could match.

To determine what was considered tall in 1841, I searched online and found that the average height of women then had been five feet, two inches. The specimen was three inches taller than average. To confirm Mary's height, I'd need her in a picture with something of known size. Furniture provided a reliable comparison if it was of standard build.

"Beauty is so subjective," I said to Sophie.

She lifted her head, then dropped it and closed her eyes again.

Feeding the skeleton photos into facial reconstruction software might reveal a beautiful woman, but that could take months and a large budget unless Sam's longtime buddy and geek friend, Greg Olsen, had such a program in his tool chest. I'd check with him first once I found decent photographs of her.

I pawed through Carver's files until satisfied I'd found the meat, then returned to my online due diligence to make sure I'd collected everything mentioning Mary, regardless of how insignificant it might seem. In a literature search, I found an additional source, *The Beautiful Cigar Girl* by Daniel Stashower. Since Srebnick had linked Mary's story to the changing times in New York and Stashower had related her story to Edgar Allan Poe, it was possible I'd find a unique reference in his bibliography. I ordered the book.

I also captured two lithographs and a print of Mary from different articles. She didn't look beautiful to me. In one, she resembled a young Eleanor Roosevelt. However, in a story written by Thomas Duke, he suggested her beauty included her pleasing manner.

Maybe beauty standards differed back then.

Then again, the beauties of today had the advantage of skilled cameramen and professional makeup artists. Plus, Mary's likeness in the lithograph would have depended on the artist's talent. Mary could have looked like Gal Gadot for all I knew.

I saved them in digital format for Greg.

Next, I checked a database of historic newspapers and

found an interesting article that appeared two years after Mary's death in a *New York Tribune*. The headline read, "Mary Rogers Mystery Explained." Fredrika Loss, a known abortionist, dying after an accidental shooting by a son, had confessed. The paper's source was a judge named Merritt. Loss stated Mary had visited her tavern that day with a young man, who'd performed the fatal abortion. Loss's sons disposed of the body, a deed they refused to admit for fear of self-incrimination.

The story, however, was retracted within days when the *Tribune* refused to name the source and the judge denied the facts. The police dismissed it as the *Tribune* trying to sell newspapers using false information.

* * *

At five o'clock, I joined Sam on the deck. He was already waiting with two glasses of Malbec.

"I'm glad you rejected the early retirement option." Sam leaned in and kissed my cheek.

"It was time." I sipped my wine. "It's odd, though. The previous genealogist quit. Carver kept saying *she*. It could be Claire. I've called her, but she hasn't responded."

"That is odd." Sam frowned.

"Yes, Claire usually calls right back. I'll try again tomorrow." I smiled. "You won't believe what I'm getting as part of my compensation."

"Let me guess." Sam's eyes twinkled. "A free course at the college."

"No, silly. An antique ladies secretary desk."

"Wow! Nice." He perked up. "Think it's a collectible piece?"

"It might be. You'll have to see it. Professor Carver said

it isn't worth what he could pay me, but I fell in love with it."

"Serendipity. You needed a desk. Time to trash your old hollow-core door from school."

"No kidding." But I'd miss it. I'd earned two advanced degrees studying at that desk.

My mind wandered at Sam's mention of college. We'd met in graduate school at Yale. His master's degree in art history led him to antiques. I'd studied genetics, but genealogy was my passion. Being practical, I used my master's degree in clinical genetics to earn good money working for the FBI, interpreting complicated DNA groupings.

But I'd also fallen in love with history in high school–or maybe I just fell in love with the way the teacher taught it. Either way, Mr. Stamos had brought history alive for me, assigning a term project to construct our family tree, beginning with the first immigrant of either parent. My Irish father disappeared when I was five, so I chose him. No luck. Apparently, he'd drifted into our lives for a few years, then drifted back out to oblivion.

Tracing my mother's side proved easier. Her large Italian family immigrated during the late 1800s to escape poverty and famine, entering the States through Baltimore, settling in the city's southeast Little Italy, where I grew up.

Sam covered my hand with his. "You okay with this project? You're awfully quiet."

"I'm not worried about the project, but I do have reservations about the client." I sipped my wine. "Professor Carver's a middleman. The actual client wants to remain anonymous and is convinced the remains are Mary Rogers."

"Sounds challenging." He rubbed his neck. "Not a typical case. There won't be much data."

"True. It's a challenge, but you trace the provenance of antique furniture. Surely, I can uncover historical documents about people."

He laughed. "People conceal things, move around. My furniture, not so much."

I shrugged. "If I get stuck, you can give me a few tips."

He leaned over and whispered in my ear. "Bet on the horse that wins."

"You're silly." I laughed, letting him kiss me again before heading inside to feed Sophie.

Chapter Six

By morning, I still hadn't heard from Claire. I tried calling and left a voicemail. When she didn't respond to that, I texted. After several hours and no reply, I shot off a desperate email. I was worried, but she was a grown woman. So, I decided to give her the benefit of a few more days. Maybe she was out of town. Maybe.

* * *

The DNA results in Carver's file matched both Rogers and Mather families based on scores greater than seventy-six centiMorgans, units of genetic linkage between individuals. A score that high on such old samples surprised me. Scores above sixty indicated virtually a hundred percent likelihood of being related, eliminating doubts of bloodline.

I emailed Carver, requesting a map of the Rogerene cemetery with detailed plot locations. Next, I searched online for church records or public documents to verify Daniel and Phebe Rogers were Mary's parents. Like everyone else, I didn't find a birth report in Lyme's public records or Presbyterian church documents. It was as if Mary had emerged from under a toadstool.

Family trees sometimes revealed alternative relationships not mentioned elsewhere. It was time to construct the Rogers and Mather family trees to see if the remains could belong to Mary or possibly one of her close relatives.

A few articles claimed Mary was related to the infamous Cotton Mather. Curious to confirm this, I started with the Mathers. I'd studied the Salem Witch Trials of the 1690s in high school history. Cotton had tested his witchcraft theories on thirteen-year-old Martha Goodwin and concluded the devil had indeed possessed her. Fixated on Satan and eternal damnation, Cotton hoped to witness the second coming of Christ. Unfortunately for Cotton, that didn't happen.

I searched using Mather as a keyword. A family website entitled Mather Clan topped the list of results. The website included a contact page for the website manager, Rose Martin. I shot off an email asking about Mary Rogers and if any new family documents had surfaced.

The site allowed me to print an eleven-generation family tree. The top-level family member, Reverend Richard Mather, immigrated to the American Colonies in the 1600s. A pop-up note indicated he'd been banished from the Anglican church for refusing to follow the dress code. He had five surviving sons, four of whom entered the ministry.

His youngest son, Increase, fathered Cotton. His second son, Timothy, was the branch that led to Ezra. At this point, I realized that any relationship Mary Rogers had to Cotton Mather was distant at best.

Ezra Mather, found in the seventh generation of Timothy's, wedded Phebe. The couple had four sons. Three had no offspring, but their youngest had two sons of his own. Another avenue for me to search for a living relative. Ezra and Phebe's only daughter, named after her mother and nicknamed Bea, died unmarried at age thirty-one.

The autogenerated Mather tree included birth, marriage, and death dates that I might find useful for future reference. I taped the Mather tree to my whiteboard. As an afterthought, I circled Bea's name.

Sophie stood by the doorway, yipping.

"Let's go," I said. "I need tea, and you need out." She barked all the way down to the kitchen and out the back door.

The fifteen-minute break helped me to get my second wind. Back at my computer, I dug into Phebe's family, resorting to the major genealogy websites. I was freelancing on this project and only had access to public sources. I wasn't sure of what I'd find, but if Carver had matches, there had to be some very early DNA information for the two families, maybe from the 1960s when test results first became reliable. Still, few, if any, historical contemporaries would exist. In 1841, the NYPD worked solely with physical evidence. So, that's what I had. I continued to search.

Zurviah Calkins Wait and Lowen Wait had Phebe in 1778. Neither parent had an obvious source for Mather markers for four previous generations.

I reached down and patted Sophie. "It's possible that Daniel carried the markers."

Daniel's bloodline led back to James Rogers, a Congregationalist who'd immigrated to Boston in the 1600s seeking religious freedom after leaving England's Roman Catholic Church. James challenged beliefs about the Eucharist taken in the sacrament. He rejected the concept of transubstantiation, believing the ritual only represented the body and blood of Christ.

I stretched both arms overhead, weary. Although interesting theological history, this sidebar of information wasn't getting me closer to solving the case.

I refocused on the James Rogers family. Once in New England, James settled in New London, where he opened a bakery, supplying biscuits to the military and commercial shipping companies.

"Sophie, get this. James's oldest son, John, founded the Rogerenes and was joined by a younger brother, James Jr."

I'd discovered the man behind the Rogerenes.

Sophie didn't seem intrigued. She stood, shook herself, then walked to the doorway. She'd had it.

While growing up, the Rogers boys roamed New London's international seaport. They met and chatted with a diverse population of travelers who entered the port. These interactions raised doubts about church dogma. At one point, John refused to pay church taxes, suffering public condemnation. He read and interpreted the Bible, forming his own opinion of traditional roles in marriage, which led to two divorces and a common-law arrangement with his third wife until she left him.

Conversely, James Jr. practiced the same Rogerene beliefs without fanfare. He channeled his energies and resources into shipping, beginning a long tradition of mariners. James Jr.'s branch was where Daniel Rogers appeared four generations later. With this direct-line Rogerene ancestor, Daniel could have been a Rogerene.

I found *James Rogers of New London, CT: And His Descendants* online. It listed Daniel's wife as Widow Mather. I ordered a copy, hoping to confirm my theory that

Daniel was, in fact, a Rogerene, or find a Mather in his bloodline.

When James's son, John, died, the Rogerenes moved behind closed doors. Forty years after his death, a grandson, John Second, reignited a Rogerene insurgency, which continued into the nineteenth century. Based on timing, Daniel could have joined the second wave.

By Mary's time, outlandish Rogerene behavior had gone underground. Fraternizing with boarders like her fiancé, Daniel Payne, a known drinker, suggested she had a liberal side. Unable to find anything private about her, I presumed the politicians and journalists had washed her squeaky clean and buried her past along with her body.

If the true Mary was hidden in personal papers, then interviewing a living Rogers or Mather relative was an obvious next step. Juicy scandals and legends tended to pass from generation to generation, becoming folklore. Perhaps Rose Martin, the Mather website manager, would reply.

Sophie whined from the doorway.

"You win. Time for your supper. And I'm late for cocktails."

The following day, I called Greg about a facial reconstruction program. He predicted it would take a few days, but I sent him my digital files, anyway. After we disconnected, I drove to the Jenkintown Library, keen to search for information on the Wait family, Phebe's ancestors.

I didn't find a Wait genealogy, but I found and leafed through Horace E. Mather's 1890 copy of the *Lineage of Rev. Richard Mather* to double-check my Mather tree. If

Mary had Mather genes, she was likely on Timothy's branch because of Ezra, but it was possible she had a completely different lineage.

The idea of Phebe and Daniel as Mary's parents bothered me. So far, it didn't fit.

Disappointed, I packed up and headed home.

Chapter Seven

Between the hubbub of the office remodel and my online due diligence, the days passed with fewer sad moments. Unlike the darkest months of my depression, riddled with grief and utterly miserable, the bouts were now fewer and farther between, occurring mostly as sharp pangs when I passed by the room next door to my office and witnessed the crib still in its box.

I checked my inbox daily. Nothing but junk mail. No reply from the Mather Clan website manager, and it had been nearly two weeks.

I tried Claire again. No answer. Hopefully, I hadn't alienated myself with my sloth behavior. She and her daughter, Emma, had always kept busy, and I'd been no fun to be around. I checked her Facebook, Instagram, LinkedIn, then Twitter. She hadn't posted in two weeks.

* * *

On Wednesday, the work crew completed the remodel, two days ahead of schedule. My phone vibrated in the middle of inspecting their work. Greg's name appeared on the display.

"How's the case going?" he asked.

"Slow. What've you got for me?" I moved to my desk and grabbed a pen and paper.

"A reconstruction from the skull photo. Got lucky. I found free software online that produced a digital copy. I'll send it over."

"Fantastic. How did it look?" *This could be a break-through.*

"Inconclusive." He sighed, then continued. "However, a comparison of the two photos from *Alchetron*, the online social encyclopedia, scored seventy-eight percent. But the confidence score combining all photos was pretty low. I'm sending you what I have."

The photo arrived within seconds. After a quick look, I moved it into my Mary Rogers photo file. "Kind of looks like her."

"I thought so, too, but the confidence score makes it questionable."

"Bummer. Oh well, it was worth a try. Thanks for the help."

After Greg and I disconnected, a text message arrived from Professor Carver.

The desk will arrive Friday.

I wasn't superstitious, but Friday being the thirteenth gave me pause.

* * *

When the doorbell rang on Friday morning, Sophie barreled toward the foyer. The cacophony of door chimes and dog barking nearly deafened me. A man in brown stood outside, balancing a large box on a dolly. My antique ladies secretary had arrived.

"A delivery for RaeJean Hunter." He smiled and handed me an iPad.

Sophie pestered him, nipping at his heels as he wrangled the carton through the doorway. She belly-crawled toward him as he handed her a biscuit. They'd met more than once.

I signed for the item while he unloaded it.

After he left, I studied the carton. The boxed secretary didn't provide the same quiet I'd experienced in Carver's office. I wanted it, but with its arrival came sadness.

The empty nursery. A new office.

I blamed myself for the loss. I still hadn't—couldn't—let go of the guilt eating away at me. I retreated to the library, burrowed beneath a blanket, and cried myself to sleep for the first time in weeks.

* * *

Sophie's yips woke me. Annoyed, I trudged to the foyer and found her sniffing the box.

"There might be something inside besides a desk." I tapped its top, listening for movement.

Sophie's entire back end wagged, including her docked tail. The large carton had handling dents, but no holes from an intruder. My canine detective scratched at one corner. I shoved her aside and sliced open the carton with a utility knife. The same fishy odor I'd detected in Carver's office drifted out. I checked for stowaways, but there was no sign of rodents.

Sophie wound around my legs, her breath steaming my

ankles.

One tug on the twine released the bubble pack. It slithered to the floor, revealing the desk in all its glory. The sight jolted me back to life. "Amazing."

Lifting the wood cylinder, the lid disappeared into its cavity and exposed the writing surface. Carver had cleaned the crystal tulip and green knobs until they sparkled.

When I touched the leather blotter, the tulip flickered. My neck hairs lifted.

Sophie bristled, too. Her nails tapped on the cardboard as she sniffed, reared, and pounced. Her behavior upset me. Rattled by the recurrent phenomena, I hastily retreated back to my nest in the library while Sophie remained with the delivery.

Sam would help us finish the unpacking.

* * *

Later that afternoon, the foyer chandelier clinked and woke me. Sam was home from his overnight business trip. Paul Logan, the owner of Beacon Hill's Elegant Antique Furnishings, had asked him to identify and date a sideboard recently acquired in an estate sale.

I laughed from the doorway when Sophie greeted Sam with her version of a triple Axel.

"How was the piece?" I asked. Hints of citrus and spice drifted into the room, reminding me how much I'd missed him.

"It was beautiful, but Paul misidentified it. It was actually a credenza, not a sideboard. No floor cabinets and no hutch." The rogue lock of hair covered his eyes when he leaned down to pat Sophie. Straightening, he wrapped me in his arms and rested his chin on my head.

Sophie stood on point once more, ears back, completely fixated on the carton.

After a few seconds, Sam pulled away and approached the partially opened box. "Your new desk arrived."

"Yup, and Sophie's obsessed. She camped here all afternoon."

"Let's unpack it." Sam began removing the carton.

My gut tightened. I loved the desk, but it mystified me.

He stepped back to admire the piece. "Simple, yet elegant."

"It is. As soon as I saw it, I knew you'd like it."

We hauled the four-piece ladies secretary upstairs, one section at a time. It was frosting on the remodel. As I admired the new look, the setting sun projected onto the crystal. The hazy image I'd seen in Carver's office reappeared.

I froze, then pointed. "There's a face in the tulip."

Sam leaned in. "Where?"

I fingered the crystal facets. "It was here, in the middle. It feels warm."

He shrugged. "The sun must have heated it."

Sam touched the tulip. "It's quartz. What a great piece. The intricate carvings suggest the early 1830s. I bet the quartz crystals created an optical illusion."

"Maybe." I wasn't ready to offer Sam a different explanation, not until I understood what had happened.

"What else could it be? A ghost?" Sam laughed.

I forced a laugh to match. "No way."

I'd had so many bad days in the previous months, between depression and a reaction to the anxiety and antidepressant drugs, that now I wondered if I was hallucinating.

Or seeing ghosts.

Chapter Eight

Saturday morning, I climbed the stairs, arms loaded with books. Sam would be pleased I was moving my project materials and supplies from the library.

As usual, Sophie trailed me. She dashed to the desk and pawed its side, her ritual since it had arrived. "What is it, girl?"

I dropped my armload onto the worktable. Her behavior had to stop or the desk would soon be ruined. "Down, girl. Leave it. Let's go find Sam."

We found him in his office. "All moved in?" he asked.

"Almost. But Sophie keeps pawing at the desk."

He stood. "I need a break. Come on, Sherlock, let's find the big attraction."

Sophie scrambled into my office ahead of us and repeated her scratching. Sam lifted her, burrowing his face in her fur. Hair clung to his lips. "Dogs have a highly developed sense of smell."

I inhaled the faint fishy aroma seasoned with nutmeg that hung in the air surrounding the desk. "Well, it does smell funny."

"Smells like old furniture to me. Could be the finish, or the builder's glue concoction. Not uncommon for a piece this old."

"It smells like spiced fish." It was hard to believe the odor remained after almost two centuries.

"A little." Sam smiled, then whispered in Sophie's ear. "What's the big attraction? Did an owner's dog lift a leg on it?"

I laughed. "I don't think so. It would smell like ammonia, not fish." Sam watched me remove the drawers and reach into its innards, rummaging for something that would account for the smell. My small hand easily slipped behind the rolltop. "Got something. It's a piece of paper." Pinching it between two fingers, I wiggled it out. "An invoice."

Sam leaned in and smelled it. "I doubt this is what bothered Sophie."

I read it aloud.

Frank Cordts Furniture Co. Date of Sale: July 10, 1927
200 Washington Street
Hoboken, New Jersey

1 - Cherry Ladies Secretary, circa 1830......... $25
Owned by: Alonzo Mather (orig. stored 1883 - C.S.)
Deliver to: Connecticut College for Women
Mohegan Avenue
New London, Connecticut

"The date suggests it's been in there for nearly a century and was owned by a Mather."

"Interesting." Sam glanced at his watch. "Yikes, Paul's calling in five minutes. He spotted a drop-leaf table at a show. I've got to go." He pecked my cheek, then rushed back toward his office.

Once settled at the new desk, I drank in my surroundings. I loved my office, the way the cream wainscoting complemented the blue-striped wallpaper.

Fabric swatches I'd taped to the bare window frame caught my eye as they fluttered. Homes like ours, built in the late 1800s, harbored untold drafts. In winter, we fought the cold, and in summer, we tolerated the heat. Our friends called us crazy for feeding the money pit, but Sam and I couldn't destroy the house's historic features.

The *ding* of an incoming email broke the spell I'd fallen under. Rose, the Mather Clan website manager, had finally responded. Her email included information that her family originated from Timothy Mather, the same as Ezra. She mentioned a recent find somewhere in New Hampshire. While cleaning out after her mother's death, a relative found journals from Dr. Augustus Mather, Ezra's nephew. Rose didn't say who had them.

I requested the relative's contact information. A living relative with historic journals could provide invaluable information. The journal may contain private accounts of Mary's story.

Assuming Mary carried Mather DNA, I searched for Mather cousins who might have known her. Proximity eliminated most, but I came up with four candidates. Obviously, Augustus because of his journals, but also three others who lived near Mary in Lyme and Manhattan.

Two Mather sisters, Louisa and Frances, also descendants of Timothy, grew up in Lyme. Living there allowed Mary's half-sister, Bea, to maintain ties to the Mather family. Bea might have taken her to their family events where Mary could play with Bea's young cousins.

In tracing the girls, I found Louisa had married Richard S. Griswold in 1835, the same year Mary and Phebe moved to Manhattan. Prior to the marriage, Richard had spent two years in China agenting for his father's import business. Once married, he moved Louisa to Brooklyn and curtailed his travel, making only brief buying trips to China.

Five years into their marriage, Louisa and her infant son died in childbirth.

A cold melancholy washed over me. Guilt. I walked to the window, hoping the sunlight would warm me. Sophie joined and peered out, looking for birds. Her wet nose print added to the dry ones already on the glass. She looked up and yipped. "I know, you want out. Soon."

Returning to my reading, I learned that soon after Louisa's death, Richard married her younger sister, Frances. The couple lived in New York for a year, then returned to Connecticut. Five years into their marriage, Richard died suddenly, leaving Frances with three children.

Another cousin, Frederick Mather, practiced law within a block of Mary's boarding house on Nassau Street. Also, a descendant from Timothy, Frederick grew up in Windsor just north of Hartford, close enough to attend family gatherings in Lyme. Although eleven years Mary's senior, his proximity to her in Manhattan piqued my interest.

Then, there was Dr. Augustus Mather himself, the author of the journals and the New Hampshire cousin beginning his medical career when Mary moved to New York.

I recalled the information from the online blogs and newspaper article reporting that several years after Mary's death, a Hoboken innkeeper, Fredrika Loss, made a deathbed confession about Mary's demise. Witnesses reported seeing Mary with a young man in the vicinity of Loss's inn that Sunday. If it was Augustus, his journals could provide clues to Mary's reinterment.

On a hunch, I searched public databases for anyone named Mary Rogers who bore children between 1835 and 1841. The U.S. Presbyterian Church had recently uploaded marriage and baptism records from New York City historical files. On the second to last line of a hand-written log, I found an entry for an infant named Iantha, born on May 12, 1835.

My eyes drifted down one more line. Two days after Iantha's birth, the minister had baptized a woman named Mary Rogers.

It could be the same Mary Rogers, and she delivered a baby girl at fifteen. This may have been an additional motive for Phebe and Mary to move to New York that year.

Interesting questions, but I was getting way off track. I needed proof that Mary could have been buried in New London. Proof I might find in Augustus' journals.

Without a Rogers genealogy, I couldn't identify any Rogers cousins close to Mary's age. I'd have to wait.

Sophie barked. She'd relocated to the door.

"I know. I promised. Just a few phone calls first to reserve rooms for a trip."

Ears flat, Sophie sighed, plopping to the floor.

So far, my only lead was Augustus' journals and the relative in New Hampshire. I'd visit there first to find and read the journals, then go to Connecticut to identify possible cousins in the Rogers family.

I booked a room at a bed and breakfast in Keene, a city large enough for a home base. From New Hampshire, I'd drive south to the Connecticut seacoast near New London, where Ezra Mather's and Daniel Rogers' families had first settled.

Once I finalized my itinerary, I tried Claire again. Still no answer. My concern mounted. I could swing by her house in Longmeadow, Massachusetts, while on my trip. I'd feel better checking on her in person.

Next, I called Professor Carver to ask him a few more questions.

"Ms. Hunter, what can I do for you on a Saturday?"

My face burned. So much for credibility. I didn't even know the day of the week. "Sorry to bother you. I called to see if you had received the genealogist's work files yet."

"Sorry. Nothing yet. She hasn't returned Bradley's calls, either. He suggested a stern letter."

My stomach tightened. If it was Claire, she would have had a good reason to resign. She wouldn't succumb to pressure. "I'm going to stick out my neck. By chance, is this woman Claire Allen?"

Carver cleared his throat. "I can't say."

"Odd. I've tried to contact her ever since I took the case, and she hasn't responded."

"Sounds like you two are friends."

"We've been friends for years. We went through the genealogy certification process together. I'm her daughter's godmother."

"Hmm, that does seem strange, then. I'm sure your friend will explain once she calls."

Something about Carver's reaction suggested Claire had worked the case. Now, I was determined to track her down. "While I have you on the line, any insights as to why Mary's family would move her remains to New London as opposed to another New York cemetery?"

"Not really. Perhaps her family felt she'd rest easier in Connecticut's peaceful surroundings where she grew up."

His answer didn't help. It sounded more like a wild guess than one based upon facts and deductive reasoning.

As soon as Carver disconnected, my computer dinged. Another message from Rose Martin. She didn't provide a surname for the relative with Augustus' diaries, but she said a woman named Bonnie from Lempster had found them when her mother passed away.

"I'm going in circles, Sophie. This case is anything but easy." I stood and leaned against the desk. The afternoon sun reflected off the quartz tulip. It sparkled. For no apparent reason, a calmness radiated through me, along with renewed confidence.

"I can do this, Sophie. I'm going to figure this out."

Chapter Nine

On Sunday, I concentrated on the Rogerenes. The sect didn't keep complete records, but I found a few new sources.

I'd learned how John Rogers split from the Congregational church in 1677 and spent his life challenging the system. After his in-depth study of the Bible, Rogers concluded that polygamy was legitimate behavior.

"Polygamy. Now, that's interesting."

His grandson, John Second, also practiced polygamy and fathered twenty children by the time he died in 1753. Daniel's great-great-grandfather, William, also a Rogerene, fathered eleven children. Between the two of them, they'd had thirty-one children. I would have been happy with one.

It was hardly a stretch to assume the practice didn't stop with that generation. In fact, I suspected it continued until 1890, when polygamy became outlawed in the United States.

Otherwise, why pass a law?

I'd discovered what it really meant to be a Rogerene.

And, if familial beliefs transcended generations, I'd nearly concluded that Daniel was a practicing Rogerene.

Distracted by Sophie's barking as she spied a bird outside the window, I lost focus, which was something I'd struggled with since beginning to take an antidepressant.

Forging on, I browsed the library's online index for books about the Rogers family. No luck. Plus, I'd lost my momentum. Time to quit. Tomorrow, I would visit the Jenkintown Library. A change of scenery might clear my head.

* * *

When I arrived at the library the next day, I collected and carried several Rogers books to the lyceum. The serene atmosphere improved my concentration, but it didn't make reading *The Rogerenes* by John R. Bolles and Anna B. Williams any easier.

Bolles, also a Rogerene, defended Rogers' actions, including John's refusal to pay church taxes, working on a Sunday, and John's nude entrance to church while pushing a wheelbarrow and declaring he was the human body of Christ. Williams concluded that Rogers' bizarre behavior exemplified his defiance of the current regime. Not an earth-shattering conclusion.

I crawled through pages of exposition. Rogerenes married first cousins and believed women deserved their own voice. If Mary was a Rogerene, her move to New York provided freedom and anonymity in the crowded city.

During childhood, Mary might have witnessed liberal practices. If one of the male Mather cousins showed interest in her, specifically Augustus, she may have accepted the invitation. If she did, I hoped it was him. He kept journals.

In the 1800s, it was common for cousins to court, and

even marry. So, if Augustus did have an interest in Mary, he could have easily boarded a Mather-owned ship bound for New York and visited her from either New Hampshire or Boston.

To stimulate my creative juices, I arranged my index cards for Mary and Augustus. No amount of shuffling produced a supportable link. My data didn't hint at romance, but my gut suspected a strong connection.

Next, I spread out cards for Frederick Mather. Based on proximity, with his office only a block from Mary's boarding house, his relationship with Mary held promise. But proximity wasn't enough.

"Okay, that's it. Take a walk between the stacks."

Outside the conference room, shelves of historical records surrounded me, filling thousands of cubic feet of the library basement. I wandered through the aisles. At the spot where the *Lineage of Rev. Richard Mather* should have been, it wasn't there. I searched tables and reading nooks. No genealogy. So, I headed to the front desk. "The *Lineage of Rev. Richard Mather* isn't on the shelf. I thought it might have been checked out."

The librarian's keystrokes echoed throughout the quiet room. "It's on loan to Middletown Public Library."

"Do you get many requests for this book?" I'd seldom encountered a rare book on loan.

"Not really. Our director approved a special request to be used for verification of a family tree. No name listed."

With databases available online, family genealogy had become a favorite pastime for many. But the director wouldn't have approved the request from a casual researcher. I had a suspicion. "Does Middletown have its own copy?"

She logged onto the Middletown site. "Actually, they

have two.' She squished her eyebrows together. "It seems odd that they'd ask for our copy if they already have their own."

"Margin notes." *Someone's looking for a family secret.*

"I don't understand," the librarian replied.

"Early genealogists' work contained errors. They depended on oral histories. People's memories sometimes altered the facts. Or the interviewer heard it wrong. When knowledgeable family members discovered mistakes, they would write corrections in the margins."

The librarian looked shocked. "And here I've been grousing when people write in these old books."

Back in the study room, unable to concentrate, I thought about Sophie, home alone. My progress didn't justify her solitude. I surrendered after a half hour.

During my drive, I contemplated the idea of margin notes. My previous examination of the Mather genealogy appeared clean, but now that it had been checked out, I had doubts. I needed a second look to be sure.

Sophie turned herself inside out when I entered the kitchen.

"No more work today." I clipped on her leash and headed out for a long walk.

* * *

The deeper I dug, the more intrigued I became with the case, and with Mary. Although more complicated than I first imagined, it didn't pose constant threats like my former projects working with the FBI. I felt safe. The case was more like a puzzle or scavenger hunt. My biggest threats were my growing inability to focus, mysterious vibes, and the fishy odors coming from the desk. Of all those things, the first item was the only thing I might be able to fix on my own.

Not for the first time, I wondered if maybe it was time to reduce the dosage of my antidepressant.

Chapter Ten

The afternoon flew by. So far, nothing I'd found hinted at solving the case or indicated Augustus and Mary were close. The New Hampshire trip could be nothing more than a fishing excursion. The existence of journals didn't guarantee useful information. Still, a business trip might restore my work rhythm. Sam would be pleased to see me back on the road.

Lost in thought, I flinched when the grandfather clock in our foyer chimed six times. "Crap, tonight's my night to cook."

When I leaped up, my chair rolled back and crashed against the table. Startled, Sophie barked all the way downstairs.

Sam appeared in the kitchen doorway. "What's all the commotion?"

"I scared Sophie when I stood up from my desk."

A year ago, an explosion wouldn't have disturbed him. But in the last six months, Sam didn't miss a move or sound I made. He hovered. Sam patted the dog, then shooed her outside while I poured wine.

"I've exhausted my available resources. I've planned a field trip, leaving on Wednesday for New Hampshire, then Connecticut. I'll stay in Keene first, then Old Saybrook."

Sam's brows furrowed. "Are you comfortable going alone?"

I shrugged.

He took my response as affirmative. "Check out Keene's antique shops while you're there. See if it's worth a second visit."

I sipped my wine. "My main objective is to read Augustus Mather's journals. And there's a memoir by Ammi Rogers at Keene's historical society. Ammi's not in Mary's direct line, but he might have mentioned her."

Sam studied me. "You're sure you're ready? I'm not seeing a lot of sparks here."

"I'm fine. Besides, I'm not hunting a suspected criminal on this case."

"I know, but I worry." He checked his watch. "Oops, another conference call with Paul in three minutes. He found a pair of carved Romweber chairs and needs a ballpark value. It won't take long."

* * *

At dinner, Sam didn't mention my trip. There was no reason to worry. A link between a hundred-eighty-year-old body in New London and Mary Rogers wasn't life threatening.

Afterward, I initiated a video call with Caitlin. She answered with her usual line. "Hey, Cub. What's the news?"

"Did I catch you at a bad time?" She'd wrapped her head in a towel.

"No, perfect timing. I just showered and started to do laundry. What's up?"

We'd shared everything since our father disappeared. Mom worked full-time, leaving us at home alone with our beagle, Radar. At age ten, Caitlin babysat me, and I babysat Radar. His uncanny ability to predict Mom's arrival got him his name. He'd bark before we spotted her car, like he had radar or could tell time. Radar stuck. The other option, Rolex, didn't have the same ring. I loved that dog and cried for months when he died of old age.

Caitlin removed the towel, shaking out her long hair. "There, I'm ready. Give me the hard news."

"I'm going to slowly taper off my antidepressant. I'm moving on. I'm ready."

"Maybe you shouldn't get off your meds so soon. You could have a relapse."

Caitlin's mothering annoyed me. "Why would you say that?"

"Epigenetic memory."

I rolled my eyes. "You read Nessa Cary's book, didn't you?"

Irked by my reaction, Caitlin came at me full force. "You're the DNA expert. Inheritance of paternal, stress-induced traits which have nothing to do with DNA can cross generations. You look like Dad, and you've inherited his susceptibility to depression. For all we know, maybe more."

"They haven't proven that cross-generation stuff to be true beyond a doubt."

The only memory I had of my Irish father was his broad smile and curly red hair. Whenever I visited a new city, I'd search for Patrick O'Leary. So far, I hadn't uncovered a single clue about him, but I'd never stop looking. Especially now, after losing the baby.

My doctor had mentioned genetics could cause an early stillbirth. Just thinking the words made my throat ache. "I'd need Dad's health history to know what caused his depression, but that requires finding him."

"It was probably the booze." Caitlin's attitude was all too familiar when I mentioned our father.

"Hard to say, since Mom refused to discuss him." We'd lost her in a car crash the year Sam and I married.

"Why else would a man abandon his children? Read Cary's book. Then, see if you disagree."

I gave her the Smothers Brothers line. "I'm depressed because Mom always liked you best."

Caitlin laughed. "Quit that. That's not true, even though it should be."

Her teasing didn't bother me. We'd bantered all our lives. I'd worry if it stopped. "Let's talk about you. What's happening in the world of journalism?"

She shared a funny story about covering a town meeting in Granby. Two men got into a fist fight. Small town politics didn't interest me, but the way Caitlin told it made me laugh.

"Hey, I've got to do laundry, or else I'll be wearing sweats to the office tomorrow."

"Now, that's funny." I laughed at the image of Caitlin at work in sweatpants. She was a power dresser. Tailored suits, heels, silk blouses. I dressed for comfort in jeans, sneakers, and T-shirts. My one formal outfit included a blazer with worn elbows and black slacks. I wouldn't know what power style was if it stared me in the face.

* * *

When I entered the bedroom, Sam was asleep.

I slipped into bed, trying not to wake him. I couldn't count how many times in the last six months he had done the same. When we lost our son, I withdrew from everyone, including him. The library became my sanctuary. I'd sneak food between meals to avoid interaction. Sam ate alone most nights. When he came to bed, I'd pretend to be asleep. He never complained.

Now that I was more or less back on track, it dawned on me that Sam had never shared his feelings about the still-birth. I'd focused inward for months. But I hardly knew how to express my own feelings, much less urge him to articulate his own.

Hopefully, getting off my antidepressant—and some time away—would help me sort things out.

Chapter Eleven

Traffic was light on Wednesday afternoon in Keene. Colonial homes lined the city's tree-canopied Main Street. I fell in love with the city as I circled the North Common in my Mini Cooper. Two blocks west, I recognized the Colony House Inn at the corner of West and School Street. The building nearly filled the lot.

"Crap, no parking!" Panic crept in—not my usual style. I spotted a sign indicating parking behind the bank on the opposite corner. "Phew."

The main door to the bed and breakfast was unlocked, but the place appeared empty when I entered the front parlor. After introducing myself to two friendly house cats, I wandered into what might be a private suite. One cat circled my legs as I passed through an updated kitchen into a living room. Washable throws covered two chairs.

I patted the affectionate feline. "Those must be your seats."

The cat purred like a well-tuned Chevy.

To my left, a similar-sized room overlooked Peoples

Bank and the shared parking. Based on the décor, I surmised the room served a dual purpose—an office and a reading room.

A second door looped back to the kitchen.

"Whoa." I did a double take. A desk identical to mine filled one corner. Mesmerized, I approached it and lifted the cylinder top. Same two drawers, five pigeonholes, and the pullout writing surface hid beneath its hood. This desk had a new leather blotter. The hutch sported a tulip inlay, and green pulls embellished the drawers. I snapped a photo with my phone, then checked the tulip for warmth.

"May I help you?"

The woman's voice startled me. I stepped away from the ladies secretary and held out my hand. "RaeJean Hunter. I have a reservation."

Smiling, the woman shifted her frame, shook her ponytail, then reached out her hand. She reminded me of a dancer, delicate yet strong. "Fran Collier. I manage the inn. We've been expecting you. This is my aunt's private apartment."

"I'm sorry, I was admiring the historic decor." Embarrassed, I closed the desk.

"It's nice. I love that piece, too." Fran smiled.

"Beautiful. I have its twin sister. How long has your aunt owned it?"

"I'm not sure. She moved back to Keene five years ago when she bought this property. She arrived with a truckload of antiques."

I almost asked if the desk emitted any fishy odors or projected hazy images, except that I knew she'd think I was crazy. "Where did your aunt find it?"

The innkeeper placed her hand on the ladies secretary as if to protect it from my swoon. "I'm not sure. She accumulated furniture pieces from all over the northeast. I'll ask her."

"I'd appreciate that. My desk had an invoice trapped behind the cylinder top. Purchased in 1927 from the Cordts Furniture Company in Hoboken, New Jersey."

Her face lit up. She removed a drawer, flipped it over, and pointed to a faint brand on its bottom. "Then yours is most likely a Van Boskerck."

"I'd like to see it."

She turned the drawer so I could read the marking. *John Van Boskerck, CABINET MAKER, No. 58 Broad Street, New York.*

"Van Boskerck branded most of his furniture."

"Mine could be signed. I'll have my husband check tonight." My heart tap-danced.

"If he built your desk, he probably did."

I followed her through the modern kitchen into a small galley. "This is the original kitchen, and this is the guest lounge."

As she continued the tour, I admired the floor-to-ceiling, glass-front cabinets, soapstone counter, and sink. In a small sitting area off the galley, she pointed to a sideboard. "In the morning, I'll lay out breakfast on the buffet. The dining area is through that door."

Two round tables, each with four chairs, filled a small room, hardly suitable for a full inn.

She handed me a business card. "Your room's up the stairs on the right side of the hall. I'm a phone call away if you need anything."

* * *

Before dinner, I called the Historical Society in Marlow.

"Marlow Historical Society, this is Annie speaking."

I introduced myself and explained the purpose of my visit.

"Say no more," Annie began. "We have a marvelous collection of historical documents. We have—"

Realizing she was a rambler, I jumped in. "I'm looking for material about the Mather family who lived there in the 1800s."

"You've called the right person. I was about to say we have a small collection of diaries and genealogies. I'm busy tomorrow, but if you're still here Friday, I'll open the building."

"Thank you. Friday sounds great."

"Yes, yes. Friday. See you then." She disconnected.

It was too early for dinner, so I logged onto the inn's Wi-Fi to research Van Boskerck. The search resulted in dozens of pages. The homepage for The Museum of the City of New York looked most promising, so I followed the link. It contained photos of their antique furniture collection, including a branded Van Boskerck ladies secretary. I made a note to visit the museum during my inevitable trip to the Manhattan public records and archives.

On my way to dinner, I bumped into Fran again. "Is there a restaurant you'd recommend? This is my first visit to Keene."

"There are plenty of good places. What foods do you like?"

"Everything," I laughed. "I've been craving beer and a burger."

"Try the Elm City Pub. Good food, a young crowd. Plus, it's a five-minute walk." She accompanied me outside and pointed west. "That red brick monster over there is a pub. It's also a microbrewery. The building housed a woolen mill in the 1800s. My ancestors supplied fabric for Union soldiers' uniforms."

"You're a student of local history." *Fantastic!*

"Not just a student. My family *is* the local history," she replied. "I'm a Collier, but my mother and aunt are grandchildren of the Honorable Horatio Colony, Keene's first mayor. History's my passion, second only to ballet. I'm happy to help in any way I can. Just ask."

She'd given me a lead on my desk. Why not? "I'm working on a case concerning hundred-eighty-year-old female remains, possibly from the Mather family who settled in Lempster in the 1800s."

She beamed like she'd won the New Hampshire lottery. "What a coincidence. One of our guests is a Mather descendant."

My stomach fluttered. "A tourist?"

"No. This woman's attending a DAR State Convention at the college. She's staying upstairs in a spare bedroom." The innkeeper chuckled.

I smiled, but I'd missed the humor.

"She's at a board meeting right now. She called two days ago and begged for a room. Having forgotten to make reservations and not being able to find a vacancy, my aunt gave her the front bedroom. We don't typically rent it. It's part of her private residence." The innkeeper hesitated. "She's returning this evening."

"I'd love to meet her if you could arrange it."

The innkeeper smiled. "I'll leave her a note."

On my stroll to the pub, I contemplated the coincidence. She was hardly a typical DAR board member if she forgot to make reservations for an annual convention. All the same, she might know something.

Spirits lifted, I approached the pub. A large tree

obscured its main door, and a footpath led past tables where patrons swilled beer as their gliding settees swung back and forth.

I entered the restaurant. It was noisy and filled with college kids.

After a beer and burger, I headed back to the inn. I smiled as I passed the gliders. Sam would love them.

* * *

Fran Collier had slipped a note under my door, citing the name Lillian Baxter and a phone number. She also mentioned that her aunt purchased the desk at Fairfield Auction House in Connecticut a few years ago. She gave me her aunt's phone number as well.

It was nine o'clock. Lillian could wait until morning. I'd promised Sam I'd call.

He answered right away. "Hey, Sherlock."

"I need you to check my desk for a brand," I blurted.

"Right now?" He sounded tired.

"It's important. I might learn who built it."

I heard him trudge up the stairs and rummage around. "Nope. No brands."

"There's an identical desk here, built in Hoboken by Van Boskerck. I was hoping."

"Nope. Sorry, there's no signature on your desk."

"The builder didn't sign all of his pieces. You won't believe my luck. A Mather relative is staying here." I told Sam about Lillian Baxter.

"Hmm, that's an odd coincidence."

"Yeah, I thought so, too." I'd met relatives while traveling for other cases, but I'd never had a family member booked at the same inn. My eyes burned from the heavy meal and alcohol. I yawned.

"Whoa, what was that?" Sam's voice elevated.

My body jerked upright. "What? Are you okay?"

He grunted a few times. "Phew. It's nothing. I thought I saw a face in the tulip on your desk. Must be a reflection from my flashlight."

"You sure?"

"Pretty sure. The tulip is a crystal structure. Light refraction, that's all. Depending on its angle of entry into the crystal, it forms a shadow."

"A shadow of a face." I swallowed.

"Yes, it's nothing. Prisms playing games."

Sam could have seen the same ghostly image that I'd seen. I didn't want to speculate. I needed sleep. "Thanks for looking. I'm bushed."

"Go to bed. Call me tomorrow."

After we disconnected, I nestled into the pillows. I wasn't sure how I felt about Sam seeing an image in the tulip. As unsettling as it had been, I'd thought seeing the image was a kind of superpower, a force between me and the desk. I thought maybe Caitlin was right, that I carried an epigenetic tag that made me inherently different. Special.

I wasn't sure what it meant if just anyone saw the images.

Chapter Twelve

I wasn't the first person at breakfast. A white-haired lady wearing a Giorgio Armani outfit occupied a dining room chair. I estimated her black satin-piped pants, two-button matching blazer, and white silk blouse were worth more than my first car, a Ford Escort costing fifty-five hundred dollars. I wouldn't have recognized the clothing except that I had seen a newspaper ad for sixty percent off at Neiman Marcus before my pregnancy. Considering an upgrade to my wardrobe at the time, I drove a half hour west to their closest store in King of Prussia. The first item I liked, a silk blouse, was twelve hundred dollars on sale.

I left the store empty-handed.

When the woman sipped her coffee, a diamond cocktail ring with a stone the size of Plymouth Rock nearly blinded me. Although she hardly looked athletic, a diamond-studded tennis bracelet dangled below the cuff of her blouse. A blue sash draped across her heart held a DAR pin, announcing an ancestor of hers was a patriot who'd fought in the Revolution.

The woman had a remarkable resemblance to Betty White.

When she looked up, the hair on my arms raised. Her steel-blue eyes sent a cold message. Betty White once said you could always learn about somebody by the way they put their hands on an animal, but not this woman. I doubted she went near animals at all.

She motioned for me to sit opposite her. "Please, join me for breakfast." Her voice suggested I'd be a fool to refuse.

"Of course. Thank you."

I surveyed the sideboard, then piled my plate high. At the end of the buffet, I glanced into the dining area. The woman averted her eyes and sipped her tea.

My cranberry bread dropped onto the tablecloth as I seated myself. The woman smirked but had the good manners not to comment.

"Oops. Sorry." I rescued it, brushing the crumbs into my napkin.

She spoke first. "I'm Lillian Baxter."

"RaeJean Hunter." I pretended to brush away more crumbs when she ignored my outstretched hand.

She feigned a smile. "RaeJean. An unusual name."

"Both parents wanted me named after their mother. They compromised. Combining Roisin, my Irish grandmother, with Gianna, my Italian grandmother, I became RaeJean."

"So, you have a made-up name."

All names are made up, I thought to myself. "I guess you could say that."

"Hmm. Well, my name derives from Lily and means purity." She dabbed at her mouth between each bite of her granola, blueberries, and yogurt.

I bit my lip. "I intended to call you after breakfast." I gave her my best ice-melting smile. Apparently, it was a dud. Her likeness to Betty White ended with her looks. Undaunted, I continued. "I'm researching the Mather family."

She nodded as she hoisted a gorgeous embroidered overnight bag onto her chairback.

I couldn't help myself. "Your bag is lovely."

She glanced at my shabby crossbody bag from Walmart, then said, "Johnny Was."

I nodded, pretending I knew who or what she meant. "Did the innkeeper tell you I'd like an interview?"

"I don't do interviews."

"Oh." So much for that. If she refused interviews, there was a slim chance I'd have a breakthrough. Then again, I had nothing to lose. "I'm researching Augustus Mather."

She sipped her tea, eyeing me as if I'd stolen the last muffin. Without provocation, likely to fill the silence, she began to prattle on about herself. "Even though I was raised in Hartford, I've always loved New London."

Unsure of the correct response to keep her talking, I replied, "New London's a great little city. Not as impersonal or hectic as Hartford."

"So true. A host of my Mather ancestors lived in New London." She emphasized the name Mather. "They dominated the shipping industry." Her cheeks took on a pink glow as she talked about her heritage. "What did you want to know about Augustus?"

"I'd hoped you'd have insights about him or his family."

Chest inflated, she straightened. "I *am* the family expert."

Once she began spouting the Mather genealogy, her claim proved correct. She was a walking encyclopedia. She named her direct descendant path from Reverend Richard Mather through eleven generations.

At first, I listened with rapt attention. Lillian's cheeks glowed as she rattled on without a word about Augustus. She wasn't giving me anything new. I'd been through the entire Mather lineage multiple times. But out of respect for her advanced age, I hid my boredom.

Finally, she paused to take a breath, and I jumped in. "Are you familiar with Augustus' journals?"

"I'm aware of everything about my family." She squinted at me. "What have you read?"

"*The Lineage of Rev. Richard Mather*, most of the histories of Connecticut, including *The Witchcraft Delusion in Colonial Connecticut, 1647-1697, Connecticut in Transition, 1775-1818, Hidden History of Connecticut, The Rise of Liberalism in Connecticut, 1828-1850*, and more. As part of my due diligence, I consume everything I find, even if it's only vaguely related." I smiled. Another hopeful icebreaker.

Lillian remained unmoved. "How did you hear about the journals?"

"From the Mather website manager."

She shrugged. "Those diaries are public."

I nodded. "Yes, but—"

"There's nothing noteworthy in them."

"You might be right, but as I said, I'm thorough."

She fiddled with her napkin. The corners of her mouth twitched. "By all accounts, Augustus was a dedicated physician. My family produced generations of doctors, lawyers, ship captains, politicians, and teachers. I don't think my ancestors missed a profession."

I pressed on despite her previous objection. "Your knowledge could be helpful—"

The woman stood. "Excuse me. I have a meeting with the DAR finance committee."

I relaxed when she tossed her napkin onto her plate. I'd had enough of Lillian.

Using both hands, she lifted her purse onto her shoulder. "I'll be home tomorrow. Call me, and I'll check my schedule."

Shocked, I responded, "I'll do that."

I watched the Betty White look-alike strut from the room. I couldn't hold back a smile when her Johnny Was bag caught on the colonial-sized door opening.

Out of habit, I cleared the table of our dishes. While rinsing them in the galley sink, I noticed the open door into the aunt's private apartment. Temptation won out. I had to see the desk again. The gray cat spotted me and wrapped around my legs as I tiptoed into the sitting room. The quartz tulip shimmered in the sunlight.

"I see you've met Maggie."

Startled, I turned to face an elderly version of the innkeeper. "I'm sorry for the intrusion. The door was open —I saw the cat."

"No problem. Lillian must have forgotten to close it."

"I'll close it on my way out." I slinked back to the galley, closing the door behind me.

I needed to learn to mind my own business.

Chapter Thirteen

The New Hampshire Historical Society opened at nine o'clock. Their website boasted having the state's most extensive collection of historical documents. A fifteen-minute walk took me to the red brick building where I planned to spend the day.

A stand of giant oaks shielded the two-and-a-half-story brick colonial. A woman watched me from an eyebrow window on the second floor, and then met me at the door. "Welcome. I'm your docent today."

"I'm looking for Augustus Mather's journals. Someone named Bonnie has them, but my source didn't specify a location."

"They aren't here. And Bonnie would be the librarian in Lempster."

I sighed. "So, they're probably in Lempster."

"Yes. Anything else I can help you with?"

"There is. I'd like to see your copy of *Memoirs of the Rev. Ammi Rogers.*"

"Of course. It's in mint condition. A gift from Keene's

Rogers family. I'll fetch it." The woman disappeared into a secure area.

After she returned, I settled in at a window seat with Ammi's memoirs. Although unsure where he fit in the Rogers family tree, his story intrigued me. During his eleven-year tenure as an Episcopal minister in the early 1800s, Ammi ministered at several New York churches.

In his memoir, he argued his innocence after a jury found him guilty of seducing an underaged woman. He received a two-year jail sentence and cried foul, claiming local Congregationalists had pressured the unmarried—and by that time, pregnant—girl to accuse him of rape. Witnesses swore under oath that Ammi was in Vermont when the alleged incident occurred.

Partway through his book, my suspicions grew. *He who doth protest too much.* A quick Internet search uncovered an alternative view of Ammi's situation. My sympathies for him faded when an article described his Rogerene-like indiscretions.

Charming Ammi had collected a following of women who loved him, and he loved them back. His downfall came at age fifty in 1820, the year Mary was born. He'd loved and impregnated a teenager named Asenath Smith. If he'd resided in Lyme instead of New York, I'd have suspected he fathered Mary.

But I still believed Daniel was Mary's father.

By noon, I admitted defeat. Other than Ammi Rogers' memoir, the general nature of the materials provided nothing new. On a whim, I checked their catalog for my father, Patrick O'Leary, and found very few Irish immigrants. None were named O'Leary. I packed up.

The docent closed her book. "Done so soon?"

"Yes. I'll need to examine Augustus Mather's journals."

"Maybe I can help." She made a quick call. "All set. Bonnie's expecting you this afternoon. She has the journals."

"Fantastic." Thrilled, I hurried back to the inn. *It's strange that the website manager didn't know the journals resided in Lempster.*

* * *

Highway 10 cut through forests, bordered small ponds, and passed through the tiny hamlets of Lower Village, Gilsum, and Marlow. The clear water and tree-lined shores at Stone Pond reminded me I missed home and Sam. Together, we kayaked on clear lakes like these.

Lempster's Miner Memorial Library, a former church and meeting house, filled the southwest corner at Highway 10 and Turnpike Road. I parked across the street next to the Town Offices.

Once inside the library's foyer, I peeked into an area slightly larger than my living room. It wasn't the smallest public library I'd seen, but close. A gray-haired woman I assumed was Bonnie smiled. "Welcome. You must be Ms. Hunter."

"I am. And you must be Bonnie. Not too busy today, I see." The place was empty.

"Everyone came this morning," Bonnie replied with genuine enthusiasm, as if throngs had marched through.

"Wow," I exclaimed when I saw their collection. Tall bookshelves lined three walls. Her desk abutted the foyer. Narrow aisles lined with stuffed shelves crowded a central table. Vaulted ceilings allowed the books to breathe.

Her eyes gleamed. "Our library has six thousand books. Excuse the mess. We're preparing for a weekend craft fair."

Handmade spring wreaths adorned the shelves. "You host a fair in here?"

"Not the whole fair. The Historical Society sets up tables, too." Bonnie pointed toward a white-steepled building across the street.

"Is that building open to the public? It looks fascinating." I'd originally pegged it as a church.

"Only on special occasions, like during the fair. It is this weekend, if you're around."

"Afraid not. Maybe some other time. Where's your historical section? The docent at the historical society said you have Dr. Augustus Mather's journals."

"Follow me." Bonnie hustled to the west side of the library.

Their collection filled two shelves. Lempster town reports dating back to 1940 formed the bulk of the works with a few histories of other nearby towns.

Bonnie handed me a stack of leather journals. "Here they are. I'll leave you to do your research. Oh, and here." She grabbed a magnifying glass from a shelf. "Use this. It will help you decipher the cursive where the ink has faded."

The journals were smaller than I expected. Their wear suggested Augustus had carried them with him. The entries in the first book dated 1838 documented his travels, but also included observations about his patients. He mentioned Lyme multiple times in relation to family funerals or weddings, but he mainly traveled to New York City.

The next two years had similar entries.

Before reading his 1841 journal, I took a break and browsed the wreaths. Standing on my tiptoes, I stared at a particularly hideous one.

Bonnie joined me. "We let the kids participate. A second grader made that one."

I laughed. "I was beginning to wonder. Will it sell?"

She beamed. "They all sell. The kids' wreaths go first. Our town fathers and police officers buy most of them. Then, the parents purchase the rest. It builds the kids' confidence."

Bonnie's knowing smile suggested she was a mother. A twinge of sadness reminded me I wasn't. "I'd better get to it. One more diary to go."

The hand glass slid over what looked like a routine entry in his 1841 journal before my brain caught up. Augustus had written an entry the day before Mary was last seen alive.

24 July – Sent medical student to New York to perform a procedure.

My heart raced as I snapped a photo. Its significance took me a minute to digest. My gut said this was related to Mary and might be the cause of her death. No further entries clarified the specific procedure or the name of the patient.

Still, I didn't believe in coincidences.

As I finished reading the journal, Bonnie approached. "We close in five minutes."

It was almost six. "Wow, it's late. I'd hoped to interview you since you have the diaries."

"You can, but I don't know much about the family, even though I am a Mather. My aunt was the family historian. Mother had the journals for years, but we never read them."

Disappointed, I stuffed my notebook into my bag and left.

* * *

Behind my parked car, cemetery headstones and plot markers shimmered as the sun set. Not wanting to miss visiting the graveyard, I tossed my bags onto the front seat. I'd make a quick sweep for Mather and Rogers gravesites.

As I navigated the incline to the first row of markers, I caught a movement at the rear of the cemetery. My neck hairs lifted. A man wearing dark clothes slipped behind a fieldstone building. The silhouette of a baseball cap poked from under a hood. He reappeared at the opposite edge, then disappeared behind trees at the crest of the hill.

He'd been watching me.

My hands and legs shook from the cold night air and the realization that I wasn't alone. Being petite, vulnerable, and three hundred and fifty miles from home and Sam, I got scared. I pointed my phone in the man's direction to take a photograph.

Rats! Too late. He'd vanished.

Shaky but determined to continue, I investigated a white marble obelisk marked Rogers, definitely not a Rogerene. Darkness crept in fast. My camera flash engaged when I took a photo. Chilled by the evening air and spooked by the mysterious man, I bolted toward my car.

When I slid into the Mini, I noticed my computer bag was tipped at an odd angle. I'd rushed and tossed it onto the seat. It must have toppled over from its own weight.

The corgi fob of mace hanging from my keychain reassured me I wasn't defenseless. Nonetheless, the fellow in the shadows had upset me. I scanned the cemetery one last time. He was gone.

Light from the rising moon reflected off the markers,

giving the graveyard an ethereal glow. I backed out, spun around, and sped down the highway toward Keene.

To relieve my tension, I pushed the Cooper. New Hampshire's rollercoaster roads provided the perfect diversion. Sam wouldn't have approved, even though he admitted the car was the right size for me. He didn't like speed.

Back at the inn, I paced, thinking about tomorrow's visit with Annie at the Marlow Historical Society. I flipped through an old issue of *New Hampshire Magazine* left on the dresser, glanced at an article featuring Marlow's Murray Hall. The journalist said it was one of the state's most notorious, haunted buildings. In 1624, a fire at a Halloween party killed seventy people. For three hundred years since the tragedy, locals have reported ghost sightings there.

Ridiculous. I didn't believe in ghosts. Or did I? My firm conviction regarding spirits had wavered since owning the desk with the quartz tulip.

Anxiety pricked at me, making me shiver. Grateful I was tapering off my meds and not going cold turkey, I decided to take a hot bath. It'd worked before, and it would give my mind a rest from the case.

Chapter Fourteen

On Friday morning, I called Lillian Baxter. She didn't answer, so I left a voicemail asking her to contact me. I doubted she would. I'd try her again after visiting Marlow.

***

Once in Marlow, I exited the highway and cruised along Forest Road, a narrow slice through the center of town. A white-haired woman with a bun at her nape waited on the stoop of the historic whitewashed building. She waved as I parked on the grass next to an old Volkswagen.

"Annie." I approached her.

"Yes, and you must be RaeJean Hunter." Her bulky sweater hung awry as she stood. She'd misaligned the wooden toggles by a loop. I liked her right away.

"I'm researching the Mather family from the 1800s."

She stopped short. "Right. You mentioned that on the phone. Are you another relative?"

"No, why do you ask?"

Annie opened the door as she spoke. "Monday, a lady visited, researching the same family. Claimed she was updating the family tree."

"Did she resemble Betty White?"

She raised her eyebrows. "Actually, yes, yes she did. She identified herself as a Mather descendant but didn't offer her name."

Meeting Lillian suddenly felt even less coincidental. What was her game?

Annie chattered on as she propped open the door with an antique flatiron. An escaping gust of air smelled of turpentine. "Let's leave it open. The building needs airing."

We passed two rooms. Raising her arms, Annie proclaimed, "This is the Great Hall."

"I can see why." I smiled and walked over to a horse-drawn hearse trimmed with gold filigree. My chin barely cleared its iron-rimmed wheels. Vintage furniture and glass-covered displays lined the side walls. A drop cloth anchored by paint cans covered the floor at the back.

"Follow me. We store our historical documents in my office."

Annie had a copy of *The Lineage of Rev. Richard Mather* in her bookcase. My pulse fluttered as I reached for it, then hesitated. "May I?"

"Of course. The Mather lady found a handwritten entry."

"Interesting." I flipped the pages, looking for the margin note. It was in the fifth-generation section beside a listing of Ezra Mather's children.

—Daughter born in 1820, verified with Lucy M. George's diary.

. . .

I took a picture. Mary's supposed birth year! This could be her. "It doesn't say who bore the child. I don't suppose you'd know who."

"No. But the answer might be in one of these." Annie handed me a box of diaries.

I picked one from the top. The author's name and year appeared inside each book cover.

—Lucy Mather George, 1815.

"Lucy was Dr. Augustus Mather's sister," she explained.

Time wouldn't allow me to analyze all of Lucy's diaries today. Still, I skimmed them, looking for references to Daniel Rogers, Phebe, Bea, Mary, and any mention of an illegitimate daughter or the Rogerene cemetery in New London.

In the 1814 diary, Lucy mentioned happenings in Lyme that caught my attention. She fretted that a widow's second husband had been *"familiar with both the daughter and the mother."* She didn't mention names, but based on context, it could have been Phebe and Bea.

After Phebe Mather and Daniel Rogers married, Lucy wrote that she doubted their union would last since Phebe was eleven years older than Daniel. *"He'll leave her when she's wrinkled and gray."* Apparently, she sensed unrest even though Daniel's marriage to Phebe *"...was the honorable thing to do."* I wasn't sure what Lucy meant by that entry.

Lucy documented her routine over the next ten years.

Apparently, she'd had little time for gossip. Then, in the 1830 diary, she mentioned Bea Mather and her tragic death from *"bad blood."* My breath caught. Bad blood, in those days, typically referred to sexually transmitted diseases.

Bea could have been a Rogerene who shared her stepfather's bed. That would explain why the tests revealed Mary possessed both Rogers and Mather DNA. Several pages later, Lucy worried about Bea's *"bastard daughter."* This evidence, combined with another source, could prove Mary was Bea's daughter.

In 1835, she wrote about a cousin who tended to Ezra Mather's farm animals so Phebe and Mary could travel to New York and visit Phebe's sister, Mrs. Downing. Maybe this was a scouting trip for the women to find a place to live.

A final entry suggested Phebe Mather Rogers had renounced her faith. Maybe she joined the Rogerenes. I was convinced Daniel was one. If so, Mary would have been raised one, too.

After two hours, I took a break in the Great Hall, poking around the hearse and admiring its intricacies. Tattered remnants of velvet drapes hung in its windows.

Annie looked up from her box of treasures. "Anything in particular you're looking for?"

Balancing on one foot, I shook my legs to increase the blood flow. "No. I'm stretching. I've been hired to confirm the identity of human remains found in Connecticut. Lucy's diaries haven't helped yet."

Annie straightened. "I believe the margin note about the daughter born in 1820 refers to Ezra Mather's daughter, Bea, having a child."

"Why her?"

"I read all donated materials and trace family travel.

Traveling back then was difficult. I've logged all the prominent families' trips, including the Mathers."

"That's awesome. What prompted you to start a project like that?"

She smirked. "A society member made an offhand remark suggesting women in the 1800s lived a boring existence. We had a heated debate about how they passed the time. I wanted to prove they had no spare time after caring for their family." She grinned. "I love a good challenge."

Annie didn't button her sweater right, but she was no fool. "Good idea, studying their travel habits. What did you find?"

"A pattern. Every family traveled for weddings and funerals. Weddings in the summer or fall to avoid bad weather, and funerals in the spring and summer, after the frost. Then, early fall before the freeze."

"Makes sense. Winter travel in New England—the snow." I made a face.

"New Englanders stored bodies from winter deaths in vaults. Once the ground thawed, they held multiple funerals a day, sometimes over several days. Everyone who could attend, would." She laughed. "Things in Marlow haven't changed much. Nobody misses a funeral."

Annie still hadn't explained her assumption, so I prodded. "What convinced you the margin note meant Bea Mather?"

"Something my Monday visitor said," Annie replied. "I quote, 'Ezra's daughter. Just as Grandmother said.'"

"You're sure she was referring to that note."

Annie shrugged. "I believe so."

Not conclusive, but Ezra only had one daughter. "What else do you know about the Mathers?"

"In May 1831, three families traveled to Lyme, including the Mathers. Care to see my work?"

"May I?" This information could clarify the meaning of Augustus' journal entry.

She beamed. "I'll be right back."

I wandered to a window and viewed an adjacent Victorian home. A pang of loneliness sent me to Wyncote and Sam. He'd sounded cheerful on the phone last night, so I didn't bother him with the cemetery sighting. A rustle snapped me back to Marlow and Annie.

She waved a notebook about an inch thick. "Here's what I've done."

Annie's timeline began in 1790 with columns for each family, including the names Huntley, Mather, and Gee. Augustus married a Gee a year after Mary died. She pointed to the chart. "This is where three families traveled in the spring of 1831."

Bea passed away in December 1830. The trip could have included a spring funeral for her. I'd check my research to see if any other Mather family members died that year.

Annie's logs confirmed the New Hampshire Mathers traveled to Lyme when Mary was ten, the spring after Bea died. Farther down, I noticed the same families traveled to Lyme in the fall of 1841. Could that have been to reinter Mary? Was this the elusive connection to Augustus' entry?

As I flipped through the pages, I noticed another pattern where different families traveled at the same time. "Travel seems to come in waves of families."

"Absolutely. A funeral was a big event. Entire towns attended. Families with resources made the effort."

"Devout families, like the Mathers, with financial means and Christian beliefs."

"True, but..." Annie hesitated, unbuttoned, then rebuttoned her sweater, this time in the correct loops. "In that era, funerals weren't religious events. The opposite. They celebrated life. A family in mourning would provide a feast. And there was never a sermon. The burial service was silent."

"I've heard that before." My throat tightened at the memory of the service in the hospital chapel for our baby boy. We'd been given a choice to let the hospital handle the tiny body or to have a small service. We elected a service. It felt right, and I'm glad we did.

Annie stared at me. "Are you okay? You suddenly turned pale."

I nodded, then swallowed. "Memories, that's all."

Thankfully, she didn't pry.

Annie winked. "And liquor flowed freely."

I laughed. "Like an Irish funeral."

"And, by the way, Lucy George wasn't the only Mather who kept diaries."

"What do you mean?"

"The Betty White lady mentioned a set of missing diaries as if they still existed, too. Apparently, one of Ezra's five sisters kept them. Ezra was Augustus' uncle."

I nodded. This was more than I'd hoped for. "You've been a great help."

She rolled her eyes. "Thanks. But you know family gossip. Stories can get embellished."

"True. Any idea which sister?"

"No. However, I'm sure the lady knew. She kept saying, 'I thought so'."

"That could mean anything. I'd better finish reading these journals."

"Usually, I'd say take your time, but I have a quilter's meeting in an hour."

"It shouldn't take long." I skimmed the last documents and didn't find a solid link between Bea and the daughter mentioned in Lucy's 1820 diary. After a quick farewell, I headed back to Keene. If the missing diaries existed, I had to find them.

Chapter Fifteen

Back in Keene, I grabbed a sandwich and walked to Keene's North Common for a late lunch. Once settled on a bench near the bandstand, I tried Lillian again. This time, she answered. "Ms. Baxter, this is RaeJean Hunter following up about an interview."

"Let me see what's available." Paper rustled in the background. Lillian cleared her throat. "You're in luck. I'm available tomorrow at two o'clock if you work on Saturdays."

"Yes. That's fine with me." Brushing aside my concerns about her intentions, I jumped at the chance.

"Let's meet at my place in Rocky Hill, Connecticut." She gave me the address.

"I'll leave for there in the morning." Before I had a chance to thank her, she hung up.

Her abruptness suggested I'd better prepare for the interview. I spent the next hour developing a list of questions about Mather family cemetery plots and the diaries. Being the family genealogy expert, she'd hopefully have located family graves.

My mapping program found Rocky Hill east of I-91.

When I zoomed out, orienting my destination within the state, I spotted Middletown south of Lillian's home. The Jenkintown copy of the *Lineage of Rev. Richard Mather* had gone to their library. I checked the travel time between Lillian's place and Middletown—fifteen minutes. Lillian could have requested the book through the interlibrary loan system.

"Interesting." I added a question to my list to see if she'd asked for the book.

A girl wearing a baseball cap disappeared into a shop. Her hat reminded me of the previous evening at the cemetery. I scanned Keene's tiny common. All clear. I relaxed.

Based on Annie's description, the most recent visitor at the Marlow Historical Society was Lillian. Claire would have made the trip, too, if she was the other genealogist.

And I was pretty sure she was.

Another worry surfaced. Claire still hadn't contacted me. She and Lillian traveled the same paths not long ago. I wondered if Claire being out-of-pocket was another coincidence.

After lunch, I called Professor Carver to update him on my progress. He answered immediately. I briefed him on my visits in New Hampshire. "I'm headed to Connecticut tomorrow. Were you aware someone else is working the case?"

"No. Could be the original genealogist. Bradley's still trying to get whatever she may have."

"I hoped you'd have the data by now." I slumped in my chair.

Professor Carver cleared his throat. "I gave you everything. She just called one day and resigned for personal reasons. When she said that, I didn't press. End of story."

If it was Claire, she'd tell me why she resigned. Something was wrong.

I told Professor Carver about the two sets of Mather diaries, the clues regarding Bea Mather in Lucy's journals, as well as the possibility of missing diaries. "Are you familiar with the theory that Mary died of an abortion? And that her cousin, Augustus, was a doctor?"

"Yes, and yes. You think Augustus may have been involved?" Carver's voice raised.

"It's possible. Augustus made a journal entry the day before Mary died, indicating he'd sent a medical student to the city. So, I doubt Augustus performed the procedure."

"Interesting. Anything else?"

"That's it." I sipped my water. We talked for a few more minutes before we disconnected, then I returned to the inn to pack for my morning departure.

Maybe it was meeting Lillian Baxter, or the man in the baseball cap, but I sensed danger. Claire had to be the other investigator, and I needed whatever information she'd found.

* * *

In the morning before leaving Keene, I tried Claire again. This time, she picked up and I could hear her breathing. "Where have you been? I've been calling for weeks."

She didn't respond.

"Claire? Are you there?"

She cleared her throat. "I'm here, sorry. Things have gotten complicated."

"What things?" My stomach churned.

"Work and home." She inhaled, then exhaled a deep breath. "I quit a case."

My stomach fluttered again. "I'm guessing it was the New London case."

"Yes. I didn't find much." Her swallow sounded like a gulp. "At least, nothing I can share."

I'd known Claire long enough to recognize insincerity in her voice. "You went to New Hampshire, didn't you?"

Her breath caught. "Yes."

"And you found something. Relevant documents or photographs. Something."

"I can't discuss the case." Her voice trembled.

"Claire, what's wrong? You sound scared."

"I'm sorry, Rae. I can't talk right now." She hung up.

I shivered. My hands shook so badly I dropped my phone. No question about it, I'd swing by Claire's en route to Old Saybrook. She was scared, and I had to find out why.

* * *

After our conversation, the ninety-minute drive to Claire's Longmeadow home felt like an eternity. She peered out her front window as I parked behind her Prius.

"You shouldn't be here. But I knew you'd come." She ushered me inside, scanning the yard as if expecting someone to pop out from the shrubs.

"What's wrong? You sounded upset on the phone. You scared me." My hands were still shaking slightly. I held them to my sides.

"It's that damn case. Drop it, Rae. Nothing good will come of it."

"What do you mean?" *Why is she reacting this way? It's just an identity case.*

93

"What I said. Trust me, drop the case." Her lips quivered.

I was baffled by her staunch position. Usually, we shared everything. "Why?"

She sighed. "I can't explain. It's too dangerous."

"The bones are nearly two hundred years old. What's so dangerous about them?" I pressed her, as I still couldn't grasp the reason for her stubbornness.

Claire glared at me. "I don't know! Just quit the damn case! They've got compromising pictures of Emma, okay? They've threatened her. Please quit the case."

I gasped. "Who's threatening her? Why?"

"I don't know. They said if I talk to anyone, Emma's in danger. Please, drop it."

"What kind of danger?" I couldn't imagine Emma doing anything to bring harm upon herself or Claire. They had the kind of relationship I wished I'd had with my mother. She was a precocious child who could read, write her name, recite the alphabet, and count to a hundred by age three. Claire and I had always treated her as an adult. We took her everywhere and never coddled her.

Before I lost my baby, I'd spent the weekend with them. We hiked on Saturday at a nearby wildlife preserve. Claire and I had laughed because Emma wouldn't let me carry my own lunch. That's the kind of kid she was. That's the last time I'd seen her.

"They took pictures of Emma and her boyfriend having sex."

"Who took pictures?" My head began to throb.

"I don't know. Someone spied on them through the bedroom window. Now, I'm being blackmailed. Whoever they are, they don't want Carver's investigation to continue.

They threatened to post the photos online." Claire covered her face, sobbing.

I put my arm around her and guided her toward the couch. "Calm down. Tell me what you know." I respected Claire more than anybody. A high school student when Emma was born, Claire graduated without help from her parents. And she never married Emma's father. Emma had just taken her PSATs and was looking forward to college. If compromising photos ever got posted online, it could ruin her future.

Claire sniffed. "If you don't stop working on this case, these people will threaten you, too. They don't care who they hurt."

I handed her a tissue. "What a mess. Let me think."

Claire's hands shook as she blew her nose loudly, letting out a frantic giggle. "Excuse me. I don't seem to have control of my body. I sound like an alarm honking."

When she mentioned an alarm, she triggered a thought. "Maybe you uncovered something that scared them." I thought about it for a minute. "If you tell me what you found, perhaps we can figure out why they don't want the case solved."

Claire wiped her nose while she pondered that. "I found quite a few interesting things about Mary Rogers. You've probably already seen them. Lucy George's diary, Augustus Mather's journal. Oh, and best of all, I found a letter from James Mather to Henry O'Reilly, the Irish American telegraph pioneer. I'm not sure which James Mather. A half dozen men with that name lived in America in 1842, including Ezra Mather's uncle. The letter's contents spoke of Mary's death, including that she died of an abortion, and it made me think he might have been Ezra's uncle, Louisa and Frances Griswold's father."

"That's fantastic. It solves the mystery of her death. Do you still have photos of the letter and your field notes?"

"No. I burned the hardcopy and deleted my digital files." She began to cry again.

"It's okay. Don't worry. I photographed the diary and journal entries. All I need is the letter. The original must still exist. Where did you find it?"

"The New York Historical Society—O'Reilly collection in the Klingenstein Library."

"Tell me about the person who threatened you."

"It was a man's voice. The call came in while I was at New York Public Records. The man described Emma—the birthmark on her thigh, what she and her boyfriend were doing in her bedroom. He was outside my house."

"God, you can't be serious." My heart ached for Claire and her daughter.

"When I threatened to call the police, he laughed. He said he'd leave her alone if I dropped the case." She hesitated. "I told him to consider it dropped."

"What else did he say?"

"Nothing. He hung up. So, I called Professor Carver and resigned."

"Did the man call again?" *It could be the same man that's been following me.*

"One more time, the next day. He said he'd emailed me the photographs. Then, he made me promise not to assist with the case or he'd ruin my daughter's life." She quickly added, "He had a Boston accent and used a kind of Italian slang."

"Why didn't you call the police? Report the emailed photos? They'd have brought in the FBI to track them. It's a federal offense."

"I didn't want them to see the photos." She sniffed again. "I know. That's stupid."

I thought for a minute. "Did you ever sense someone was following you?"

Claire shook her head. "No. The first hint of trouble was the phone call."

"I'd like to consult with Grace Walker and see what she suggests."

"Why didn't I think of her? I've been so upset. My mind isn't working right." Claire blew her nose again, this time more quietly and in control.

"I'll contact Grace. She'll know what to do." I checked the time. "I've got a drive ahead of me."

"Thank you. Please tell me what she says." We hugged, and I left.

I mumbled to myself as I wobbled back to my car. "Right, RaeJean. A hundred-eighty-year-old cold case. No threat. No stress. Take ten deep breaths."

Claire had to protect her child, but I didn't have that worry. My eyes filled as I recalled the tiny white casket that held our son. These people couldn't threaten me.

Then, I thought of Sam and Sophie, and I realized they could.

My hands shook as I started the car. There was no denying the coincidences now that I knew Claire was the previous genealogist. The man wearing the baseball cap in the Lempster cemetery had been watching me. Meeting Lillian at the Colony House and her being one step ahead of me in Marlow was deliberate.

I was scared. I reasoned that I should call Professor Carver, quit the case, and go home. That would be the smart thing to do.

When I left Longmeadow, I considered driving straight

to Wyncote. It would take five hours without stopping. But an accident had turned I-91 into a parking lot, giving me time to think. Although Lillian made me uncomfortable, she might have information that would help Claire and Emma. Plus, I could quiz her about her New Hampshire visit and verify it included more than the DAR conference.

Despite Claire's warning, I concluded that stepping away wasn't an option. At the Rocky Hill exit, I made a split second decision and left the highway.

Chapter Sixteen

Lillian lived in Zachary Estates, a high-end subdivision where they measured house lots in acres, not square feet, like ours. The deeper into the community, the more elaborate the homes. When I turned onto her street, the opulence nearly blinded me. Manicured lawns and gardens accented each mansion. Most were colonial style, with a few modern homes interspersed.

Lillian had described her place as the first of two estates in a large cul-de-sac surrounded by forest. I wasn't prepared for the expansive building she called her Connecticut home. With her obsession with history, I'd expected a colonial or Victorian, or at least a replica. Instead, the daunting two-story modern sat behind a circular drive that spun off toward a garage large enough to hold a fleet of buses. A tennis court in the rear answered why Lillian wore the diamond bracelet.

As I reached for my purse, a woman opened the front door, a promising sign that Lillian was home. Not that I believed she'd stand me up, but after her comment about not doing interviews, I'd harbored doubts.

"Come in. Mrs. Baxter will be right down." The housekeeper led me across the marble floor of a two-story foyer with a cut-glass chandelier as big as a piano that had to cost more than my Mini Cooper. We passed through an area with solid hardwood floors, plastered walls, and crown-over-crown wood trim. The smell of cinnamon and freshly brewed coffee surrounded me as we passed the kitchen.

"Make yourself comfortable. Mrs. Baxter prefers to sit by the pool."

I gawked at the Olympic-sized pool with an adjacent outside kitchen. Wrought iron lights hung from a redwood porch ceiling sheltering a granite bar.

"Coffee? Fresh baked blueberry scones?"

"Sounds great." Ten-foot kitchen doors swallowed the woman. I felt small, vulnerable. As I roamed the pool area, it occurred to me that this visit may have been a bad idea.

After five minutes, Lillian appeared, accompanied by the housekeeper. "I see you found my humble home."

"Yes. It's lovely." I chose an overstuffed wicker chair and nearly drowned in the throw pillows. I wedged several behind me to prevent my legs from sticking out straight. Lillian settled into a chaise lounge.

She spoke first. "Let's begin."

After gulping coffee to wash down my second scone in as many minutes, I retrieved my recorder from my bag. "Do you mind?" I held up the device.

"That's fine."

Tread lightly. Don't let Lillian clam up or spew a rerun of the Mather family tree. "Let's get into specifics since you've already shared your lineage."

She straightened her coral embroidered T-shirt. Johnny Was, I guessed.

I smiled my ice-breaker smile and began. "What do you know about Ezra Mather?"

After several sips of coffee, she cleared her throat. "Ezra earned a living with land investments in Connecticut and New York. Dabbled in imports and exports through the port of New York."

"What about family?"

"Let me see. He married Phebe Wait, Lowen Wait's daughter. They had five children. Of his four sons, one died young, and three sons outlived him. Ezra left his eldest son the farm. Phebe and their daughter, Bea, resided there free until Phebe remarried. Bea never married, and she died at thirty-one."

"Do you know anything about Phebe's family?" I'd already researched them, but I wanted to keep her talking.

"Only that the Waits had money and social status." She shrugged and took a deep breath, as if unsure she wanted to share. "Phebe had a distant uncle who was a New York City judge."

"What do you know about Phebe's life after Ezra died?"

"Not much. In the early 1800s, respectable widows kept a low profile."

I nodded. "What about Phebe's daughter, Bea?"

"All I know about Bea is what I've already told you." Her mouth twitched.

Nothing new yet. An entry in Lucy's diaries prompted my next question. "Did Phebe Mather travel to Manhattan frequently before she moved there?"

She shook her head. "I have no idea. Why do you ask?"

"Lucy George, Augustus' sister, mentioned in her 1835

diary that a cousin tended to the farm animals in Lyme so Phebe could travel to New York."

"I didn't catch that when I read them."

Apparently, the Mather family expert had missed a clue. "Did you visit Marlow, New Hampshire, recently?"

"Since I was in Keene, I decided to confirm an item Grandmother had mentioned. We shared a passion for family history. One of her diary entries said Phebe traveled to New York in 1821. We believe she visited Lucy George in Marlow during that visit, which I couldn't confirm."

"You have your grandmother's diaries."

Lillian's eyes became slits. "Yes. But I promised Mother I wouldn't share them."

"A promise you won't break, I assume."

"That's right." Lillian set her chin.

Not only did Augustus Mather and Lucy George keep journals, but Lillian's grandmother kept a third set. Not to mention, there was a set of missing diaries. My brain raced. I needed to convince Lillian to share her grandmother's journals.

She broke the silence. "I have the guest register from Grandfather's funeral in 1937. I'll dig it out tomorrow. It might help."

She'd dodged the diary topic by offering the funeral register. I doubted its usefulness but feigned interest to gain her confidence. "Great!"

"Why the interest in Phebe Rogers and Bea Mather?" Lillian's face was stoic.

"An entry in Lucy's diaries implied a widow's second husband was familiar with both the mother and daughter. Lucy never revealed the widow or explained what she meant."

She stiffened and arched one eyebrow. "And?"

"I have a theory. I think Daniel Rogers, Phebe's second husband, was a polygamist, and he was intimate with both Phebe and Bea."

"Polygamy was unlawful. No Mather would have married a woman who would violate the law, God's law, after he died. It's an impossible notion." Lillian's disgusted look could have soured milk.

I changed direction to prevent her from shutting down. "Not until 1890."

"If you say so." Her offended posture remained unchanged.

I moved to the next topic. "It's possible Phebe socialized with the Mather family after Ezra died."

"Yes. I believe up until she remarried, then only a few members remained friendly. After..." Lillian repositioned herself in her chair as if she could distance herself from the past by her movements.

"After what?"

"After Phebe and Daniel had a child, most of the Mather family grew distant. But they included Bea in their family gatherings."

"Could Mary have attended with Bea?" This could link Mary to the Mathers.

"Yes. Especially when Bea visited her Uncle James Mather and Aunt Caroline. Their girls, Frances and Louisa, were close to Mary's age. Grandmother mentioned seeing them play Graces. You know, French Hoops."

I recalled Ammi Rogers' memoir, and the illegitimate baby. "Do you believe that Daniel Rogers was Mary's father?"

"She carried the Rogers name. Why are you asking?" Lillian's eyes remained narrowed as she awaited my next question.

"Without a birth certificate, nothing is certain." I tried to ease her back into the conversation about Daniel.

"Why are you curious about him?" She seemed to relax.

"I'm tracing Ezra's descendants and his widow for a client. There's no record of Mary's birth." Suspicious and uncertain of Lillian's interest in my project, I withheld my project's bonus goal: Identify how Mary Rogers died.

"Documents get lost. Mary wasn't a Mather, anyway. Will you publish a case report?"

Interesting. Lillian believed Mary wasn't a Mather. She probably didn't care where Mary was buried. My reports belonged to the client, so I'd never publish, but I decided to lie to see her reaction. "I might. The Mather family history fits my vision of a publishable story."

Lillian squirmed in her seat. "I see."

I had a feeling her disquiet didn't arise from questions about Mary. But I had no idea what other reason she might have. "Are you aware of certain missing diaries?" I studied her face for a tell.

Her lips twitched again. "It's a family rumor. Nobody's ever found them. They belonged to Martha Wade, Ezra's younger sister."

I waited. Lillian might divulge more.

"You should try to locate them," she added.

"Then, you believe they exist." I smiled inside. I'd caught her in a fib.

Her voice disagreed with her smile. "It's possible."

"Any suggestion of where to search?" *She knows more.*

"No. Well, it's probably nothing, but after Grandfather died, my father shipped boxes of family records to New York City." Lillian's voice faded at the end of the sentence, as if she'd just remembered something.

"What kind of records?"

"I have no idea. At ten years old, I didn't pay attention. Father also mentioned a key. Let me think." She gazed at the floor for a moment. "What did he say?"

I waited.

She checked the time. "Oh my, it's nearly five o'clock."

"Two more questions. I'll be quick."

"Go ahead. Ask."

"Did you request the Jenkintown copy of the Mather genealogy?"

Her eyes narrowed again before she answered. "Yes, I did. I check for margin notes in every copy I find."

"Right. You're thorough. How about locating family graves? Much research there?"

She nodded. "I've personally visited several cemeteries in Connecticut, and I use a feature on Ancestry.com called *Find a Grave*. Saves time." Lillian rechecked her watch.

I didn't pursue the grave issue since Lillian didn't recognize Mary as a Mather, and she appeared anxious to end the interview. I turned off my recorder. "Wow, where did the afternoon go?"

She smirked as I slid from the chair and stood, catching a rogue pillow before it hit the floor.

"I appreciate your time. I'd better head out." Hoping to catch her off guard, I added, "I think another Mather is trying to identify remains found in New London. The discovery made the news."

An insincere smile crossed her face. "I doubt it. Why? Do they suspect it's a Mather?"

"Some believe it's Mary Rogers."

Her smile vanished. "That's ridiculous. Who believes it's her?"

"Just rumors among graduate students." I lied again, uncomfortable about revealing my client.

"Please keep me informed of your findings." She forced another smile. "If Mary Rogers was a Mather, I'd need to know."

"I'll definitely do that." Another lie. I suspected she knew Mary's lineage very well.

On the way to my car, I texted the innkeeper at Pratt's in Old Saybrook to advise her I'd be there in an hour. She assured me the Library Room was ready.

Claire's warning nagged at me during the drive, but I wasn't ready to quit. Lillian had confirmed the existence of Martha Wade's missing diaries. Plus, she'd alluded to a key.

Claire may have hit a nerve with a Mather or Rogers family member, but I doubted I'd rankled someone this early in the case, unless it was Lillian. She was an odd one, for sure, but she was a knowledgeable source.

If I could believe her.

Chapter Seventeen

When we spent a weekend in Old Saybrook a year ago, Sam and I had walked past the Deacon Timothy Pratt's Bed & Breakfast. Deacon Pratt's father had built the two-hundred-seventy-year-old parsonage on Main Street adjacent to the First Presbyterian Church. Years later, they moved the church across the street.

The bed and breakfast stood next door to Katharine Hepburn's old stomping ground, the James Pharmacy & Soda Fountain. Built on the former church lot, it had been owned and operated by the first black American female pharmacist, Anna Louise James, in 1922. Anna James was a groundbreaker in her profession, for both her gender and her race.

During check-in, the innkeeper waxed on about the recent remodel, incorporating reprints and furniture from past owners. She wanted the house to tell its own story. Family pictures from five generations decorated the walls.

"This way." She led me to a suite she'd named the Library Room. My quarters faced the street.

"Oh my." She looked at me, then surveyed the elevated canopy bed. "I'll fetch a step stool from the sitting room."

The top mattress of the four-poster reached my armpits. "What a magnificent bed!"

"Yes. It is spectacular. It sits well above the floor drafts. Heat rises."

"It's great." I inhaled. *A fall from this bed would hurt.*

"During the renovation, we tore out the bookcases, except those." She pointed to a display of antique bottles and letters. "We kept the items found in the walls."

I examined a hand-blown bottle. A glass neck protruded from a leather case.

"That's a laudanum bottle, a solution of opium." The innkeeper lifted her eyebrows.

Mary's fiancé, Payne, came to mind. He'd overdosed on laudanum after Mary died. If Mary succumbed to poison, we'd never know. Opiates were undetectable after a hundred and eighty years.

"Be right back with a stool." The innkeeper disappeared through a second door, back into the dining area. She'd toured me full circle instead of taking the direct route to my room.

I waited at the front window until she returned, carrying an antique bed ladder, which was basically a fancy stool with three steps.

"Nice ladder," I said. The solid mahogany piece showed wear on the treads. Otherwise, it was mint. Sam would've loved it.

"Thank you. It came with the property. They used the house as a children's school before I bought it." The innkeeper exited back into the dining room.

I checked my phone for messages. Nothing from Sam. Then, I texted Grace. *Can we talk? I need your help. It's related to Emma, Claire Allen's daughter, and blackmail.* The chime indicating the message was sent relieved my tension and renewed my determination.

Grace could calm a storm with her ability to synthesize data into significant facts. A career woman with the FBI and single by choice, her work schedule made mine look part-time at best. Grace was amazing. She'd help.

My stomach growled. Lillian's scones had long worn off. I headed to Liv's Restaurant, a place Sam and I had wanted to try but ran out of time. Lost in thought, I strolled north on Main Street.

Music boomed from a former retail store. Movement inside caught my eye. I peered inside. Women in leotards danced, flexing every muscle as they gracefully moved to the melody.

When I turned to continue, I ran smack into a man wearing a Yankees baseball cap. My breath caught. "Oh! Excuse me. Sorry."

He turned away. "No problem."

The guy looked familiar. I glanced back, watching him stroll south. Same build. Right height. He could have been the man I'd seen in Lempster. I quickened my pace toward Liv's Restaurant.

The coliseum entrance with tall pillars, a rotunda ceiling, and a seaside mural above the door reminded me of a classic movie set. A couple drank wine at an outside table. I chose to dine inside. The man by the fitness center had unnerved me.

When I entered, the warm air smelled of Italian spices with a hint of seafood and anise. Customers chatted at small tables. I requested a window seat. I'd barely landed when a waitress swooped in for my drink order.

"A Muscadet and fresh oysters, please."

"You sure? We have Prince Edward Island mussels tonight. They're going fast."

"No, I have my heart set on oysters on the half shell." My mouth watered.

Her eyes widened. "Okay, but you don't know what you're missing."

"I'm a bit of an oyster connoisseur." I'd acquired a taste for them early in life, a taste my dad and I shared. He told me it made me special, along with my curly red hair. At four years old, I'd believed him and slurped one down to make him happy.

"Then, you've made the right choice. You won't find better oysters anywhere."

I smiled. "That's what I'm hoping for."

While waiting for my oysters, I read Grace's response. *I'm in for the night. Call when you can.*

The waitress emerged from the kitchen as I replied to Grace that I'd call in two hours. En route to my table, she visited an elderly man seated alone at a corner table. His leathery face suggested he'd spent his life on the water. He was a story ready to be written, a relic from a Winslow Homer painting.

A voice boomed from an adjacent table. "Hey, Rogers, don't you ever go home?"

"When I fill up," the old salt responded.

My antennae lifted. *Did I hear that name right?*

A burst of laughter and loud comments ensued. I couldn't understand anything else, but I wondered if he might be a Daniel Rogers descendant. He looked old enough to be worth interviewing.

"Do you know the gentleman at the corner table?" I asked my waitress when she delivered my oysters.

She smiled. "Sure, that's Ezekiel Rogers. Zeke eats here almost every night."

"Is he related to the Rogers family who helped settle Lyme?"

The waitress threw back her head, laughing. "Are you kidding? Everyone in Connecticut is related. My aunt is Zeke's cousin. And yes, our family helped settle this area."

"I'm researching a member of the Rogers family. I'd love to talk to him."

"No worries. Zeke talks to anyone who'll listen." The waitress swung by Ezekiel's corner on her way to the kitchen. She gestured toward me while she spoke. Ezekiel waved, nodded, and smiled. I took that as a yes.

After the waitress cleared my table, the man stood and shuffled toward me, visiting with customers along the way. He knew everyone in the restaurant, it seemed.

At my table, he leaned on one hand. "Young lady, I hear you'd like to have a chat."

My breath caught, momentarily mesmerized by his deep blue eyes and the shock of white hair dusting his shoulders. "Yes. Did the waitress explain that I'm researching the Rogers family?"

"She did." He sat opposite me, folding his weathered hands on the table.

I began with an open-ended request. "Great. Tell me about yourself, your life."

He squinted. "Not much to tell. I was born in Old Saybrook in 1938. Quit school when I was old enough to sail with my father. I've been a commercial fisherman all my life."

The waitress's comment suggested he was talkative, so I waited.

And he waited.

I tried another approach. "What about your family?"

"I had a brother and two sisters." He pursed his lips as if that's all he wanted to reveal.

I tried again, this time asking about his mother. "Tell me about your mother."

He frowned. "What do you want to know about Mother?"

"Did she come from this area? What was her maiden name?" I smiled, hoping to gain his trust.

"She was born and raised in Lyme. My mother was a Mather."

The waitress had joked that everyone in Connecticut was related. I hadn't considered the current generation, but Ezekiel Rogers had a tie to the Mather family. "Which branch of the family?" *Maybe he was related to Bea Mather.*

"No idea. I'm not much for the family tree stuff." He looked away.

Frustrated, I rethought my approach. This man defied the waitress' description. He responded to open-ended questions with single words. I needed him to talk.

"Excuse me. I need to use the ladies' room." I pointed at my empty water glass.

I lingered in the restroom, formulating a strategy. Yankees tended to be tight-lipped, as he'd proven. Diplomacy, that's what I needed. Smooth-talk him a bit. I formulated a few slick questions to soften him up.

Chapter Eighteen

When I returned, Ezekiel was roaming the dining room, socializing. He lumbered back to my table when he spotted me. "Catching up on the news," he explained.

On intuition, I blurted my burning question. "What do you know about Mary Rogers?"

He grinned. "It's about time you got to the point, young lady."

My face burned. "Okay, you win. Tell me what you know about Mary."

"She died mysteriously. At least, that's what all the books say." His blue eyes twinkled.

"Did anyone in your family ever discuss the cause of her death?"

"No, even though I'm pretty sure my folks knew."

"Why do you suspect that?" My stomach fluttered at the prospect of him finally opening up.

"In the tenth grade, our teacher had us read stories by Edgar Allan Poe, including *Marie Roget*. She said Poe based his story on a real person, Mary Rogers." Zeke scowled.

"Then, she asked me if I knew how Mary died since I was a Connecticut Rogers."

"You're kidding."

He shrugged. "After school, I asked Mother about Mary. Her face turned white. She denied knowing anything, but her expression said she had a secret."

"Do you think anyone recorded Mary's real story, not just what the papers printed?"

"No idea. Could have. If accounts exist, nobody's checked the right places yet." He winked. "And..."

"And what?"

"And you seem like the kind of gal who doesn't quit." He smiled. "So, start with family trees."

"I have."

"Okay, then you know everyone in Connecticut's related. And one of these relationships should lead to the answer." Ezekiel signaled to the waitress for a coffee refill while I formed my next question.

"Which family relationship?"

He squeezed his eyes shut. "Trace the Mather women, not the men."

Tracing maternal lines presented a challenge. Surnames changed through marriage. It wasn't impossible. I'd done it enough times. Plus, I'd gotten the most titillating information from Lucy George's diaries. And if I located Martha Wade's, maybe I'd learn more. Lillian had implied they held promise.

I asked a few more questions, but Ezekiel had regressed to single-word answers once more. At least, until I mentioned the Rogerenes, then the stories began to flow one after the other about their radical behavior. He laughed so hard over a Rogerene attending a traditional church service naked that he almost choked.

"My Rogerene ancestors used their liberal beliefs to justify immoral behavior and host wild parties." He offered me a grin full of mischief. "Of course, I'd never do that."

Ezekiel was shrewd. He played the ignorant old salt, but it was just that, a part he played. "So, you behaved for your entire life."

"I didn't say that, but I don't blame my misdeeds on religion."

"I've been hired to confirm the identity of human remains found on campus at Connecticut College. My client believes they were dislodged from an upstream cemetery."

"The Rogerene burial ground north of the boathouse."

"Most likely. The professor thinks they belong to Mary Rogers. DNA results showed both Mather and Rogers markers."

He raised an eyebrow. "If your client's right and it's Mary, there's a problem."

"What's that?"

"Those Rogers were Presbyterian. They'd never bury her in an unhallowed grave."

"I have evidence her father came from a Rogerene branch." *This isn't good.*

Ezekiel rubbed his chin. "Maybe, but I'm positive Daniel's grandfather, Ebenezer, worshiped with the Presbyterians, same as my relatives."

"Maybe Daniel's father, or Daniel himself, joined the Rogerenes." *I believed he did.*

"Maybe. Don't know much about Daniel's father, Amos. He drowned in a squall in Long Island Sound, sailing home from New Haven on a Russian-made yacht he'd bought. Darnedest thing. Wasn't a single nail used to build the boat. A work of art. The boat didn't fail. Amos misjudged the sea."

I drew on my napkin. "Ebenezer was Daniel's grandfather."

"Yup. We all descended from James, the Rogerene. Daniel's family descended from James's youngest son, William. But I heard Grandma mention Ebenezer served as a Presbyterian church deacon, so he wasn't a Rogerene."

Ezekiel Rogers knew more about family history than he realized. Not uncommon in most families. I scribbled notes and muttered, "Oral history."

"Oral history! It's nothing but family gossip." He slapped the table, laughing.

"There's often a fiber of truth in family stories. It's the thread that ties us to the past."

Ezekiel shrugged. "Maybe."

"Do you know if Phebe was Mary's mother?"

"No. If the remains are her, Bea had her. It's the only thing that fits."

"Why Bea?"

"Gossip. When I was a kid, I heard Grandma talking about Mary's death. She said if Phebe had left Mary with the Mather relatives who'd wanted her, none of that would've happened."

"So, Phebe was her grandmother."

"That's what Grandma believed." He tapped the table with a leathery finger. "Grandma said Mary was a winter baby. Small, not expected to live. So, the doctor didn't record her birth. Never did because he died that same winter."

I checked my notes. "Did your grandmother mention why Phebe refused to leave Mary?"

"Grandma said she was Phebe's meal ticket."

"How so?" This was new information.

"I didn't get her meaning at that moment. Everyone talked about Mary's beauty. I overheard talk about parties at the farm after Ezra died, but Grandma shushed everyone if I was around. She called it an adult conversation."

If Ezekiel Rogers believed Bea was Mary's mother, I was on the right track. To confirm the Mather connection, I needed documented proof if I was ever going to use any of the information to prove the bones could be Mary.

Ezekiel scanned the near-empty room. "It's closing time. We're the only ones still here. If that's all, we should probably settle up and leave."

"Just one more. Do you know Lillian Baxter? I interviewed her this afternoon."

Ezekiel's facial muscles tightened. "Yup, she's a relative. We don't share the same views. I don't obsess over history. It's a living thing, always one second behind you. Never disappears. Just gets larger and deeper over time."

He didn't elaborate about Lillian. I sensed no love lost between them. But he was right about the past being eternal. Finally, I spoke. "Mr. Rogers, I'd like to phone you if I have more questions."

He scribbled his number on a napkin, then struggled to his feet. "By all means. And call me Zeke. Everyone else does."

Calling him by his nickname—I'd penetrated his defenses, finally. "I will, Zeke. Thank you for your time."

"Time's what I've got since I'm not fishing." He hesitated. "You be careful of that Mather woman." He turned and walked out the door.

As I left, the scent of licorice lingered from the night's special. Was Zeke referring to the dead woman, or Lillian Baxter? I shivered from cold and residual fear as I hurried back to Pratt's. Once there, I called Grace. She picked up after a couple of rings.

"I have a situation that could use your help," I said.

"Okay, shoot." Grace didn't carry a gun, but she got a kick out of talking the talk.

"Claire Allen's teenage daughter is in trouble. Someone photographed her having sex with her boyfriend. Claire was told to drop a recent case, or else they would post the pictures on the Internet."

Grace paused for a moment. "I haven't heard of anything like that. But this kind of thing can ruin a kid's life. I'll check. Have Claire send me the pictures. Our guys may be able to track information from them."

"Thank you. I appreciate your help." We ended the call, and I immediately sent Claire a text about the photographs.

An hour later she replied. *Done, but I'm not telling Emma. She'd die of embarrassment.*

I wanted to believe Emma would trust her mother's judgment, but Grace was probably right. Thinking of poor Emma's humiliation only made me want to find out who was responsible for all of this even more.

Chapter Nineteen

In bed, planning my visit to the Phoebe Noyes Griffin Old Lyme Library, I realized tomorrow was Sunday. They would be closed.

"What an idiot." My travel planning skills needed dusting off after a seven-month break. The innkeeper kindly extended my reservation for two more nights, and I called Sam about my change in plans.

"No problem," he said. "I'll call Greg. Maybe we can catch tomorrow's game. The Pirates are in town. Why don't you connect with Caitlin?"

"She's covering an event in Granby. I'll keep busy, you know me."

"Okay. Be careful."

I fell asleep the minute we disconnected the call.

* * *

When I awoke, rain pounded at the windows. I passed the day rehashing Mary's story on the off chance I'd missed a clue that would solve the mystery.

Mary had disappeared for a week during her employment at Anderson's Cigar Emporium. A reporter from *The Sun* claimed she'd left a suicide note, but Mary had returned home alive and well after supposedly visiting a friend in Brooklyn.

After that, she became overwhelmed by the publicity. Papers published her every move for financial gain. Ultimately, she quit her job at Anderson's to run their boarding house. It was then that Mary had become engaged to Daniel Payne, the cork cutter and current boarder.

On Sunday morning, July 25, 1841, she told Payne she was visiting her aunt, Mrs. Downing, on Jane Street. That was the last time her family and friends saw her alive. When Mary hadn't returned by Monday night, Phebe placed an ad in *The Sun* asking anyone who'd seen Mary to contact her. Friends and family searched until Wednesday, when two men spotted a body floating in the Hudson River near Elysian Park in Hoboken. They used a small boat to drag the woman's body to shore. The police and a coroner were involved. Then, as Carver mentioned, Crommelin happened upon the scene and identified Mary based on the hair pattern on her arms.

And they believed him. *Not very thorough police work, if you ask me.*

After the fact, information emerged that Mary had visited Crommelin daily for two weeks before her death, leaving a rose in the keyhole at her last visit.

I suspected he knew Mary had gone to Hoboken.

The journalists went wild. If it had been any other working girl, the story would have died quickly. But John Anderson had introduced her to the heartbeat of New York City.

The coroner ruled Mary's death suspicious rather than

accidental, implying she'd died either by an unnatural cause or by murder.

The police investigated, while the *Herald*, the *Tribune*, and *The Sun* sensationalized the homicide possibilities. After numerous interviews with Mayor Isaac Varian, his successor, Robert Morris, and the NYPD, they concluded it was a murder.

I tapped the table. There had to be more. "A mayor wouldn't typically be involved in a case like this."

Police had three suspects, including her fiancé, a sailor named William Kiekuck, who was also a former boarder, and a neighboring wood engraver named Joseph Morse. Both Payne and Kiekuck produced supportable alibis. Wanting to hide infidelity, Morse fled to Worcester, Massachusetts, soon after Mary's body was discovered. When the police caught him, he confessed to a tryst with a young woman. In the end, all three men were cleared.

The *Herald* suggested a gang had murdered Mary and her male companion because within days of finding Mary's body, a man's body also floated ashore down river. Kids found Mary's clothing and her parasol strewn around Sybil's Cave. The reporter deduced the assault had occurred there, and the assailants had dumped both bodies in the Hudson.

Police dismissed this theory as a coincidence.

Politicians also used Mary's tragic end to pass two important laws in 1845; the NYC Police Reform Act to modernize their police system, and a state law criminalizing abortion.

I seethed. "Right. Outlaw the solution, not the cause of the problem."

* * *

Monday morning, I crossed the Thames River to Old Lyme. Massive oaks and maples lined the streets, providing a natural canopy for the parking spaces near the library.

Stepping from my car, I checked for people wearing baseball caps. None resembled the man I'd previously seen. I released the breath I hadn't realized I was holding.

Once inside, a librarian directed me to the resource room. The *Barbour Collection of Connecticut Town Vital Records* verified the Mather family tree I had developed. Area cemetery records in *The Hale Collection* included the primary Mather family burial site in Duck River Cemetery. I located Ezra Mather's grave, but no records for Mary or Phebe Rogers.

The library's historic church newsletters confirmed that soon after Ezra died, Phebe disappeared from the social columns. Several listed couples included women with escorts, but none were Phebe. Lillian could be right about widows and single women in the early 1800s rarely appearing in public unescorted.

An article about the Rogers family's absence from the social columns after Ezra died hinted that Phebe's activities had become "unbecoming of a widow," which reminded me of Lucy George's diary entry stating Daniel and Phebe's marriage was "the talk of the town." Lucy may have meant the age difference, but it could have been more than that. Whatever happened, Phebe's name never appeared in the columns again after her marriage to Daniel.

I found it strange that Lucy hadn't mentioned Bea. At fifteen, the age of maturity, Bea should have debuted, entertaining suitors. It was a juicy topic for Lucy to write about. Something could have happened on the farm to impact Bea's marriage prospects.

Later in her diary, Lucy did mention Bea died of bad

blood. This cause of death, combined with Phebe's disappearance from the social scene, smelled of the Rogerenes. When I mentioned polygamy to Lillian, she'd claimed ignorance. But I'd seen her mouth twitch.

The library's collection of Rogers family genealogies and memoirs focused on the Rogerene split from the Congregational church and the schism's drama. I was able to verify the Rogers family tree and Zeke's information regarding Ebenezer Rogers being a Presbyterian. If Daniel was a Presbyterian, my theory didn't fly. I had more digging to do on that idea.

At closing time, the librarian and I walked toward the parking lot.

"Good day researching?" she asked.

"Not bad. I don't have conclusive evidence yet."

She smiled. "I'm sure you'll find it."

"Maybe." I still had Lillian's grandfather's funeral register to examine.

* * *

Duck River Cemetery was less than a mile from the library. With several hours of daylight left, I drove to the memorial park to stroll among the Mather graves, a pastime I'd previously found peaceful until seeing the man in Lempster.

The cemetery entrance opened into a nature preserve sandwiched between two housing developments. Century-old elms had invaded the gravesites near the front where I parked in a turnoff inside the gate. Heavy vegetation hid nearby homes, but it didn't block the traffic sounds.

As I climbed out of my Mini, a vehicle pulled in behind me. A quick look assured me the driver wasn't familiar, and he wasn't wearing a baseball cap. Relieved, I ignored him and wandered into the old section of the graveyard.

History engulfed me, its silence disturbed only by the *scrape, scrape* of workers shoveling gravel for a new grave. I strolled along paths flanked by markers, visiting a handful of the sixty-six Mather graves before I spotted a tall obelisk marked Griswold jutting from the center of a plot near Ezra's grave.

I crouched for a closer look. My eyes filled, hands shaking as I traced the tiny letters below Louisa Mather Griswold's name.

And Her Infant Son

Unlike Louisa, I'd survived. But my baby didn't see life outside my womb. I covered my face and cried. These moments had become rare, but when they hit, they hit hard.

After a few minutes, I wiped my eyes and blew my nose. Then, I stood and headed toward an arched stone bridge spanning Duck River, a small tidal estuary flowing into the Connecticut River that fed Long Island Sound. The river swirled as I crossed the bridge into a newer section of the cemetery. Brackish water licked the road's edge, creating a foamy swale. Further up the incline, moss covered the headstones protruding from the ground next to a pretentious white cross.

A muffled voice drifted in the wind as I leaned over to clean a ground-level marker and check the name. With a glance uphill, I saw a man resting against a tall marble marker while he chatted on his cellphone. He wore a black baseball cap with white lettering. His build looked similar to the man in Lempster and the guy in Old Saybrook. I leaped to my feet, backpedaled, then tripped and fell. Pain shot through my head.

* * *

Someone touched my shoulder. A man's voice asked, "You all right, Miss?"

I opened my eyes. A man in blue coveralls leaned over me. I couldn't read his nametag.

"I'm not sure. I tripped and bumped my head." My eyes began to refocus.

"Lay still." He kneeled beside me. "I'll help you up when you're ready."

"Do you work here?" A silly question. Where else would he work?

"Yes, ma'am. I saw a little fluff of color over here on the ground. When it moved, I realized it was you. I'd seen you earlier at the Griswold monument."

My head hurt. Reaching back, I felt a hard lump behind my right ear. "No blood. I guess I'm going to live."

"You might have a concussion. Sit for a few minutes. Can I contact someone?"

"No. I'll be fine, but thank you. I'm staying ten minutes away at Pratt's in Old Saybrook."

The man lifted me like a ragdoll and stood me on my feet. I wobbled. I was physically fine, but emotionally, I was a wreck. I'd seen a man wearing a baseball cap. "Did you see anyone enter the cemetery today wearing a black ballcap?"

"Nope. Let me walk you to your car." He pointed toward a man loading tools into a truck across the river. "We're done for today."

I felt dopey as I stood next to the Mini and fumbled for my keys.

"There's a doc-in-the-box not far away. I'll take you to the clinic."

"Thank you, but I'll be fine." I'd had worse bumps.

After the worker left, I noticed the car behind me had disappeared as well. As I grabbed the door handle, I spotted an envelope tucked under the windshield wiper. Plucking it off, I flopped into the car and threw it onto the empty passenger seat where I'd left my computer and purse. Scanning the interior, bile rose in my throat. I jumped out of the driver's seat and shouted to the caretaker. "Wait a minute, please."

He turned, heading back toward me. "What's the matter?"

"Did you see anyone around my car earlier?"

"No, I was busy digging. I didn't notice anything." He scowled. "Why?"

"My computer and purse are missing." Besides a headache, my stomach began to roil.

"Was it locked?" He'd asked the obvious question.

"I don't recall locking the car. Not that it matters now." My own carelessness disgusted me.

"Sorry, Miss. I hope you still have your keys." I raised my key ring and he nodded. "Well, be careful driving. You had a nasty fall."

"I will." *Crap. No computer, no money, and no ID.*

Unsure of what else to do, I tore open the envelope to reveal a blank sheet of paper. *What the heck? Is this some sort of creepy game?* I stuffed it back into the envelope and shoved it into my pocket. I'd check for a hidden message later once my head stopped throbbing.

At Pratt's, I reported my stolen purse and laptop to the police. Then, I called Sam.

"Didn't you lock your doors?"

"I must not have. I can't remember," I lied, too embarrassed to own up to it. While Sam and I talked, I realized I'd forgotten something else as well. "Darn, I forgot to report the note."

"What note?"

"Someone stuck an envelope under my wiper." I patted my pocket. It was still there.

"Did you see any kids around?" Sam asked. "Could be a prank."

"Maybe. But blank paper? Seems lame for a prank. Kids are more creative than that." My pounding head made it difficult to think. "I saw a guy talking on his phone before I fell. He looked familiar, but I didn't know him."

"Are you sure you're all right? If you feel dizzy, get to a clinic." Sam's voice cracked.

"I will." His concern was salve in my wound. "There's one five minutes from here."

"Call before you leave tomorrow." He'd regained control of his voice. "Love you."

"I will. Love you, too." We disconnected and I wrote myself a note so I wouldn't forget.

After taking pain pills to dull the headache, I rested back on the pillow to rehash the cemetery event. It all happened so fast, and a thought hadn't occurred to me at the time.

Was I clumsy, or had someone pushed me?

Chapter Twenty

Light traffic made the four-hour trip home a breeze, thank goodness. The conk on the head had dulled me, but my fuel-efficient Mini made it home with ease and, with his usual resourcefulness, Sam had followed through on his promise to cancel my credit cards.

As I pulled into the driveway, I spotted Sophie chasing a tennis ball across the yard. She propelled into a corgi-sized leap, caught the ball in midair, and landed on her stubby legs.

Sam sauntered over to my car. "Did the Mini grow wings?"

The egg on my head complained when I smiled. "I'll never tell."

Once inside, he inspected my wound. "Still swollen. Do you need to wear a helmet?"

I laughed. "According to Caitlin, all the time. I've always been accident prone."

"Let's relax on the porch and you can tell me about your trip. Want anything to drink?"

I automatically shook my head. "Ouch. Just water."

Sam returned with a beer for himself and ice water for me. I recounted the tidbits of information I'd found about a scandal involving Ammi Rogers and a teenage girl who'd delivered a baby the year Mary was born, Mary and Augustus' relationship, as well as the journal entry the day before Mary died that said he'd sent a medical student to the city.

"To perform an abortion." Sam took a sip of his beer.

"Could be. It didn't say. Mary might have had a fatal abortion, but I've got no hard evidence supporting it."

"Why not?"

"It's a long story. But the crux of it is, I finally talked with Claire. As suspected, she was the previous genealogist. She hung up when I asked her about the case. So, I swung by her house on my way to Old Saybrook. And she warned me to quit."

"Why?" Sam's eyes narrowed.

I hesitated. My neck felt hot. "I promised Claire."

"Surely you can tell me. I can keep a secret." Sam stared at me, his eyes now mere slits.

"It's about Emma. Someone photographed her having sex with her boyfriend. The perpetrator spied through her bedroom window. And if that's not horrifying enough, the pervert threatened Claire, saying he'd post them on the Internet if she didn't drop the case."

Sam rubbed his forehead. "God, at her age, this could scar Emma for life. And the boyfriend, too."

"I know. Claire's scared. I've never seen her like this." Telling Sam only amplified my fears.

"If quitting the case could help Emma..." His face paled as the realization dawned on him. "Does that mean you're in danger?"

I replied, fingers crossed behind my back. "Not really. If

I'm discrete, my research shouldn't attract Claire's blackmailer."

Sam arched an eyebrow. He wasn't buying it.

I inhaled, then blurted my suspicion. "I think I'm being followed. I keep seeing the same guy, or a similar looking guy, wearing a black Yankees baseball cap. I'm probably imagining it."

Sam's brow remained arched. "Maybe, but you still need to be careful."

Nervous, I prattled on. "In Old Saybrook, I met another Rogers—Ezekiel—at Liv's. By the way, we've got to go back there. The food's fantastic."

Sam ignored my aside. "You need to conclude this case before something bad happens. Between Lillian Baxter and this Rogers guy, you have two living relatives to interview. They might be able to corroborate your findings. Maybe move things along."

"I'm pretty sure Ezekiel Rogers will. But I'm not convinced of Lillian Baxter's sincerity. There's something about her. She runs hot and cold. Mostly cold. First, Lillian says she doesn't do interviews, but then she invites me to her house. She offers information, but not about what I asked. Plus, she's been one step ahead of me at every stop. I think she's making sure no embarrassing family secrets get revealed."

"It sounds like a fruitful trip except for the protein on your head." He touched my bump, making me wince slightly.

"Food analogy. Really?" I laughed.

"Where's the note? Maybe there's a hidden clue. In Boy Scouts, we used lemon juice to write coded messages." Sam smiled at the memory.

"In my briefcase, by the door."

"I'll get it." Sam returned holding the note with tweezers, a lighter in his other hand.

"That's it. What's next, Watson?"

He held the paper above the flame. "Nothing."

"It could be a threat about something. But what?" I suddenly felt ill again.

* * *

The next day, I submitted an online request to replace my genealogist certification ID card. It would take four weeks. Then, I called Grace at her private number. She didn't get much private time, but I was anxious about the note. She answered after a few rings.

"Hi. It's Rae. Sorry to bother you."

"No problem at all. I've actually been meaning to call you. Emma's situation doesn't look like anything other than blackmail."

"Thanks for the update. That's a relief, at least. I have something else to ask you. On Monday, someone left a blank note on my windshield and stole my laptop."

"And you're just calling me now?" Grace sounded exasperated. "Send me the note. We've seen this MO before, a month ago in Rhode Island. I'll have the lab check for prints. If you can, send me the serial number for your laptop. I'll review our list of recovered goods."

Working with Grace felt good. I retrieved a phone photo. "I just emailed a picture of the laptop label. And I'll mail the letter tomorrow."

Chapter Twenty-One

The following day, en route to get a duplicate driver's license, I swung by the post office and mailed the blank note to Grace. I checked myself in the rearview mirror. My hair had exploded into a bird's nest of curls from the humidity, and I'd forgotten makeup. Another ugly picture on my license.

Once legal to drive again, I shopped at my favorite computer store for a new laptop. Groaning, I thought about the thief reading through the private stuff in my daily journal. I kept personal notes, secrets about my past, and confidential information from previous cases. Plenty of fodder for a blackmailer. Fortunately, I also stored everything in the cloud.

Once I finished my errands, I returned home. Scooting past the nursery, I entered my darkened office. When I opened the new curtains, a light beam struck the quartz tulip. A blurred image appeared, disappearing just as quickly.

"Sam says it's the crystals, Sophie. Or he might have said prisms."

Sophie ignored me and claimed a spot on the stuffed chair.

Dense air surrounded me as I sat. Air moved across my shoulder. The ceiling fan was off. I shivered, then touched the quartz tulip. It felt warm.

"Come on, you don't believe in ghosts." My mouth felt dry. "Has to be my meds or my mind playing tricks on me."

Shaking off my misgivings, I pulled out my interview notes with Zeke. His answers filled a few gaps. Genealogists didn't consider oral histories conclusive or fully reliable on their own, but people's stories often led to solid evidence. I had a question for him about the absence of Phebe in the church newsletters.

When I called, Zeke answered right away. "Hmm. Not even forty-eight hours. I haven't lost my charm."

The old sea dog relaxed me. "You haven't lost an ounce."

He laughed.

"I have questions after reading some historic church newsletters. Not about their content, about what wasn't reported. Did your grandmother ever mention after Ezra died that Phebe disappeared from the Lyme social columns?"

"Can't say I remember anything like that."

"When Daniel Rogers married Phebe, the ceremony wasn't published. Weddings usually made the headlines. I expected an announcement in the paper or the church news."

"Grandma said the community shunned them, but she didn't explain why."

"That's interesting. Bea could have been pretty. I thought maybe Daniel had become attracted to her as she matured." After six years of marriage, Phebe would have aged, her looks faded. She was eleven years older than Daniel.

"No idea. I grew up in the Rogers family. Bea was a Mather, so she was rarely mentioned."

"Any stories about Phebe joining the Rogerene sect?" My gut said she did.

"Nope. I'm curious. Where'd you dig that up?"

"An entry in Lucy George's diary. It mentioned a widow who'd shamed the family and renounced her faith."

Zeke chuckled. "I bet one of the Mather women started a rumor. They loved to gossip."

"I'm not the only researcher who read Lucy's diary recently. Lillian visited the Marlow Historical Society a week before I did."

Zeke sniffed. "She's been obsessed with the Mather bloodline for years."

"What do you mean?"

"Lillian bragged to most of Connecticut after her acceptance in the DAR. She even called Mother after ignoring her for years. Remember, everyone in Connecticut's related somehow."

"Right. You did mention your mother."

"Lillian is supposedly my cousin." I could hear his fingers drumming.

"You don't sound convinced." Zeke's doubt caught my interest.

"I don't know. There was an offhand comment from Grandmother about Lillian's mother."

"She'd need an official birth certificate, marriage licenses, and church records to be accepted into the DAR. She must be a Mather."

"Maybe. But Lillian uses money and influence for personal gain." He drummed louder.

I couldn't imagine the DAR being fooled with forged documents. My remaining questions were best suited for Lillian. I'd have to avoid the topic of keeping her informed. She'd never cooperate if she knew I couldn't update her.

"Thanks, Zeke. That's it for now." I chewed my pen.

"Call anytime." He chuckled, "I haven't had this much fun in months."

We disconnected.

Refocusing on my case, I considered Zeke's conclusion about Bea. It made sense. If Bea had Mary out of wedlock, then Phebe and Daniel may have agreed to raise her as their own. And Bea being Mary's mother didn't guarantee Daniel was the father. It's possible that Bea got involved with a different Rogers.

As the anecdotal evidence mounted, I was sure Phebe and Bea had become Rogerenes. Phebe could have rein- terred Mary in the Rogerene cemetery. Historians had found evidence of wild parties at the Mather farm after Ezra died. That, combined with a resurgence of the Rogerenes in the mid-1800s, suggested a Rogerene house- hold. Zeke had mentioned parties, too.

And Daniel Rogers descended from James, a confirmed Rogerene. Srebnick had cited R. B. Wall, a 1910 New London reporter who referred to Daniel Rogers as "a heavy drinker and the ne'er-do-well son of his respected parents." I'd found a similar comment in Caulkins's book, *The History of New London*. Daniel sounded Rogerene to me.

I continued to chew the end of my pen, wondering what other Rogers men Bea might have hooked up with. The gatherings at the Mather farm may have led to indiscretions. So, someone other than Daniel Rogers could have fathered Mary.

No. A different father didn't sit right in my gut.

According to Lucy George's diary, the Rogers marriage was one of convenience. Society had considered twelve-year-old girls to be women. Boys were deemed men at twenty-one and were usually older than their wives. Seldom was a wife older than her husband. Phebe's eleven-year seniority was rare.

But Bea Mather had been ten years younger than her stepfather, Daniel. A more likely pairing. The marriage described as convenient may have actually meant one that covered scandalous behavior. And Daniel, the party animal and drinker, needed a place to stay in Lyme. This very well could have been the basis of Phebe and Daniel's marriage.

I sat back down at my desk. The tulip didn't glow, and I didn't lapse into a trance or have any bright ideas. But I did feel calm. Perhaps, a spirit on the other side had reversed the flow and extracted my anxiety. The idea made me laugh aloud. "Now, you're a believer."

Sophie lifted her head and yawned.

Chapter Twenty-Two

My attempt to reach Lillian on Friday failed, so I left a message.

Splaying Phebe and Bea's index cards on my table, I rehashed the data. I needed irrefutable evidence that they were Rogerenes. First, they lived with Daniel, possibly a Rogerene himself and reportedly a heavy drinker. Second, Zeke had provided oral evidence of wild parties at the farm. Third, Lucy George's 1820 diary entry said a Mather bore an illegitimate daughter. And finally, the margin notes next to Ezra Mather's name in the Mather genealogy indicated a daughter was born in 1820.

Bea *had* to be Mary's mother.

Arranging and rearranging the cards didn't help. My mind drifted. No historical researcher ever had perfect proof. With previous cases, I recognized sufficient data to support a conclusion. Not today. I quit and set the cards aside.

Trying a mind-cleansing technique that had worked for me in the past, I switched my focus to the ladies secretary. Van Boskerck operated a large woodworking shop in Hoboken. The hidden invoice. The quartz tulip. The aura. Somehow, I felt the desk and my case intersected.

Next, I moved to a process that I used to identify family clusters, but I applied it to case locations. By late afternoon, I'd covered my table with maps flagged with anything remotely related to Mary or her case. I even included the false sightings after the tabloids reported her suspicious death, and her aunt Mrs. Downing's place on Jane Street, even though she denied a planned visit.

As I studied the map of Mary's neighborhood, I thought about Phebe's response when told that her daughter had disappeared. She'd bluntly said, *Mary will never return,* instead of asking the more expected question, *What are you doing to find my daughter?*

She already knew the outcome.

Recounts of events leading up to Mary's death implied Phebe had convinced Mary to break her engagement to Payne in favor of Crommelin. Phebe's influence and firm control suggested knowledge of Mary's whereabouts on that Sunday.

I reviewed the case's geography. In Hoboken, the proximity of Van Boskerck's woodshop to the body recovery site formed a fragile link between Mary and the desk.

I realized I needed to visit Sybil's Cave where kids found her parasol. Walk the banks of the Hudson where men dragged her ashore. Gain insight into Mary's world.

I retried Lillian's number. No answer.

"What do you think, Sophie? Is Lillian keeping secrets?"

Sophie shook herself, then gave me a corgi smile.

"You're right. She's hiding something. I'll reveal it, even if it kills me. Let's go, it's quitting time. Mail, then lunch."

Sophie ran out the door and down the stairs.

A legal-sized padded envelope filled our mailbox. The return address indicated the funeral register had arrived along with a Next Day Mail envelope from the FBI.

Lab results.

I didn't have high hopes for the register, but the lab results regarding the blank page held promise.

Once inside, I ripped open Grace's envelope. Her hand-written note said, *No prints, but DNA on the paper. Report and database access codes included.*

The genetic markers could point to the culprit who left it. I wondered about the similar note Grace mentioned during our phone conversation. I shuddered. The blank letter reminded me how twisted and dangerous perpetrators could be.

I loaded the DNA report into the FBI databases and GEDmatch, a public online database. It would take hours, but the resulting matches might form a cluster or identify a relative.

When I entered the kitchen, Sam was munching on an apple. I wrapped my arms around him, inhaling deeply. He smelled delicious.

He kissed the top of my head. "How's the case going?"

"Okay. Well, to be honest, nothing's gelling like on previous projects."

"Keep digging. You'll figure it out."

Sam gave me an opening, so I laid the groundwork for another trip. "I've planned a visit to Manhattan and Hoboken. I've exhausted the Internet."

He took another bite of the apple, chewed and swallowed. Then, keeping a somber face, he asked, "Mind if I go with you? I mean, after the tumble in the cemetery, you're hardly a candidate for unescorted travel."

His answer surprised me. "I'll be fine."

"I'm serious. What will you research in New York?" Sam didn't smile.

"First, the O'Reilly letters. Claire found proof of Mary's cause of death in them. After that, I'm not sure. I have gaps in my data. I've found possible leads not mentioned in the literature or police reports, but I'm stuck."

"Stuck on what?" Sam tossed the apple core in the trash.

"For one thing, I'm convinced Phebe knew Mary's fate before Crommelin delivered the news. And I sense the desk is part of the mystery. I think Mary or someone close to her owned it."

"The old gut. Women's intuition. Voices in the dark," Sam teased.

"I can't explain it. I guess it *is* the old gut." I stuck out my tongue at him. Still no smile from him. "But unfortunately, I've found nothing that puts Mary in the Rogerene cemetery."

"Maybe it's time to switch gears. Clear your head. Go in a completely different direction. Like, study the desk. What have you discovered about it?"

"Maybe Van Boskerck built it." *Maybe Sam is on to something.*

"Start there. Look for buyers. That's what I'd do."

"Right. And I'll try Lillian again. She knows something about Martha Wade's diaries."

"Stay on track. Desk first, diaries later. Besides, Lillian makes you uneasy."

For no apparent reason other than he was right, my blood boiled. Nothing fit. And Claire's warning haunted me. I wanted to blame the reduced levels of my antidepressant on my behavior, but the truth was, I felt overwhelmed at everything that was happening. My life felt out of control.

Sam's voice interrupted my thoughts. "What did I say?"

"It's not what you said. It's how you said it." I bit my lip. My anger vanished as quickly as it had sparked. Lately, my emotions ran the gamut—scared, confused, stymied. Afraid for Emma and myself. Confused by the ginormous puzzle of a case with few pieces fitting together. And now, I was ashamed that Sam had become my punching bag.

He held his arms up in surrender. "I'm innocent."

"Sorry. I want this project to end. Lillian said to call anytime. She never hinted she wouldn't answer." A thought popped into my head. "And Zeke thinks Lillian may have lied about her lineage to get accepted into the DAR."

"Whoa. That's a whole new line of inquiry. Another distraction. Focus on the desk."

His tone annoyed me. My eyes burned as I turned to leave. I'd lost my appetite, even for M&M's. And now I was angry with Sam again over nothing.

"I'm sorry if I said something that upset you, Rae."

I worried myself all the way to the foyer. Sophie nearly knocked me over at the stairs, charging the incline like Teddy Brewster in *Arsenic and Old Lace*. In my office, I avoided the desk and decompressed at my side table. It took all of fifteen minutes to realize Sam was trying to help. I glanced at my watch—afternoon pill time.

Getting off an antidepressant wasn't as easy as I had thought. Now, I could sympathize with my mother's struggles after my father left. At the time, I just thought she didn't like me. She took medication until she couldn't afford it. It was either them or food for the table. "Enough. Back to work."

Sophie licked my sneaker, then laid her head across my foot.

I dialed Lillian. Still no answer, so once again, I left a message. "I received the register today. Thank you for your help." Maybe a gracious attitude would elicit a return call.

I thumbed through the leather-bound funeral register where attendees had written notes and memories, checking names by using the Mather website. Mr. & Mrs. Kenneth Seggerman turned out to be Zeke's grandparents.

An intriguing Bible quote followed the signatures. *Whoever welcomes this little child on my account is welcoming me. (Luke 9:48)* An Internet search didn't produce an interpretation meaningful to my case. This guest hinted that someone at the funeral had welcomed a child into their family.

I checked for a penmanship match. The closest was Zeke's grandparents' signature. I emailed photos of both to Greg, asking for help. He responded immediately with a thumbs-up emoji. Then, I called Zeke.

"Hello again, young lady."

"Did you know your grandparents attended Lillian's grandfather's funeral in 1937?"

"No, but I'm not surprised," Zeke laughed. "Back then, everyone went to funerals. It was the easiest way to keep up with the family gossip."

"By chance, do you have handwriting samples for either of them?"

"Not me, but I might be able to get some. It'll take a couple of days."

I was on to something meaningful, but it would have to wait for the handwriting examples to truly analyze what was in front of me. Until then, I decided to work on Frederick Mather's file since I hadn't finished researching him.

Before I began, I relocated to my desk. The clutter on the table from the historical maps and printouts frustrated me. Everything seemed to make me feel that way. I hated feeling so raw, but I was determined to eventually get off the meds.

At the desk, a sense of calm settled over me. My mind felt free, natural and unnatural all at once. Dense air brushed my cheek.

Sophie's gentle snoring emanating from beneath my feet was soothing.

Based on my research to date, Frederick had been invisible in Mary's case. He likely frequented Anderson's cigar shop like other professionals in the neighborhood and would have known John Anderson. Born in Windsor, Connecticut, Frederick grew up there and moved to New York in 1835, the same timeframe as Phebe and Mary's move. He had to have known them. Phebe had married a Mather. Plus, the Rogers boarding house was a block from his office.

It's conceivable that Frederick provided Anderson with legal services. A trip to New York's public records could solidify the connection between the two men and form another loose connection to Mary. I added the task to my work plan.

By late afternoon, I had written a dozen report pages and developed a relationship chart. I'd already traced both Daniel and Phebe Rogers' lineage back four generations, enough to verify neither side had connections to a Mather except the tangential relationship of Phebe's marriage to Ezra Mather. The apparent explanation for Mather DNA markers was Bea. But I hadn't proven that the family had moved Mary's remains from New York to New London.

One thing had become clear. All roads led to New York City.

Done for the day, I closed the curtains and glanced at the desk as I left, a habit I'd developed since my first vision. Nothing glowed, flickered, or glittered, but the quote from Luke about one such little child suddenly niggled at me.

Sam poured wine as I entered the kitchen, then saluted me with his glass. "You look better."

"I am. My evidence is mounting regarding Mary's maternal bloodline, but I still have nothing concrete. No birth certificate, church record, or diary confirmation."

Sam raised his glass again. "You'll find something. You always do."

"Sorry I let my frustrations get the best of me earlier. Weaning off an antidepressant isn't easy, but that's no excuse. I'd love your company on my New York trip."

Sam set his wine on the counter, picked me up, then planted a juicy kiss on my lips. "I'm sorry, too. I was meddling in your business. It's my Robin Hood complex. It'll take more than prickly behavior to drive me away." As he twirled me around, Sophie barked and nipped at my heels. Sam laughed. "I'll subject you to corgi torture before I give up on you."

He always found ways to smooth things over. I'd try harder in the future. Maybe my quick temper came from my Irish father's genes, or from my Italian mother. She held her own in their fights, which probably contributed to their divorce.

After dinner, I checked the progress of the DNA matching program on the blank note. It had another five or six hours to go. A cluster was forming in Rhode Island in an area reputedly home to several notorious mafia bosses.

I planned to call Grace once I pinpointed the neighborhood, but until then, my only plans included spending the rest of the evening holding hands with Sam during a movie, reminding him that he was my rock through the toughest of times, and that I adored him for his patience and unwavering devotion.

Chapter Twenty-Three

The first thing I did Sunday morning was recheck the DNA comparison program. It had finished in the middle of the night. I had a cluster showing around Lower South Providence.

Crap. Mafia!

It was too early to call Grace, so I texted her to call me as soon as possible.

While strategizing, I fiddled with the small drawers on the desk hutch. I slid one out and flipped it over. Color variation revealed a series of slats in a patterned veneer. Out of curiosity, I removed the matching drawer. Same surface, but it felt lighter. "Hmm."

Sam never mentioned the veneer. I barged into his office and held out the drawers. "Look at these bottoms. Pretty fancy to be hidden."

"I saw the veneer when I searched for a brand." He shrugged.

"You never mentioned it. The signature could be hidden." My Irish temper was coming out again. *Back off. Sam's trying to help.*

He rubbed his chin. "Sorry. I was tired. Besides, a builder wouldn't conceal his signature. Let me see it."

He tapped the bottom of the drawer.

While he studied it, I pulled up the photo of the desk in Keene. "The innkeeper didn't say Van Boskerck signed all of his work, but it's an identical desk. He must have built it."

"Let's check the other drawers."

We returned to my office, removed them one by one, placing them on the side table. We also checked under the hutch for veneer or a brand. Only two small drawers had veneer bottoms. I grabbed a ruler and measured the depth on both. Then I hefted the left one. "This one's an inch shallower, and it's heavier." I handed it to Sam.

Holding it to his ear, he tapped the bottom. "Thicker." He tapped it again. "Hollow. A hidden compartment."

"You're kidding." I leaned in.

Sam picked at a slat. "Nothing moves."

His picking upset me beyond reason. "Don't destroy it!"

"I won't." He flipped it over. "I think it's a Chinese puzzle box."

He shoved the drawer toward Sophie. She backpedaled, reared up, and licked a corner.

Sam laughed. "Built with a glue Sophie likes." He gave it another shake. "It's empty, or whatever's inside fits tight."

An odor wafted toward me as he handed it back. "Smells like spiced fish."

"That's why Sophie's so interested." He patted her head. "If it's a puzzle, we should be able to open it without destroying it by sliding the slats in a specific sequence."

"We need the move sequence to get in." I grabbed my laptop. "Let's search online for a solution." We tried all suggested move combinations, but after an hour, we quit. Nothing worked.

Sam grasped the drawer's sides. "Let's break it open."

"Absolutely not! We could ruin the contents." My hands shook.

"Okay, calm down. I understand. It could be evidence." Sam retrieved his phone. "I'll call Greg. He has a buddy in Chinatown who works at Wing Kee's in Philadelphia and collects puzzle boxes. He might be able to help. Claims he's never found one he couldn't open."

I exhaled, trying to relax. "Good idea. While you're at it, check Greg's progress on the handwriting analysis, please."

Sam retreated to his office to make the call. Five minutes later, he returned. "Greg's on top of it. Plus, he'll have the handwriting results to you in a day, two at most."

"Fantastic." I was pretty sure it was Zeke's grandmother, Sarah Seggerman, but I'd wait to see.

* * *

Sam's scent lingered around the desk as I combed through copies of the police reports again, answered a handful of questions, and gained ground on the family connections. After an hour, I refocused and searched for information about desks and puzzles. Nothing.

Closing the barrel top, I laid my forehead against the cylinder and rehashed the invoice where it said, *Owned by Alonzo Mather (orig. stored 1883 – C.S.).*

I sat up. But Alonzo couldn't have been the original owner. He wasn't born until 1848, and the desk was built in the 1830s. Whoever owned it first might have known Mary. I couldn't explain how Alonzo ended up with it.

The person who stored it had the initials C.S. Possibly a

worker at the warehouse, or the person who paid to store it. More unknowns to research.

There were still so many unanswered questions.

The tulip flickered. Replanting my forehead on the desk, I shut my eyes. Maybe with contact, I'd form a spiritual link. Other than goosebumps on my arms, nothing happened. No link. No ghost.

"If you're watching me, you could help with this case," I suggested into thin air.

Still nothing.

Crap, now I was talking to my desk.

Chapter Twenty-Four

The next day, I decided to follow up on the Cordts invoice. I retrieved it and smoothed out a wrinkled corner. The high quality paper had remained in excellent condition after decades inside the desk.

Professor Carver implied that his predecessor had coveted the ladies secretary. Maybe he would know why Dr. Isabelle Kemp believed that this particular one was important. I called him.

He answered immediately. "Hello, RaeJean. I hope you're calling with good news. The Budget Review Board meets next week. I'd love to report you've solved Mary's mysterious death." He laughed. "I know. Not your priority."

"It's not, but I've made progress." I'd wait to tell Carver I'd solved the bonus question when I had a copy of the O'Reilly letters.

"Great. How can I help you today?"

"I've hit a roadblock. I need a map of the Rogerene cemetery grave locations."

"I have a grid diagram, but we never completed the aerial photo overlay. Why?"

"Well, if I find evidence Mary was buried there, I'll need a reference point to determine her grave location. A plot number or an abutting marker."

"Right. Geez, that's a tough one." He thought for a moment. "I'll see what I can find. I do recall several plots had site descriptions."

"I appreciate your help." I crossed my fingers. Historic cemetery records didn't include much, but maybe I'd get lucky.

"Anything else?" he asked.

"Tell me what you know about the desk."

"Not a lot. Is it important?" He sounded confused.

"I'd like to know its history, if possible." I wasn't even sure why at this point, but the desk felt vital to the case.

He shared what little he knew. "Dr. Kemp found it at Cordts in Hoboken, where it had been stored for years. Apparently, well-to-do Manhattan families rented storage space there. After items sat for years, the warehouse owner would seek permission to sell them."

"I found an invoice inside," I explained, "indicating Alonzo Mather owned it, and that it was originally stored in 1883, along with the initials C.S. Do you know anything about that?"

"Nothing." He sounded surprised. "When Dr. Kemp died, she left the college a few items. Called them notable artifacts."

"Notable artifacts." I wondered if their notability was the original owner. My stomach fluttered.

"Yes. The Dean asked me to evaluate them. Decide what to keep since the college didn't have room for it all. Antique experts appraised everything. The only valuable artifact was a complete set of Woman Suffrage Buttons, which we donated to the Smithsonian. The few items you saw are the last of her belongings."

"The desk didn't intrigue the appraisers." That surprised me.

"Not really. They said it was one of hundreds made in the 1800s."

"But Dr. Kemp thought it was special. Did she know its original owner?"

"She believed a women's rights advocate owned it, Ann Lohman. But I'm sure you've already discovered Lohman's connection to the Rogers case."

"Right." Lohman's name had surfaced in more than one article about Mary.

"Isabelle worshiped Lohman," Carver said. "The college has Kemp's unpublished manuscript, detailing Lohman's mistreatment in the mid-to-late 1800s by the New York judicial system."

Pieces started to fit. "What was Dr. Kemp's political position?"

"She saw Lohman as a visionary for women's health and freedom of choice."

The thought of another potential lead excited me. "I see. I'd like a copy of her manuscript, if possible."

"I'll check. If so, I'll overnight it."

"I'd appreciate that. Did your sponsor know Dr. Kemp?"

"I promised not to disclose details about my sponsor," Carver responded.

His non-answer made me suspect this shadow client was somehow affiliated with the college.

After we disconnected, I researched Ann Lohman, also known as Madame Restell. Historians described her as a self-taught midwife. In *The Sun*, her ads said that Madame

Restell's potions helped women experiencing female trouble. Lohman claimed to have a concoction to prevent conception and aid with "private difficulties." She opened a women's lying-in hospital on Greenwich Street for complicated pregnancies. Plus, Lohman claimed she could remove "obstructions," a euphemism for abortion.

I hadn't decided if she was an angel or a villain. Her dedication to women's health issues tipped me toward angel, but her prices for Preventative Powder at five dollars per package or Female Monthly Pills at a dollar each suggested that her practice leaned toward the commercial side. She targeted people with money, and it worked. She and her husband became rich.

Ann's life was filled with drama. Press articles named her "the wickedest woman in New York City." According to Amy Srebnick's book, rumors circulated about parties at her Fifth Avenue mansion. One night, a journalist watched carriages drop off notable New York City men without their wives. A penny press printed an unsubstantiated article that Lohman's parties involved gambling and prostitution. Tight-lipped city officials put a lid on the story.

Anthony Comstock, a dogged reformer in the mid-to-late 1800s, visited Ann, pretending to be a concerned husband seeking birth control help for his wife. Lohman, sympathetic to his problem, provided pills and a pamphlet. Deeming it obscene literature, he returned the next day with a search warrant, collected additional evidence, and arrested her.

Lohman's charge was possession of "materials used for immoral purposes." Outraged journalists dubbed it moral entrapment. Ann made bail and returned to her mansion to await trial. Sadly, her life ended in tragedy. Early on the morning of her trial date, she drew a warm bath, slipped into the water, and slit her own throat.

Comstock, a special agent for the U.S. Postal Service and secretary for the New York Society for the Suppression of Vice, used and abused his position as a special agent to "uphold Christian morality." Called a moral hysteric by many, he blatantly violated the First Amendment.

I scribbled the information about Lohman on a card and added it to a pile labeled, *Desk*.

Out of curiosity, I visited the Connecticut College website to see if a Mather worked there, but none were listed. Notable adjuncts lectured for the English department, including William Pence, who taught the course, *Documented Research, Getting the Facts Right*.

I'd read his articles in *The New Yorker* and *Time*. Over his thirty-five-year journalism and writing career, he'd mined the city records for graft, collusions, and fraud, and wrote scathing stories about powerful officials. When he turned his stories into books, they topped the *Times* Bestseller List their first week out and made millions.

Maybe if I solve this cold case, I thought, *I could write a book. Make millions*. I wouldn't count my money yet. After being unsolved for a hundred and eighty years, my prospects remained slim.

I found myself sidetracked again. I hadn't identified the person whose initials were C.S.

* * *

The next day, Sam and I discussed the case. "I suspect Ann Lohman owned the desk. So, I called Professor Carver. His predecessor, Dr. Kemp, was convinced it was her desk."

"So, there's a possible tie between this Lohman woman and Mary Rogers."

"Yes. And Claire found letters confirming Mary died from complications after an abortion. And Lohman provided women with a way to remove obstructions." A weak link between Mary and Lohman was forming. My mind swirled as Sam mumbled in the background.

"Or she fell into the Hudson while walking along its banks. Or she was mugged in the Elysian Fields and thrown into the river. Or she ran off with a sailor. Or she disappeared into the desk. It could be like the wardrobe in Narnia—"

"What about Narnia?" I'd been lost in thought.

Sam laughed. "Go back to your investigation."

"I'm sorry. I was processing the theory about Lohman owning the desk. My gut says she wasn't the original owner."

Sam poked my side. "Your gut's been busy. Just focus on the facts, Sherlock."

"The desk holds a clue to Mary's death. I can feel it." Sam didn't understand, but I knew.

"It shouldn't matter. You weren't hired to determine her cause of death."

"True. But if I do, I'll get a big, fat bonus."

Sam studied me. "There's more, isn't there?"

I hesitated for a moment. "I can't figure out why the puzzle box was inside my desk."

"You believe it holds a clue to Mary's death."

"My gut says yes."

"There goes that gut again. The only way to find out is to open it."

"Hopefully, the puzzle expert Greg mentioned will be able to help."

"Let's hope he can. For now, I have an appraisal to finish." Sam turned to leave, stopped, and pointed to an Overnight Priority Mail delivery envelope. "I almost forgot. A package came from Connecticut College."

"Ah, speak of the devil. Isabelle Kemp's manuscript." I opened it, skimming a few pages. It was going to be a challenging read. "Wordy."

Chapter Twenty-Five

Once back in my office, I returned to the Cordts invoice. This time, I vowed not to get sidetracked. I reread the document for the umpteenth time.

"Alonzo Mather!" I'd been so focused on the desk belonging to Lohman that I'd overlooked the obvious. He had to be someone of importance.

According to the Mather Clan website, Alonzo's ancestral branch also sprouted from Timothy. Born in 1848, he appeared in Mary's generation, a distant cousin born after she died.

Out of curiosity, I searched for information about Alonzo's wives, who might have used the desk. Nothing on his first wife, but I found paydirt with his second one, Louise Eames. Part of the Fairfield Collection at Syracuse University in Utica had eight boxes belonging to Alonzo, including correspondence and journals belonging to his wife.

I contacted the university and spoke with a docent familiar with the collection. I explained I was looking for a link between the Mathers in Fairfield and the Mathers in Lyme.

"I'll have an intern review their personal correspondence. Any specific Mathers?"

"Yes. Louisa Mather Griswold, Frances Mather Griswold, Frederick Mather, or perhaps, Dr. Augustus Mather." I'd almost forgotten. "And also, Mary Rogers."

"There's a nominal research fee, but we can have this for you in a few days."

We disconnected the call after I gave her my credit card number, genealogist certification number, and email. "Yes! This could be it!"

Sophie jumped up and barked at my exclamation. I threw her a mini milk bone, and she settled back onto the chair.

The invoice questions seemed unanswerable until I found that the Hoboken Historical Museum had boxes of woodworking shop invoices, including Cordts. Maybe I'd find out how Alonzo got the desk, or who stored it. Like Sam had said, look for the buyer.

I added the museum to my list of places to visit when I was in New York.

* * *

A few hours later, my phone rang, and Zeke's name scrolled across the screen.

"Greetings, young lady."

"What's up?" I hoped he had handwriting samples.

"I have a letter Grandma Sarah wrote, but nobody has one from Grandpa Ken."

"Maybe we'll be lucky. I'd be grateful if you'd mail me a copy as soon as you can or send a picture from your phone."

"I'll get it copied at Staples today and mail it. I'm not tech savvy."

My phone vibrated. It was a text from Lillian.

"Gotta go. Lillian's messaging me. Thank you again."

"Lucky you. I'll get right on this." Zeke disconnected.

I read her text. *Don't overlook the Wade diaries.*

I dialed her number immediately, hoping to catch her. My call went to voicemail. *Crap.*

While typing a response to Lillian's text, my phone vibrated again with a call from an unknown number. The male caller left a voicemail, asking to call as soon as possible, so I hit callback.

"Hello?" The man's voice matched the voicemail.

"What number were you calling?" I wondered if the caller had misdialed, since I didn't recognize his voice.

He repeated my phone number. "I'm surprised you contacted an unknown caller."

"Your voice indicated it might be an emergency. I was concerned you'd mistakenly dialed the wrong number." This time, his voice sounded vaguely familiar, but I couldn't place it. "Have we met?"

"I'm not ready to divulge my identity. And no, we've never met. I'm the one funding your current case. A friend discovered something that might help you."

"Is this a ploy to lure me out? You could be lying to me." Images of the man wearing the baseball cap fed my doubts.

"That's an odd thing to say. What's going on?" The man paused. "I hired Professor Carver as a go-between to maintain my anonymity."

"Anyone could say that." Well, not anyone, but that didn't mean he was the client.

"What proof will make you comfortable that I'm Carver's sponsor?"

"Tell me something nobody else would know." I'd have him on that.

"Easy. You coveted a desk in Carver's office and took the case when he agreed to give you the old relic instead of more money."

I vividly recalled that day. "Okay, that's true. I doubt Carver would have shared that information with anyone else."

"So, do you want what I have discovered or not?" He sounded perturbed.

"Of course, if it will help with my case."

"It might. It's Louisa Griswold's photo album." He emphasized her name.

"Louisa Griswold." I thought of the marble obelisk in Duck River Cemetery, inscribed to include her infant son. I shook off a wave of sadness. "A Mather cousin."

"Yes. Louisa's mother remained friends with Phebe Rogers for years. Even after Phebe fell out of favor in Lyme."

"Interesting." *Strange that he would know that.*

The man cleared his throat. "My friend said the album is full of notes, cards, and newspaper clippings. It also includes a few old photos."

"I can't believe I'm hearing about this now. Did you have it all along?" My mind raced at the possibilities. I couldn't fathom anyone overlooking such a valuable artifact.

"Lord, no. I wasn't aware it existed until I spoke with my friend today and was telling her about the case. She found it in a trunk in her deceased mother's attic."

An image of the Mather attics full of old trunks and boxes danced through my head. Attics like theirs would contain treasures, descending from an illustrious religious leader, unlike one owned by me. Being a third-generation Irish-Italian-American, the only heirloom I had was a rusty colander from my grandmother that I used to drain spaghetti.

"Should I send it?"

"Absolutely." I didn't want to mention I was leaving on Monday. Hopefully, the album would arrive before then.

"I'll send it out today, priority mail. You should have it by Saturday."

"Great. By the way, I met a woman named Lillian Baxter during a trip to New Hampshire. She claims she's an expert on Mather history."

The man's volume increased. "Lillian! Attending another DAR event, I presume."

"That's what she said. Coincidentally, we stayed at the same bed and breakfast."

"Beware. There are no coincidences with Lillian. She definitely wants something." The foreboding in his voice was disturbing.

"I doubt she wants anything from me. I simply inter-viewed her."

"Did she offer worthwhile information?"

"Not much. She asked to be informed of anything I uncover."

"I'll bet she did." He chewed his words.

"I didn't agree to anything. My contract's clear. Any and all disclosures require my client's permission."

"Well, you've asked, and the answer is an emphatic no. Don't share a thing with Lillian."

I didn't mention the puzzle box. I'd wait until I knew its contents. It might not even be relevant.

And for all I knew, the caller was the man wearing the

baseball cap. Except, he knew about the desk. And he obviously knew Lillian. It was getting harder and harder to believe anything, or trust anyone.

Chapter Twenty-Six

Louisa's album wouldn't arrive until Saturday, so I spent the next three days reading Dr. Kemp's manuscript. Her degree in archaeology didn't temper the flowery description of her antique collection. Her writing was downright tedious.

After the first half hour, my attention span had reduced to that of a gnat. During her pontification on women's rights, I nearly fell asleep. When I reached her description of the desk, I snapped to attention. She wrote, "based on a spiritual connection, I conclude Ann Lohman had owned the secretary at some point."

"Oh, boy!"

According to Dr. Kemp, Lohman's clash with the law after Mary died wasn't a coincidence. Without tying Lohman directly to Mary's death, Kemp wrote how Mary's celebrity status and suspicious death had brought attention to Lohman's practice, resulting in police harassment.

She was rehashing what I already knew about Mary, so I set the manuscript aside and turned to my index cards. I'd taped a photo of the Bible quote to one of them. It caught my attention. I picked it up and stared at the signature.

To the naked eye, the writing appeared a perfect match to Sarah Seggerman's sample that had come in the morning mail. If I was correct, she'd signed the register, then returned later to add the scripture.

Why?

Since Sarah was Zeke's grandmother, I'd call him and see what he thought.

Before I could dial his number, my phone vibrated. It was Greg.

"Sam says you're expecting an artifact related to the case."

"I am. A photo album. Why?" I suspected natural curiosity, but I waited for his answer.

"Sam's description of the mystery hooked me," he laughed. "And I miss Sophie."

"You're either bored or easily hooked." It was my turn to chuckle. "Sophie would love to see you."

"My schedule's clear this weekend. I'd like to join the welcoming party."

Greg was like family. He and Sam met years ago at the Oaks Gun Show in the Greater Philadelphia Expo Center. Although a software engineer by profession, Greg loved antiques, especially weapons. He and Sam converged on a matched set of English Clough & Sons duelers that ended up selling for eight thousand dollars. They'd been buddies ever since.

"Absolutely. The album should arrive by noon on Saturday. I'll plan an extra for lunch. By the way, Sarah Seggerman's writing sample arrived today. If it matches the signature and the Bible quote, we've confirmed it was her."

"Cool. Send me a digital copy."

After we ended the call, I sent the copy to Greg, then immediately called Zeke.

"RaeJean Hunter here. I got your grandmother's writing sample. It looks like a match to me, but I'm waiting for an expert's opinion. I have a few questions."

"Go ahead and ask away."

"Can you recall anything else about the Mather farm parties?"

He thought for a moment. "A riotous coming-out party for Bea Mather's fifteenth birthday. Hundreds of friends, relatives, and strangers attended all weekend. The tale took on a life of its own. By the time I heard the story, it made Woodstock sound like a family picnic."

I laughed.

"Grandma said it was the first of a litany of wild parties. Called them free-for-alls. It got so wild that respectable folks stopped going. Uncomfortable with the moral direction, she said."

"Would Lucy George have attended?" Lucy's entries hinted at more knowledge of Mary than she'd recorded in her diaries, and her diaries indicated she traveled to Lyme regularly.

"Augustus' sister? Possibly. Most eligible bachelors and debutantes attended the first coming-out party." Zeke was quiet. "Where're you going with this?"

"I'm not sure. Lucy's diary mentions an illegitimate daughter, so maybe Mary *was* Bea's daughter and Lucy left out the details."

"Sounds like you're closer to solving Mary's mystery than any other researcher has been."

"Maybe. But I'm positive someone's one step ahead of me." As I related my cemetery saga, I touched the tender spot on the back of my head.

"Careful, girl!" He clicked his tongue. "Lillian will never let you uncover shameful family history. She'll do anything to hide the truth. As hard as she's worked to prevent a leak, I'd say she has a body in the basement."

Thoughts of the guy with the ballcap and the DNA cluster in South Providence's mafia territory made me shiver. "What do you mean? Would she murder to keep a family secret?"

Zeke laughed. "My father used that cliché when he believed someone had a secret. I'm not sure about murder. But be careful. That chin-wagger, Lillian, doesn't play by the rules."

"I will." I'd underestimated her, fooled by her advanced age, her DAR membership, and her passion for family history. *If* history was even her passion. Perhaps, she had a hidden agenda.

"Anything else?" Zeke asked.

My mind was wiped clean. "That's it for now. I'm sure I'll call again."

Usually a calming exercise, recording data on index cards failed me. I fanned them as I contemplated Lillian's willingness to break the rules. The man in the cemetery. And Claire's situation. My anxiety was at such a high level it could ring the gong at a country fair.

A big unknown loomed ahead.

* * *

Sophie barked. I heard Sam shout from the back porch, "Greg's here!"

Hefting a platter of sandwiches, chips, and pickles, I joined him outside.

"Let me help." Sam grabbed the platter and placed it on the table.

Greg straightened after patting Sophie, then hugged me. "Looks like I timed it right."

"You did, but we'd have waited." I sat with my back to the wall.

"Dig in," Sam said, piling his plate high.

During lunch, a FedEx truck entered our driveway. Sophie went nuts. Like the UPS guy who delivered my desk, this guy also brought dog treats. He joked about changing vehicles to surprise her.

I set the package aside. "Let's finish eating. The album isn't going anywhere."

The guys gobbled their sandwiches, gulped drinks, and stood. "We're ready."

With half a sandwich left, I stuffed all but the crust into my mouth. "Be right there."

Sophie drooled at my feet. "Sorry, girl, I almost forgot." I slipped her a piece of crust. It disappeared like a bug on a frog's tongue, then we joined the men in the library. Hopefully, the album held answers. I needed a break.

Chapter Twenty-Seven

I scrunched between the two men on the library couch while I unwrapped the album. The sponsor had included a note. "He wants this item kept confidential for now."

"What's all this Darknet stuff about?" Greg asked.

"It's a long story. My theory? The sponsor doesn't trust his relatives. Promise not to share what we find."

"Who would I tell?" He rolled his eyes.

He had a point. Greg worked from home and gossiped with Sam.

Louisa had laced the embossed leather cover with a blue silk cord and fastened a daguerreotype print to the front flap. I patted the thin pewter photo. "Richard and Louisa."

Greg scowled. "Look at those sourpusses. They didn't get enough likes on Facebook."

I chuckled. "Don't be fooled. Rich people in the 1800s believed only the lewd, the drunk, and the entertainers smiled in portraits. Richard Griswold was filthy rich. He inherited his father's Chinese import business and supplied items to dozens of small businesses in Chinatown."

Greg's head snapped in my direction. "Like Chinese puzzle boxes?"

"Tea, silk, and Chinese laborers mostly. But he may have brought in puzzles."

Sam pointed to a single tab in the middle of the album. "Turn to that page. It's marked."

I pulled myself from the photo and tipped the album to view the tab. It read, *Louisa at her desk.* "Interesting. But skipping ahead is cheating."

Instead, I opened the front cover. Louisa had penned her name and the year, 1835, in white ink on black paper. She'd added the picture later when daguerreotype photos became available.

"Come on. Just a glimpse," Sam begged.

"No. Reviewing historical documents is my specialty. Patience. We'll get there."

Clippings from family announcements of marriages, births, and deaths filled most pages. The few interspersed pictures depicted a proud, frail woman.

"It's more like a scrapbook than a photo album," Greg observed.

"In the 1800s, people called them keepsake books." Carver's sponsor had called it a photo album.

Sam leaned in to face Greg. "Daguerre didn't commercialize photography until the late 1830s. Before his discovery, everything was a lithograph and looked like a newsprint."

"Oh, right." Greg nodded. "Keep going."

Sam groaned. "Come on. Turn to the tab."

I shushed him. "Patience. I've missed clues before by getting over-anxious and skipping ahead."

Greg bumped me with his shoulder. "Come on, Rae. You're killing us."

"I have a piece of history in my hands. Don't rush me." I wanted to savor the experience. The album held a slice of Louisa's life. I'd walk through her significant moments, not race to the conclusion. Besides, I already knew her ending from the monument at the cemetery. A lump formed in my throat.

Crispy brownish black flakes dropped onto my gray sweats as the page edges disintegrated with each turn. Most of the foil corner mounts had fallen off. Names written in white ink identified the people and places. Sometimes, Louisa wrote poems to finish out a page. I was a voyeur peeking through a keyhole into her world. Her life revolved around family and the desire for babies. She'd miscarried at least twice based on her notes. Notes that described baby gowns trimmed in blue silk thread.

Unaware that I'd hesitated, Greg nudged me once again. "Keep going."

Louisa had included a handmade valentine from Richard. The watercolor depicted a heart surrounded by a wreath of roses. I slipped it from the page to view the back, reading aloud Richard's note declaring his undying love.

I smiled at Sam. "Nice."

"Ugh. Sappy, if you ask me." Greg wrinkled his nose.

Sam reached over and tapped Greg's head. "That's why you're still single, pal."

Louisa had clipped social columns from the *Olde Lyme Gazette* and the *Long Island Star* whenever mentioned in them. By the end of 1839, she included brown printed photographs, now faded and blurred. Richard's wealth had allowed her access to calotype salt prints.

I turned the page and saw the next photo. My breath caught. I squinted to read Louisa's caption. "It's Mary with

John Anderson in front of the Cigar Emporium. Not a great picture."

She'd subtly linked Mary and John Anderson as a couple, information missing from the police reports.

"Is Anderson someone important?" Greg asked.

"Mary worked for him. Anderson used her to gain publicity for his business. He fed false news to the newspapers about her disappearing. With Mary's celebrity status, her every move became news. Papers sold and Anderson's business boomed, but the truth was never revealed."

"Sometimes, it never is." Sam stared blankly at the floor.

His expression and comment disturbed me, like he knew I had a secret. I continued. "Newspapers hinted that John and Mary were lovers when she first moved to New York. At first, thinking of Mary with Anderson bothered me. He was eight years her senior, and she was a teenager. Then, I recalibrated my thinking to 1839."

"She was considered an adult," Sam said. "Sounds like Anderson's worth investigating."

I nodded. The center tab was next. I hesitated. "Ready, guys? Ta da!"

The monochrome photo concealed colors, but Louisa's desk matched mine—pulls, tulip, and all. A journal lay open on the leather writing surface. Louisa stood next to it with her hands clasped at her waist. Sunlight poured through a window, casting her shadow onto the hardwood floor. A mirrored dresser reflected her left side and revealed a headboard, confirming she was in a bedroom.

Sam poked the print with his finger. "That's your desk."

"It might be. But Van Boskerck sold hundreds of them." My heart skipped a beat. Dr. Kemp believed Ann Lohman had owned my desk.

A dainty floral ring dominated Louisa's spider-like finger.

"She's frail. Look at her boney hands," Greg said. "Where was this picture taken?"

I looked closer at the personal items, a ladies bone hairbrush monogrammed with LG, a pitcher and glass of water, a pill case, and a *New York Herald Tribune*. The date was difficult to read. I grabbed a magnifying glass. It looked like March 1840, but the day was difficult to see. "The date on the newspaper looks like the year Louisa died." My hands shook. "Her initials are on the hairbrush."

Sam squinted at the faded photo. "LG. Louisa Griswold."

"Which suggests the photo was taken in her bedroom, or a bedroom where she stayed." My gut thumped a silent message. *It was her desk.*

"I have software that will enhance this. Maybe I can determine the exact date." Greg used his phone to take a digital copy. "What do you know about Louisa?"

"Not enough. She grew up in Lyme and was Bea Mather's first cousin. After Bea died, Louisa married Richard Griswold and moved to Brooklyn in 1835. That same year, Frederick Mather, Mary, and Phebe moved to Manhattan within two blocks of each other." I sucked in a breath as the realization struck me. "Mary knew Louisa. A photo of her in Louisa's album suggests they were close."

I'd connected a set of dots.

"What does that prove?" Sam wasn't convinced.

"I'm not sure. But the connection to the desk is getting close to Mary."

We studied the photos on the page. The New York paper, the initials on the hairbrush.

"This looks like the same room." Greg pointed to the

second photo of Louisa where she stood beside a table set with an oil lamp and knick-knacks.

"Looks like it. It's the same bed in the mirror, and a dark wood floor." From this angle, Louisa looked nearly full-term. I'd ask Lillian about the Griswolds and see how she reacted. She had me chasing the Martha Wade diaries and a supposedly important key, but she'd never mentioned Louisa.

"I need a copy of the desk photo." If this was my desk, I'd found the furniture necessary to confirm Mary's height.

Sam raised his eyebrows. "Okay."

I studied Louisa's face as I pried off a corner and removed the picture. The old photo felt heavy and thick compared to today's one-hour prints.

Greg scowled. "She looks unhealthy."

"She was. Sadly, she died in childbirth. This photo might have been her last. She never fulfilled her dream of becoming a mother." My stomach knotted. I didn't look at Sam.

Sam gently took the photo. "I'll make a copy."

Greg cupped my hand in his, winking at me. "Are you okay?"

"Mostly." I shrugged. "You know."

Greg gave my hand a soft squeeze. "Keep the faith, Rae. You'll be a mother someday." He reached over and wiped a tear from my cheek.

Sam returned, bowed, then handed me the photos. "Ask and ye shall receive."

I couldn't help but laugh. "My manservant, right?"

"Of course." He slid in next to me, wrapping his arm across my shoulders.

"Look at the similarities." Sam pointed at my desk. "Same top, the same number of drawers, same knobs, and an inlaid tulip. I could go on."

It looked identical to mine. "I'm not sure about the knobs. The photo is black and white."

Sam passed me the copy. "Knobs are easy to replace. Someone may have changed them. That doesn't make it a different desk."

"What do you need for a positive ID?" Greg asked.

"Conclusive evidence the desk came from Hoboken and that Carver's predecessor purchased it." I hesitated. "And a trip to Manhattan."

He stood. "I'll enhance the newspaper photo with my laptop. Try to decipher the date."

"I'll go with Greg," Sam said.

I laughed. "In other words, you've both had enough."

They nodded.

"Go do whatever you need to do. I've got this." I didn't have to offer twice.

After they disappeared, I scrutinized every page. Several group shots showed Mary, Frances, and Louisa picnicking with others, adding to the evidence that they were close. Louisa had a picture of Augustus holding a diploma. The photograph confirmed their friendship. Augustus had logged visits to New York in 1839, likely to care for Louisa during the final stages of her pregnancy.

My phone vibrated. Greg had texted, *The date is March 7, 1840.*

Two weeks before Louisa died. I looked down at Sophie. "Well, girl, the album proves Augustus, Louisa, and Mary socialized." I snapped my fingers. "Sophie, I almost forgot!"

Sophie opened one eye, then yawned.

I needed to measure my desk, then scale it down to photo size. I could determine Louisa's height using the photo in the album.

I rushed to my office with Sophie at my heels and fumbled through my field equipment for a tape measure. Sophie jumped at my legs, no doubt expecting a treat. I measured the desk's height, width, and depth. "That ought to do it."

Using ratios and a few assumptions, I calculated Louisa's height to be approximately five feet two inches, which was average for a woman in 1841. This allowed me to estimate Mary's height at five feet five inches from a photo in the album of them side by side. Mary was taller than average, which was consistent with the newspaper's description of her. More importantly, it was consistent with the bones in Carver's office. "Bingo! It could be Mary."

And she definitely spent time with Louisa.

I made digital copies of the photos with Mary and sent them to Greg's email to feed into his facial reconstruction program.

He sent me a thumbs-up and a selfie of himself at the poolside in our backyard. He and Sam had gone from work mode to leisure, it seemed.

Opening the album to the center, I studied the desk photo again. The puzzle within it could reveal a family secret someone would do anything to keep.

And my involvement could very likely have put a big, terrifying target on my back.

Chapter Twenty-Eight

Early Monday morning, we took the train to New York City. I carried the drawer with the Chinese puzzle box in my large bag. I'd made reservations at The House of the Redeemer, locally known as The Retreat. A college friend had raved about it after attending a writer's seminar organized by the late Lady Barbara Wedgewood, a well-known author and playwright.

I hadn't stayed there before, but I'd chosen it for two reasons beyond my friend's infatuation. First, I wanted a place close to Central Park, and second, it billed itself as a place apart, a place where all may find spiritual refreshment during their visit. I wasn't a religious person, but I was thirsting for some spiritual refreshment. I figured it was worth a try.

Sam was excited about its historic library room, which included panels from the Palazzo Ducale di Urbino in Italy and a 1916 Aeolian Opus organ.

When the Uber dropped us at the 1914 Italian Renaissance and Baroque-style building, goosebumps lifted on my arms. A Vanderbilt had constructed the four-story townhome on the east side of Central Park for his great-granddaughter. I hoped to jog the mile-and-a-half trail around the Jacqueline Kennedy Onassis Reservoir. Maybe I'd bump into Bill Clinton. I'd heard he jogged there.

We dragged our luggage up stone steps to a massive oak entry. I punched in the entry code provided, and inside, marble steps led to wrought iron doors opening into a large foyer.

A woman appeared from nowhere, greeting us. "Mr. and Mrs. Hunter."

"Yes." I stepped forward.

"Your room's on the fourth floor. The elevator's next to the library, or you can take the stairs." She handed me the keys and pointed to a small door.

"This way, Sam." We headed toward the elevator.

Sam drew back the tiny entrance gate. "Looks questionable."

"I'll check the stairs." I opened the door to a narrow stairwell with a steep incline. I'd seen treacherous flights of steps like these leading to an attic, but never in a public building.

I wasn't about to carry a purse, a carry-on bag, and a large rolling American Tourister up three flights, so we took the elevator. The trip to the room was an adventure. The elevator stopped at the third floor. We walked the hallway twice before finding the cage to the top.

Our room looked as if time had stood still. Clean, small, and essential, I surmised it had once been a maid's quarters. The brass bed and oak dresser could have been original.

"Good thing you're small," Sam said as he flopped onto the bed. The box spring squeaked, blowing a puff of air around the room.

A dank odor drifted by my nose. "Something smells bad."

"The room's just stuffy." Sam opened a window and switched on the small ceiling fan.

I went into the bathroom. "The funky smell is coming from in here." Nothing obvious jumped out at me. I grabbed a towel and gave it the sniff test. It smelled fresh. A lonely soap bar sat on the sink. I congratulated myself for packing shampoo and lotion.

Sam leaned in and looked around. "Looks clean. Ahh, no vent."

Once settled in, I booked another Uber. Our first visit was to the Hoboken Historical Museum. A response indicated a driver would meet us out front in five minutes.

When we left, Sam glanced at the elevator. "Let's try the stairs."

It took a few false tries on the middle floor to locate the lower flights. Like the elevator, we found them on opposite ends of the hallway behind what looked like a narrow closet door.

Our ride pulled to the curb as we walked out the front entrance.

"RaeJean Hunter?" the driver asked. He looked like somebody's grandfather.

"That's me." We climbed into the rear seat of the clean, nondescript, blue sedan.

When we crossed the Hudson, I closed my eyes and leaned back against the seat. I envisioned Mary's likeness from the lithograph on a penny press brochure, face-up in the river, her hair a halo of dark tentacles swirling with the current.

"This is it," the Uber driver said, bringing me back to the present.

The museum hours posted on the door indicated it opened at two, and it was barely noon. We decided on a leisurely lunch in Hoboken.

Sam checked his restaurant app. "There's a cool-sounding coffee shop down the block."

"You pick. I'll eat anything right now. I'm starving."

Sam hovered at several storefronts as we walked down Hudson Street. "Let's come back another time and look for antiques."

Mesmerized, I nodded. I was seeing what Mary had once seen. *Mary walked these streets. These same brick buildings with ground level shops lined the streets back then.*

I finally said, "Let's go find something to eat."

Chapter Twenty-Nine

After coffee and a sandwich, we returned to the museum. Lingering in the pass-through between Hudson Street and the Bernard McFeely Shipyard, we waited for the doors to open.

I wandered to the east opening. The Manhattan skyline provided a spectacular backdrop for Shipyard Park. Meanwhile, Sam snapped photos of the murals boasting workmen swarming half-built vessels, a poster of Frank Sinatra, and the first baseball park in 1847.

At exactly two o'clock, a security guard appeared and unlocked the doors. His keys rattled as they retracted into his belt clip. "Come right in."

We wove through a small gift shop to a room displaying artifacts and documents. A docent approached. "May I help you?"

"I saw an invoice on your website for a sale from Frank Cordts to a Mrs. Bracken."

"Yes. We have banker's boxes of Cordts records that are still out. A recent visitor traced items to Cordts from a boarding house on Nassau Street. You can look at them if you want."

My body stiffened, and Sam squeezed my hand. "Was it a woman?" I asked.

The politely curious docent answered. "Yes."

"Did she look like Betty White?"

She didn't hesitate. "There was a strong resemblance."

"Lillian," Sam and I said in unison. She had beat me again.

"Was she looking for the desk?" Sam asked me.

"No idea. I've never mentioned it to her." I was stumped.

After a short presentation about Hoboken, the docent showed me the box of invoices and explained that the Klingenstein Library had most of the collection.

Sam viewed the displays while I plowed through files. I was well into the final box when he reappeared. "Find anything?"

"A receipt for several pieces of furniture, including a mahogany bookcase, a small table, and a ladies secretary desk with a description matching mine that was stored by C.S. in 1883."

"Who was C.S., a person of importance?" Sam asked.

"I'm not sure, but they could be. The initials match the ones on my desk invoice."

"Anything else?"

"Only that Lillian searched these boxes last week. But you already knew that."

On our way out the door, Sam grabbed a map for the self-guided walking tour. "It's almost four-thirty, but we have time for half the route. If we hustle, we can visit the Elysian Fields, the riverbank where they recovered Mary's body, and Sybil's Cave."

"You know this case better than I do."

"Not really, but I listen well."

We wandered east to the intersection of Sinatra and Hudson to Elysian Park, then entered and traversed the park on a gravel path.

"Not much left from the past." Sam kicked a stone. "All I see are a few basketball courts, an enclosed dog park, and a kid's playground. The grassy fields are gone."

"Yup. Swallowed up by progress," I said, staring at the street lined with multi-story apartments that funneled visitors into the park. A woman approached, leading a golden retriever. Sam saw her, too, and took my hand. "I miss Sophie."

In five minutes, we exited the park through an east gate and crossed Sinatra Drive, following the waterfront south to Castle Point.

"Look at that hill." Sam pointed toward a giant knoll on the west side of the street. It loomed a hundred feet in the air, overlooking the river. A green-veined outcrop formed a bluff at its apex. "Henry Hudson noted Lookout Point in his log when he sailed upriver in *The Half Moon*."

"Cool." I stared up at the natural barrier. Contemporary Hoboken faded behind the mound as traffic wound along the narrow road between the hill and river. We stayed on the broad path by the water. Halfway to Eighth Street, we spotted an arched façade.

"There's Sybil's Cave." Sam picked up his pace.

"Kids found articles of Mary's clothing and her parasol scattered near here. The gang theory suggested this is where she was violated, killed, then dumped into the river. The police concluded the site was a false trail, but they never elaborated."

Sam continued to read from the brochure as we walked.

"In 2007, the city rediscovered the cave and barred its entrance to prevent digging by curiosity seekers. For forty years after Mary died, people visited to drink the spring water, believing it had healing properties. Then, in the early 1880s, city officials, concerned about pollution, closed the attraction. It wasn't a natural spring. It was a man-made cave that collected water, which turned out to be sewage seepage."

"Oh no." I swallowed the rising bile. The thought of all those people drinking polluted water turned my stomach.

"Too bad it's closed." Sam peeked through the bars and pointed his phone light into a corner. "There might be old beer bottles or kegs in there."

"See anything?"

"Not really. Old bricks and stones." He turned off the light.

I remembered reading something about the site. "An article I read said that eventually, someone built a tavern here and used the cave to store food and beer. It became a gin mill for dockworkers and closed in 1937."

Sam paused for a moment. "Lillian's grandfather died that year."

"How do you remember such details?"

He tapped his head. "To quote Hercule Poirot, *it's the little gray cells.*"

I paced in front of the cave opening. "Lillian's father traveled to New York City around the time they closed the spring. Maybe he carried the Wade diaries to New York and hid them here. No, that's silly. He wouldn't have known about its closing."

"He might as well have burned them if he planned to do that." Sam peeked into the grotto once more.

"Right. Lillian's father wouldn't hide family records in a

cave. With his wealth, he'd have them stored somewhere safe, like a bank or law office. Besides, Lillian said he shipped them." Just the same, I made a note to compare his travel schedule with the spring's closing date.

Once back on the riverbank, I booked another Uber. While we waited, I photographed the old Hudson Tea Buildings on Weehawken Cove, the site of Nick Moore's Tavern. Modern residential complexes occupied the former pastoral riverside. As I stared at the water, I thought about details in the police files.

"A tipster in 1841 claimed he saw a woman fitting Mary's description that Sunday walking with a male companion near Moore's Tavern when a thunderstorm struck. Speculators suggested a gang of drunken men leaving the tavern killed both Mary and her companion. But the police never followed up. They didn't see a connection. And I haven't found anything to suggest otherwise. Except..."

"Except what?"

"A contemporary researcher found a police report for a man's body discovered downstream two days later. Based on river currents, he concluded the bodies could have been dumped together, but admitted there was no other evidence."

"Interesting." Sam stared out at the Hudson.

"It is. Those were rough years in New York City. It was common to see bodies floating around. And there weren't enough police to handle the rash of suicides, accidental drownings, and foul play." I shuddered at the thought.

Sam repocketed his phone as we moved toward the gate. "Ready for dinner?"

"Of course. I'm always hungry and I have a spot in mind. There's a pub in Jersey City I'd like to visit, O'Leary's

Publik House." Sam was used to me searching for my father. He knew by the pub's name what I had in mind.

Sam sighed. "You think you'll find your father there?"

"No, but we're nearby. And, you know me, I have to keep looking." I glanced across the street toward Sybil's Cave. My heart momentarily skipped a beat when a man wearing a baseball cap leaned against the fence. He turned, and a car headlamp revealed his face. Not the same guy as in Connecticut. I stuffed my phone into my pocket and breathed a sigh of relief.

"What's up?" Sam wrapped his arm around my shoulder.

"The guy by the cave looked familiar. But the body shape's wrong and he's Chinese. Here comes the Uber."

The twenty-minute ride to Jersey City took us south. We passed Liberty State Park and entered into an aging industrial neighborhood. The inside of the establishment turned out to be cozy. We joined a group of what looked like blue-collar regulars at the bar. Sam grabbed a menu tucked between a jar of pickled eggs and an empty beer bottle.

I leaned across his arm. "What looks good?"

"The burger and beer special."

"Sounds perfect."

The bartender approached as Sam closed the menu. "What can I get you?"

"Two Hoboken 902 craft beers, burgers, one medium and one well done, both with fries," Sam replied.

The bartender yelled over his shoulder toward the kitchen door. "Two specials, torch one burger." He handed us each a cold mug of beer. "You folks new in town?"

"Visiting." I took a sip, then asked, "Are you an O'Leary, or is that just the pub's name?"

He reached out a hand. "Kevin O'Leary at your service. I own the place."

I shook his hand. "My birth name is O'Leary. We could be long lost cousins."

He grinned. "Could be. My sister Aileen did one of those DNA tests a month ago. Not sure why. All of us Irish are related, so she isn't going to learn anything new."

"You never know. A stray gene might reveal ties to the King of England." I grinned.

The guy on my right leaned in and whispered loudly in Sam's ear. "If he's related to the King of England, then I'm Hannah's pup." He raised his beer, chugged it, then slammed it on the bar for a refill.

Sam laughed. So did I. We lingered over the meal while we enjoyed the friendly atmosphere.

"All set, folks? Or can I get you another beer?" Kevin wiped the bar in front of us.

"All set." Sam paid while I booked another Uber.

"Good luck with your family search," O'Leary shouted. "Come back soon."

The Uber driver pulled up within minutes.

"You didn't learn much about the Jersey City O'Leary family except the DNA test by Aileen." Sam climbed into the backseat.

"Not much. It's a stretch, but I might have found my first real lead to my father."

"I hope so, for your sake."

"I'll resubmit my results to GEDmatch. With five thousand new tests being uploaded every day, I might find a match. Maybe Aileen will show up."

"Stranger things have happened." Sam didn't smile.

On our ride back to The Retreat, Sam received a text message from a regular client in Manhattan, Valerie Von

Royer, who often asked Sam to verify her unusual finds. She and I had clicked at our first meeting.

"Do you mind if I meet Valerie for a drink when we get back? She found an interesting antique furniture piece she needs appraised. Since I'm in the city, it'll save me a trip."

"Go ahead. I'll work on my notes." I'd looked forward to an evening with Sam. I was a little disheartened at him leaving, but I understood. I concluded I could use some quiet time. "I have a lot of information to absorb. Maybe something will connect."

"Thanks. I won't be gone long."

Sam arranged to meet Valerie at Earl's Beer and Cheese on Madison Avenue. When the Uber driver dropped us at the main entrance to The House of the Redeemer, Sam headed off to meet her.

The sudden appearance of an interesting antique felt off. Having it show up at Valerie's shop the same day we visited the city didn't feel like a coincidence.

Chapter Thirty

Stuffed from dinner and slightly down from Sam's leaving, I lingered outside a moment to appreciate the building's architecture. Each level's unique window style should have been gaudy. Instead, the white brick window frames produced an elegant effect.

As I stepped inside the front lobby, voices emanated from the reception room to my right. I slipped into a folding chair inside the door, where arched ceilings and rounded windows wrapped me in their arms and warmed my soul. I closed my eyes, eavesdropping on a Bible study group listening intently to the minister-in-residence.

He opened with a question. "Who's familiar with Esther's story?"

I opened my eyes to see if anyone volunteered. A few hands lifted. Not mine. It had been years, but vague memories from Sunday school surfaced. Neither Caitlin nor I considered church as much more than an outing with friends. Our mother lost the battle when we reached our teens.

My mind wandered to Mary. Like Esther's life change

from marrying a king, Mary had moved into a new world from rural Connecticut to city life. Adjusting to an urban environment must have offered freedoms and perils. If raised a Rogerene, the city dwellers' open lifestyles would have eased her into New York's evolving free society where women challenged traditional roles.

A cough followed by murmurs broke the prolonged silence, yanking me into the present.

A woman spoke. "Esther kept a secret from the king when she married him."

The minister responded. "True. Why did she keep it from him even after they wed?"

It was a man who replied. "Because she was a Jew, and the king had ordered all Jews to be killed."

"Exactly. But shouldn't Esther have been honest with the king before their marriage?"

I'd kept a secret about my past from Sam. But now, I needed to share it with him, so he'd understand my recent struggles. Riveted to the chair, I barely breathed. When the minister asked the next question, my stomach knotted. I wasn't religious, but I wasn't a nonbeliever, either.

"Esther's secret meant she'd be killed, so she kept quiet. Does anyone know why?" The minister's gaze skimmed the crowd.

The same man responded. "Because her cousin told her not to tell the king."

"That's true. What does the Bible say about keeping secrets?"

Once again, the room fell silent. The minister smiled at the group. "The Bible teaches us that keeping secrets can be both good and bad. We have to decide their right or wrong use on our own. In Esther's case, she kept the secret until she needed to save her people."

"So, she revealed it out of necessity," a woman said.

"Yes. Esther used her influence to save her people. Because the king loved and respected her, he withdrew his order to kill all the Jews, which would have included his wife."

The discussion continued, but I'd heard enough. I slipped from the library and climbed the stairs to my room. After two flights and some soul-searching, my flimsy excuses for keeping my past from Sam had evaporated. A healthy marriage hinged on honesty. *I'll tell Sam as soon as possible. He won't hate me for it. Right?*

The event had remained a part of me, not impacting my life with him. But now, to move forward, I needed to face the one thing I'd withheld from him. "God, I haven't been a faithful servant, but I've never asked you for anything. Please, listen to me now. Make Sam understand."

Once in the room, I checked my email. I had a message from Syracuse University. They stated they would email their results from examining the diaries written by Alonzo Mathers' second wife. I should receive the reports by Friday, or Monday at the latest. Apparently, the student was struggling with cursive.

I slipped into pajamas and tried to prepare for tomorrow's visit to the New York Historical Society. My inevitable conversation with Sam wound through my head like an earworm. My hands shook. Doubt and fear surged through me. Finally, I threw my notebook onto the table and simply waited for him.

I didn't wait long.

He burst in, grinning from ear to ear. "Did you hear me hooting?"

"No. Why were you doing that?"

"You wouldn't believe what Valerie found. The

matching Regency hall chair that Paul at Elegant needs for an order. The client has offered a hefty finder's fee to Valerie and I." Sam danced around the room, singing, "We're in the money!" He bounced onto the bed, waving his phone. "Look at this specimen. It's mint."

"Wow. I remember the chair. It's gorgeous. A swag back with a shell crest rail. So unique." My shaking ceased. I shoved the difficult conversation onto the back burner. I wouldn't ruin his mood tonight. The timing had to be perfect. Hopefully, soon.

Sam locked me in a warm kiss.

"I love it when you talk furniture." He kissed me again.

"I love it when you kiss me like that." His excitement kindled my fire. We kissed with more heat, ending all discussion of chairs, and commencing a sultry night of bliss.

Sam and I slept late, then headed out for brunch at a coffeehouse on Madison Avenue.

"You never told me about your evening while I was with Val. What did you do?"

"Rehashed the case." My stomach knotted. I was such a coward, but I couldn't ruin Sam's mood. "I don't think Lillian's recent travel was triggered by the discovery of the remains. And I'm not sure what it could have been. While you showered, I checked Claire's invoices in Carver's files. Lillian's excursions mirrored Claire's field trips. Lillian could have been worried that Claire had unwittingly uncovered scandalous information. I hope to learn more at the New York Historical Society this afternoon."

"Will they have information about who owned the desk?" Sam ordered a second coffee.

"They might. Lillian being at the Hoboken Historical Museum means she likely visited the New York Historical Society, too. If she did, I'll see if she asked for anything in particular."

"Like what?"

"I'm not sure. I'm going to check in with Claire." A concern nudged me. I didn't share it with Sam. If this museum visit set the blackmailers on Claire, I could be setting myself up. Worse, I could be further endangering Claire or Emma.

"Anything new about the desk?"

"Not really. Ann Lohman and Louisa Griswold are the closest links. And I think Ann may have owned it."

"Sounds like a long shot."

"Welcome to forensic genealogy. Usually, I'm dealing with the living, not the dead."

"Not just dead. Dead for nearly two hundred years." Sam gulped his coffee.

"Yup. With a deliberate coverup."

Sam's coffee mug stopped in midair. "Where is that coming from? Coverup by whom?"

"Mary's relatives. Recall that Phebe was a Wait. Two New York lawyers, John and Morrison Wait, formerly from Connecticut, had just begun their practices when Mary died. A connection to the case could have stifled their successful careers."

Sam nodded, a silent nudge for me to continue.

"Eventually, Morrison served as the seventh Chief Justice on the U.S. Supreme Court."

"Morrison could have participated in a coverup."

"Maybe. Or maybe the Presbyterian Rogers relatives who didn't support her lifestyle. If the remains are Mary, we can also include the Mather family. It would take a bunch of people to make her past disappear."

"Hard to believe they wiped away her life." Sam shook his head.

"She became a woman with no history. No records in Lyme or Manhattan. The city swallowed her up, and the newspapers spit out whatever sold copy."

"Any other explanation?" Sam asked.

"Not yet. It's just a theory. Actually, a feeling." And my desk held a clue.

"The old gut again." Sam smiled.

"It makes sense. New York City was a melting pot." I waved my arms. "Except in 1841, the pot still boiled. Anti-slavery sentiments surfaced. Female wage-earners like Mary had newfound freedom, the start of the women's rights movement. In the liberating environment, Mary might have found herself pregnant and had an abortion."

"And a family would want those events covered up," Sam added.

"Exactly. From what I've read, being pregnant at your wedding was acceptable back then, but having an illegitimate child or getting an abortion wasn't viewed the same."

"Sad." Sam finished his coffee. "Let's return to the room."

"I'm ready." Fatigue overtook me as we returned to The Retreat. My legs felt like lead.

Sam noticed, lacing his arm around me. "We have time for a nap."

"That sounds great. We didn't get much sleep last night." I smiled at the memory.

Sam's eyes softened, and he leaned over to kiss me. "But it was worth it."

The sounds of Manhattan traffic knocked Sam out. His

snoring lulled me into a restless semi-sleep, but a recurring dream slipped in. The dream was my secret.

Caitlin and I sat parked at the Planned Parenthood building in New Haven, Connecticut. We remained in the car while Caitlin reasoned with me. Her argument made sense. At fifteen, I wasn't ready to be a mother. We both believed in a woman's right to choose.

Once in the building, I stared at the floor. The white tile needed washing.

"Don't worry. Nobody knows you. Wait here." Caitlin collected a clipboard and returned. "Fill this out. They'll call when it's your turn."

I answered what I could, then returned the clipboard. My hands shook as I presented a copy of Caitlin's ID with my photo. I'd need Mother's approval if I gave my correct age.

The receptionist checked it. "You don't look eighteen."

"I get that a lot."

She turned over the ID, never lifting her eyes from the information sheet. "Take a seat. Someone will be with you shortly."

My knees wobbled as I returned to my chair. I was sure she knew it was a fake, but she also knew I needed help.

A woman dressed in scrubs leaned out a doorway. "Caitlin O'Leary."

Caitlin pulled me to my feet. "Come on."

The doctor talked me through the exam. When she finished, I sat up on the edge of the examination table. "I can do the procedure today, unless you want to think about it more."

I'd thought about it long enough. Any doubt I had was gone.

When my friend, Mary Helen Jones, became pregnant,

she wasn't allowed to attend school. She became hall talk for months. Everyone whispered, "How awful." She cared for her baby girl, worked, and studied for her GED. I didn't want her life. I had plans.

"Today." Relief spread through me as I laid back down on the table.

A chunk of Caitlin's college stipend solved my problem, and the procedure was over within an hour.

"Where's Mom?" Caitlin asked as she turned into the driveway of our home.

For once, I was thankful for an empty house. "Working."

"I'll stay. The doctor said to watch for heavy bleeding. Let's find a movie." Caitlin flipped through DVDs and waved *Titanic* at me. I nodded. Our taste in films differed, not that it mattered. I closed my eyes.

Caitlin immersed herself in Rose and Jack's tragic love story, but I wasn't sucked in. Life wasn't like the movies. I curled into a ball and slept. Caitlin woke me when the show was over.

"I've got to study." At the door, she turned and locked eyes with me. "This is our secret. I won't tell a soul, and don't you, either. And for God's sake, either stop having sex or protect yourself."

"I will. I promise. I'm sorry, Caitlin. I'm sorry—"

"Rae, wake up. Wake up."

I opened my eyes to see Sam leaning over, gently shaking me.

"You had a nightmare." He scooped me into his arms. "You're alright. I'm right here."

I cried on his shoulder for a few minutes until I was wide awake.

Sam brushed the hair off my forehead. "Do you want to talk about it?"

"I don't really remember it," I lied. I wasn't ready to talk yet.

"Those are the worst kind." His kiss brimmed with concern, not passion.

I closed my eyes. He was right, I'd had a nightmare. Unfortunately, it was far from over.

Chapter Thirty-One

The hum of Fifth Avenue traffic vibrated our top-floor windows as I stepped into the shower after a rough night. While the warm water ran down my back, I lamented the mess I'd created by keeping my abortion from Sam. But at the time, I was sure my past procedure wouldn't matter.

When I'd discovered I was pregnant with Sam's baby, I'd read every study I found about the aftereffects of abortion. Nothing suggested the procedure caused problems in future pregnancies, so I decided the secret was mine to bury.

My doctor believed chromosomal abnormalities caused the stillbirth. Maybe I'd inherited something from my father. Perhaps, it was an epigenetic tag. Regardless, if I'd shared my first pregnancy with the doctor, he might have run further tests.

My aching heart told me I hadn't given our son a chance. I'd caused his death.

"Are you trying to use all the hot water?" Sam asked through the door.

"No. I'll be right out." I turned off the water and wrapped myself in a towel.

"Mmm, you smell like lilacs," Sam said as I hurried into the room. "Ready?"

"Just about. What's your plan?" I tied up my hair.

"It's late for breakfast. Let's do an early lunch, then I'll return to The Retreat to call Paul Logan. I'm sure he'll buy the chair, but I don't want to leave it to chance." His eyes sparkled. "How about dinner tonight in Chinatown at that restaurant we saw in *New York Magazine?*"

"Yes, Nom Wah's! Great."

"That's the one. Maybe you'll meet a craftsman who builds puzzle boxes." Sam winked. "Text me whenever you're done at the Historical Society."

* * *

After lunch, I caught an Uber to the New York Historical Society on Central Park West, and Sam returned to The Retreat. It wouldn't take long to photograph the O'Reilly letters. The harder task would be examining a ton of woodworking shop invoices.

Between lack of sleep and worry, I'd failed to check my messages until I was at the museum. Grace had texted, asking me to call. She'd have to wait. This was the only available appointment here for a week, and the two-hour slot would barely be enough time as it was.

At the museum, I went directly to the Klingenstein Library on the second floor. "I'd like to see the Henry O'Reilly papers, please." I presented my identification as a qualified researcher.

The archivist checked her computer. "Here they are.

Interesting. It's been fifty years since anyone reviewed this box. Now, you're the third request in two months."

Claire was one of them, but it unnerved me to think someone else would want to see them. "Did you know the other researchers?"

"Not offhand, but I'll check. Be right back." She disappeared into a back room, then returned carrying a box. "You'll need to sign for this."

I signed, slipped on a pair of gloves, and began flipping through the files. Immediately noticing an interruption in the filing sequence, I returned to the desk with the box.

"The file with the O'Reilly letters is missing." I showed her the gap in the file numbers.

The woman waved her hands. "I don't understand. I doubt they'd be misfiled. I'll ask the other assistants. The letters might be out." I watched her hustle off. She returned quickly, bewildered. "They aren't signed out."

I listened to her keyboard click as she checked the registration log.

She looked up, eyes wide. "The last person who signed in was you on April twenty-fourth."

"What?" My mouth dropped.

"It wasn't you?"

"No. I wasn't in New York in April. I was home. Someone stole my purse the previous day while I was in Connecticut."

The archivist frowned.

"Did you work that day?" I asked.

"Sorry. That's my day off."

"Is the archivist who worked then available?" Uneasy, I scanned the room. All women. No ballcaps.

"I'm sorry, she's out on maternity leave. We record

everything we pull. Let me check with one of the other docents."

"Thank you. I appreciate your help." My hands shook as I fiddled with my purse.

The woman printed a list and handed it to a coworker. "Check the other cartons we pulled on April twenty-fourth. Perhaps, the O'Reilly letters got put into the wrong box."

"I'm on it." The archivist hustled toward the storage room.

"It shouldn't take long. Is there anything else while you're waiting?"

It took me a minute to refocus, upset by the O'Reilly situation. "Yes, actually. I'd like to see the records from John Van Boskerck's woodworking shop."

The archivist returned with a dolly full of boxes. "All of Van Boskerck's ledgers as far back as 1830."

"Thanks." I opened the first box. They'd filed records by address. I found a desk delivery at 146 Greenwich Street in 1839. Toward the end of 1840, he'd delivered a desk to 132 Nassau Street, Frederick Mather's office. I photographed both invoices. Deliveries after 1840 fell outside my timeframe.

It was possible Frederick Mather owned my desk or accepted its delivery at his office. And Ann Lohman had a clinic on Greenwich Street, but I wasn't sure of the exact address. I checked the internet. Bingo!

The archivist signaled me to join her, frowning. "We didn't find the missing letters. I can't imagine where they went."

I suspected foul play, but I didn't tell her. "I'm sure the letters will show up." I texted Sam. *I've been outmaneuvered. The O'Reilly letters are missing.*

His response was quick. *Meet me at Nom Wah's in forty-five minutes. And be careful!*
I packed up and left.

Chapter Thirty-Two

Outside the building, I merged into a late afternoon crowd headed toward the Eighty-First Street Station. When the train arrived, we moved en masse into a cramped car, standing together like sardines. After eight stops, the train eased into Grand Street Station, a ten-minute walk to Nom Wah's.

New York Magazine had described the place as a ninety-year-old, ongoing eatery. A Chinese social club had met there since 1925. I was hopeful one of the members might know of a nineteenth century cabinetmaker who also made puzzle boxes.

Heading east into a section of Manhattan known for its high crime in the 1800s, dark doorways near the curve nicknamed The Bloody Angle provided ideal stalker hideaways. I squinted into the shadows, searching for secret passages in the Chinese Theater on Doyer Street. My pulse quickened at a spot where gangs had once ambushed their rivals.

I increased my pace and caught movement in the doorway of an unlit shop, gasping at the profile of someone in a baseball cap. The person faded into the shadows, but the body shape resembled the man in Lempster, in Old Saybrook, and in Duck River Cemetery. Same build and hat, now four times. No coincidence.

I had a stalker.

I moved into the light, sprinted to Nom Wah's, and practically leaped into Sam's arms.

"Whoa, are you okay?" Sam held me tight.

"I am, now." I looked around. "Someone's definitely following me. Let's talk inside."

The tiny vestibule led into a dated but clean dining area. The black and white tile floors reminded me of a Norman Rockwell cover for *The Saturday Evening Post*. Half a dozen booths on our left lined the wall below a photo gallery of famous patrons. Groupings of Formica tables and red-cushioned chrome chairs filled the center. The rear area had several more booths.

"Feels like we've walked back in time." Sam grinned.

A waiter approached us. "Sit wherever you'd like."

We chose a seat near the back since people-watching was a favorite pastime of ours.

Sam relaxed in his chair. "You seem upset."

I sighed. "I'm frustrated and unnerved. It's been a crazy day. The O'Reilly letters are missing, and even worse, whoever took them used my ID."

"You're kidding. Any idea who?"

"No. The archivist who worked that day is out on maternity leave. My gut says Lillian is slippery enough to steal them. Plus, she's beat me to every other location."

"Could be." He picked up a menu.

A smiling waitress approached us. "Are you ready to order?"

"Dumpling soup to start, please." Sam nodded toward me. "She takes forever to decide. Bring me a pork sandwich when you deliver her order."

"No problem. I'll get the soup." The waitress scurried off.

"Forever?" I made a face at Sam.

He laughed. "A long time, okay?"

Rattled from my baseball-cap fright and the missing letters, I chose an old favorite, ignoring the rest of the menu. Then, I searched for a back room. The only visible doors led to the kitchen on one side of the rear booths and restrooms beside a padlocked storage area on the other. There was no observable private area or meeting room.

"What are you looking for?" Sam craned his neck.

"A backroom or something private. This place was a gathering spot for Chinese woodworkers in the early nineteenth century, but I don't see another room."

"Me either."

I took a couple of interior photos, then checked my photo library.

Sam spotted the puzzle box. "That's a good picture. Why don't you send it to Greg to show his friend at Wing Kee's?"

"Good idea." I forwarded the picture to Greg.

The waitress delivered Sam's soup. "It's very hot. Be careful." Her eyes strayed to the puzzle box photo. "You're ready to order now?"

"I'm ready. Rice roll with spareribs, please." I handed her the menu.

Her eyes barely moved as she glanced down at the photo. "You're a photographer? We have many famous visitors."

"No, I'm a genealogist." I looked around. "But I under-stand a men's social club meets here."

Her smile faded. She glanced toward the kitchen. "No."

I wasn't sure if she meant it wasn't a social club or if she couldn't talk about it. I waited for more, but she scurried off. As she passed a tall Chinese man, she nodded, and I suddenly realized he resembled the man from Sybil's Cave. He followed her into the kitchen.

I leaned over to Sam. "Did you notice the tall Chinese man by the kitchen door? He resembles the man at Sybil's Cave yesterday, except no ball cap."

"Is he the same guy you just saw outside?"

"No. Too tall."

Sam took my hand. "Not everyone in New York wearing a baseball cap is following you. But if they are, I'm here to protect you."

I laughed. "I know. I feel silly, but—"

"But what?"

"I don't know." I picked up my phone, browsing through my photos as something niggled at me. Sam ate his soup.

In my photo of Sinatra Drive's waterfront, I'd captured a man smoking a cigarette next to a group of tourists. His silhouette, including a ballcap, matched the guy from The Bloody Angle.

"Sam, look at this." I showed him the photo.

"This is definitely not the tall Chinese guy." Sam finished the last of his soup and put down the spoon.

"I know, but he's built like the man I saw in the Lemp-ster cemetery, in Old Saybrook, at Duck River Cemetery, and now just outside here."

The waitress delivered our meals. "Anything else?"

"I'm looking for help opening a puzzle box," I blurted.

Sam's eyes widened.

The waitress' gaze shifted to the tall Chinese man, now standing a few feet away. I saw his eyelids flutter and his mouth twitch. Maybe a signal.

After an awkward moment, she answered. "Sorry. I can't help."

The tall Chinese man moved out of earshot.

I locked eyes with her. "Are you sure you don't know anyone who can open a puzzle box? What about one of them?" I pointed to the elderly Chinese men sitting at a rear table.

Sam covered his mouth with his napkin.

"No. The old men don't speak English. And don't talk to strangers."

"I could hire a translator."

Again, she glanced toward the tall man, now by the front register. Did I detect a slight head shake? "They don't talk to strangers," she repeated, refusing to budge.

I slid my phone to the edge of the table, exasperated. "Have you ever seen a puzzle box like this?"

She shook her head. "I can't help."

"You can't help, or you won't help?"

"Rae!" Sam leaned in and whispered, "You're getting pushy."

I forced a weak smile at the waitress and apologized. "I'm so sorry. I've had a frustrating day. There's no excuse for my behavior."

Her expression relaxed a bit, then she muttered, "Ting's Gift Shop on the corner of Pell Street sells puzzle boxes. Try there."

Dinner sat like a stone. As Sam settled the bill at the checkout, he grabbed two fortune cookies. Afraid to read the message inside, I refused mine. "You can have it." I waved my phone at him. "If the guy wearing a baseball cap is outside, I'm calling the police." Glancing back, I noticed the tall Chinese man disappear into the kitchen, his phone against his ear.

Chapter Thirty-Three

The glass door creaked as we left Nom Wah's. Neon signs flashed pink, green, and blue, illuminating family groups drifting by as they chattered in their native language. Even though nothing unusual presented itself, my hands trembled. I shoved them into my pockets. The man in the baseball cap had disappeared.

Sam looked both ways. "The coast is clear, Sherlock. It's thirty yards to Ting's, right over there." He pointed to a red door, wrapped his arm around my shoulders, then used his officious voice to say, "You're safe now, Tess."

"Oh, stop it. You're not Dick Tracy." I punched his side, laughing. Sam and I loved the comic book movies, even the ones filmed before our time. *Dick Tracy* was our favorite. Sam always teased that I could out-eat The Kid.

Bells on the door jingled as we entered. The store was empty except for an elderly gentleman, who greeted us. "May I help you? Are you interested in something special?"

"Yes, a Chinese puzzle box."

"A puzzle box! Ahh, *Himitsu-Bako*." He grinned and

led us to a display at the rear of the cluttered store. "A local craftsman builds these for me."

The puzzles of varying sizes and designs filled two shelves. The clerk handed me a particularly intricate-looking box.

"Beautiful." I rotated it. "Can you open it?"

"Yes, but only if I buy it." He showed me a sealed envelope taped to its bottom. "Only the owner gets the moves."

"What if you lose the code? Could someone else open it?"

The shopkeeper shook his head. "Not me. I sell them. Only the craftsman who made the box could open it." He hesitated. "Or perhaps, someone who learned from the craftsman."

"Has the artisan of this puzzle made boxes for a long time?" Sam asked, picking up another small chest.

The shopkeeper's head bobbed. "Oh, most certainly, yes. Lin Chen learned from a master. Many Chen ancestors crafted puzzles."

I handed him the box. "Did the Chens live in New York?"

"Many generations. Businessmen brought boatloads of our people to work in the wood shops." The shopkeeper rummaged in a drawer, then handed me a business card printed in Chinese.

"I can't read Chinese."

He grinned. "Turn it over."

The card listed Lin Chen at Artistic Woodcraft in Brooklyn and a phone number. "Ahh."

"It's best to visit the shop. Chen doesn't hear his phone when he's working."

Not wanting to be rude, we stayed a few minutes longer, then left.

"If Greg's friend can't help, this Chen guy sounds promising." I slipped his card into my purse, and we headed back to The Retreat.

* * *

Back in our room, I called and talked with Grace.

"My team still doesn't believe Emma's case is anything more than blackmail." Grace sounded confident. "But we recently arrested mob members holding five teenage girls in a Lower South Providence hotel during a recent sting. They believe the traffickers are working with someone else. These guys freelance."

Her confidence in blackmail momentarily relieved my anxiety, but when she added the part about freelancing, my heart raced.

"We think that's what's happening here. Several of the same perpetrators are working a side job," she explained.

"You mean they could be working for someone besides a mob boss?" I wasn't sure this revelation made me feel any better.

"Possibly. If you stick with the case, we might get a break. A chance to nab them. Especially if they don't know we're watching."

Knowing Grace's team was out there helped. Still, things were getting dicey. "Okay. I'll hang in there."

Grace cleared her throat. "And someone needs to bring Claire up to date."

My heart sank. I knew it had to be me. "I'll call her right away."

"Great. Tell her to call me anytime. Gotta go. I have another call."

"Thanks." A sick feeling lingered after we disconnected.

Sam emerged from the bathroom. "You look like you've seen another baseball cap."

"I just spoke with Grace. There's been a sting in Lower South Providence, the area of the DNA cluster—human trafficking. I'm not sure what that means for Emma."

"Maybe she's a target. Claire's threat could involve more than photographs." Sam shook his head. "If these mob guys are connected to the blackmailer, sexual photos going viral are the least of Claire's worries."

"I agreed to call her."

"You'd better do it now. Otherwise, it will eat you up."

Claire answered right away. "Hi, Rae. Any news from Grace?"

I took a deep breath, then blurted out what little I knew about the human trafficking ring, the mob, and the potential threat to Emma. Claire remained silent on the other end of the line.

"Claire, are you alright?" She had to be dying inside. Most mothers would be. But it was all I could think of to say.

Finally, she spoke. "Yes...no...I don't know. Is Grace handling it?"

"Yes. She's leading the case. She said to call her anytime. And I'm pushing ahead with the project to see if I can flush them out."

"I've got to talk to Grace." Claire's voice cracked. "Let's talk later."

She hung up before I could reply. I glanced over at Sam. "I'm running out of time."

Chapter Thirty-Four

After a sleepless night, I'd barely dozed off when the ringing of Sam's phone woke me.

"Hey, Greg. What's up?" Sam checked his watch. Five-thirty. "It's early, even for you." Sam put his phone on speaker.

"My friend said the puzzle has a release pin. He suggested moves if you find it. I'll text them to you."

"We'll give it a try."

"If that doesn't work, we have another lead. A woodworker in Brooklyn. His family specializes in custom furniture and puzzles," Sam explained.

"Let Rae know I haven't run the photos yet, but I'll get on it later today. Oops, my toaster oven just buzzed." Greg disconnected the call.

The puzzle box peeked out from under a shirt I'd thrown onto the dresser. Sam reached for it, and we turned it every which way until we found what we thought might be the pinhole.

"There's a needle in my travel sewing kit. Maybe that will work."

It didn't.

"That's it," I sighed. "We'll have to wait until we can meet with Lin Chen."

Sam put the box back on the dresser, leaned in, and kissed my cheek. I grabbed him and placed a long, passionate kiss on his lips.

His eyes showed hope. "I'll shower now, unless of course..."

"Better wait." I wrapped my arms around him, and we fell onto the unmade bed.

* * *

We shared grins as we ate our takeout breakfast in bed. Work awaited us both, and it was getting late after a luscious start to the day. Afterward, Sam went to the library to phone Paul Logan.

I ran through the leads. The desk was on hold until I could visit Lin Chen. Augustus Mather's journals intrigued me, but his entries didn't name Bea or Mary. They did, however, point me in a direction connecting him to New York. And then there was Lillian, the Mather family expert, and a prime suspect for my troubles, who wouldn't answer my calls.

"What did you do while I was gone?" Sam had returned.

"Same old, same old. Rehash. Catalog. Look for a connection. It's time to widen my search."

"How?" The bed squeaked as Sam sat.

My body heated, thinking of our pre-breakfast lovemaking, but I stuck to the case. "John Anderson."

Sam nodded. "The cigar store owner. Not a bad idea. If I remember right, he may have provided Mary money for the abortion."

"The newspapers suggested he had funded an abortion, but some evidence points to Crommelin, the guy who identified Mary."

"You're thinking that Anderson and Mary's relationship went beyond business."

"Looks that way. An 1885 *New York Times* article said he changed after Mary died. He fled to Europe. Plus, those pictures in Louisa's album connected them."

Sam shrugged. "He could have just liked Europe."

"Maybe. But Anderson claimed Mary's ghost visited him multiple times. That's what drove him over the edge." Fortunately, my sensations from the desk were nothing compared to seeing a ghost. I might have felt a little unnerved, but I certainly wasn't close to the edge of madness.

Sam peered out the window. "It's too nice a day to be inside. Let's take a break from work. It's nine o'clock. If we quit around ten, we can take a walk in the city."

"Sounds perfect. It shouldn't take more than an hour to consolidate Anderson's notes. A break might do me good."

"I'll be downstairs in the library." Sam shrugged. "I doubt I'll read all their books, but I'll give it my best shot."

I laughed. "There's over a thousand. Get out of here. I'll meet you in the foyer at ten." I set my phone alarm for an hour and finished Anderson's cards quickly.

Next, I reviewed my notes from Augustus' travel journals. His regular trips to New York could have been to visit his cousin, Frederick Mather. Since he was building a medical practice, he'd want to take advantage of Frederick's social connections. Or he might have stopped by the boarding house to check on Mary and Phebe.

I found it odd that Frederick's name never appeared in

the police reports or the papers. And his office was only a block away. I made a note to follow up on him.

My phone alarm sounded. I grabbed my Manhattan historical map and headed downstairs to meet Sam. He was waiting in the foyer, staring at a recent map of the city.

"I have an idea."

"Back to bed?" Sam smirked.

My emotions said yes, but my logic said no. So, I slapped his arm. "Unfortunately, no. It's a perfect day to trace Mary's likely route on that Sunday in 1841." I'd been wanting to visit Mary's neighborhood, and this would be a good time. I handed Sam the historical map. "This map shows lower Manhattan in the 1800s. I can get a feel for distances, the proximities."

We compared the two, placing them side by side on the table in the foyer. "Not much of the old city remains. Maybe the inner streets," Sam observed.

"I know, but distances haven't changed. Wall Street, Nassau Street, still here." I tapped their locations on both maps.

We exited the subway at Wall Street and encountered Federal Hall, the former U.S. Customs building completed the year after Mary died. "It's impressive. Probably the largest building in its day."

Sam tilted his head back. "Doesn't look so big sitting next to those skyscrapers."

We cut over on Pine to Nassau. All the while, I carried on like a tour guide. "Nassau Street was the hotbed of 1800s publishing."

There was no evidence of Mary's boarding house. A Petland store had replaced it.

"The Silk Shop is where Frederick had his office."

We walked in silence as we moved along Greenwich Street toward Lohman's clinic.

Lost in thought, I imagined what the boarding house and Frederick's office might have looked like in 1841. Then, I noticed that Sam kept glancing west. "What are you looking at?"

"Don't you feel it?" Sam rubbed his arms as if he was cold. "The loss. The sadness. Two thousand seven hundred and twenty-six people died there. I'll never forget that number. It's like their spirits are closing in on me."

I gazed toward Ground Zero. My throat ached, remembering that terrifying day.

"The air feels dense." Sam shivered.

"I know." *Like the air around my desk.* Anxious to change the subject, I prattled on. "Nothing remains of Lohman's clinic or Poe's rental house. They've been gone for years. One's a parking lot and the other's a commercial building."

Sam silently stared as the distant trees bordering the 9/11 Memorial swayed, maybe from the wind, or maybe something else.

"One more detour—a stop at 657 Fifth Avenue. It's practically on our way."

We rode the green line from Fulton to Fifty-First Street.

"This is it." I pointed to a corner building with several businesses.

Sam narrowed his eyes. "Salvatore Ferragamo Shoes, Som Kim Pillows, and La Grenouille's. What's so important about these shops?"

Retrieving a photo from my bag, I showed him Ann Lohman's mansion. "This."

"That's what used to be here?" Sam stared at the buildings. "It must have been amazing."

"Yup. The Lohman stables are all that remain. They're now La Grenouille's. A developer replaced the mansion with a loft building in 1911."

Ann took her life there rather than face another prison term for helping women. During my recent depression, I'd had dark days, but I couldn't imagine considering suicide.

We caught a bus to Central Park and bought hotdogs and lemonade from a street vendor. Sam held up his half-eaten hotdog. "To us!"

I mirrored his salute. "Here, here! Amid happy families, smells of coffee, and onions."

"Couldn't be better." As Sam stuffed the last of his hotdog into his mouth, his phone rang. He mumbled through a mouthful, "It's Logan. I'll take it over there. Don't want to spoil the magic of the moment." He grinned and walked away. Food flew out of his mouth as he chewed and talked.

I shook my head and took another bite of my lunch. Closing my eyes, I leaned back against the bench, basking in the sun. I'd just begun to drift off when a voice startled me.

"You look lonely." An elderly woman's friendly face blocked my view. My hotdog had mesmerized her corgi.

"I'm missing my dog. She's a corgi, too." I lifted the hotdog a little higher out of the dog's reach. His eyes never left his target, while his ears stood tall.

"I'm sorry, I've spoiled him. He's adorable when he begs."

I laughed. "Tell me about it."

She patted the hotdog-blinded canine. "Do you care if I join you? I usually sit on this bench. Eli likes to watch the families."

"Of course not." I finished all but a small piece of the hotdog. "May I?"

"Yes. He'll be your friend forever."

Eli nibbled the scrap from my fingers. "Nice manners. My corgi isn't quite as gentle."

"I've worked hard with him. He's learned patience."

I scratched Eli's rump. He groaned with delight.

We chatted about the park's history. The woman pointed to a wide street leading east across the park. "We might be looking at Dorothy Arnold's route home from shopping the day she disappeared in December of 1910."

I'd seen Dorothy Arnold's story on the Smithsonian website when reading about Mary. "What do you know about her disappearance?"

"A little. Only what I've read."

"Are you interested in local unsolved deaths?" I was surprised she mentioned the Arnold case. Although high profile at the time, it wasn't as well known as the Rogers mystery.

"I am. I enjoy family histories." She looked down at her hands.

She looked tired and lonesome, so I continued to make small talk. "What about yours?"

"I don't know my family. My parents adopted me from New Zealand when I was four."

I didn't usually hand out business cards to strangers. There was something about this woman's sweet, melancholic demeanor that touched me. I handed her a card from my purse. "If you're interested in learning more about your ancestors, here's my contact information."

She smiled as she read the card. "Bloodline Forensics. A snappy name."

"Thanks. It's a grabber for online search engines."

"I have a Kindle, but I'm not much of a computer person." She glanced toward the park.

Sam approached, offering a smile and nod to the woman.

She stood. "Time for us to head home, Eli." The dog stood by her side waiting for his signal. "Let's go, boy." She smiled at us. "Enjoy the rest of your day."

"I will. You, too." I watched her stiff gait as she limped away. I suspected it was she who needed to get home, not the dog.

Sam sat down. "Who was that?"

"A lonely lady and her dog. Nobody I know."

Sam looked like he had something to say but was worried about my reaction.

"Do you have gas, or is there something you want to tell me?"

Sam burst out laughing. "No, I don't have gas."

"So, is Paul interested in the chair?"

He exhaled. "More than that. He wants it tomorrow, and he wants me to deliver it."

"Why you?" I didn't want Sam to leave, but his excitement silenced me.

"These chairs are worth a lot more than we thought. A buyer is willing to pay seven thousand dollars per chair if we can deliver the pair by Friday, plus shipping or travel expenses."

"Cripes, that's great. But what's the rush?"

"No idea. But I can't refuse that much money for two chairs. Plus, it's a visit to Boston."

I faux pouted. "So, you're abandoning me. Shirking your bodyguard duties over a chair."

"Are you okay with it?" Sam shifted his gaze from me to a passerby. "I'll rent a car. The chair is small and easy to carry."

"Of course. I'll be fine for two days. I'll still leave for

home on Friday. I can make a side trip, have lunch with Caitlin, and still be there in time for supper, which you will cook, of course." My surface bravado remained intact, but fears crawled under my skin.

"Deal. What do you want on your pizza?" Sam laughed.

Chapter Thirty-Five

Torrential rain canceled our evening walk. While Sam arranged for a car and to collect the chair, I called Caitlin.

"Give me the nut graph," she said. Caitlin used her journalism jargon whenever she got excited. I'd heard it enough to know she meant a summary.

"If you're available for lunch on Friday, I'll swing by on my way home from New York."

"I'm free all day. Text me when you get close. Anything new?" Caitlin loved to hear about my cases.

I told her about the Chinese puzzle box we'd found attached to a drawer of the desk. It led to reminiscing about when our mother used to put them in our Christmas stockings and how we'd hide things inside, forget the combination, and then have to break them open. "Sam and I haven't been able to open this one yet. Whatever's inside doesn't make noise when we shake it."

"Maybe it's money, and you'll never have to work again."

We both laughed.

"It could be anything. I'm hoping it reveals the original owner."

"Don't worry about who owned the desk."

Caitlin's indifference annoyed me. "But it might have belonged to Ann Lohman, an abortionist in the 1800s."

Caitlin groaned. "Rae, come on. Not that."

Surprised by her response, I snapped, "It has nothing to do with *that*."

"Easy girl. Sorry, I misinterpreted. Why does it matter, then?"

"It matters because Mary went missing for a week while working at Anderson's and rumors circulated suggesting she'd had an abortion. Plus, one theory implied she died due to complications from the procedure." My hackles settled.

"I thought you were supposed to confirm she was buried in New London, not solve a mystery."

"Yes, but Mary's cause of death might reveal how she lived, and who she was."

"I don't see how Mary having an abortion could help you." Caitlin returned to business.

"It loosely supports my theory that Mary lived in a Rogerene household. It would make sense for her to have been interred in a Rogerene cemetery."

"The sect from Mamacock Farm in New London?" Caitlin sounded surprised. "Our paper ran a piece recently about that farm and Pilgrim Hill."

"Yup. Rogerenes. I think her father, Daniel Rogers, was a member and a polygamist."

"That's a bit of a stretch."

"A relative, Lucy George, kept a diary. She inferred that Mary's half-sister, Bea, who was possibly Mary's birth mother, died from bad blood. You know, syphilis. That fact, along with Mary's alleged abortion, suggests liberal views held by the Rogerenes."

"I see your slant. Liberal sexual conduct. But it's flimsy, Cub."

"If the evidence keeps piling up, I could be right."

We discussed the various clues and deadends I'd pursued. When I told Caitlin about two more living relatives I'd met, Lillian Baxter and Ezekiel Rogers, she laughed at my story about Zeke, then admonished me for trusting Lillian, a total stranger. She couldn't help herself, so I let it go. However, I reminded her I was approaching my thirty-third birthday, hoping she'd realize I wasn't a child anymore.

After telling her about Augustus' journal entry and the unnamed medical student, she agreed it was a useful clue. "There must be someone else in her family who's newsworthy."

"There is. Frederick Mather's law office was a block from Mary's boarding house. Proximity makes him interesting. I haven't researched him yet." I paused. "Or the New York City Waits, minus Phebe's sisters. Most of them cut ties when she married Daniel."

"Skip the Waits. It's the lawyer. It's always the lawyer." Caitlin laughed.

"Right. The law profession touches everyone. Plus, interactions are verifiable. He'd have been listed on legal documents like wills, deeds, or family trusts."

Caitlin spewed reasons to suspect him. "Frederick may have been counsel to someone involved in Mary's death. Or advised in a family conspiracy or coverup."

"Maybe. It's a big family."

"Six degrees of separation. We could be related to the Mathers."

Her comment stirred thoughts of epigenetic tags. "I doubt it. Mathers were English Protestants. We'd be Catholic descendants of the only Italian Puritans," I laughed. Caitlin didn't understand the inference. She'd skipped most of her Early American History classes and hadn't paid much attention at church.

"What's your next move?" she asked.

"Phone calls. I've compiled questions for the two living relatives. Lillian Baxter, a Mather, acts helpful but isn't. Zeke Rogers is more forthcoming. I'll call him first."

When I rattled off questions for Lillian, Caitlin suggested an approach. "I've dealt with a hundred people like Lillian. They love the limelight. Make her feel important."

"That won't be difficult. Lillian thinks she's the queen of the DAR."

"You get my drift. Tell her she's instrumental in solving this case. She'll open right up."

"I'll try." I yawned. "Sorry. Excuse me. Hopefully, I'll be revived by tomorrow. Sam and I walked all over the city today."

"I'm booked this weekend, but I'd love you to spend next weekend with me. Ask Sam and Greg to join us. It'll be fun."

I missed her, and I welcomed a break from the case. "Sounds great. I'll check with Sam. We can plan it during lunch on Friday."

We disconnected as Sam stuck his head in the door. "Check with me about what?"

"We've been invited to Caitlin's next weekend, and she asked me to invite Greg along."

"Caitlin included Greg. That's a surprise."

"Not really. I can't believe you didn't notice the spark

between them at our last gathering. This could become news." I loved Sam to pieces, but he missed the subtle vibes between people.

"I don't know. Greg's been a confirmed bachelor ever since I've known him."

"We shall see." *I'm right on this one!*

I read while Sam researched the chair, my mind bouncing in a million directions. I'd forgotten to tell Caitlin about the O'Leary family in Jersey City. Just as well. I'd wait and see if it turned out to be anything. I had upset her more than once with deadends.

Unable to concentrate, I closed the book.

Chapter Thirty-Six

S am left early. At his insistence, I got an Uber to the New York Genealogical Society and arrived as the doors opened at nine. They'd pulled the Griswold boxes, so I went right to work.

The records included wills, deeds, and legal documents for business transactions. I checked for grantors, grantees, trustees, and executors, anything that might link Frederick to Mary. Midway through one of the folders, I spotted Frederick's signature on Richard Griswold's will.

I officially had irrefutable evidence that the two men knew each other.

An entire box contained documents Frederick had prepared and filed for other Griswold family members. My phone vibrated as I photographed Richard's will. It was Lillian.

"Hello." I couldn't imagine what she could possibly want now.

"Have you made progress tracing Ezra and Phebe Mather?"

"Hold on. I can't talk here." I smiled at the docent, then

exited into the hallway. "I'm back. And yes, I've made some progress."

"Great. Tell me what you've discovered." Lillian pressed as if expecting me to share what I'd learned.

"I'm sorry. I can't disclose my findings. It's in my contract." I didn't tell her I could with my client's permission, but I already knew the answer.

"Too bad. We could have collaborated. Regardless, I'd suggest you find the Wade diaries instead of wasting time on other deadends. Martha's diaries have answers."

Her attempted redirection annoyed me. "Maybe."

"I'm trying to be helpful. You'd be wise to listen."

Her harsh reprimand irritated me. "For the record, I'm not wasting time. I like being thorough."

"Right, thorough. If I were you, I'd press for my inclusion. My knowledge could solve your case." She'd softened her tone.

Rattled by Lillian's demands but determined to learn what this helpful knowledge might be, I scrambled for a response. "It's clear you want to help, but I'm bound by my contract."

"I repeat, inform your client that I have a lot of family information I can contribute. Surely, you can make a convincing argument since that's what you do for a living. Excuse me, I have another call."

Her abrupt dismissal and tone alarmed me, but the latter snide comment annoyed me. Her insistence on being involved didn't feel helpful. In fact, it felt intrusive. She rarely answered her phone. Now, she had called me and was being both pushy and obstructive at the same time. Pretty impressive when I thought about it.

I returned to the library. By noon, I'd abandoned my search since the remaining materials were dated beyond the

1860s. Skipping lunch, I went directly to the archived public records on Chambers Street. Allowing myself thirty minutes to research O'Leary, I found nothing.

Switching to Mary's case, I quickly found a dozen Mather family documents Frederick filed. I also unearthed Frederick's name on a deed record for the Fifth Avenue land purchase and a building permit for the mansion where Ann Lohman had taken her life. I took photos of everything and uploaded them to the cloud.

Hoping for a breakthrough, I kept my late afternoon appointment at the New York Historical Society to examine the shipping manifests from Griswold Imports and the Rogers Family Papers, which included an 1898 diary by a woman named Harriet Rogers. When I arrived, the archivist led me to a table covered with boxes.

"You're kidding." There was thorough, and then there was this. I'd need to eliminate boxes outside the date range.

She smiled sympathetically. "Have fun."

I hoped the Griswold manifests would identify who built my desk or the puzzle box, or both. I dug in. A Customs House broker on Wall Street kept detailed records for Griswold's Shanghai cargo—Griswold imported tea, silk, porcelain, and nankeen, a durable cotton cloth. There was no mention of puzzle boxes.

By five o'clock, I had one box left containing Harriet Rogers' diary. Though she was born after Mary died, Harriet was a Rogers who kept journals, so I reviewed hers on the off chance she mentioned Mary or Phebe. But Harriet only recorded personal thoughts, nothing helpful. It turned out to be another deadend.

As I was packing up, an email arrived from the GEDmatch site where I'd run my comparison to Aileen O'Leary. I would wait to open it. Disappointment was getting harder to swallow these days. If there was a gene match, I'd take it to the next level and call Caitlin.

I packed and returned to The Retreat, feeling as though my day had been a success.

Sam called. He'd delivered the chair to Paul to complete the order and was spending the night in Boston after returning the rental car and taking the train from Boston's South Station to Philadelphia.

"Who is this client that's willing to overpay for two antique chairs?" I asked. Another niggle. The coincidence that Sam and I happened to be in New York City and now he was being offered a price above market suggested to me that something was definitely off.

"No idea. Valerie's working through a broker."

"Not another shadow client." All of this secrecy was making me uneasy.

"Apparently. By the way, Greg said yes to Caitlin's offer about next weekend."

"Great. I'll let her know." *She'll be excited, but I bet she won't show it.*

"He also said to tell you he hasn't run the photos yet. Maybe tomorrow."

"I hope so. The album photos might be a better match."

I texted Caitlin after Sam and I disconnected. She responded with a dancing Snoopy dog.

One more night alone at the House of the Redeemer. Shivers ran down my spine as I thought about the man who had been following me, and about Lillian pressing me for information. Tomorrow, I would be safe at home with Sam. It was less than twenty-four hours.

But it felt lightyears away.

Chapter Thirty-Seven

"Crap! Crap! Crap!" I leaped from my morning shower. The lukewarm water had turned ice cold. Shampoo dripped down my back as I slipped into my terry robe and stuck my head under the ice cold spray. So much for a relaxing shower. Before I could straighten up from toweling my hair, my phone rang. Lillian Baxter's name scrolled across the display.

"Hello." I wiped a stray drip from my forehead.

"Meet me at noon in Hartford at the Connecticut State Library. I have something important to share." Typical of Lillian, no introductory etiquette.

Confused, I asked, "What's this about?"

"Nothing I can discuss over the phone."

Her abrupt answer annoyed me. It felt like an order. My knee-jerk reaction was to refuse. But she'd said it was important. "I assume it's regarding my case."

"Of course."

My instincts warned me it was a trap, but my commitment to Grace and my unabated curiosity won out. "Okay. I'll be there in three hours."

"I know." She disconnected.

My arm hairs lifted. Lillian knew my drive time, that I was in New York. But I relaxed, remembering that the State Library was staffed with full-time security guards. Plus, it would be broad daylight and parking was nearby. I arranged for a rental car to be dropped off outside The Retreat.

* * *

Slipping my stash of M&M's into my pocket, I prepared for the drive. Once on the highway, I accelerated to a speed just over the limit where state cops wouldn't stop me. I wanted an edge, and that meant beating Lillian to our rendezvous spot.

Trees and guardrails blurred as I focused on my destination. Checking for a possible tail reminded me of my vulnerability. A line of cars followed me. Plus, I wasn't confident I'd be able to spot one. Halfway to Hartford, it dawned on me that I'd forgotten about lunch with Caitlin. I'd text her from the library. Sam, too, if time permitted.

The Colt Armory's blue onion dome signaled my arrival to Hartford. Colt had long since ceased operations in the stunning white elephant that clashed with the city's traditional New England architecture. Like many abandoned facilities, it now housed offices.

After circling the buildings twice at the State Library in search of a parking space, I parked two blocks west. The walk to the library relaxed me.

At the building, I gazed up at the grandeur of the Italian Renaissance pillars and sweeping arches forming the library entrance. Inside the door, a guard directed me through a metal detector into a spacious and empty lobby. On my right, the door to the State Supreme Court stood open.

231

Court wasn't in session. A sign resting on an easel indicated after today the building would be closed until May twenty-first for maintenance.

Two lawyers or legal aides poured over casebooks in the law library to my left. The stacks of books filled me with a familiar comfort. God, I loved libraries!

My footsteps echoed as I rushed downstairs to the historic document section. Lillian would arrive in thirty minutes. Not enough time to review the entire Mather and Griswold collection, but I'd have time to check for new documents.

I ducked into the stacks and located their copy of the *Lineage of Rev. Richard Mather*. Habit forced me to review it for margin notes. A crossed-out scribble in the margin next to Bea Mather's name roused my interest. I thought of the other note I'd found in Marlow and snapped a photo with my phone. Maybe Greg's handwriting analysis program could decipher it.

A new book entitled *History of Mather LifeWays* caught my eye. The first page had a photograph labeled Alonzo Mather, the name on the desk invoice. He'd owned the desk at Cordts, where Dr. Kemp had found it.

I learned from the introduction that in 1941, eight years before he died, Alonzo bequeathed his fortune to a foundation. Concerned over widowed friends unable to support themselves, he wanted to provide *a home for aged ladies of refinement and from good families*. Originally called the Mather Home for Aged Ladies, it was later renamed Mather LifeWays when the services expanded to include men.

When the clock chimed, I checked my watch. Time was running out. I flipped to the appendix, a document section many researchers tended to ignore. Like bibliographies, my best leads were often found there. The first page included a list of corporate officers and a financial statement with a footnote, submitted by Empire Auditors.

"I figured I'd find you here." Lillian's voice cut like a knife.

Startled, I turned and found myself nose-to-chin with her.

"Hello again." I extended my hand, receiving the same brushoff I did in Keene. During my visit to Rocky Hill, Lillian had switched on the nice-lady act because she wanted something. But here, she felt in control and wasn't compelled to play nice. She strutted toward the door of a reading room.

I replaced the *History of Mather LifeWays* and made a mental note to check Empire Auditors.

Lillian led me into a private resource room, a clean room used for handling primary documents. She toted her usual Johnny Was bag where she probably stashed case-related information. Taking the chair facing the door, I sat and watched, expecting her to produce a historic document. Instead, she seated herself, then placed both hands on the table. The chair screeched as she drew it in. No rare document. I'd either waltzed into a trap, or this was an interrogation.

Lillian cleared her throat. "What would it take to convince you to drop your current project?"

Her question left me speechless.

Outside the door, motion caught my eye. Two swarthy men peeked through the glass door as they passed. The heavy set one wore a baseball cap. I thought of Emma, the DNA cluster in Rhode Island, and its connection to this case. The threats and the photographs. When I looked into Lillian's unsmiling face, I swallowed hard. "Why?"

"Continuing this could end badly for you." Her face twisted into an ugly sneer.

I locked eyes with her. Claire's warning echoed in my head as Lillian continued. "Mary's been dead for centuries. She's nothing to you."

My hands shook from her biting remark. "What makes you think she's nothing to me?"

Her eyes narrowed. "I'll double the contract amount if you'll abandon the project."

Her offer hit me like a punch. I couldn't think clearly, so I stalled. "I'd need to talk with my client first." I really wanted to call Grace, but I couldn't tell Lillian that.

She raised her eyebrows. "What's to discuss?"

I searched for a response, hissing the only retort that came to mind. "You don't even know my contract price."

She shrugged as if the amount didn't matter, or she'd suspected it wasn't a bundle.

"My contract is a hundred and twenty-five thousand dollars," I lied. "Are you willing to double that?"

"Of course, money's not an issue. Drop the case." Arms folded across her chest, she glared at me.

Lying under pressure helped me regain my composure. I stared back. "I repeat, I'd like to talk with my client."

"Go ahead. You have ten minutes." Lillian stood and left the room.

Surprised, I fumbled with my phone. Once I'd confirmed she was out of earshot, I dialed Grace. My call went to her voicemail. "Grace, call me right back. It's important." I tried Sam, then Caitlin. Neither answered. I didn't bother to leave Caitlin a message in case Sam tried to call back.

While I waited for someone—anyone—to call, the man wearing a baseball cap passed the glass door again, this time heading toward the exit. I recognized him as the man I'd bumped into in Old Saybrook. There were no coincidences when Lillian was involved.

Her preposterous offer floored me. If I accepted, we'd have money to finish the house. Or, if we had a baby, it would provide enough for me to stay home for a few years. But I thought of my promise to Grace, to help catch the bad guys. This wasn't just about money.

What was so bloody important to Lillian about Mary Rogers?

She returned before anyone called me back, so I made my own decision. I had every right to pursue the case and help catch the men who'd threatened Claire and Emma.

"Your ten minutes are up. Give me your answer."

My Irish stubbornness took over. I stood my ground. "I'm not ready to surrender yet."

"You've nothing to gain by continuing the case. You could ruin me, or my family's reputation."

I didn't believe Lillian's hogwash about her family's reputation. I was positive she had something to hide. Something worth a quarter of a million dollars. "I'm close to discovering what happened to Mary Rogers. That's enough for me." I stayed on the path of Mary even though I doubted her life had anything to do with Lillian's offer.

Lillian played along, but her eyes suggested she didn't believe me. "You never will. Experts have failed, and you're only a genealogist." Her mouth twisted into a sneer as she spoke of my profession. She whipped around and left the room. The hallway echoed with her arrogance as she stormed away.

"I'm a *forensic* genealogist!" I hurled the words at an empty space.

My blood boiled. At last count, over seventy cold cases

had been solved through genealogy, including the Golden State Killer and a sixty-five-year-old Montana case of two teens. I'd show her.

Still fuming, I decided I had time to revisit the *Mather LifeWays* book and look up Empire Auditors, so I returned to the stacks. I hadn't heard back from Grace, Sam, or Caitlin. As I reached for the book, strong hands grabbed me from behind, covered my mouth with a moist cloth, and pulled me backward. My nose prickled. My eyes watered. The cloth smelled slightly sweet. I kicked and flailed.

And all went dark.

Chapter Thirty-Eight

"Oh." My moan broke the silence. A faint echo resounded as I pried open my eyes. Light entered from beneath the door of an otherwise pitch-black room. Numb from the cold damp air, I tried to move. My abductors had taped my wrists in front. When I moved my legs, I realized they'd also bound my ankles. The metallic taste in my mouth reminded me of sucking copper pennies. Once, when I was a kid, I'd accidentally swallowed one. It hurt all the way through, especially its exit the next day.

My tongue held back the bile rising in my throat as I struggled to stand. After several attempts, I succeeded. Left shoulder braced against a concrete wall, I bunny-hopped toward the light. Objects in my zip-up sweatshirt pockets thumped with each jump. A solid door blocked my escape route.

"Get me out of here! Somebody, help!" Frustrated and angry beyond reason, I yelled and pounded the door, a useless tantrum. Exhausted, I slid to the floor. The aroma of red wine, rotting paper towels, and biology class wafted from my hoodie's neck opening.

I'd been had. *Chloroform!*

A brief rest on the cold concrete reset my senses to something closer to normal. My heart quit racing. My nose stopped running and I could hear again. "Relax. Use your head." My voice echoed. My hands shook as I picked at my ankle bindings. "Crap."

I'll die if I don't do something. Inhaling a deep breath relaxed me a little.

Upright again, I fumbled toward the opposite wall. Between hops, I heard a faint *plink, plink.* The further I went, the louder the sound became. On my next jump, my knees collided with an object. The tinkle of breaking glass resonated in the chamber. I slid to the floor, fingering the debris. I'd smashed the glass in a picture frame.

I pawed around, feeling for a large shard. "Ow! Gotcha."

A knife-sized shard stabbed my palm. I clawed at it and grabbed it with two fingers. Rotating it toward my bound wrists, I jabbed at the tape. *Come on! You can do this.*

I poked and poked at the material. The shard slipped as my hands grew slick with blood from self-inflicted wounds. My fingers cramped, but the fabric held firm. After a few more jabs, I stopped.

Think. You can get out of this. Then, it came to me. In my self-defense training required by the FBI, I'd watched a video on how to escape from duct tape. Hands overhead, I thrust downward onto my thigh as I raised my knee. The tape broke with a *snap.* Tears formed as I freed one hand, ripping off skin, hair, and tape. It stung, like removing a Band-Aid slowly, only worse. Blood oozed from the raw spots created by the adhesive. Next, I freed my ankles.

Then, I checked my pockets. M&M's on the left side, and the keychain penlight, minus my keys, on the right. Why take my keys and leave the light?

Using the penlight, I panned the room. Curved walls formed an arched chamber the size of an average Burger King. Industrial lamps hung at intervals on the opposite wall above a narrow platform. A deep trench, about ten feet wide, dissected the room. A wooden pallet spanned a corner of the channel, and the shattered picture frame lay next to the wall.

I knew this basement. I'd seen it in a photo collection showing the State Library as it was being built. I was locked in the unfinished subway station beneath it with only one way out—the solid door.

"Oh no. Now what?"

I tapped my watch, surprised I still had it. Probably an oversight. Or maybe one more way to torture me. *Great. Now I'm scaring myself.*

"Six o'clock. The library closed at four." Lillian and the man in the ballcap had left hours ago. "Trapped, alone, with nothing but a bag of M&M's, a watch, and a penlight." Talking aloud helped, so I babbled on. "Caitlin expects me for lunch. She'll check her phone tracker app. She follows me like Big Brother. She'll call. Wait, crap. I turned off the ringer during my meeting with Lillian. I doubt anyone will hear it vibrating in the stacks."

Just when I thought things couldn't get worse, I remembered the notice at the entrance. Today was May eleventh. The library would be closed until May twenty-first for maintenance. "Ten days." My panic turned to despair as I edged along the wall. "Think of survival."

After a tortuous preteen year in Girl Scouts, I'd quit. But in one year, I'd learned I hated cooking and sewing, and that an average-sized person could survive three weeks without food, and three or four days without water. Sadly, I was sprite-sized, so it could be less.

A *drip, drip, drip* suggested I had the means to stay alive. All I had to do was find it.

I panned the room again, this time focusing on the trench. The light reflected off an iridescent, greenish-purple slime. I scuffed debris into the water to break the surface tension. Between the odor and the slime, my desire to drink vanished, but my mouth was dry. Back at the wall, I scuffed the glass and kicked the frame again. Then, I sat it upright.

"It's dry, not damp like everything else in here." I recognized the print. "A Cassatt!" The scene depicted a naked infant being held and kissed by its mother. Not only was it a heartbreaking picture, but also, when I broke the glass, a shard gouged out the baby's nose.

Someone wants to torment me. Someone wanted to remind me of my failure, my inability to become a mother. And the only way *that* someone would know my fears was by reading my daily notes.

Whoever put me here had my laptop.

"What an idiot. You walked into a trap and you're going to die if you don't do something. Think, RaeJean, think!" My voice cracked. "Oh, sure, this case will be an easy segue back into the working world." My sarcasm echoed in the darkness.

Nothing about Mary Rogers warranted this drastic action. But refusing a quarter of a million dollars might have. *Mary, what's Lillian hiding?* I yelled, "If it's you, Lillian, you'll be sorry! You won't get away with this! I have the FBI on my side!" Exhausted, a bit delirious, and a lot angry, I collapsed, drifting into a fitful nap.

Later, the coldness woke me. The Cassatt had warmed

my chest. I lifted it, touching the infant's face. "I'm not going to die here. Someone planned this, but I'll survive if I use my head."

I inventoried my survival tools, and double and triple-searched the accessible areas. A penlight, the Cassatt printed on canvas, a wooden pallet, and a seven-ounce bag of M&M's. That was it, all I had.

Thinking about the M&M's made me hungry. I fought my inclination to stuff my mouth full of chocolate, choosing instead to read the label. "Twenty calories for four pieces. No wonder I've gained weight." I dumped the bag onto the floor and counted its contents. "Two hundred and ten pieces. If I start eating them tomorrow at a meager twenty-one a day, or a hundred calories, I should be fine. Mahatma Gandhi fasted for twenty-one days. All I need to do is stay alive for ten until the library reopens."

Tempted to pop a few in my mouth, I resisted, instead scooping them into the bag. Feeling their familiar size and shape reminded me I'd taken my antidepressant that morning and still required two more weeks at lower doses. I shrugged. "So much for tapering off."

Crawling to the channel, I swiped my hand along the damp wall and licked the foul-smelling moisture from my fingers. It tasted earthy with sprinklings of salt. "Could be toxic. Crap! If I'm not found, I'm toast, anyway." I swiped and licked again.

My mind churned while I resumed my blithering. "Obviously, Lillian's behind this. She set me up, and the guy with the ballcap dragged me down here. Okay, Einstein, why'd you refuse Lillian's offer? Because the FBI had your back. Duh! Where's Grace now?"

Like Claire, I'd hit a nerve and a knee jerked...hard. Blinded by my own confidence in Grace, I never expected to get into a worse predicament than Claire. A few keystrokes might ruin Emma's life, but my situation indicated that Emma could be in more danger than a ruined reputation.

"Get me out of here!" Only my echo responded.

Shivering, I dragged the pallet onto the concrete floor. Although warmer, the slats dug into my back as I drifted off.

* * *

Three days passed while I rationed M&M's, licked stinky water from my hands, paced, slept, and shivered. Antidepressant withdrawal symptoms—tremors, muscle pain, and dizziness—added to my discomfort.

Now, when my eyes opened, my lips refused, sealed with dried blood. By moistening them with the stagnant water, I was able to consume my daily candy allotment.

The catnaps conserved my strength, but the cold air weakened me, so I paced for warmth. Moving burned calories and increased my thirst. I needed more fluids.

"Drips!" I fumbled for my penlight. Water beads ran down the trench wall. "Where are you coming from?" I may have missed an escape route. I looked closer. "Crap. Seepage, not a stream."

Water condensed into droplets and slid into the pool. No hidden escape route. Moisture oozed from a seam where the platform met the side of the trench. Slimy, single-celled organisms clung to the wall like a living drape. When I touched the goo, my whole body shuddered. The residual odor on my fingers caused an involuntary dry heave.

* * *

On the morning of the fourth day, my thirst won the battle. "It's now or never, Sherlock." My eyes teared up at the sound of Sam's pet name for me. "No time to wallow. Slime or no slime, you need fluids. Hand licking isn't enough." I debated hanging my hoodie by one sleeve into the trench. The cuff might reach the water. Fabric acted as a wick. Then again, I could drop it and lose it altogether. I'd have no way to keep warm and could die from exposure.

"Oh, heck. I'll give it a shot." I draped the shirt over the edge. The cuff was dry when I retrieved it. All my fretting didn't matter because my kindergarten-sized arms weren't long enough to reach the bottom.

I flopped onto the cold floor. Panic warred within me. "Don't cry. Think. You can figure this out." I rechecked my tools. A pallet, M&M's, and the Cassatt. Lifting the picture, I fingered its center. As my hand moved over the baby's face, a familiar sensation of fibers tickled my fingertips. It was a print, sprayed on cotton canvas.

"Fabric!" Canvas held water.

I removed the residual shards, then hesitated, not wanting to destroy the painting. "Oh well. It's you or me." The frame held tight to the canvas. Using a glass shard, I scored the edge, then ripped it free, gathering it into a pouch before holding it up. "It's big enough for a water bag."

With string, I could gather it and create a pouch or bowl. I needed the hoodie tie to extend my reach when I lowered the pouch. My brain worked slowly to reevaluate my cache. I thought about the clothes I was wearing. Then it dawned on me.

"Sam's gonna love this. " I pulled off my jeans, intent on repurposing my favorite thong panties. The polyester lace fought me, but I chewed until it broke. "Gotcha."

Next, I punched eyelet holes at intervals along the

edges of the canvas. Feeding the lace through the holes, I drew it in. Once tied to the sweatshirt sleeve, I lowered the crude bowl into the pool.

"Crap! It floats!" I retrieved it, weighted it with hunks of glass, and tried again. This time, it tipped enough to collect dribbles of water. I inched it up, tipped it to my mouth, held my nose, and sipped. After a third sip, I dry heaved, but the M&M's and water stayed down. I'd drink again later. No point in overindulging. I would wait and see how my body reacted.

Back at the pallet, my body curled into a fetal position. I whispered, "I'm going to die, Sam..."

Chapter Thirty-Nine

My watch battery died while I slept. I continued to alternate between pacing for warmth, eating M&M's, sipping groundwater, and sleeping. My pacing, now a shuffle, took me to a corner where I eliminated a blob of flux. Urinating was a no-go. I'd lay beside the door in case I heard voices.

* * *

A muffled sound woke me. Was I moaning? Something nudged my back. Light shone in through a wide crack. Someone had partially opened the door.

A man's voice said, "Door's blocked. Anybody there?"

"Me, RaeJean Hunter," I croaked after my swollen tongue managed to press my bloody lips open. Crusty eyes sealed out the world as I clutched my remaining M&M's.

"It's her. She's alive." The man's voice floated over me as he gently nudged me along with the door. A light beam stabbed the one eye I'd managed to pry open.

"Oh, geez, she's just a kid," another man said.

A shadow loomed over me. A hand touched my face, then my arms. "She's freezing." The shadow wrapped me in a blanket and gently lifted me.

The next thing I knew, a needle pricked my arm. My eyelids fluttered, too weak to stay open. A blur of people filled the room. Unfamiliar voices said my name, leaned over me, and asked questions I couldn't understand.

Then, a familiar spicy smell filled the air by my bed. "Sam? Is that you?"

I felt a kiss against my forehead. "Hey, Sherlock."

My attempt at a smile split my lips. They tasted salty as I ran my tongue over them. My eyes barely focused. "Sam."

"You're going to be okay. You need to rest."

* * *

Sandpaper eyelids rubbed my eyeballs as I forced them open. Two blurry figures stood beside the bed. I tried to focus. "Sam. Caitlin."

"Hey, Sherlock." Sam took my hand. "Good to see you again."

Confused about my surroundings and afraid that I was dreaming, I said the first thing that came to mind. "How'd you get here?"

"I flew to Hartford from Boston. Caitlin met me at the airport."

"You had us pretty scared." Caitlin's voice quivered.

"Where am I? What day is it?" I had to be sure it wasn't a dream.

Sam pulled me to his chest, burying his face in my hair. His chest shook as he cried.

"Move, you big oaf." Caitlin elbowed her way in and kissed my cheek as we both cried.

Sam wiped his eyes and sniffed. "You're in the ER at Saint Francis Hospital in Hartford. It's Wednesday, May sixteenth."

"Oh, Sam." I wrapped my arms around him and sobbed into his shirt.

"I should have stayed with you. I'm a lousy bodyguard." His voice cracked.

"I thought I'd be okay. It's not your fault."

"I shouldn't have left you alone." He brushed hair from my face.

"Enough." Caitlin stepped in, straightening the blankets. "You'll need to stay a few days. The doctor says you're severely dehydrated. You have nasty wounds on your wrists."

My raw fingertips stung when Sam kissed them, but it was a good sting. I was still alive. "I did that to myself, removing the tape."

"You'll be fine." Sam sat on the edge of the bed. "No kayaking for a while, though."

"I can live with that." The scent of Sam's aftershave reassured me.

A nurse winked at me as she entered my room with a food tray, pointing at Sam to get off the hospital bed. Sam's face reddened, but he obliged, and hopped down. "All kinds of good stuff," she continued. "Lime Jell-O, beef bouillon, tea, skimmed milk, sherbet." The nurse placed my meal on the table.

"I'd prefer a steak." Too weak to sit on my own, Caitlin raised the head of my bed.

"It might taste good, but believe me, you wouldn't enjoy the outcome," the nurse replied.

"Milk?" Caitlin handed me an open carton, and I started to guzzle.

"Whoa, small sips." She grabbed it back. "I'll meter it, or you'll vomit again."

"Again?"

Sam pursed his lips, then said, "You've been like a volcano."

"News bulletin, Cub. Both ends," Caitlin added.

"You had to tell me that?" I poked at the green Jell-O. "I'll try this." After a few bites, I tried the sherbet. The bouillon vapors turned my stomach. Consumption of a cup of food exhausted me. My eyes drooped, but I fought the sensation.

"Sleepytime." Caitlin lowered the bed as Sam tucked in the sheets.

I clutched his hand. "Don't leave me."

* * *

Sounds of a baby crying in the next room disturbed me. A breakfast tray sat on my table. Sam lounged in the recliner by the bed, where he'd spent the night.

When the shift nurse entered my room, I questioned her. "I thought I heard a baby crying."

"You did. The first available bed was here in the pediatric wing," she explained.

"Right. Another case of mistaken identity, I suppose."

"Sort of," Sam said. "The ER nurse identified you as a young teenage girl."

"Oh, for Pete's sake. Not again."

Sam winked at the nurse. "Better than the geriatric wing."

The nurse checked my pulse. "No matter. This wing's fun. Kids get special treatment."

Sam interrupted her. "The police want to interview you."

"Is that my special treatment?" The nurse laughed at me. Nothing looked good on the food tray. "May I have ice cream?"

"Absolutely." The nurse winked at Sam. "I'll be right back."

"Great." My mouth watered at the thought.

"If you're up for the interview, I'll tell the officer outside your room." Sam nodded toward the door.

"An officer's guarding my door. Why?" I didn't feel safer with him on guard.

"Protection. We don't know who did this. That's why the officer is out there."

I'd expected him to say Lillian and was surprised when he didn't.

While Sam fetched the officer, I surfed TV channels and thought about ice cream. Sam and the nurse returned at the same time. She delivered a heaping dish of vanilla.

"All set," Sam announced, taking a seat. Fifteen minutes later, the state trooper joined us. I'd recovered enough to be embarrassed by my disheveled condition. I needed a shower, so badly that I wanted to cover my head with the sheet.

The officer introduced himself as Trooper Janco and removed his tan campaign hat. "This shouldn't take long. I just need a brief statement." He produced a mini recorder. "Are you okay with this?"

I nodded.

"Do you remember how you got into the train station?"

"I'm not sure. I was in the stacks when someone covered my mouth." My hand touched my lips. "That's all I remember."

He looked up from his notetaking. "Why were you at the library?"

"I went to meet Lillian Baxter. We met in New Hampshire four weeks ago. She called me in New York, said she had something important to discuss." She'd tricked me. I felt stupid telling the story.

"What was it?"

My fingers caught in a snarl as I ran them through my hair. "Nothing related to my case. She offered me money to quit doing research."

Janco's eyebrows arched. "How much money?"

"A quarter of a million dollars. But I refused."

He scribbled something, then asked for Lillian's address.

I gave him the street name and described her house. "Trust me, you can't miss it."

"Anything else?"

"Two men peeked into the room while Lillian and I met. They'd left by the time we finished."

Sam leaned toward me. "Was it the guy wearing the baseball cap?"

"I think so. He left before Lillian did, but I'm not sure if the guy left the building. I never saw him again." I tried to remember, but my mind was blank.

Janco interrupted. "What guy with a baseball cap?"

"I think he's been following me since I visited Lempster, New Hampshire, four weeks ago. I've seen him in several different cities. Actually, there might be two men. One's Chinese, and the other—I'm not sure." I described what I could recall, like his hooked nose and small chin.

"We may need you to look at mugshots. Any idea why someone would want to harm you? This research, perhaps?" Janco asked.

"No. I've been working on a hundred-eighty-year-old cold case, the death of Mary Rogers. Hardly a threat to the living." I swallowed to relieve my parched mouth. "But I'm pretty sure it's related. Lillian doesn't want me to tarnish her family name, or so she says. I think there's more to it."

"Like what?" Janco looked confused.

"They're Mather descendants, and she's a muckety-muck in the DAR."

He wrote something down, but I couldn't tell what. I laid back on the pillow, then added, "It's complicated." As if that explained everything.

"It usually is." His sympathetic look reassured me.

"I was hired to verify the identity of some old human remains found at Connecticut College. Actually, I was the second genealogist hired. The first one quit." I didn't tell the detective Claire's name or anything about her daughter, not wanting to involve them. Besides, the FBI was already on it.

"And that's it?" Janco straightened himself, readying to leave.

"Actually, my client suspects the remains are Mary Rogers, a Mather descendant."

"Why would that be a problem?"

"Because Mary likely died from an abortion. And I'm guessing Lillian thinks her cause of death would tarnish the family name." Saying it aloud made Lillian's reason sound flimsy. There had to be more to it.

"That's hardly a reason for kidnapping and attempted murder."

"I thought so, too, but you'd have to meet Lillian. She identifies with her ancestors. The DAR, you know. All that family history."

Janco grunted. "There's definitely got to be more to it."

I shrugged. My mind went blank as I watched him put

away the recorder. "If you don't have any questions for me, I'm done."

"What about my purse and phone? Did you find them, or the car keys?"

"All accounted for, doggie fob of mace and all." He smiled. "We found them stuffed in a trash barrel in the Capitol Building parking lot. Unfortunately, they smashed your phone."

"How'd you know to check the library?"

"Your husband and your sister. He said you couldn't drive past a library without stopping. Plus, your sister's phone tracker placed you near the library the last time she checked."

"Sam's right. And I knew Caitlin would be tracking me." I smiled, then closed my eyes.

Sam touched my hand. "You okay, Rae?"

"Tired."

"That's enough for today, then. You can collect your items once we've finished processing them for prints." Trooper Janco handed me his card. "If you think of anything else, call me."

"I will, but I'll need a phone." I squeezed Sam's hand. "Right now, I need a nap."

"Go ahead. I'll update Caitlin and Greg. They're driving me crazy." Sam kissed me, and I fell asleep before he and the detective left the room.

Chapter Forty

By Saturday, I'd recovered enough to realize how much I disliked hospitals, especially the pediatric ward with its poor sick babies. I couldn't wait to get home and shower. Sponge baths to avoid the wounds on my wrists and ankles prevented infection, but they didn't trump a hot shower.

Awake since four in the morning, I performed an abbreviated set of yoga exercises. I was exhausted after only five minutes, and I took a break that lasted until the doctor arrived for his six o'clock rounds.

"Good morning, RaeJean." He smiled as I retrieved the bedsheet from the floor.

"I see you're feeling better."

"Getting there. When can I go home?"

He checked my wounds, wrote on my chart, then looked up. "How does today sound?"

My heart raced. "Fantastic."

"I figured you'd say that." He grinned. "I'll authorize your release. Everything looks good. If the wounds become inflamed or you run a fever, contact your regular doctor.

You may have ingested some nasty bugs, but so far, all the tests have been negative."

The nurse delivered my breakfast tray after the doctor left. "You're dressed early."

"The doctor says I can go home today." I ignored the tray. I was too excited to eat.

"Great. Your husband called a few minutes ago. He said he'd be here by nine."

"That's three hours from now. I'd like my release papers once they're ready, thanks."

"No problem. It takes an hour or so after the doctor's seen you." The nurse returned at eight o'clock, paperwork in hand. She set it on the nightstand.

Sam had spent the night at Caitlin's after getting minimal rest in the hospital chair. The minute he arrived; my feet hit the floor.

"You're anxious to get out." He hugged me. "I'll check for discharge orders."

I snatched them from the nightstand. "All set. I got them after the doctor's morning rounds."

An orderly brought me out in a wheelchair, and Sam collected me at the hospital entrance with my Mini. "You've got my car."

"Greg drove it up and flew back to Philly yesterday. He didn't have time to stop."

"Nice."

* * *

Janco had requested we stop at the station on our way home to sign my statement. Sam slung his arm around my shoulders while we waited in a small interrogation room. We didn't talk. The institutional beige paint reminded me of the clinic in Hartford seventeen years ago.

When the desk officer returned, I read and signed the statement. "I assume you don't have any mug shots for me to look at."

"Not today. Don't have enough to go on, yet. We'll call you when we do."

I appreciated his confidence, suspecting that whoever had abducted me had already left the state.

"We can eat now or wait and eat at Caitlin's." Sam said as he opened my car door.

I slumped against the seat, in no shape for the public eye. "Caitlin's."

"Caitlin's it is." Sam climbed into the driver's seat and called her. He glanced at me while navigating the sleepy streets of Granby. "You look tired."

My eyes watered, and I nodded. I couldn't wait to get home.

He reached over and squeezed my hand. "We'll talk later. Someone's waiting for you at Caitlin's."

My stomach tightened as I closed my eyes. No offense to Greg, but I hoped it was Sophie. I missed my dog.

Now on the mend, I realized how careless I'd been. I couldn't imagine what was motivating Lillian. It wasn't the family's reputation. She wanted me to drop the case. I'd refused and almost died. As I retraced those last few moments at the library before being drugged, I remembered seeing the appendix in the *History of Mather LifeWays* with an account payable to Empire Auditors.

Sam turned off the engine. "We're here."

I lifted my head in time to see two dogs fly out from Caitlin's side door. Sophie's jump-spins nearly knocked me over. Caitlin's ten-year-old Yorkie, Nellie, stood there, watching in what I could only guess was disbelief. When I knelt, Sophie smothered me in dog kisses. Life was good.

Sam held the door open, kissing my head as I slipped by him with both dogs at my heels. Together, Caitlin and Sam fixed breakfast. The smell of bacon made my mouth water. I rested on the back stairs and sipped orange juice. When they'd finished cooking, we moved into the dining room.

The ride had exhausted me. We forced small talk, but mostly ate in silence. Still not ready to share my experience, I was grateful that neither one pressed. About to suggest that we head home, Sam broke the silence. "Greg's joining us for a cookout."

"He called earlier and wants to see you himself," Caitlin smiled at the thought.

I grinned at her. "I don't think it's me Greg wants to see."

"Greg's smart. I like smart guys." Her eyes sparkled. Color crept into her cheeks.

"He's not too shabby to look at, either. Reminds me of a heavier Bradley Cooper."

Sam feigned jealousy. "Not better looking than me!"

I stood and cleared my place. "Nobody's better looking than you."

He rose from his chair, dishes in hand, and winked. "Right answer."

I raised up on my tiptoes, kissing his ear as I passed by. "I'm ready for a nap."

Caitlin stood, reaching for her purse. "Sam and I are headed to Geissler's Market to buy food."

I stiffened at the prospect of being left alone.

Sam caught my reaction. "I'll stay if you'd feel better."

"No, you go. I'm okay. I have Sophie and Nellie to protect me."

"You're sure, Sherlock? Here, take my phone and call Caitlin if you need anything."

"Thanks." I wasn't sure, but I nodded anyway. I couldn't live my life afraid to be alone.

"We won't be gone long." Caitlin flashed a list. "I want Sam to pick out the sides."

"No green Jell-O!" I yelled over my shoulder, earning me a laugh from both of them.

I climbed the stairs to Caitlin's guest bedroom. Both dogs tagged along. Too tired to shower, I slid into bed fully clothed. As I lay there, I realized it had been eight days since I'd taken an antidepressant. Other than being tired, I felt fine. Nearly dying wasn't the best way to wean off a drug, but it'd worked.

Sophie curled at my feet, and Nellie claimed the adjacent pillow. I might have been exhausted, but I couldn't fall asleep immediately. I doubted I'd ever feel safe again.

Chapter Forty-One

A booming laugh from Caitlin's front room rattled the half-open bedroom door. Greg had arrived.

As I checked the clock, my hand touched a warm spot on the bed. Sophie had abandoned me, no doubt anticipating a dog treat from Greg. An unpleasant odor escaped my hoodie as I threw off the blanket. While I was sleeping, Caitlin had set out fresh clothes across a chair. *Thank you, Caitlin.*

Before I joined the party, I took the shower I'd dreamed about for days. The warm spray ran down my face and body. My wrists stung when water soaked the gauze, but I was finally able to wash away the odor of fear with her honeysuckle bath soap.

Rested, showered, and dressed in Caitlin's oversized clothes, all I needed was a hearty meal to restore my resolve. Everything suggested that I was close to a solution.

I hobbled toward the living room, feeling conspicuous in Caitlin's St. Moritz athleisure suit, black with white splatter and green lettering, instead of my usual Old Navy gray sweats. Sam watched from the doorway. When I reached him, I wrapped my arms around his waist, resting my head against his chest at armpit height.

He pecked my cheek. "You look better."

As I reached down and patted Sophie, my eyes watered. "I'll make it."

Caitlin waved from the kitchen doorway.

"I hope you're planning an early dinner," I said. My stomach fluttered, a recurring sensation since my entombment. Unwilling to admit my trauma until now, I realized the hollow feeling came from almost dying, not hunger. Still, I searched the room for M&M's. Caitlin always had a dish available when I visited. I didn't see one.

"Got you covered. We're having a late lunch." Caitlin disappeared into the kitchen and came back with a partial bag of the colorful candy. "I bet you're looking for these. They found you clutching them."

I laughed. "Always." I opened the folded bag and took out a handful of the remaining pieces.

"They're white," Greg observed.

"The color wore off from daily counting." I popped one into my mouth. "Still good."

"Don't spoil your lunch." Caitlin echoed our mother's familiar warning. "It's almost ready." We followed her into the kitchen, which smelled of freshly sliced onions. Caitlin took charge. "Everyone, grab a dish and head to the back patio."

Greg and Sam drank beer and talked baseball while the burgers cooked. Caitlin and I went about setting the table with outside dishes, but I struggled to place the forks.

Caitlin took the utensils from me. "Sit, Cub. I'll do that."

"Sorry. My brain is on overload." I slumped in the chair and watched her, feeling loved and grateful.

"Wine?" Caitlin held out a bottle of Catena Malbec. She'd splurged for my homecoming.

I loved good wine. But today, my body rebelled against itself. I shook my head. "No thanks."

Caitlin sipped the violet drink while she chattered about her work. I barely listened. Instead, I contemplated my next steps in the case. I needed to convince Sam and Caitlin I had to continue.

Sam placed a heaping platter on the glass table. "Burgers are ready."

Conversation stopped while we consumed our food. I hunched over my burger. The outside tasted of charcoal, but the center was juicy without a hint of pink, just the way I liked it. Sam had toasted the rolls. I ravaged it like a half-starved dog. When I looked up, I caught my husband staring at me.

Sam arched an eyebrow. "Don't worry, we won't take it away."

Embarrassed, I straightened. "Food tastes so fabulous." My whole body prickled. New taste buds, fresh eyes, and a vivid world full of clear sounds. I felt like Saul in the Bible, who'd gained sight as if scales had fallen from his eyes. I was ready to confess my past to Sam. Just not here. Not now. I resumed the attack on my lunch. I didn't ever remember enjoying a plain burger so much.

Halfway through, my stomach cried enough. I broke the meat into pieces and slipped them to Sophie, who sat under the table, drooling on Caitlin's oversized sneakers.

We chatted about the weather and other meaningless topics. Finally, Greg gave me a questioning glance. He'd waited as long as he could, trying to give Caitlin, Sam, and I space to recover.

"I guess you're curious about what happened."

He nodded. "Tell us about it."

"Give us the scoop." Caitlin sipped her second wine, not that I was counting.

"I don't remember much. I slept a lot and was always cold. I dreamed about food. Whenever I was awake, my head pounded." My hands shook. "I'd agreed to meet Lillian at the library."

I answered their questions for a while.

"Sam said you refused a quarter of a million dollars." Greg sipped his beer, but he eyed me like I'd lost my mind.

My stomach lurched. "Yes. And I got entombed for my naiveté."

Caitlin waved a fork at me. "What were you thinking? Why didn't you quit the case?"

"The outrageous offer convinced me I was close to a big discovery." I looked at the three sets of eyes, riveted on me. "Sam would have asked me if the case was all about money." I turned to Sam. "I know I'm right."

"I might have said that." Sam's eyes darkened. "I should never have left you in New York. Those stupid chairs. Your life's worth more than them or Lillian's offer. You could have died in there." He gulped his beer.

We remained quiet for a few minutes, then I spoke. "I thought I would die."

Nobody uttered a word for a few minutes. Sam leaned over and kissed my cheek, while Caitlyn patted my shoulder.

Finally, Greg said, "Thank God, you didn't!"

"I'll toast to that." Sam raised his beer, then chugged it down.

I cringed as Greg asked how Lillian had reacted when I refused, recalling the ugly sneer on her face as she left the room. "She stormed out, leaving me wondering what happened. So, I went to the stacks to retrieve a new book I'd found, the *History of Mather LifeWays*. The next thing I knew, I felt something over my mouth. Then, I woke up in the train station."

Caitlin set her wine glass on the table. "And you think you hit a nerve with Lillian. She was worried about tarnishing the family name."

"Yes, but she stumbled over her words. She said it would *ruin me*, then corrected herself to say *ruin my family's reputation*. Zeke warned me about her."

Sam grabbed another beer. "You trusted Lillian, even after being warned. Martha Wade's diaries are probably one of her wild goose chases."

"Possibly. I've never trusted Lillian, but she's a living relative. I guess I need to find one who doesn't want me off the case."

"What's your alternative?" Caitlin asked.

"More phone calls." I shrugged. I hated cold calls to relatives, with their unpredictable reactions. Everybody remained quiet. "Lillian's hiding something. And if it's as big as I suspect, we ought to be able to spot it. I'm convinced the answers are in front of me. All I have to do is recognize them."

Over the next hour, we discussed the countless possibilities.

"It can't just be about the family name." Lillian had all but admitted she didn't care about Mary.

"Why not?" Caitlin finished her wine and set the glass down.

"Money has to be involved. The Mather name has been dragged through the mud before. Cotton Mather, and the witch trials. Why would Lillian offer me a quarter of a million dollars to save a family name? It doesn't add up." As I yawned, I thought about Empire Auditors again.

Caitlin stared at me. "You look exhausted."

"I am. I'd really like to go home." All I could think of was my own bed. I turned to Sam. "Do you mind?"

"Not at all." He stood. "But we can't leave Caitlin with the cleanup."

My sister looked about to protest, but Greg interrupted.

"You go ahead," he offered. "I'll stay and help."

I peeked over at Sam. He winked. "Okay then. We're off."

We packed up the Mini and headed home.

Sam unloaded the car while Sophie patrolled the backyard. I climbed the stairs to put away my laptop. The nursery door was ajar. I hadn't been inside since before my trip. My fingers curled around the doorknob, but I hesitated and pulled it closed, unable to enter. My eyes filled as I continued on. Being a functional human being again was proving difficult.

When I walked into my office, the tulip glowed. I didn't flinch. The mysterious visions had become almost ordinary. Instead, I plugged in the laptop.

"We'll visit tomorrow, whoever you are."

Sam peeked in the doorway. "Who are you talking to?"

"The ghost in the desk." *The ghost who's a friend.*

He shook his head. "Let's go to bed, Sherlock. I'm wiped."

"Me too." Bravado had exhausted me.

Under the covers, I was almost too tired to sleep. Instead, I made a mental list of things stolen from me while

I was entombed and from the break-in of my car. Thanks to Sam, I already had a new laptop. My house keys needed to be rekeyed, my smashed phone needed to be replaced, and I could dig an old purse out of my closet to replace the one that now stunk from the trash can, but I'd need a new travel bag.

Suddenly, I sat up in bed and nudged Sam. "Are you awake?"

"I am now." He rubbed his eyes.

"They never touched the puzzle box. It was on the front seat, too." My gut said it was connected to the case. "If Lillian was worried about Mary Rogers, she would've taken it."

Chapter Forty-Two

The following evening, Sam and I sat on the porch, sipping our evening wine after spending the entire day flitting around the house.

"I wasn't surprised that Greg stayed to help Caitlin clean up." I smiled.

"I was. A little, anyway." Sam sipped his wine.

"To be honest, I wasn't sure he liked women. He's never brought a date around. But he seems interested in Caitlin."

"Oh, he likes women. He just hasn't found his soulmate."

"Maybe he's like Caitlin. Nobody meets her high standards."

"She's right to be picky. Finding the right partner isn't easy."

"Our parents exposed us to violent arguments during their divorce," I reminded him, my eyes tearing up. "We'd hide from their yelling. Caitlin would hustle me out when things got outrageous. She protected me, and she believes their arguing traumatized me, kept me from growing."

"Momma bear and her cub. You're her family."

"I guess, but Caitlin deserves more. I want her to be lucky, like I am." A warmth spread through me.

He glanced at me. "We all have hang-ups. Even me."

The moment had arrived. I prayed for courage, then swallowed. "We do."

Sam brushed a tear from my cheek. "Something's been bothering you for a while, Sherlock." He set his wine on the side table. "Come on, spill it."

The trees in the yard blurred as I searched for the right words. Words I'd rehearsed in the underground train station, the hospital, at Caitlin's, on the car ride home. Words I could no longer find. Panic and frustration turned my stomach.

"Come on."

My nose began to drip. "I'm not sure where to start."

"Start at the beginning." He swallowed. The look on Sam's face sent a chill through me. His pupils were constricted, and his mouth had a strange twist to it. I didn't know how to read him, even after ten years together. We'd always planned to have a family, but not until we'd established ourselves and owned a house. Now, I was about to tell him I may have messed up our chances. I gulped wine to steady my nerves.

"Okay." I set down my glass. "You have to know why I fell apart so badly after we lost our baby."

His eyes softened. "I assumed the reason was pretty obvious, Rae. I'd never seen you that messed up, but I certainly couldn't blame you for it."

My eyes blurred. I pinched my leg—Caitlin's trick.

He waited, fingers steepled against his lips.

I lifted my glass again with trembling hands, spilling the wine. "It's a long story."

He sat back in his chair. "We've got time. Tell me what's

going on."

I shook from head to toe. "I'm trying." He reached out and brushed the drops of wine off my sweatpants.

"The summer before my sophomore year of high school, I slept with an older boy."

Sam nodded, urging me on.

"My mother worked, and Caitlin spent the summer as a counselor at a girls' camp. Most days, I had the house to myself, so I'd invite this boy over. We experimented." I met Sam's gaze. "I became pregnant. I was fifteen."

Sam's eyes widened. His expression became impossible to read.

"The boy returned to college after Labor Day, and I attended high school. By late September, I knew I was in trouble. I panicked and called Caitlin at college. She—I mean, I...I had an abortion." I started to cry, then caught myself. My heart pounded so loudly I could barely hear myself. "And now, I think it was my fault that we lost our baby."

Sam blew out a gust of air. He'd been holding his breath. "No, sweetheart. The doctor told us it was because of abnormal chromosomes."

"I lied when the doctor asked if this was my first pregnancy."

"He'd have kept it confidential. Besides, he probably could tell."

"Maybe, but I didn't think it would matter. I never saw a doctor for my first pregnancy, except for the abortion."

"You didn't trust your OB to do his job?"

I closed my eyes. "I didn't believe it would matter. Not until after our baby died."

"I don't know what you mean." Sam's voice was a whisper.

"It took months before my body straightened out after the procedure." I shook uncontrollably.

"Your body was probably still growing. You were just a kid, Rae. Your hormones were probably all over the place, pregnancy or not."

"Maybe, but I could have a genetic defect, an epigenetic tag, or worse. I could have inherited it from one of my parents...stress caused by my father's drinking."

Sam grabbed a tissue and wiped my nose. "Maybe, maybe not. But you can't change the past. Let it go. Remember what you said about Mary when you began the case. You wanted to learn who she was, not let her death define her life."

I forced a smile. "Right, I did say that. Like Mary, I dealt with the problem and then moved on. But she died from it, and now I've hurt you. Us."

Sam sighed. "You still don't get it."

Unable to respond, I stared up at the single cloud in the sky.

Taking my hand, he asked, "Do you trust me?"

This time, I whispered my reply. "Of course, I do. But do you trust me?"

"Yes. I probably have things I've never told you. I won't know until a situation presents itself. Like, um, who was that Jewish woman in the Bible who married the king?"

"Esther. She kept her secret until she needed it to save her people."

Sam looked surprised. "That's the one. Esther. Well, you're my Esther. We'll find out together if the abortion caused the stillbirth, but I doubt it. I wanted our baby as much as you did." His voice faltered, then he drained his glass. "Remember our marriage promise."

I spoke into my lap. "Always be honest with each

other."

He wiped his cheeks. "Promise me you'll visit your doctor and explain the whole story."

My lips quivered.

"When we confirm why you didn't carry to full term, we'll consider our future plans."

Slumped in my chair and unable to talk, I prayed. *Thank you, Sam. Thank you, God.*

Sam picked me up from the chair and cradled me to his chest like a baby. "You scared me. I thought I'd lost you."

In his lap, my arms wrapped around his neck, I kissed him. "I love you."

He kissed me back. "I love you, too."

After finally sharing my secret with Sam, I felt ready to revisit the nursery. To sit and rock, to reflect about a baby, maybe touch the fuzzy wallpaper. Everything was as we'd left it. A crib box leaned against the wall. A changing table with the small toy.

We might someday use the nursery, after all.

Sophie interrupted my musing with a yip from my office. "Coming." Relief spread through me as I headed toward her. "I need to love myself, right, Sophie? Move on with life. I can't change the past, nor do I want to. But I should've been honest with Sam."

Zeke had said the past was a living thing, always one second behind us. He was right. I needed to focus on, and deal with, the present. In my case, that meant moving forward, finding out what Lillian was up to.

I stood, put my fears behind me, and headed to my office.

Chapter Forty-Three

My inquisitiveness returned after ten days of rest. Life was good since I'd shared my secret with Sam. I rewrote my to-do list of unfinished case tasks, then started completing them one at a time.

Greg hadn't sent results using pictures from Louisa's album for the reconstruction photo. I texted him and received a reply almost immediately. *On the road. Home late Friday. Will run a comparison program then. I'll send over the results ASAP.*

A cemetery map arrived from Professor Carver. He'd identified a few plot locations, but it wouldn't help without a legal description for Mary's gravesite. *If* she was there. I set it aside.

Next, I grabbed the remaining index cards of untested leads. The first three were Baby Iantha, Lin Chen, and C.S. All three originated in or around New York City. My stomach knotted at the thought of another trip. But I'd gotten this far, and I was so close to a solution. I pinched my arm to reduce my fear and anxiety. It took a fingerprint bruise and a few minutes, but my stomach settled, and I was able to plan. "I can do this."

I would research the 1835 birth records. Mary may have stayed with her aunt, Mrs. Downing, and delivered a baby named Iantha, the baby listed in the Manhattan Presbyterian Church records. However, it could be a coincidence that a woman named Mary Rogers was baptized the same day. This clue might not pan out.

My phone vibrated. Lillian's name glowed on the display screen. I was stunned she'd call after the library incident, figuring she'd gone underground with the involvement of the police. Dread filled my veins, but I answered, stuttering out a greeting. "Hello, Lillian. You have some nerve calling me after...after having me dumped in a basement."

She spluttered. "I didn't...I mean, you...you don't have to get snippety."

"You sicced thugs on me." My hands shook as I relived the days and nights in damp darkness.

She hesitated. "No, I didn't sic anyone on you. I called because I wondered if you'd found anything useful in the funeral register."

Right. There was no way that I believed her, but this was my opportunity to snare her. "I can't believe you care. You made it clear you want me off this case."

"It's pointless to continue, but I regret my behavior. Being a member of DAR, I should want to preserve all history." Her voice dripped with insincerity.

I blurted out my reservations about her purpose. "You know this case has nothing to do with the American Revolution."

Lillian tittered. "I know, but I'm a family history buff. We're a lot alike."

Her nervous giggling annoyed me, and I wanted to

scream that we were nothing alike. But she wanted something, and I needed to know what. So instead, I said, "True. We both like history."

She asked again about the funeral register.

"Nothing case related." I lobbed the ball into her court. "Tell me about the documents your father sent to New York."

She scoffed. "That was years ago. I didn't pay attention."

"I bet Martha Wade's diaries were among those records."

"Possibly. I hadn't considered that." Her voice elevated with the lie.

Fingers crossed, I asked, "Your father probably stored them at a New York bank or law firm."

"I doubt it. Father banked in Connecticut."

"He could have shared a vault somewhere else."

"I'd know about a vault in the city." She hesitated. "Unless...hmm. Possibly. The Mather Family Trust could be paying rental fees. I don't see those transactions. They're managed by a New York law firm. I withdrew my trust funds when I married my late husband."

"What law firm handled the trust?" The firm could lead to more living relatives.

"I don't recall. If you mentioned a few, I might recognize it."

"Andrews, Atkins, Yardley, Twist, or McClane." I listed the ones that immediately came to mind from previous inheritance cases.

"None sound familiar. I doubt they'd have kept them for a century." Lillian sounded like she wanted a reason to quit looking.

"As long as the rent's paid."

"Whatever you say. I have no idea."

She was toying with me, but I continued the game. "I'll do some digging and get back to you. The law firm may still exist."

"It was years ago. I doubt I'll remember," she replied, playing the old-age card.

"I'll compile a list of New York banks and law firms operating when your grandfather died. A name might trigger your memory."

"Anything's possible. I'll wait to hear from you." She hung up.

Within an hour, I had four law firms that operated in 1937, but tracing banks turned into a crapshoot. None of the 1937 financial institutions still operated under their original names. They'd been bought, sold, consolidated, and renamed. Tracing would require OCC and Federal Reserve filing history. I'd wait. The information might not be necessary.

Frustrated, I narrowed the law firms to one large international outfit dating back to 1866 and still headquartered in New York. It had been sold multiple times, renamed, and currently provided services under Murbeck, Twist, Hanley, & McClane, commonly called Murbeck. Still, having the documents was a longshot. But that was genealogy, the finding of lost records.

Murbeck advertised services for "clients of means." Austin Bradley worked there.

I called Lillian. My call went to voicemail. "Crap." While plugging my phone into the charger, the desk's tulip glowed. Room lights were off, and the sun wasn't shining in the windows. The office air had gone still. The tulip flickered.

All my doubts vanished, and I knew two things: The

desk had a role in the case, and I had to revisit New York City to open the puzzle box.

* * *

While heading to the kitchen for an M&M's fix, I called Lin Chen at Artistic Woodcraft. "I'd like to meet with you soon about the puzzle."

"Thursdays, my wife and I have lunch at Big Wong's. We could meet there if you like Chinese food."

"Hang on. I'll check with my partner." I covered the phone and leaned into Sam's office. "Are you up for a bodyguard assignment in New York the day after tomorrow? Lin Chen's available for lunch."

Sam turned around. "I'd love to guard your body." He mimed a Marx brother eyebrow wiggle. "Can't dally. An English Pembroke table needs to be valued."

Back on the phone, I told Lin, "We love Chinese food. Thursday's fine." We set a time, then disconnected. Relieved Sam had agreed, I smiled all the way to the kitchen.

M&M's in hand, I wandered from room to room like a fly searching for a landing spot. Thursday, Sam and I would visit New York City and meet with Lin Chen. My head swirled with ideas. Questions. Leads to follow. Standing outside our library, my legs balked. My entombment in Hartford had sullied my sanctuary. I retreated to the living room and into Sam's chair to call Zeke for his reaction to Lillian and the funeral register. There was no answer.

Dr. Kemp's manuscript lay open on the table, reminding me that I hadn't finished it.

In 1920, after a seventy-two-year battle, women won the right to vote. Kemp was an impressionable fifteen-year-old, and the event shaped her life. Not only did she collect campaign buttons, but she also dedicated her life to teaching young women their worth.

I picked up the manuscript and skimmed to where she discussed *Marie Roget*. She wrote, "I believe Poe solved the mystery. Mary died from a fatal accident, and someone dumped her body in the middle of the river." Kemp believed Poe knew more than what was published. She also suggested Ann Lohman and Mary knew each other through their shared societal contacts at Anderson's Cigar Emporium. The same men who flirted with Mary at the cigar shop had attended parties at Lohman's mansion. Kemp went further, saying Mary likely participated in Ann's parties. Her logic fascinated me.

She connected Mary to Lohman's husband, Charles, a printer at the *Herald*. Because Charles frequented the cigar shop with their employees, she concluded Charles knew Anderson. That's something I'd never confirm, but it made sense.

Kemp shared Lohman's position on birth control. Whether with preventative potions or clinical procedures, Kemp believed a woman should be the master of her own body. She cited a statistic that thirty percent of pregnancies in the early-to-mid 1800s in New York City ended with abortion regardless of social or marital status. I checked online, finding support for her statement.

In 1829, Lohman's practice opened when only post-quickening abortions were a felony. She swore she refused to help women if they had felt movement. Then, in 1839, pre-quickening abortions became a misdemeanor, making a big part of Lohman's practice illegal.

Kemp suggested Ann Lohman's association with wealthy, powerful men was strategic. Ann wanted change, and she understood social change was political. She needed support from the men she entertained. Kemp wrote, "Lohman challenged the laws of men, and the men didn't like it." In the end, those same men abandoned her. Alone, in despair, her ultimate act was suicide.

Kemp began the chapter on women's suffrage with a quote from Sarah Moore Grimke. "I know nothing of man's rights or woman's rights; human rights are all that I recognize." She raged over marital rape not being a crime until the 1980s. Her tirade stirred personal feelings. I closed the manuscript. This line of inquiry wouldn't help identify the remains.

Opening my laptop, I reviewed the case data. Maybe I had enough evidence to support my hypothesis that Carver's student had found Mary. First, my client believed it *was* Mary, which was the basis for my thinking. Second, circumstantial evidence indicated Mary was a Rogerene. Thus, she could have been buried in the Rogerene cemetery. Lastly, the physical attributes of the remains matched her build and stature.

Unfortunately, I didn't have a deed to a cemetery plot or a burial record naming her. I also didn't have proof through marriage records that Mary carried both Rogers and Mather markers, like the DNA of the remains indicated.

I needed more.

Chapter Forty-Four

Fortified by the breakfast of sausage, eggs, and toast Sam prepared, plus a good night's rest, I boldly entered our library and called Lillian. Surprisingly, she answered.

"I may have identified your family's law firm. Have you heard of Murbeck?"

"Of course. Everyone's heard of Murbeck. They handle the Rockefeller and J. P. Morgan accounts. My lawyer, Austin Bradley, works there."

Concerns surfaced when she mentioned Bradley's name. Coincidences. Her stay at The Colony House Inn. Him being her lawyer. After a moment, I responded, "Great. Did your father ever mention Murbeck?"

I could hear her breathing. Maybe she was composing her next lie.

"No, I don't believe so. But I did remember Father's lawyer. Werner."

"That's it, then! The original partners included someone named Werner when two law firms merged in the

1930s to become Murbeck. They might have the Wade diaries."

"It's possible. That would be great!" The excitement in her voice confused me. Maybe she knew I couldn't get access without special approval.

"Why don't you call Mr. Bradley since I'm not family? He won't be able to discuss your family's affairs with me."

"I'll call early tomorrow. How grand!" She sounded euphoric.

The hairs on my neck lifted. Her delight could mean that she believed finding the diaries would throw me off her trail, the reason she wanted me off the case.

"I would call today, but I have a lunch date and a shopping trip."

That was the Lillian I knew and distrusted. "I have a few more questions."

"Okay, but I'm leaving in thirty minutes."

The list of questions I'd been holding trembled in my hands. "This won't take long. It's about family relationships. I found several new names at the New York Historical Society."

"Go ahead. If the people are my relatives, I'll recognize them."

"Tell me about Frederick Mather."

"General Frederick Ellsworth Mather," she stated. "Of course, you already knew his rank." She spouted his life history, both significant and insignificant accomplishments, all of which I'd found online weeks ago.

"Are you aware of any correspondence between Frederick and Augustus?" I slipped this question in hoping she'd add to what I already knew about them.

"No."

I fished a little more. "Did Frederick advise John Anderson?"

She hesitated. "John Anderson wasn't family."

"I know, but Frederick might have visited Anderson's cigar shop."

"Of course, Frederick frequented the place. Augustus mentioned a visit in his journal."

Darn! I'd overlooked a significant entry. "I don't recall any mention of a cigar store."

"You missed it. In April 1841, Frederick took Augustus to J.A.'s to buy a humidor."

The entry had preceded the medical student's visit, which I'd almost missed, too. "You're sure it was Anderson's?"

"Positive. No other cigar shop with a J.A. existed in 1841 within New York." Lillian had done her homework. That said, acting nice didn't mean she was nice. First, she didn't do interviews. Then, she did. Claimed she had vital information to share, but instead offered whatever price it took to quit the case. Stomped off, and I got entombed. Now, she'd become Miss Congeniality.

I planned to call Bonnie in Lempster for a copy of Augustus' journal entry to assure myself that Lillian wasn't lying.

"I hope we're almost finished. My friend will arrive soon."

"What about Richard Griswold?"

"He married into the Mather family. Richard inherited his father's import business. Mostly goods from China."

"He married a Mather." I reached down and patted Sophie.

"Actually, he married two sisters. When Louisa Mather

died in childbirth, Richard married her younger sister, Frances."

"Louisa lived in Brooklyn across the East River from Mary, and they likely socialized." A connection would support the evidence in the album.

"I have no idea. But I doubt it. Mary Rogers wasn't a Mather."

"True. But both women grew up in Lyme. If they were childhood friends, I think Louisa would have contacted Mary in Manhattan." So, Lillian truly believed Mary wasn't a Mather.

"No way," she replied. "Louisa's family wouldn't have approved. Mary frequented the Bowery and lived near the slums." Lillian enunciated the Bowery like it was a dirty word. "Also, Phebe Rogers fell out of favor with the Mather family when she remarried."

My client had suggested that Louisa's mother remained friends with Phebe for years. Even after Phebe fell out of favor in Lyme. I waited. Lillian didn't continue, so I tried another approach. "I suspect Louisa Griswold's husband frequented Anderson's Cigar Emporium."

"Of course, he did. If you had researched the cigar store, you'd know that most prominent gentlemen relaxed there."

Her scolding irritated me. Of course, I knew the cigar store clientele, but once again, I wanted to keep Lillian talking. "You're right. One more thing. I've been reading about Ann Lohman."

"Madame Restell. The abortionist." Lillian choked on the last word.

"You've heard of her." I braced myself for the next question. "I think Louisa Griswold or Phebe Rogers may have associated with her."

"Oh, for heaven's sake! Absolutely not! You're talking

about my family." Her tone indicated she'd had enough. Before I could thank her for her time, she disconnected the call.

I'd touched on a topic Lillian refused to discuss. The Griswolds. More specifically, Louisa's connection to Lohman.

Sam walked in while I was still staring blankly at my phone. "You look confused."

"Lillian hung up in the middle of a conversation."

"I'm not surprised."

"She bristled when I asked her about the Griswolds and Anne Lohman."

"A clue. Keep beating the bushes," he encouraged. "See you later. Work's calling."

I climbed the stairs. Sophie drafted me, head-butting my calves with each step. At the top landing, she scooted into the office. I swiped the nursery door with my fingers on the way by.

Once in my office, I called Bonnie at the Lempster library. She emailed me a photo of the journal entry mentioning Augustus' trip to Anderson's cigar store for a humidor. It was precisely as Lillian had said. She hadn't lied, but it still might be a false lead.

I typed the Griswold name into my search program. Nothing new resulted. Then, I called Zeke again. Still no answer. I didn't want to read too much into it, but I felt uneasy.

Chapter Forty-Five

After lunch, I returned to my office, where the quartz tulip flickered as I drew in my chair. I touched it, feeling its warmth. Sophie settled in at my feet.

A cursory investigation of the Griswolds pointed to New York public records. I grabbed the stack of index cards for persons of interest. Before I delved more deeply into each card, I'd weed out people who didn't support my hypothesis.

The first card belonged to Daniel Payne, Mary's fiancé. Ten weeks after she died, police had found Payne's body on a bench in the Elysian Fields, a drug overdose. A note stuffed in his pocket spoke of regrets, but no murder confession. Unaware of Mary's change of heart about marrying him, he'd died before her reinterment. He wouldn't have known where Mary ended up. I laid his cards aside.

Arthur Crommelin's cards came next. At one point, both Payne and Crommelin boarded at the Rogers house at the same time. In his official statement, he explained that he'd moved out after Mary's attentions turned to the other boarder, Daniel Payne. Phebe didn't approve of Payne. Present at the boarding house when Mary announced her engagement to Daniel, he claimed that Phebe flew into a rage.

Crommelin had walked onto the scene by the river where Mary's body lay. He identified her for the police from the hair pattern on her arms. Mary had visited his new residence on John Street the week before she disappeared, leaving notes requesting a meeting. The day before Mary disappeared, she placed a rose in his keyhole. He told police he wasn't open to reconciliation.

Crommelin, not the police, delivered the news of Mary's death to Phebe. Intimately involved in the Rogers tragedy, I suspected he knew of her final disposition. I kept his cards.

Although a potential source of the Mather DNA, Bea Mather's cards held chiefly hearsay. If Bea was Mary's mother, proving a conjugal relationship between Bea and a Rogers man would be impossible. Circumstantial evidence in Bea's cause of death, so called bad blood, pointed to Rogerene beliefs. Also, opportunity by cohabitation was a strong indicator, but family gossip wouldn't support a kinship argument if contested. Besides, Bea died long before Mary, so I set her cards aside.

Now, there were Phebe's cards. Six years into her marriage to Daniel Rogers, she supposedly had Mary. In her first marriage to Ezra Mather, she'd delivered Ezra Jr. in their first year together and bore the next four children two years apart. Statistics indicated she'd have conceived earlier in her second marriage, and the two-year birth pattern would repeat itself. Unless Phebe lost babies before Mary, or aborted earlier pregnancies, her birth pattern indicated she was not likely Mary's mother.

Confident she knew where Mary was buried, I kept her cards.

"Augustus, you're next." I reached for his pile.

He had established his initial medical practice in Boston after graduating from Harvard, but he logged frequent travel to New York in those early years, implying something or someone required regular attention.

The day before Mary disappeared, his journal entry indicated he'd *sent a medical student to the city in his stead.* He could have arranged Mary's abortion. Still, I doubted he directly participated, or that the diary entry was coincidental. He hadn't mentioned Mary's reinterment in his journals, but he may have recorded it elsewhere. I kept his cards in the active pile.

"Okay, Frederick. I bet you know where Mary was reinterred." Frederick's pile was small. Proximity was the most compelling argument for his involvement. Based on delivery records, he also held a connection with a desk through an invoice from Van Boskerck, but I wasn't sure if the desk was an important link yet. His profession involved him in family issues. I kept his cards, too.

The last card belonged to John Anderson. A copy of his statement to police indicated they'd questioned him for hours. Curiously, his statement never made the newspapers. In his only printed remarks, Anderson claimed he had nothing to do with *it,* but he never publicly said the Rogers case. Not being a family member, he likely had no input into her reinterment.

Anderson had migrated to New York City as a young man and worked various jobs before he opened his first tobacco store. At his retirement, he and his second wife moved to Paris to escape the gossip about his strange behavior after Mary died. He lived the rest of his life abroad.

In his book, *The Beautiful Cigar Girl*, Stashower had described Anderson as an old man haunted by Mary Rogers' apparition. Apparently, her death left a deep, lasting wound. A wound which may have been inflicted during a romantic relationship. Or a trauma caused by his attendance at her gruesome death. Or the heavy burden of guilt for the way he'd used her. If he'd known Mary's burial location, I doubted he would have recorded it. I set his cards aside.

I'd narrowed my field down to Phebe, Crommelin, and Frederick as the most likely sources for information about Mary's final resting place. Another person I'd left out of my research was Phebe's sister, Mrs. Downing. I made a card for her but decided to pursue it later.

It was late, and I was about to finish up for the day when my index card stating *"orig. stored 1883 - C.S."* slipped out from under a piece of paper. A thought occurred to me. C.S. could be someone's initials, or a company name. Kemp believed Ann Lohman had owned the desk. I'd start there.

I searched using the date of 1883 from the invoice and Ann Lohman's name.

"Paydirt!" I exclaimed, leaning closer to the laptop screen. A blogger had posted an article about Ann's grandchildren, Caroline Shannon and her brother, Charles, and how they had turned the mansion on Fifth Avenue into a hotel. This had to be C.S. Either Charles or Caroline had stored the furniture at Cordts when they built the Langdon Hotel in 1883. "At last!" I'd connected Ann to the desk.

I rushed downstairs to Sam's office, waving a printed page. I handed it to him. "Ta da!"

"You're kidding. Lohman's grandson stored the desk." Sam looked surprised.

"Yup. Either he or his sister, Caroline. I'm getting closer! I'm not sure to what, but the puzzle box is looking more important than ever."

Chapter Forty-Six

Thursday at noon, Sam and I approached the Big Wong restaurant on Mott Street. An older couple waited out front. The man waved, smiling. From his voice, I'd envisioned a younger man.

"I'm Lin Chen. This is my wife, Mei."

"This is Sam, my husband and honorary partner on the case. He's an antique furniture expert, so he's helping me to trace the desk's provenance." We shook hands.

"Lin's excited about your discovery," Mei said. "He's spent his life around puzzle boxes. Our basement is filled with exotic woods in various stages of treatment." She waved her thin arms and spoke with a wispy voice. Sam towered over her tiny frame.

We entered the restaurant, and Lin selected a table along the wall. The clean but dated interior was packed. Aromas of ginger root, garlic, and onion, along with a steady stream of takeout traffic, suggested excellent food.

After ordering, Sam shared information about the desk. "We're almost certain the secretary came from Van Bosker-ck's woodshop, but the puzzle box was added later. Rae suspects finding who built the puzzle box might lead us to the original owner."

"Do you have the puzzle box with you?" Lin asked.

I removed it from my bag, handing it to him.

He examined it. "The design resembles my ancestor Chen's workmanship. He sold hundreds of boxes. Crime in the 1800s was horrific, so people hid their valuables."

With their sincerity and attentiveness, the Chens quickly gained my trust. I explained the mystery, the unidentified remains in New London, and my inexplicable attraction to the desk. "My client suspects the body is Mary Rogers, a woman who died in 1841. The cause of her death has never been determined."

Lin frowned. "And I take it you believe the desk is related to your case."

"Yes. Someone close to Mary must have owned the secretary." I didn't mention names. The Chens didn't need that information.

"What makes you think that?" Lin scowled.

"A photograph in a cousin's album. Plus," I sucked in a breath, "I'm drawn to the desk. I know it sounds silly, but I want to know its secrets."

Mei and Lin looked at each other, then Mei whispered in his ear. He nodded. "*Jingshen*. Spirits."

I continued. "I'm sensing a spiritual element to it, maybe through the quartz tulip."

Sam spoke up. "I don't believe in spirits."

Lin turned to him. "Believing or not believing won't change that they exist."

Mei nodded emphatically in agreement.

"Who else might have built the puzzle?" Sam asked.

"There is another possibility," Lin explained. "My

mother's relative, Ah Ken. He owned a cigar shop and also imported Chinese goods. He could have imported it."

"Maybe, but it was built into the desk." I doubted it was imported.

Sam spoke up. "I'm convinced someone at Van Boskerck's made the desk. Rae has pictures of a sister piece he branded."

"It's possible." Lin shifted his weight.

"Your grandfather, Ken Lin Sou, might know something." Mei turned to me. "He is old, but his memory is sharp. Most of the men in Lin's family worked in woodshops."

"I'd like to talk to him, if possible. Or call him."

Lin hesitated. "I'm not sure. You can try. You'll find him at Nom Wah's Tea Parlor every Friday morning by nine o'clock. He sits at a rear table with a group of his cronies."

"That's tomorrow. I could visit him there." Anticipation raised my confidence. There was a real chance that I could know the puzzle's secret by tomorrow.

"He won't bite, but there's no guarantee he'll cooperate. He has his code of honor. He lives by ancient rules." Lin paused. "Most of his friends also worked in the furniture industry. One of them might remember something."

The waitress's warning came to mind. "Will I need a translator?"

Lin chuckled. "No. He's a third-generation American and bilingual."

Mei frowned. "Why did you ask?"

"We dined at Nom Wah's last time we were in town. The waitress said club members didn't speak English."

Both Lin's and Mei's eyes narrowed. Finally, Lin spoke. "The waitress misled you."

"When I asked about puzzle boxes, she squirmed and

glanced at a tall Chinese man I'd seen before. When the tall man left the room, the waitress told me about Ting's."

Lin shook his head. "I have no idea why they weren't more helpful."

"I suspected her reluctance was connected to—" Sam nudged me, indicating he didn't want me to mention the man wearing the baseball cap. "—something else."

We spent the rest of our lunch in casual conversation. The Chens, both fourth-generation Americans, had children of their own as well as a new grandson who, based on their description, sounded like a child prodigy.

Sam called for an Uber while I told Lin I planned to visit Nom Wah's tomorrow when the social club met. Our ride pulled up outside, and we said our goodbyes, thanking the couple profusely for their help.

I turned to Sam. "You obviously didn't want me to mention the guy in the baseball cap."

"You don't know these people. You're too trusting. Like you said, the tall Chinese man and the guy in the ballcap are working together. The Chens could be a part of the threat, too."

"They seemed so sincere and innocent."

"And that's why I'm the bodyguard and you're the researcher. Teamwork!"

Maybe Sam was right. Perhaps, I was too trusting. But the Chens? I had a hard time seeing it.

Chapter Forty-Seven

riday morning when we entered Nom Wah's, the tall Chinese man stood at the front desk. The same waitress from our previous visit waited beside him, wearing a grim look. She started toward me, but I waved her off, strolling toward the group of Chinese men at a rear table.

"Good morning. I'm RaeJean Hunter, and this is my husband, Sam. We're looking for Ken Lin Sou." Black eyes stared back at me long enough to make me wonder if they truly spoke English.

Finally, a shriveled man responded. "I'm Lin Sou. Lin called last night to tell me you might visit. Please, sit." He gestured to an empty chair next to him. "Tell me about your mysterious puzzle box and desk."

My stomach fluttered as I slipped in beside the man. I glanced at the other faces as I showed Lin's grandfather the photos of the box and desk, hesitant to reveal the box until he agreed to open it. Nobody looked like they harbored anything beyond curious interest in the items. Sam pulled up a chair next to mine.

Lin Sou studied the pictures, then passed the phone to his left. "*Himitsu-Bako.*"

"Puzzle box." I translated for Sam. He winked at me.

Each man nodded, repeating the phrase I'd heard at Ting's.

The farther the phone traveled, the more chatter arose. The room bubbled over with singsong phrases. I had no idea what they were saying, but I recognized it as Mandarin from what little I'd acquired through a Chinese roommate in college.

When the noise subsided, I asked, "Do any of you know who built the desk or attached the puzzle box?"

Lin Sou gestured toward the men around the table. "Many of our family members have worked in woodshops and could have built the desk. But only one could have built that puzzle box. My great-great-grandfather. He worked at Van Boskerck's."

I smiled at the sea of unblinking, dark eyes. Nobody challenged his declaration. I'd officially confirmed someone at Van Boskerck's had built the desk and that Lin Chen's ancestor probably made the puzzle box. Excited and eager for help, I blurted, "We need help opening it."

The room went silent. Heads turned toward Lin Sou.

"I cannot help you. We never share family secrets with outsiders." The old man closed his eyes, crossing his arms on his chest.

Under the table, Sam grabbed my hand and gave it a squeeze.

I took a deep breath. "Never?"

He opened his eyes, staring into mine. "Rarely. You must have a compelling reason, or have something worthwhile to trade."

Lin Chen hadn't warned me that Lin Sou would want

to haggle. My excitement faded into the grim realization that I needed to outwit the old man and find a way to get him to cooperate.

"It's important that I learn what the box contains. It could solve a very, very old mystery."

Lin Sou shook his head. "Curiosity is not a compelling reason."

"It could help to identify a body. That's a good reason." I unzipped my jacket to release the heat building with each refusal. Sam squeezed my hand again.

Lin Sou shook his head once more. When he grinned, the expression exposed gaps in his teeth. "The body knows who it is. We don't need to know."

This wasn't going well. I'd run out of arguments. I hated to barter, but I'd have to give it a try. "What could we provide in trade?"

"We'll talk." At that, Lin Sou turned toward the others. They chattered until he slapped the table and said a few crisp words in Mandarin. Everyone nodded except one fellow, who instead chirped a retort. All eyes turned on him. He lowered his head.

Lin Sou addressed me. "You find missing relatives."

"That's one of the things I do." He wanted me to look for someone?

The old man placed his hands on the table. "Find my twin sister."

"And then you'll help open the puzzle box?" I knew his response could seal the deal.

"And then we'll talk again about opening the puzzle box."

Crap! Murmurs around the table filled the silence as I deliberated. I'd learned from my Chinese friends that they valued honesty, commitment, and maintaining face. If he said he'd reopen the discussion if I found his sister, then he would. I figured my client's generous fee would cover additional research costs, but I'd need a beginning point and a name, or a last known residence. "Okay. But I'll need—"

As if reading my mind, Lin Sou interrupted me. "Her name is Ming-Yue. She went to Philadelphia in 1917." He drew an envelope from his pocket. "This is all I know of her."

The envelope contained a black and white photo of two young children, hands clasped. The boy was slightly taller than the girl. I smiled, thinking that the old man had planned this from the beginning.

"That's you and Ming-Yue." I smiled.

He nodded, trying to hide his pleased look.

As I studied the photo, a tinge of sadness nipped at me. I thought about my own father, how I wanted to see him again someday. Or at least know what happened to him.

In the photo, Ming-Yue tipped her head and wore a crooked grin. The envelope also contained what looked like a handwritten contract. I held it up. "What's this?"

Lin Sou took the paper. "It's a contract for indenture to a man in Philadelphia. Ming-Yue was eight years old when she left New York."

"It's a place to start. More than I get sometimes." But I wasn't sure it was enough. He was my first Chinese client, unfamiliar territory for me. That said, I was excited to learn about their ancestral records. Very few were available for Chinese immigrants due to the 1882 Chinese Exclusion Act. Until it was lifted in 1943, ship manifests contained the only records with names. Otherwise, they were referred to as a Chinese man or a Chinese woman in most publications during that timeframe. Those manifests were only recently digitized and available online.

The old man smiled. "You will find her."

"I'll do my best." I had one more question. Hopefully, I wouldn't have to find another relative for an answer. "Any ideas about who might have originally purchased the desk?"

Blank faces answered my question. Lin Sou shook his head.

"Any idea how to find out?"

Nobody volunteered.

When Sam and I stood, all the men rose. Lin Sou agreed to meet with us again at the tearoom once I had information about his sister. I arranged to call Lin Chen first.

"Seeing the sunrise each day is a gift," the old man said. "I don't want to pass through this phase of my journey before I find my sister."

The men took their seats.

I thought of Caitlin. "I understand."

Sam bought the men a pot of tea before we left Nom Wah's.

Finding the old man's twin and opening the box could identify the human remains. I could also have just dug myself a deeper hole and attracted more danger. At the restaurant's front door, I toyed with letting Sam break open the box himself. My palms began to sweat.

"All clear. No Yankee baseball caps," Sam said.

We left the tea parlor and returned to The Retreat.

Back in our room and deep in thought, I walked to the window and stared out at the brownstones lining the street. One block south on Madison Avenue, high-rise apartments stood above the neighborhood. A movement across the street caught my eye. A baseball cap concealed the face of a man as he lit a cigarette. He leaned against a gnarly tree and watched the entrance to The Retreat. My heart pumped wildly. "Sam, he's outside, across the street under the trees."

I stepped aside, letting him peer out. "I don't see anyone."

I peeked around his shoulder. The man was gone. "He was there. Really."

"I believe you." Sam looked again. "I still don't see anyone."

"He probably saw my shadow and ducked out of sight."

"Maybe, but I think I'll wander out and take a quick look." Sam slipped his bare feet into his sneakers. "I'll be right back."

"Be careful. Stay on the steps. This isn't a coincidence. Someone's following us. I'm calling Grace." I shivered as the door closed.

She picked up on the second ring. "Hey, what's up?"

"Sam and I are at the House of the Redeemer in Manhattan. A man's watching us."

"Describe him."

"All I saw was a silhouette of a man wearing a baseball cap."

"I've got an agent in the area. I'll send him over." Grace added, "Be careful, but keep pushing on this case. My field agents have reported movement in our investigation."

"Okay. Thanks. Let me know what you discover." I was too anxious about Sam to ask what she meant by movement. I didn't relax until he returned.

"I didn't see anyone. What did Grace say?"

"She said to be careful but keep pushing. She's sending an agent over."

"Great." Sam looked out the window and rechecked the street. "I don't see anyone. He probably left."

I spent the rest of the day searching the Internet for

clues about Ming-Yue. We would leave for home in the morning with whatever I found online. Once there, I'd visit the Philadelphia records department. Philadelphia had its own Chinatown in Center City around Race Street, where the Chinese entrepreneur, Lee Fong, had opened a commercial laundry in 1870. According to an online article, Fong imported help from other Asian communities. A census record from the era might provide what I needed.

Chapter Forty-Eight

Once home, I resumed my search for Ming-Yue by calling Lin Chen.

"Hello, Ms. Hunter. I've been expecting your call. I talked with Grandfather. Sorry, I didn't think to warn you. He's a shrewd businessman."

I laughed. "Yes, he is! I called because I could use more background. Why, at ten, would Ming-Yue be indentured to serve in a Philadelphia laundry?"

Lin Chen sighed. "The old ways die hard in our culture. My great-grandfather worked seven days a week to support eight children. My great-grandmother was expecting another baby when he sold Ming-Yue."

"Sold. Like a slave."

"Back then, if families had too many mouths to feed, they sold the girls. The boys earned wages, helped to support the family. Women and girls earned much less for the same jobs."

"The contract said she'd been indentured to a businessman in Philadelphia."

"Yes. The contract complied with the laws at the time."

It angered me to think parents would have ever sold their children. "If girls meant so little to the family, why is Lin Sou determined to find Ming-Yue?"

Lin Chen cleared his throat. "You misunderstand the situation. It was her honor to go. She saved the family. And now, she visits her brother in his dreams. They shared their mother's womb. He wants to recognize her on the next phase of his journey."

"He said he hoped I'd find her soon. He's ill and running out of time, isn't he?"

Lin Chen laughed. "No, he's not sick. He's old and feels mortal. And at his age, he's most definitely running out of time."

"If someone else ever tried to locate her, they might have useful information."

"I'm not aware of anyone else. Until now, Lin Sou has remained philosophical about their separation. It surprised me when he revealed what he'd negotiated with you."

"I assume he's the only one capable of opening the puzzle box."

"Without a doubt. He is your only hope if you want the box to survive."

I didn't just *want* the box to survive. Something was telling me it had to. "Thanks for your time. I'd better get to work."

After an hour combing through websites, I discovered a Ming-Yue listed in the 1930 census living with a Fong family on Race Street in Philadelphia. The head of the household, Lee Fong, owned the laundry at the same address. In the next census of 1940, Ming-Yue didn't appear at that address. In fact, she didn't appear in Philadelphia at all. At twenty-one, she would likely have married, so I wasn't surprised. She would have lived else-where with her husband.

Lee Fong expanded his business into numerous urban areas across the country when Ming-Yue worked for him. I began a systematic search of each location from the east coast westward. In a group photo at Lee Fong's laundry facility in Prescott, Arizona, I noticed an Asian girl who posed with her head tilted. She wore the same crooked grin from the photo Lin Sou had provided.

I had a lead.

I returned to the 1940 census in Prescott and found Ming-Yue Wong, her husband, and their two small chil-dren. It could be the same Ming-Yue. I recorded her husband and children's names. The most recent census might show Ming-Yue still living in Prescott. Like Lin Sou, she'd be close to a hundred. But no record existed for her at the same address. Public records came up empty. No obit-uary or death certificate.

Next, I looked for a family member who could verify that Ming-Yue was still living. I started with her son, Kim. I found a phone number listed under that name and called it. A woman answered. I told her I was looking for Ming-Yue, formerly from Philadelphia. After a slight hesitation, she confirmed that Ming-Yue lived with a granddaughter in Sedona.

"I've been hired by her twin brother to locate her. They have been separated for years and he's trying to find her, if possible." The line went silent. "Are you still there?"

"Yes. Grandmother can't be that person. She's never mentioned a twin brother."

I wasn't surprised. "She has one, and he lives in New York City." We exchanged information. I explained that I didn't know her relatives, but I'd been hired to find Ming-Yue. She said she needed to speak with her family.

I called Lin Chen and updated him.

"You're an outsider," he reminded me. "I'll wait for the final word before I tell Grandfather."

Stalled until I heard back from Ming-Yue's granddaughter, I called Grace. "Update me about Claire's blackmailers."

"Nothing new. What's up?"

"The person we saw outside The Retreat was not around this morning when we left. I didn't see much of him, but he was definitely wearing a baseball cap."

Grace hesitated for a moment. "It could have been one of my agents."

"What do you mean?"

"After your call last night, I checked with my team. You're attracting a lot of attention from the same folks we've been watching. So, we put a tail on you. A couple of agents switch in and out."

"Have they spotted anyone suspicious?"

"Not directly, but we know the suspects visited New York during the time you spent six days in the old train station. We have someone on the inside." She spoke calmly, then added, "An agent swung by The Retreat last night to check on you."

Her calm voice didn't prevent the chill from racing down my spine. "Am I in immediate danger?"

"Possibly. But we need you to keep poking around. It's our best chance to force movement. To catch them so we can protect Emma and confiscate the photos."

An adrenalin spike rushed through me. "I still don't see the connection between my case and Emma, but I'm in."

"What we've noticed is that two of the same guys

fingered in a human trafficking ring keep showing up wherever you are. We don't believe it's a coincidence."

I didn't, either.

* * *

Ming-Yue's granddaughter called the next afternoon. "Grandmother admits she has a twin brother who was lost to her when she moved to Philadelphia."

It has to be her. "Did your grandmother show interest in seeing him?"

"She is interested, but she doubts he's still alive. Grandmother reached out to him in her dreams, but he never responded."

Jingshen.

"I have a digital photo of Ming-Yue with her twin. I'll send it over by email."

The granddaughter hesitated. "One moment, please." Muffled voices indicated she'd covered the phone. "I'm not comfortable sharing my email. I'm so sorry. I can't help you."

Before I could respond, she disconnected the call.

While convinced I'd found Ming-Yue, I recognized I was an outsider in a tight-knit family. Lin Chen would know how to approach them, so I called him. He answered right away, and I explained the roadblock.

"Give me their phone number. I'll speak in our language to the woman."

I had my fingers crossed as I sent the photo and number. I had to open the puzzle box without destroying it. Hopefully, Lin Sou would be satisfied that I'd found his sister and he'd agree to open it. If the puzzle was built by his ancestor, he would want it preserved, too.

The next evening, Ming-Yue's granddaughter called me. "I'm sorry I was uncooperative. There are so many scams these days. I showed Grandmother the photo Lin sent. She wept when she saw it. She said a friend took the picture on her last day in New York City before she was lost to her family."

"I understand. I'd be suspicious, too, if a stranger called claiming to have found a lost relative." Unless it was about my own father, Patrick O'Leary. Then, I'd believe anything.

After we disconnected, I called Lin Chen. "You did it! It's her. She cried when she saw the photograph of her and her brother as children."

"I'll tell Grandfather, then get right back to you."

I stared out the window while waiting, but it took less than five minutes before my phone vibrated, announcing his callback.

"He'll open the box if you bring it to Nom Wah's," Lin advised. If I arranged it, Sam and I could meet him on Wednesday. I'd check with the House of the Redeemer for an available room. "I'd like to meet Lin Sou at the teahouse on Wednesday morning at nine o'clock."

"I'll call him. I'm sure he'll agree," Lin said.

"How long will it take to solve the puzzle?"

He hesitated. "If it isn't distressed from age, I'd guess thirty minutes max."

Even though Sam thought I was too trusting, I wanted Lin to join us. "Will you be there?"

"Absolutely! I wouldn't miss it. See you then."

After we disconnected, I made my way over to my desk. The quartz tulip flickered, and when I reached out and touched it, it felt warm.

Chapter Forty-Nine

I reserved a room at the House of the Redeemer. On Tuesday, Sam and I caught the train to New York and spent the night in the city. Wednesday morning commuter traffic was heavy as usual. Still, we got to the subway station early and made it into Chinatown without a problem.

When we reached Nom Wah's Tea Parlor, we encountered a crowd. Several dozen customers spilled out the door, forming a line along the sidewalk. Sam and I joined them.

"What's going on?" I asked a man in front of us.

"Somebody's bringing in a puzzle box to open." He looked at my bag. "Is it you?"

I heard a familiar voice.

"You made it." Lin Chen smiled. As he guided me toward the door, the crowd parted like the proverbial Red Sea for Moses. I caught a fleeting glimpse of an average-sized man wearing a baseball cap. He loitered off to the side. The hairs lifted on my neck. He could be on Grace's team, or he could be a suspect on the FBI's radar.

When we entered, Greg emerged from a cluster of spectators. "Let the show begin."

Sam rushed forward and grabbed Greg's arm. "Hey, glad you could make it."

I patted Greg's shoulder. "Can't keep you guys apart."

"Let's see what you have, Ms. Hunter," Lin said. Mandarin intonations filled the room, like musicians in an orchestra pit tuning before a performance, mostly smooth with a few sour notes. The crowd quieted as I opened my bag and removed the small drawer. Lin Sou beamed as he reached for it, then gestured for me to sit next to him.

The audience oohed and aahed as the old man held the piece up to the light. He lowered the box to his nose, then sniffed. "It hints of fish, a formula our grandfathers always used."

"That's why Sophie liked it so much," Sam whispered.

Lin Sou set it on the table and brushed a finger against the green pull. "Beautiful. *Jingshen.* This knob is Apophyllite, a powerful truth stone used to connect the physical and spiritual worlds."

All heads nodded in agreement.

He touched it again and raised his eyebrows. "This stone is active with spirits."

Goosebumps formed on my arms.

The old man tipped the drawer, examining the pinhole we'd found. His eyes sparkled as he retrieved a small wire from his pocket and slid it into the tiny opening. With a gentle tap, the puzzle released from the drawer and dropped into his hand.

Faces in the crowd pressed in for a closer view. Tears brimmed the old man's eyes as he cradled the box.

"Look, Sam." John Van Boskerck's brand, now visible,

ran along the drawer's back joint. He, or someone in his shop, had built my desk. If I'd had any doubts before, they'd vanished.

Lin Sou cleared his throat. "This is a fine piece."

"Ah, yes," a spectator agreed. Others nodded. Some clicked their tongues.

"I'd like you to open it."

He smiled, and then as if in slow motion, rotated the object to what I suspected was the bottom. Lin Chen retrieved a small magnifying glass and handed it to the old man. He smiled again.

I whispered in Sam's ear. "There's something about the bottom." Sam nodded.

Lin Sou tapped the bottom corners, then slid a finger both directions across an edge. "This box requires many moves. I've only seen one other like it."

The crowd murmured. I drew in a breath. The old man pressed a corner. A wood sliver moved. From where I sat, it looked like maybe an eighth of an inch. He'd exposed a cherry-colored layer beneath the outside browns. Another murmur rolled through the crowd. I perched on the edge of my chair, fascinated. Sam dabbed beads of sweat from his forehead with a paper napkin, and Greg's pink cheeks suggested he was also warm. However, his pinched face puzzled me. Odd.

A sound from the front of the restaurant distracted me. The same waitress who'd sent me to Ting's had propped open the door with a chair. The tall Chinese man watched from behind the counter.

The old man worked across the box's surface. He moved each sliver a fraction of an inch, allowing the next piece to move. When he completed the moves on the top, he repeated the movements on the remaining three sides.

"Twenty-seven moves so far." Greg's whisper carried through the silent room. My glance caused him to blush. He'd been counting.

The old man turned the box once more and pushed. The wood slat held firm. He pulled a small bottle from his pocket and opened it. When he dipped a cotton swab into the liquid, the scent of oranges drifted my way. The wood drank the oil as he wiped each fragile joint. "This must sit while we have tea."

The tearoom bustled as the patrons and curiosity seekers bought tea and mooncakes. A lucky few, like us, had a table. Most of the patrons stood with their teacups and cakes in hand while they speculated about the box's contents.

My mind raced through the possibilities. It had to be something small. A key pressed into wax so it wouldn't rattle, maybe. Perhaps, it was the key Lillian had mentioned. It could be fabric like an embroidered handkerchief, or a piece of fine jewelry wrapped to fit tightly. Then, I thought of the flickering quartz tulip.

Jingshen. Hopefully, a demonic genie wearing Mary's tattered dress wouldn't rise from the box. "Get a grip," I whispered to myself, then sipped my tea.

After thirty minutes, Lin Sou tested the box. The only sound in Nom Wah's came from outside. All eyes watched the old man shake his head and apply more oil.

We drank more tea.

I checked the restroom. It was available. "Don't open the box until I return."

On my way back, I recognized the man from the cemetery sitting by the door. Our eyes never met as I weaved through the crowd, but he glanced toward me as I took my seat.

My hands trembled as I touched Sam's arm. "Don't look. My stalker's sitting at a front table, near the door."

Sam's eyes widened and his lips formed a thin line.

I covered his hand. "Don't do anything yet."

Sam stretched to look at the man. "You think he's the same guy?"

"Yes. I've seen him too many times to be a coincidence. I'll text Grace," I whispered.

He mouthed the words, *Good plan*, silently.

I snapped his picture and sent it with a blunt text to Grace. *This guy is following me.*

Lin Sou held up the box. "It's time." He made the final moves, eyes glistening as he tilted the box and tapped each side once more. A small case containing a scroll slid onto the table. The old man reached for it.

"Wait. Let me do it." I drew a small cosmetic bag from my purse. "Tools of my trade."

Lin Sou nodded.

I unwrapped a stylus, tweezers, and nitrile gloves, then cleaned a spot on the table. The blue silk thread around the scroll matched the ties on Louisa's album. Using tweezers and the stylus, I removed the thread and unrolled the note. The ink had faded and bled together to render the cursive message unreadable. Only the uppercase letters in the signature remained distinguishable.

"F—M—G," Greg said aloud. "Another mystery."

"Blue silk thread, like on Louisa's album." I had a suspicion, but it was too early to tell. "It's illegible."

"I can decipher it with my CR program," Greg offered. "It has a cursive library. We might know by tomorrow."

"Start with Spencer cursive. That's what Louisa would have used." I'd encountered unreadable documents before and found the slant helped to determine the method. Handwritten pages provided a large portion of evidence in nineteenth century cases.

Lin Sou spoke to the waitress. She disappeared, then returned with a glass container. He slid the scroll inside. "Now, it will be safe to travel."

Soft applause signaled the end of the show. Everyone stood, and the crowd left, except for Lin and his grandfather. "Ms. Hunter, we would like to learn the message," Lin said. Lin Sou stood beside him, nodding.

I hesitated. "I'll call you. I will need my client's approval."

"We understand."

Disappointment drained me. I'd have to wait another day to see if the note held a lead.

Sam patted his stomach. "I'm hungry."

"Not me. I'm heading home. Got a customer to visit in the morning. There's still time to catch the one o'clock to Philly." Greg headed for the door. We followed, leaving Nom Wah's together, then headed in opposite directions. Sam and I caught a train toward Central Park. Greg caught one to Penn Station.

Once back at The Retreat, Sam went to the library to make a few calls. He returned a half hour later wearing a worried look.

"You look like you received bad news."

"Tomorrow, Val's meeting the woman buying the chairs. She's from Connecticut."

"Lillian!" I could hardly breathe.

"It could be her. We need to do something." Sam paced.

"I'll call Grace." I grabbed my phone and dialed. "Hey, it's me. Did you get the picture?"

"I did. We're still checking," Grace replied. "Did you open the box?"

"Yes. It contained a blurred note. Our friend is trying to decipher it. But that's not why I'm calling." I took in a breath. "Something else has happened. Sam's been offered a crazy amount of money for a pair of antique chairs, and coincidentally, the buyer's from Connecticut."

"Doesn't sound like a coincidence to me. I'll see what I can find out, run a background check on Lillian," Grace said. "We'll see who she's been in communication with."

"Thank you." We disconnected. She'd pull Lillian's phone records as a first step; I was sure of it.

We ate early and went to bed by nine so we could catch the first train in the morning.

* * *

Wide awake at two, I wandered downstairs to the chapel. Upon entering, my thoughts turned to Esther, and how she'd kept her secret until she needed to reveal it.

I suspected that FMG was Louisa's sister, Frances Mather Griswold.

Van Boskerck's delivery ledger had shown two identical desks delivered two years apart. The first desk went to Lohman's clinic on Greenwich Street in 1839. The picture in Louisa's album *had* to be her standing next to that delivery. She'd been at the clinic at the time. I may have been wrong to assume the first delivery had been for Ann Lohman. It could have been for Louisa.

Late in 1841, after both Louisa and Mary had died, Frederick received an identical ladies secretary delivered to his office. It could have been the matching desk I saw at the Colony Inn in Keene.

I'd seen Mary and Frances together in Louisa's album. Both sisters had married Richard Griswold and would have been familiar with the practice of hiding things inside puzzle boxes. Maybe Frances Griswold, like Esther, had concealed the note from the world until just the right moment.

Chapter Fifty

By one o'clock, we'd arrived home and eaten lunch. I'd checked with Grace. Nothing new. And no word from Greg about the message on the note.

To keep busy, I sorted through two days of mail. The copies of the *Mather LifeWays* financial statements had arrived in an envelope that was thicker than I'd expected. The librarian had sent me fifteen years of history and included a note saying that a friend who works for the Foundation had suggested she send multiple years for analysis.

Each statement had a line item of steep charges by Empire Auditors, reminding me of the auditing charges I'd seen in the Foundation's annual report at the Hartford library. It's what I'd been trying to check when someone had drugged me.

* * *

At two, I'd lost my patience. "Sam, call Greg."

"Relax. He said he'd be here. It's probably taking longer than expected.".

"I'm going to walk Sophie. I'll be right back. I just need to get out of the house and get some fresh air."

Sophie led the way down the sidewalk that bordered property after property of well-kept historic homes, all built in the late 1800s. Some peeked over brick walls covered with ivy. Some stood tall at the end of a manicured lawn. Black wrought iron fences provided security for others. A mix of brick and wood clapboard siding made them unique and interesting. Being in a historic district preserved the feeling of living in another time, a feeling Sam and I loved. Any modern looks were kept to backyards or interior rooms.

I spotted Greg turning into our driveway as I rounded the block. He waved a paper at me, causing me to sprint toward the house with Sophie barking every step of the way.

"I've got it." He grinned, handing me the note. I read it while I headed inside, placing it on the counter.

Frederick Mather, an advisor and friend, preserved Mary Rogers' truth. She died young, but her life was hers to live as she chose. We loved her dearly. Her story is safely stored in a Manhattan vault for her descendants to find.

Respectfully, Frances Mather Griswold

"Frederick knew how Mary died, and he'd hidden that truth."

Sam studied the copy. "I'm not sure that's what Frances means."

"It could be something else." I shared my theory of a

coverup by the family, then added, "The truth could refer to her bloodline."

We speculated on various theories, like her having a different lifestyle from her cousins and the quandary of her squeaky-clean published version versus her behavior that appeared to be hidden. Yet, we kept coming back to the same question. Why did they love her so much?

"Maybe she helped care for Louisa when she was at Ann Lohman's," Greg offered.

I shook my head. I didn't believe that was enough. "When she said preserved, I think she meant that Frederick stored a legal document somewhere else."

"What about the boxes Lillian's father took to a New York lawyer?" Sam had rejoined us.

"She never called back. I need to call her."

Greg frowned. "I'm surprised you'd trust anything about that woman. She sounds crazy and possibly dangerous."

"I don't, but I'm maintaining a rapport in case she reveals something useful."

Greg shook his head.

I snapped a photo of the message. "Lin Sou wants to see this," I explained. "I should ask my client for permission, since it mentions Mary."

Sam shrugged. "You own the desk where Frances hid the note. There's no obvious reason to withhold the message from Lin or his grandfather."

"True. And it's incidental to the case." I didn't want to waste time getting permission for something that might not matter, but I felt a lingering uneasiness that it was no coincidence. I sent the photo to Lin and requested a meeting on the following Wednesday.

He responded with a thumbs-up and a text. *If I read it to the social club, a member may recall something.*

* * *

The next day, Sam walked into the kitchen just as I collapsed my head onto the table.

"Banging your head won't help. Val sent this." He showed me a picture of a woman with two antique Regency chairs.

"It's not Lillian, but her face looks familiar. I'm not sure why."

"Definitely not Betty White. Beautiful chairs, though." He brushed my hair away from my face. "Stop with the headbanging."

"The solution is drifting around in my subconscious, but it's still out of focus."

"Let's review your progress. Maybe there's something you've overlooked." Sam flipped around a chair, straddled it like a horse, then sat with his chin on the chairback. "First, you identified Frances Griswold as the person who wrote the message in the puzzle box. The note confirmed a friendship between Frederick, Frances, and Mary. And Louisa's album confirmed other relationships, like the photos of Augustus, Mary, and John Anderson."

We rehashed the connections I'd made. I knew I was close to a solution, and Lin believed his grandfather held a few more clues that might help. And the note implied close relationships. We sat in silence for a few minutes, both of us analyzing the facts.

Sam shifted on his chair. "We're missing something."

"Nothing serious. Just sufficient data to confirm the remains could be Mary Rogers." Sometimes, sarcasm grounded me when I suffered from monkey-mind, but not today.

Sam tapped my head. "You've been stuck before on cases. What did you do, then?"

"I didn't quit. I dug around and poked the bushes."

"Keep at it. If you think you're close, you probably are. Patience—and care."

"You're right. Sometimes, I get impatient." I looked up in time to see the corners of his mouth twitch. "Alright, most of the time. I'll call Lillian. Her grandmother's diaries might identify the reference to the truth in the message." *Unless it's a truth worth murder.*

Sam scowled. "Sounds like a longshot, and maybe a dangerous one."

"You're right, but I've got to try. Lillian's voice telegraphs answers. She's a terrible liar."

I went to my office and worked with the index cards, developed another relationship diagram, and posed a couple new proof arguments. I used my best evidence indicating that Mary was a Rogerene. These included Lucy George's snippets about Bea Mather from her diaries and Daniel's lineage, placing him in the branch of Rogerene believers.

In between creating the relationship diagrams, I called Lillian. She didn't answer.

My inbox revealed I'd finally heard from Syracuse University. Their response included a similar photo of Louisa Griswold standing next to the desk. Caroline Shannon had scribbled a note on the back, dated 1883, and indicated she'd stored the desk at Cordts because she felt it should be kept in the family, so she'd stored it for Alonzo. He would have been nearly forty by then.

Now, I knew how Alonzo came to own the desk, but before I could react, my phone vibrated. Another text message from Lin Chen. *Lin Sou called a special meeting of the social club to read the note. The Wednesday meeting at Nom Wah's is a go.*

On Saturday, I reviewed my work and reread Frances' message. As my mental debate raged on about her meaning of truth, an idea popped into my head. I might get Lillian to leak something useful. I'd promised my client I wouldn't share anything with her, so I needed his approval. I dialed Carver's number.

"Hello, RaeJean. What's your challenge today?" he laughed.

"I've discovered a note written by Frances Griswold hidden in a secret compartment of my antique desk. I think it's related to the case." I read it to him.

"Hmm, interesting."

I explained my proposed ruse. "I'll read Lillian the note. Bait her, then question her. I can ask things that might reveal what the truth is that's being referenced."

"It might work. It can't hurt to try." He didn't sound convinced. "You're hoping her grandmother's diaries hold the answers."

"Exactly. I'll call you if Lillian spills anything useful." Now, all I had to do was get her to answer my call.

Chapter Fifty-One

ours later, I still hadn't heard from Lillian, so I went to my office and called again. This time, she answered. Surprised to hear her voice, my mind went blank. Then, I jumped into gear and feigned excitement. "I found something phenomenal."

"Really. I don't know what that could possibly be." She emphasized *possibly*.

Fortunately, it wasn't a video call, or she'd have seen me biting my lip. Her doubting tone annoyed me. I relayed the drama of the unreadable scroll and how Greg had deciphered it.

"Well, read it to me." She sounded sincerely interested.

Although I hated to admit it, Lillian and I had one thing in common: curiosity.

I read Frances's note out loud. As I did so, I caught a word I'd overlooked until now. Frances referred to Mary's descendants in the message. Mary had a child. I almost choked, but I controlled myself, waiting for Lillian's reaction.

Her silence gave her away. The message must have fit

with something in her grandmother's diaries. Finally, she said, "Louisa must have hidden the note for Frances."

Her response surprised me. "No, Louisa died long before Mary."

"Then, I don't know who hid it." Lillian seemed confused.

Amazed by her response, I blurted out, "It had to be Frances!"

"Frances may have written the note," Lillian said, "but I doubt she hid it."

Maybe it wasn't a silly idea, after all. Lillian, the family expert, knew Louisa died before Mary. She'd stalled to weave her next lie, or worse. Perhaps, she'd become the hunter.

The old woman cleared her throat, then repeated the dreaded phrase, "I can't break my promise."

Right. Lillian had raised her promise shield. Apparently, this avenue of questioning held answers. I recalled Lillian's recent visit to the Hoboken Historical Museum. She'd searched the same boxes I did, looking for furniture from Nassau Street stored at Cordts. Time to test my theory. "I won't ask you to break a promise, but I have a few more questions."

"Go ahead and ask, but I can't guarantee I'll answer."

Surprise, surprise. "I believe Louisa stayed at Lohman's lying-in clinic on Greenwich Street."

"I won't confirm that."

I drew a smiley face next to the question.

"I think you visited the Hoboken Historical Museum to trace furniture moved from a boarding house on Nassau Street to Cordts."

Lillian tried to turn the allegation around. "No way!"

Another smiley face. Lillian sounded off guard.

Here's where I hoped I'd have her. My client agreed to let me mention the album. "I have Louisa's photo album. Being the family expert, I expect you are aware it existed."

She gasped, then her voice turned harsh. "No, I did not! I'm family. I should have it. Not you."

I smiled. "Actually, a Mather relative lent it to me."

Lillian growled. "Go ahead. Have at it. It won't lead you anywhere."

I pictured the corner of her lip twitching as I teed up what I thought would set the trap. "Louisa had photos of herself in a bedroom. She was pregnant at the time. I wondered if it was at Ann Lohman's clinic, that's all."

"Well, I guess I can answer this. Yes, Grandmother's diary mentioned her stay there."

Surprised she gave me a straight answer, I continued. "Here's what I think. Louisa stayed at Lohman's during her fatal pregnancy in 1839. Richard bought her a small desk that was delivered to the clinic. It's listed in Van Boskerck's ledger. When Louisa died, he left it there."

"Anything's possible." Lillian sighed.

I smiled. "Ann moved it to her mansion. When her granddaughter, Caroline Shannon, handled the estate, she stored the desk at Cordts. If it wasn't furniture, what were you looking for in Hoboken?"

"Certainly not that desk with the puzzle box. And I have no idea who hid the note."

"I think you know it was Frances." I attempted to call her bluff.

"Why would Frances hide a note in a desk at Lohman's clinic?" She scoffed as though the idea was ludicrous.

"I don't know." It puzzled me, too, but I had a theory I needed to test out. "Ann wouldn't furnish a clinic room to include a desk. Like I said earlier,

Richard bought the desk and put it in the hospital room because Louisa was anticipating an extended stay. After Louisa died, removing the desk wasn't a high priority. Richard traveled for his import business and never got to it. Plus, he and Frances married within fourteen months."

Lillian huffed. "He didn't grieve very long."

"Richard and Frances may have found comfort together." I took a breath. "Two months after their marriage, Mary died."

"Why in God's name would Frances hide a note in the desk at Lohman's?" Lillian sounded befuddled.

"I suspect Frances expected to get Louisa's desk since Richard and Louisa had no children. Plus, she was the closest female next of kin and would enjoy the beautiful ladies secretary her sister had used."

"That's an interesting theory," Lillian sniffed.

I pressed her again. "After Louisa died, do you think Richard gave Ann Lohman the desk?"

"I have no idea. Grandmother didn't mention it in her diaries."

"A lot was happening for Richard. He may have just forgotten about it and left it at the clinic." I changed topics. "Mary's behavior, her daily visits to Crommelin two weeks before her death, suggests something urgent. Maybe she was seeking money for an abortion. John Anderson could have refused to help her."

"All I know about Anderson is what I've read."

"Tell me about Mary." I threw out my last pitch.

"Gracious, I told you I don't know Mary's story. Only what I've read."

"Mary knew Ann through Louisa. I think Mary visited Ann's clinic before she died."

"I'll not answer that! Mary was..." She stopped mid sentence.

"Lillian, I'm so close!" I'd lost. Lillian had taken control once more. But still, I pushed on. "Finish your sentence."

"Mary was a nobody. You're wasting your time. She doesn't matter."

My hands shook as I suppressed my anger. "I will solve this case."

"I doubt it. Excuse me. I've got another call coming in." Lillian hung up.

I stared out my window. Lillian hadn't rejected my theory that Frances hid the note, and she'd confirmed that Louisa had stayed at Lohman's. But I hadn't learned the truth, which had been the goal of my call. What I did learn was that she didn't give a hoot about Mary Rogers. She had an entirely different motive for getting me off the case.

* * *

At lunch, I told Sam about my conversation with Lillian, and how while reading the message to her, I'd realized that Frances had referred to Mary's descendants. "Mary had a child."

Sam straightened in his chair. "That's a new path. If she did, then there'd be a record."

"There should be, and I may have already found it. A child named Iantha Rogers was born in New York the year Mary turned fifteen. But it wasn't a birth record. It was baptismal and only listed the baby and the birth date."

"What's next, Sherlock?"

"More digging. When Mary and Phebe moved to New York in 1835, I'm guessing Phebe wouldn't leave Mary in Lyme because she was pregnant. Mary delivered the baby when she first arrived." I sighed. "But I haven't linked Iantha to Mary, except on the baptismal record."

"Well, there's a twist." Sam rubbed his chin. "A baptism puts the kibosh on your theory about Mary being a Rogerene and being buried in the cemetery on the Connecticut College campus."

"Not necessarily. Mary may have been raised in a Rogerene household. Once in New York, perhaps her Presbyterian relatives converted her. Her burial location may have no relevance to her religious beliefs. Convenience and expense may have forced Phebe and her sister, Mrs. Downing, to bury her in New London. That way, at least she'd be with Daniel's family. And I'm nearly convinced he was her father."

I didn't for one minute believe Mary's burial site or religion was why Lillian wanted me off the case. She was protecting a secret, one that someone deemed to be worth murdering to keep.

Chapter Fifty-Two

My phone rang first thing Monday morning. I shuddered, seeing Lillian's name scroll across the display. I despised interacting with the woman, but I needed her. And apparently, she still needed me.

"Austin Bradley called. He took on our family accounts when he joined Murbeck." Her tone was guarded. "The Mather Trust has paid storage costs for years."

I didn't let on that I'd become suspicious. I'd bet anything Austin told her what was contained in the boxes. "Did Bradley know what kind of documents were in the vault?"

Her voice thinned with her answer. "No. He said he'd check. I have an appointment on Wednesday to discuss estate planning. He'll have a contents list by then."

"Great." *History may have been preserved.*

"When I mentioned you, Bradley had a coughing fit. I expect you two are acquainted."

"Yes. I've worked with him on several projects." There

was no point in lying about it. Lillian had called because she'd guessed that Bradley and I knew each other.

"I'll call after I meet Bradley on Wednesday." She disconnected, as usual, with no goodbye.

My conversation with Lillian reminded me of Caitlin's comment, *It's the lawyer, always the lawyer.* So, I circled back to Frederick's cards. His law office had been a block from Mary's boarding house, making it impossible to isolate himself from the events surrounding her death. Phebe must have known him. Frederick and her first husband, Ezra, were cousins.

Men from respectable families in that era dutifully cared for widowed relatives. Being a Mather, Frederick would have helped Phebe before she became Phebe Rogers or moved to New York. As would Louisa's father, James. Lucy George implied Louisa's mother, Caroline Griswold, had remained Phebe's friend, which would explain a lot as well.

Frederick was the lawyer for both the Lohmans and Richard Griswold. And he undoubtedly knew of Louisa's childbirth issues. He may have referred Richard to Lohman. Between the photos and Lillian's confirmation, I'd proven Louisa stayed at Ann's clinic.

It's also possible that Lohman had arranged Mary's abortion, and that Frances hid the note in the desk at the clinic with an altruistic hope that someone from a future generation would find it. Perhaps, Frances had agreed to a family coverup, hoping the day would come when society found the truth acceptable.

If this had happened, I had to prove it. I held out hope for Martha Wade's diaries.

Within an hour, my phone vibrated again. Lillian. "Hello."

"Bradley found diaries, wills, business documents, and bundles of correspondence in the Mather vault," Lillian tittered. "This is so exciting."

"Great." Her nervous tittering made me suspect that her sharing was a ruse to steer me from something Claire or I had already discovered since she'd made it clear that solving the case wasn't important to her.

"He's scheduled a family meeting for Wednesday to coincide with my estate planning. It saves me a trip. Let's meet in town for lunch afterward. I'll share the vault contents list."

"That works." My meeting with Lin Sou was early that morning. I'd have time for both. The vault contents could be my elusive breakthrough.

"Wonderful. Where should we meet?"

"You choose and text me the restaurant name." I'd go, but definitely not alone.

"No need to text. Meet me at Gran Morsi's," she bubbled. "It's my favorite lunch spot in the city."

"Bradley said something that excited you."

"Oh no, not really. He's invited other family members. I'm not convinced they're necessary, but that's just like a lawyer." She tittered again. "By the way, the materials are scheduled for destruction on July sixth, if unclaimed. Some internal housekeeping that's been overlooked for years."

That's only three weeks from now. "Surely, you'll claim them."

"Don't worry. We have plenty of time." She disconnected.

Lillian had found more documents and appeared willing to share them, provided the family agreed. But she never responded about the shredding. I wasn't confident three weeks allowed enough time for the legal work to save them, so I called Austin Bradley.

"Austin, it's RaeJean Hunter. I spoke with Lillian Baxter about the Mather family documents. She said Murbeck's about to shred them."

"That's right." He hesitated. "Lillian signed off on the shredding."

I nearly choked. "No way! Lillian can do that? She has the authority?"

"I'm afraid so. Since the holding time has elapsed, we only require one relative's approval to destroy materials. She said it was about time."

"We need to find a way to delay it."

"Well, other family members can object."

"Crap. This is a real mess." Lillian, the self-proclaimed history buff and family expert, approved the shredding because she didn't care a hoot about family history. Or she didn't want anyone to know what was contained in those documents.

"Maybe I can stall. You need the documents to identify the bones, I assume." Austin sighed.

"I'm not sure. It's possible."

"By the way, the first genealogist didn't retain her records. After I sent her an official request, she allowed us to search her computer and phone. She'd wiped them clean."

"I know. That's what Claire told me. She's scared." I didn't let on that Claire knew how Mary died. It wasn't important right now.

"I'll see what I can do to save the Mather documents. And you watch out for yourself."

I was relieved Austin Bradley saw through Lillian. I grabbed the stack of Mather LifeWays Foundation tax filings on my side table. It was time to analyze the numbers.

After spending the next two hours identifying line items on their income statements, I turned my attention to what seemed like excessive auditing fees. Unfamiliar with the cost components in a senior living facility, I called Austin to see if he could help.

His receptionist answered. "Mr. Bradley is in a meeting."

"I'd like Mr. Bradley to get me a copy of the Empire Auditing's Articles of Incorporation."

When I explained why I wanted them, his receptionist fell silent for a moment. "Mr. Bradley can't handle requests that might be construed as hostile to the Mather family. I'll send your request to another corporate law partner. He'll help."

After disconnecting, I reached for Mary's index cards. Still, nothing jumped out. I wasted the remainder of the afternoon reorganizing. I did that a lot lately.

Sam was in the kitchen when I came downstairs. "Where's Sophie?"

He nodded toward the backyard, where the dog sat by the pool, watching a pair of cardinals. "She's on lifeguard duty."

"I'm heading back to New York on Wednesday to meet Lin Sou. And Lillian wants to meet for lunch. I'd like you to go with me."

"No problem. I'd like to visit Valerie. She has another set of Regency hall chairs for me to appraise, and another buyer lined up."

"That's fine. You don't have to spend every minute with me. You and Valerie can meet while I visit with Lin Sou and his friends at Nom Wah's."

"Sounds reasonable. I'll let her know." He finished his beer and left.

I poured wine, sipped it slowly, and let my body relax. A familiar calm spread through me. It was the same drugged tranquility I felt at my desk. And now, without an antidepressant.

Chapter Fifty-Three

A few hours later, Sam rejoined me in the kitchen. "All set. Valerie's available. And, by the way, it's the same woman from Connecticut."

"Not Lillian."

"Nope. I'll accompany you to Nom Wah's, meet Val at Starbucks on East Broadway, and then sneak into Gran Morsi's around noon."

"Thank you."

Sam shook his head. "Lillian's two faced, a real Janus. She'll likely delay everything in hopes that time runs out and the files are shredded."

He was probably right, but I held tight to a thread of hope. "Maybe she changed her mind. She did loan me the funeral register, and solving the case isn't her concern. She acts afraid that I might stumble upon something unrelated to the Rogers mystery. A secret she doesn't want revealed."

"That's odd." Sam's eyes narrowed. "Don't forget, Lillian's the enemy."

"I won't. I don't trust her, but she's my only hope to access the Mather documents."

Sam sighed. "She's definitely hiding something."

"I agree. But I'm not sure what yet. So, I'll wrangle it from her. Make her spill her guts." I playfully bared my teeth and growled for emphasis. Meanwhile, my stomach did flip-flops.

Sam laughed, lifted me, and danced around the room. "Who let my dog out? Who, who?" Sophie joined the frenzy, barking and nipping at my dangling feet.

"Put me down. Right now!" He had me laughing so hard, I almost wet my pants.

* * *

Back at my desk the following morning, I worked on the link between Louisa and Mary. By noon, I'd posited an airtight argument connecting the two. There were enough photos of Mary in Louisa's album to confirm their friendship. I wasn't sure where that friendship would take me, but I'd closed the loop on one lead. As a reward, I needed a sandwich and some M&M's. "Come on, Sophie. Time for lunch."

I followed the dog as she waddled downstairs. With each step, my concern about Lillian's deceit intensified. My face muscles tightened. When I arrived in the kitchen, Sam had started lunch without me.

As soon as he saw me, he mumbled through a mouthful, "What's wrong?"

"Lillian's behavior is all wrong. If she approved the shredding, why tell me about it at all?"

"Maybe she thinks it will distract you. Or she's confident she has the upper hand." He chomped down on his sandwich.

"So, she's setting a trap for me. So far, I've been easy prey. Why stop now?"

Sam lifted his arms in self-defense. "You said it, not me."

I playfully grabbed his arms. "You've never complained about me being easy before."

"Nor will I ever again."

"I'm holding you to that." I smiled up at him.

During lunch, I thought about Lillian's trap. It fueled my mounting fears that someone wanted me out of the way. It had to be her. Nothing I'd learned about Mary warranted death threats. Mary seemed the beautiful daughter of a widow who'd lost sight of her maternal role.

After Ezra died, Phebe made choices that led her and Bea down a treacherous path. She married a younger man, lost her family's respect, and left the farm.

Daniel Rogers could have seduced both women, and Mary was the product of one of those seductions. Phebe could have married Daniel to cover up their lifestyle, or to provide security for her and her daughter after he got one of them pregnant. And I believed it was likely Bea who bore the child.

By the time Mary went to New York, Mary's Rogerene upbringing meant she'd seen it all. Once there, she had the chance for a new identity. Mary may have been seduced by an older man, John Anderson. Or been the seducer. She could even have been an Icarus who died young, punished for her moxie.

Or maybe she was none of those. Perhaps, in truth, she was a dangerous woman, part of New York City's thriving commercial sex industry in the 1800s. It was likely this last possibility, the Jezebel persona, that bothered the family. If so, why did her cousins claim to love her?

And Lillian. She was a treacherous woman of a different sort. Her treachery could be about preserving her wealth and prestigious lifestyle rather than her family reputation. Sam was right. She was an enemy, but she was an enemy I needed to solve the case.

I'd take Sun Tzu's advice, keep my friends close and my enemies closer.

Thinking about friends reminded me I hadn't told Claire that the O'Reilly letters were missing. I called her and explained the issue.

"I've almost confirmed Mary's burial in New London. What did the letters say, exactly?"

"They provided solid evidence that Mary was a Mather and that she died of an abortion."

"Mary carried Mather DNA. I figured as much. I get a bonus for discovering Mary's cause of death." An outcome that wouldn't matter if I failed to confirm the remains were hers.

Claire laughed. "I should get the bonus. I found the letters."

"If you sign an affidavit, I can use it as secondary evidence."

She hesitated, then said, "I can't risk it. Emma."

"I know. But I don't believe solving the case is the issue."

"I can't imagine what else it could be!"

"It's something we've both uncovered, but not recognized yet."

Claire was quiet for a moment. "Then, it's not the remains."

"It's improbable that it's them. I'm looking into other possibilities. Besides, for now, only your lawyer and I will know about an affidavit. By the time I need it, Grace will have nailed the perpetrators and found the photographs of Emma."

"All right. I'll do it. I can't just sit around worrying. I need to do something besides researching women's ancestry for membership in the DAR."

"Ugh. You've been doing that for four months?"

"Yes. Family trees. Nothing dangerous or exciting." Claire sighed. "Emma's about to go out of her mind being stuck at home. She's binge-watched every suitable series on Netflix, BritBox, and Prime. It wasn't bad while she was in school, but summer break started last Friday. She's climbing the walls."

"I can only imagine."

"What other evidence do you have to support your theory about the remains?" The old Claire had resurfaced. The one with confidence and determination.

"Mostly hearsay. I'm hoping the Wade diaries are at Murbeck and will give me another Mather link. Maybe as to how Mary's remains could have ended up in the Rogerene cemetery."

"I never pursued the Rogerene lead, but I'll get the affidavit prepared right away."

I smiled. It felt good to have Claire back on her game.

Chapter Fifty-Four

Wednesday morning, Sam and I caught the train from Philly to South Station. We hopped a subway to Chinatown, then walked the last few blocks to Nom Wah's. Sam continued to East Broadway to meet Valerie at Starbucks.

I arrived early for my nine o'clock meeting. The door was unlocked, so I entered. Lin and Lin's grandfather occupied their usual table. They stood, bowing when they saw me.

"The place is empty." My voice echoed.

The older man smiled. "They open at ten-thirty, but our club has private seating at nine."

"How'd you get in?"

"I'm friends with the owner," Lin Sou explained, bowing his head. As if to prove his point, the owner appeared from the kitchen with a tray of tea and breakfast items.

"I hope you don't mind, I ordered for you." Lin placed my favorite tea in front of me. He'd remembered the details from our first meeting. "Lin Sou knows who put the note in the puzzle box."

Lin Sou nodded.

Lin leaned forward. "It was my great-great-grandfather."

"When he built the puzzle box?"

"Yes. The story has been passed on to recent generations as a family miracle." Lin Sou nodded as his grandson continued. "After a woman died, our ancestor and his friend accompanied a lawyer from Nassau Street to a Greenwich Street clinic where they met a sad woman wearing a long black dress with a black lace veil covering her face."

"Frances, still in mourning. Why was the story a miracle?"

Finally, Lin Sou spoke. "When I was a child, my grandfather repeated the family legend of my great-great-grandfather. A large sum of money saved our family. Our ancestor earned enough to buy exotic wood and open his own shop."

"Did he talk about the man? Are you sure he was a lawyer?"

Lin jumped in. "No, but the legend implies the man came from a rich family."

The information wasn't conclusive. However, it sounded like Frederick. He and Frances succumbed to family pressures to conceal Mary's truth during their lifetime. But they believed her fate should ultimately be revealed. Perhaps, Frances had the note put in the puzzle box and hoped a future family member would find it—Mary's descendant.

At precisely nine o'clock, an entourage of Chinese men made their ceremonial entrance into the restaurant. The eldest came first, with the youngest last. The youngest was probably in his seventies.

A minute later, the tall Chinese man entered and went straight to the kitchen. My stomach fluttered. Nervous and distracted, I pretended to listen to Lin Sou chatter in Mandarin. He had a lengthy discussion with one man. I caught the name Mather several times while they talked. Finally, they smiled and appeared pleased with their conclusion.

Lin Sou spoke first. "My friend believes it was a lawyer, Frederick Mather from Nassau Street, who took the men to a clinic on Greenwich Street."

"It could have been the importer, Richard Griswold."

The old man shook his head. "No, my friend swears it was a lawyer. His ancestor read the name painted on the office window. Plus, when they left for the clinic on Greenwich Street, the man locked the door with a key from his own pocket. Our ancestors had modified two desk drawers, putting the puzzle in one and a false bottom in the other."

The legend fit what could have happened. "Your friend's sure the office was on Nassau?"

"Positive. His ancestor helped install the new drawers in the desk." Lin Sou pointed across the table to an elderly man, who nodded in greeting as Lin Sou continued speaking. "The lawyer paid our ancestors ten times the box's value in exchange for a vow of silence. In his excitement at receiving so much money, my friend's ancestor inadvertently leaked his secret by purchasing his wife some hair combs. The family still has them." He turned to an elder. "Show them the combs."

The old man produced two exquisite mother-of-pearl combs embellished with silver beads and finely cut stones. The crowd murmured as he handed them to me. I took a photo.

"They're beautiful."

He nodded emphatically. "My mother called them combs of secrets. Her grandmother wore them proudly. So did Mother."

"Did anyone utter the Mather name?"

"Yes. Silently," the old man replied.

Jingshen.

Lin Sou and his friend had identified who built the puzzle box, who hid the note, who modified the two drawers, and who installed them in the desk. For them, the combs proved that Frances and Frederick orchestrated a plan to hide a record of Mary's tragic life and legacy. But I needed more than a family miracle.

Chapter Fifty-Five

By ten o'clock, I'd finished at Nom Wah's and met up with Sam. Lillian's reservations at Gran Morsi's in Tribeca were for noon. Unbeknownst to her, Sam had also booked a table. We still had a few hours to kill, so we strolled through Columbus Park and claimed a bench in the sun.

Sam sat, stretching out his legs. "How'd the meeting with the social club go?"

"From what Lin Sou said, I believe Frederick and Frances hid the note with the help of his and a friend's ancestors."

"Any idea why?"

I shook my head. "Nothing definitive, but it smells of family differences."

Sam checked his watch. "Still an hour and a half before lunch."

"Let's relax and read."

Sam opened a digital book on his phone, and I pulled a copy of *Manhattan Beach* by Jennifer Egan from my bag. I typically loved Egan's writing, but today, I couldn't concentrate and kept rereading the same pages before giving up.

A group of Chinese elders had gathered for a game of mahjong. Each play began with silence, followed by a shrewd move, then loud chatter accompanied by wild gestures. Sam noticed. "It's like watching a foreign movie without captions," he quipped.

We watched the show until my phone rang at eleven-thirty. "Hello, Lillian."

"I'm on my way. You won't believe what else I've learned!" Her voice grew shrill with excitement.

"Tell me." I couldn't imagine a discovery that would wind her up so much.

"I'll tell you at the restaurant." She abruptly disconnected, Lillian style.

I stood and collected my bag. "Let's go. Lillian's on her way, and I want to try to get there first."

"Did she say where she was?" Sam checked his watch. "It's a fifteen-minute walk."

"No. But she's excited about something she's learned. She'll tell me at Gran Morsi's."

"Sounds like she's planning her next move." Sam's eyes had narrowed to slits.

"I don't understand why Lillian would purposefully withhold what excited her."

"Fishermen call it chumming." Sam grinned. "Once she lures you in, she'll throw out the bait and hope to hook you."

"You're probably right. She's not trustworthy." It was hardly a newsflash, but she'd been quasi cooperative lately. I needed to keep my guard up.

He didn't respond, just picked up the pace. "Maybe we'll beat her."

At the restaurant, Sam waited and watched from outside.

The maître d' met me. "I'm meeting a friend. We have a reservation."

"Under what name, please."

"Lillian Baxter."

"Mrs. Baxter is already here." He pointed toward a table, where Lillian sat facing the door. She waved me over.

"You beat me here." She'd made it a point to arrive first.

"I called two blocks from the restaurant." She tucked in her napkin, then smiled smugly.

At first, her smugness annoyed me. When I realized she'd taken the seat with her back to the wall, my imagination went wild. She could have a more elaborate plan than simply lunch and a debriefing. I scanned the restaurant. Nothing looked suspicious. She was probably like me and preferred to face the open room. Still, I knew too well that things might not always be what they seemed with Lillian.

I settled into my chair. "Tell me about the meeting with Austin and the diaries."

She lifted and waggled her favorite Johnny Was bag. "I brought a few of them with me. Austin's shipping the rest."

"Great. There must have been a lot of journals." She could carry a small child in her oversized satchel.

"Bradley didn't say how many there were. They weren't missing, after all. They'd been stored in a separate vault."

"I'd like to read every one. Will I have access to them?" I wasn't sure what to expect, but I anticipated resistance.

"I'll decide what you can read." She sipped her water. "Bradley's shipping everything to Rocky Hill. I'll decide once they arrive."

"I thought—"

Lillian grabbed her menu and cut me off. "Let's order. I'm starving."

Her plan smelled like yesterday's fish. *Don't trust her.* Zeke's warning echoed in my head. Which reminded me, I needed to check in with him.

The waitress took our order. Wine dulled the edges of my frazzled nerves. When the food arrived, Lillian ignored me while she ate.

The waitress had cleared the table and we were sipping the last of our wine when Lillian finally made eye contact and handed me four diaries. "Here. You take these."

"Thank you." As much as I wanted to start reading them right away, I slipped them into my bag and gave her my full attention.

"These diaries may solve the mystery of Mary's death, but I uncovered more at the lawyer's office."

"More what?" She was teasing. Another of Lillian's diversions.

"I'll get to that. Martha Wade kept diaries all her life. Fifty-eight all together."

She *did* know how many diaries Bradley had. I went on the offensive, hoping she'd agree and all would be well. "It could take a while to read that many, but I'm familiar with cursive and should be able to get through them quickly."

She locked eyes with me. "If we split the diaries fifty-fifty, it could take half the time."

"I really need to read them all. Without the full picture, it's difficult to know what's important."

"Don't worry. I know what's important." Her look was pure evil.

I definitely hated her plan, but I needed to see at least some of them. "And I suppose your promise to your mother applies to the Wade diaries, too."

Her mouth twitched. "No. I only promised not to reveal details from my grandmother's. I'll use discretion with Martha's. Reveal only what I feel is relevant."

"What you feel is relevant." *Censorship.* Her bargain wasn't a bargain at all.

"Yes." Lillian tidied the table. "Your client won't share, so neither will I. At least I'm sharing something."

The other shoe had dropped, and it was a size twenty, triple E. "I've already signed a confidentiality contract." I had never published my findings.

"Reassuring, but not good enough. If you want all the information in these journals, you'll have to share what you've already discovered."

I already knew the answer. "I can't do that, but I'll call my client when I get home."

"Call now. Let's settle this quickly."

I looked around the crowded restaurant. "No, this is too public. I'll call the minute I get home. That's my best offer."

Lillian made a face. "Well, if that's the best you can do. But remember, I said there's more..."

I chewed on my lip while I waited.

She lowered her voice. "Bradley has a sealed envelope from Frederick Mather dated in 1895. Frederick restricted access to its contents for a hundred years."

The envelope could contain the truth about Mary. "That's the mystery you referred to? Open it, for Pete's sake. It's been over a hundred years." I caught myself. "I assume Bradley opened it?"

The corner of her mouth twitched again. "No. At some point, someone added a restrictive clause. Three Mather descendants must sanction breaking the seal." She didn't look happy about it. "In the event of a refusal, the required number of consents will increase by one for every objection."

"You mean if one person refuses, we would need to find four consenting Mathers instead of three. And if two people refused, we would need five."

"Yes, you've got it right." Lillian suppressed a smile.

Between the wine and the emotional yo-yo, I'd become numb, but I pushed on. "Has anyone opened it, ever?"

"Once, in 1937, before the hundred years expired. The firm allowed a document to be added without revealing the envelope's contents, and then resealed it. The timing indicates it could have been my father after my grandfather's funeral."

"And Bradley wouldn't open it for you. It's been a hundred and twenty years."

"When I challenged him, he quoted a bunch of legal mumbo jumbo and wouldn't budge. Of course, I'll sign." Her smile could have melted butter. "But I'll still need to recruit two more consenting Mathers."

Dazed from the latest roadblock, I barely heard her. The envelope could contain the document Frances alluded to in her note.

Lillian tapped her chin. "But that could be challenging. We don't all get along."

I wanted to shout, *Tell me something I don't know!* Instead, I asked, "What's next?"

"Find two agreeable Mathers besides me, of course."

Even though Zeke was related, I didn't suggest him. Then, there was Carver's sponsor. I suspected he was a Mather, but if he participated, he'd be forced to disclose his identity.

She added, "Once the contents are read, all three must agree to release the information."

"What are the chances of all three Mathers agreeing?" I needed another glass of wine. Maybe a whole bottle.

"Time will tell." Lillian checked her watch. "What a day. I'm exhausted. I'm staying in town tonight."

We stood, and I walked her to the front of the restaurant.

"I'll be in touch." Lillian marched out the door.

It irked me that she thought she had me.

Sam joined me from his corner table. "If we go now, we can catch an earlier train." He slipped his arm across my back and guided me out the door.

"I'm more than ready."

I was worn out, but I wanted—no, yearned—to know the answer to one question. What other lost treasures were in the vault?

Chapter Fifty-Six

Once on the train, I shared my lunch conversation with Sam. "Lillian has custody of Martha Wade's diaries. She lent me four to read. She also has four, plus Bradley's shipping her fifty more."

Sam whistled. "That's a bunch. Is she planning to send them your way?"

"No idea. Right now, she's basking in the glory of her find. She said we'd work it out when they arrived."

Sam shook his head.

"Bradley found a sealed envelope from Frederick Mather." I explained the restrictions required to break the seal.

"The Mathers family is huge. Finding three people shouldn't be a big deal."

"True. But one decline means the stakes increase. If Lillian refuses, we need to find four people instead of three."

"Did she hint that she would object?"

"No. In fact, she included herself in the three agreeing readers."

"Interesting. I bet she has an angle." Sam shook his head.

Sam's remark got me wondering if I'd missed something. It would be just like her to take charge to prevent my access to specific information that may or may not be related to my case. For now, I'd concentrate my efforts on the four diaries she'd shared. Maybe they would provide answers.

I told Sam about Lillian alluding to more mysteries, and how hearsay in a family miracle story passed down at least three generations of Chinese-Americans was my only proof as to who put the note in the desk. Sam laughed about the miracle, but I wasn't so sure there wasn't some kind of divine intervention at work with the combs.

"Enough about my work," I said. "Anything new with you?"

"Actually, yes. Valerie met the buyer's agent for the second set of chairs."

"Is it the same buyer of the first set?" I tried to show interest even though I didn't care a fig about who bought the chairs.

"No idea, but Valerie suspects a referral from the other buyer. The delivery address is near The House of the Redeemer on East Ninety-Fifth Street." Sam stretched. "The plot keeps thickening."

We took a cab home from Philly station, picked up our car, and collected Sophie from canine camp. By the time we got home and unpacked, it was after six. I changed into sweats and met Sam in the kitchen.

"Want to eat now? Or relax and drink wine?" Sam asked.

"I'm always hungry. But after today, wine first. Lots of wine." He filled my glass, and I took my usual seat on the porch. I savored the oaky flavor of the full-bodied

Chardonnay while Sophie played land-and-fly with the birds. Her bark didn't scare them. Two cardinals taunted her from a lilac bush. After dinner, we retired to the library and read for the evening.

Sam buried his head in a nonfiction book about the Osage Indians, *Killers of the Flower Moon* by David Grann. He'd wanted to read it for a while.

I read Martha's diaries. No earth-shattering news. She described church socials and wedding preparations. The diaries confirmed large family gatherings at funerals. She belabored her aunt's death. Went on about Ezra's marriage to Phebe Wait, the births of Ezra Jr. and Bea. I drummed my fingers on the short stack of journals. Martha had waxed on about babies and her daily chores. Relatives from Massachusetts, Vermont, and New York had gathered in Lyme for a two-week stay at the family home for her aunt's funeral. Phebe came over from the farm and handled the kitchen for the large gathering.

"What's the drumming about?"

"Lillian didn't randomize her selection. I have every other year beginning since Martha Mather, Ezra's sister, married George Wade, twenty-one years before Mary's birth."

"Not much new data, then."

"Nope. Nothing, except her grocery list for her wedding party and one for a funeral."

Sam stood and stretched. "I'm calling it a night."

"Good idea. Four diaries out of fifty-eight doesn't tell the whole story."

I laid in bed, rehashing my lunch conversation with Lillian. Talk of fifty more diaries nagged at me. Unable to fall asleep, I crept into my office and checked the Mather family tree. Martha died at eighty-two. If she started keeping diaries at sixteen, at one per year, there should be sixty-six in total.

There were eight more diaries somewhere.

* * *

My second coffee was half gone when Sam joined me in the kitchen. "You're up early."

"I couldn't sleep. I need to call Lillian."

He checked the time. "It's too early."

"I know it is. But the diary count doesn't add up. There should be more. Plus, it makes sense for me to stay in Rocky Hill rather than ship diaries back and forth. With the two of us reading, it won't take as long."

Sam sat across from me at the table. "Staying near her would speed things up. What's the deal with the diary count?"

I reiterated my calculations from the night before. "Either Lillian hasn't noticed, or she's withholding eight diaries."

He stared over his mug at me. "I would assume the latter."

"I won't know until the diaries are delivered."

"You need to be careful while working with her." Sam sipped his coffee.

"I know. I'm calling Grace for protection." I shook my head. "Lillian wants to split the reading. I don't like her plan. I might miss clues if I don't read them all."

"Then, read them all." Sam spoke as if it were simple.

"You're right. I never cut corners." A formidable challenge lay ahead, convincing Lillian that I would need to see all of them.

* * *

My phone rang while I rinsed my cup. Lillian's name, again.

"RaeJean." It sounded like she was short of breath.

"Are you okay? You sound winded."

"I'm fine. The diaries are here—three boxes—and letters Bradley never mentioned."

"Wow. Exciting!"

"My housekeeper helped me drag them into the kitchen. They're too heavy to lift." The image made me grin. "It's exhilarating."

Once she quieted, I proposed my approach. "My husband and I have been discussing logistics. To save time and shipping costs, I'll stay at the Holiday Inn Express off Interstate 91."

"Gracious, no need! You can stay with me. I have plenty of room."

My arm hairs bristled at the thought. *Bad idea! Really bad idea.* But Lillian's house was big enough to host an entire football team, and the job would end quicker. Plus, Grace's team could place her house under surveillance while I was there. "Are you sure?"

"Absolutely. Get here as soon as possible. These diaries are a huge temptation."

"Hang on." I covered the phone and whispered to Sam, "Lillian offered me a room."

Sam's eyes bulged as he whispered, "Bad idea. Don't do it. Don't trust her."

I whispered back, "I know, but it's only two days. Plus, I'll call Grace."

Sam shook his head. "Bad idea. Very bad."

Determined to solve the case, I uncovered my phone. "I'll head over now and take you to lunch."

"Don't worry about lunch. Alice will prepare it for us." Lillian hung up.

Sam clutched my arm. "Rae, this is a terrible idea. The woman's a liar. She's probably behind all the crap you've been dealing with lately."

I crossed my fingers on both hands held behind my back. He was probably right. "I'll be fine. Grace will help. She'll put Lillian under surveillance."

"Damn, I still don't like it. If anything feels off, anything at all, you come home. Promise me."

I raised up on my tiptoes and kissed him. "I promise."

On my way to pack, I called Grace. "I'm going to Lillian's to read diaries. I'd like you to put her home under surveillance, if possible."

"Already have. They're the grounds crew next door. I'll call them. Do you still drive the red and white Mini Cooper?"

"I do. I should arrive around noon. Thanks, Grace."

Sophie studied my every move while I packed an overnight bag and my laptop. When I left my office, I glanced at the desk. All was quiet on the tulip front. I landed in the foyer, a step ahead of Sophie. Sam lifted her up, rubbing her belly while I juggled my bags out through the doorway.

"Call or text me. Keep me informed." He smiled, but his eyes betrayed his concern.

"I will. Nothing bad will happen."

Chapter Fifty-Seven

On the road by nine, I entered Zachary Estates at twelve-thirty. As I approached Lillian's, a member of the grounds crew working at the neighboring mansion nodded.

"Thanks, Grace."

Lillian opened the back door, waving a diary. Apparently, temptation had won, not that I had expected her to wait. Butterflies filled my stomach as I pulled my bags from the backseat and joined her.

"Your room's upstairs to the right, the last door on the left." She pointed to a set of stairs off the kitchen. "I hope you're hungry. Alice is a great cook. She's prepared my favorite lunch."

"Yes, I'm starving. I'll be right back."

A black-on-white sitting area at the landing connected two wings. Three doors on each side flanked a hallway lined with original oil paintings. I looked out a window at the end of the hall and saw Grace's crew weeding a flower bed at the neighboring mansion.

The door to my room stood open. I entered a luxurious

boudoir decorated in a European style with cherry furniture, a dresser with a beveled mirror, and a king-sized bed with a gray satin comforter embroidered with gold-threaded scrolls. A walk-in closet big enough to hold my office and a private bathroom separated the suites. I couldn't resist a few photos. "Wait until Sam sees this."

I returned to find a delightful meal of grilled Chilean sea bass, a salad of sliced baby tomatoes, grilled pineapple, spinach greens, and pink grapefruit wedges tossed in a tequila dressing, then garnished with rose petals. I wanted to lick the plate, but I held myself back. "My compliments to Alice. That was delicious."

Alice appeared as if on cue.

"We'll take our tea and dessert in the sitting room," Lillian advised her.

"Yes, ma'am." Alice started to leave, then turned. "The baby scones and clotted cream?"

"Of course. What else?"

I gasped as we entered the sitting room. Three open diaries rested on a nineteenth century, Louis XVI-style needlepoint chair. The entire room was filled with antiques. Not at all what I expected in the ultra-modern home. And thanks to Sam, I recognized most of them. Valerie's buyer may not have resembled Betty White, but the urgency, timing, and request for Sam to personally deliver the chairs didn't feel coincidental anymore.

"You have an extraordinary collection."

"Yes, I do. Chairs are my downfall. I've accumulated quite an assortment over the years."

"Nice."

Lillian stood, arms akimbo as she surveyed her work. "I've been sorting."

The sitting room looked ravaged by a tornado. A second

pile of diaries spilled over the seat of a spiral-twist-legged, Elizabethan-style chaise upholstered in Loro Piana linen. A box tied with twine sat untouched. "What was your method?"

"Method?"

"I suggest we review the diaries in chronological order, and then read the letters."

"I suppose that's your rule, or a professional standard," Lillian groused.

"My approach is based on experience. It's easy to miss things if you skip around."

"Like you did in Augustus' journal." She smirked, obviously thrilled to be able to remind me of my oversight.

I didn't react. Instead, I pinched my leg. "Exactly."

"Well, I've already started to read diary entries describing family gatherings that I knew about. Martha would have recorded family news after those events."

"Good idea. What did you find?" I suspected she'd looked for specific information for a reason I'd yet to uncover.

"I was right. Martha loved to spread scandalous rumors."

I lifted a stack of diaries and reordered them by year. "Let's start from the beginning."

Lillian suppressed a yawn.

Adrenaline had me high even though the drive and the lunch should have zonked me. "You go ahead and nap while I sort and take inventory."

"I think I will. I'm bushed." She scanned the mess. "I'll take one of my power naps. See you in a half hour."

As soon as she left the room, I dashed to the window to check on the grounds crew next door. The same guy who nodded earlier saw me and tipped his hat. Definitely Grace's team.

Surprised she left me alone with the documents, I searched for hidden cameras. Nothing. For all I knew, she was calling the mob right then.

It took me ten minutes to count and organize the diaries. As suspected, the missing eight journals created a gap when Mary lived in New York. I had time to call Austin Bradley.

"I'm surprised that Lillian didn't tell you." He hesitated, then said, "I can't release eight of the diaries."

"Why not?"

"It's in the restrictions. By the way, the FBI called. They want a list of Mathers who benefited from the trust. Any idea why?"

"Yes, but I can't say right now." Grace was looking into Lillian's affairs. "I think it's possible you also have the Griswold records."

"I'll check, but you'll need a court order if you want to see them," Austin said.

"I know."

"You know what?" Awake from her power nap, Lillian had reappeared in the doorway.

I turned around and held up a finger. "Right. I've gotta go." I disconnected.

"Who were you talking to?" She glared at me.

"Austin Bradley. He called about a box of deeds, wills, and letters," I lied.

"Why would he call you?" Her eyes narrowed.

She had me. Or did she? I'd heard the closer to the truth, the more convincing the lie. So, I shot a question back. "By any chance did you mention me at your estate planning meeting?"

Lillian hesitated. "I may have. We talked about a lot of things."

"There you have it. Bradley wondered if I'd found errors in the Mather database." Like Bradley cared.

"And you did, I suppose." She scowled.

"Actually, yes. I found a discrepancy in the data on the website. They had Phoebe Wade, not Phebe Wait, as Ezra's wife. Amy Srebnick, a professional historian, found a church marriage record naming Phebe Wait as the correct woman."

Lillian made a face. "I'll have a closer look at what's posted online."

"Bradley suggested the website manager could verify the data using the deeds and wills."

Lillian tapped an unopened box. "I haven't checked to see what's in here."

"I did. It's the deeds and wills he phoned about." I'd dodged a giant coconut.

"That's your forte." Lillian pointed to a chaise stacked full of diaries. "What's that all about?"

"I've sorted Martha's diaries into decades. The first twenty years shouldn't take long if they're like the ones I've already read. But things heated up in the second decade after Ezra Mather died in 1808."

"They certainly did. When Ezra died, his wife stayed at the farm with two of her four living children. She leaned on friends and family for help while the two oldest sons were at sea."

At a previous meeting, she'd denied any knowledge of Mary. *That's a lie.* I handed Lillian ten diaries. "Here's some reading. Are you aware that eight are missing?"

"I had no idea." Her lip twitched.

Keep my enemies closer.

By the end of the afternoon, we'd read the first twenty diaries. I didn't find anything useful to the case. All I learned was that Martha delivered four of her children and was expecting the fifth the year Ezra died. And that the babies, cooking, cleaning, and sewing wore her out.

Lillian announced. "Six-thirty. Time for dinner."

Lunch turned out to be like eating leftovers compared to Alice's dinner. She served duck breasts with a choice of apricot chutney or orange sauce. I tried both. Sides included basmati rice and broccoli with garlic butter and cashews.

We took our dessert in the sitting room. Alice rolled in a food cart containing a ginger layer cake with wine poached pears, cream cheese frosting, and blueberry lemon truffle.

"What's your pleasure?" she asked.

My hollow leg nearly full, I said, "I'll try a small serving of each."

Lillian tittered.

"A little of each, it is." Alice and I had different ideas regarding serving size.

After dessert, I was so overstuffed all I could think about was going to bed. I excused myself, retiring to the guest room. Once in my pajamas, I flopped onto the canopy bed and called Sam. I wanted to tell him he could relax, that the search was nearly over. But I feared Lillian might have an ear to my door.

"You're kidding! Austin has the critical diaries?" Sam exclaimed when I explained what little I knew about the eight missing journals.

I kept my voice low as I brought him up to speed. "Yes, and Lillian lied about knowing they were missing."

"This project is one deception after another."

"I know, but I'm too tired to think tonight. I'll call you tomorrow. Love you."

"Love you, too," Sam said, and hung up.

As I drifted off to sleep, I realized I'd forgotten to tell him about Lillian's antique chair collection. Not likely a coincidence.

As Zeke had said, there were no coincidences with Lillian.

Chapter Fifty-Eight

Alice offered me an omelet for breakfast, but I passed. "Just coffee, thanks."

Lillian strutted into the room dressed to the nines in a classic Armani suit in shades of blue.

When she finished pouring mine, she filled Lillian's mug. "I'll be right back with your breakfast, ma'am." Within minutes, she returned with a granola yogurt swirled with fresh blueberries, the same breakfast Lillian had at the Colony Inn in Keene.

We began the day reading the decade that included Phebe and Daniel's marriage in 1814. Martha described their union as a marriage of convenience. She never mentioned Mary's birth in her 1820 diary.

Bea had died three days before Christmas in 1830. In the Spring of 1831, Martha attended a family funeral in Lyme, likely Bea's. Martha wrote about how the children, Mary, Augustus, Louisa, and Frances, played Graces in the field next to the church. I remembered Jane Austen writing about the game, similar to ring toss.

After reading in silence for an hour, Lillian slammed closed the 1843 diary. "My Lord!"

"Lillian, are you okay? What is it?"

"A disgrace. Nothing about Mary." She sneered and clutched the diary to her chest. "Augustus worked with Ann Lohman."

"I suspected as much. Augustus' travel log listed regular visits to New York."

"True, but I didn't expect it of him! He was a well regarded physician."

"Working for Ann Lohman didn't change that. Frederick was Ann and Charles Lohman's lawyer, and he was certainly well respected."

"She was an abortionist!"

"Ann helped women have children. She considered herself a physician." And I admired her for that.

"With no education!" Lillian snorted. "Doctors in my family graduated from Harvard."

"Ann recognized her clinic needed additional medical expertise. Augustus provided it." I admired that, too.

"I can't imagine why he would stoop so low."

Lillian's snobbery and ignorance of the real issue made my blood boil. I'd had about all I could handle, and it took every ounce of restraint in me to keep from screaming at her. "He wasn't stooping low. He believed in Ann's cause. Women in the 1800s received little or no healthcare. I've suspected Augustus' involvement, and these diaries provide proof. Louisa Griswold also sought treatment from Ann Lohman." The Mather cousins had been far more progressive two centuries ago than Lillian was now.

Lillian huffed and returned to her reading. Around mid morning, she stood and stretched. "I've finished 1834. How about a cup of tea? I need a break."

My eyes burned and I had greedy thoughts about cookies. "I would love one."

"I'm afraid we're on our own, though. Alice is at the market."

In the kitchen, Lillian heated water and I set out cups. My stomach growled when she set out the homemade butter pecan sandies, even though I thought I'd never feel hungry again after last night's dinner. Good thing I hadn't eaten breakfast.

"So, what did you find?" I spoke through a mouth stuffed with cookies.

Lillian stared at the crumbs on my slacks before answering. "Not much. Martha mentioned Bea's death in 1830. She wasn't pleased about the circumstances surrounding the death but attended the funeral out of respect for her brother, Ezra."

"What circumstances?"

"Bea's poor health. The Rogerene belief in sexual freedom. Martha capitalized the S and the F." Lillian scowled.

"I've wondered about Bea's cause of death and her being a Rogerene." Martha's diary all but stated Mary was raised in a Rogerene household. *But that's still not confirmation.*

"Bea likely died of syphilis or gonorrhea." Lillian spit the words out as if to prevent personal exposure. I was surprised she'd used the medical terms at all.

"And Martha mentioned Mary's father, Daniel, died in an explosion. She attended his memorial service despite the family's objections." Lillian looked puzzled.

"Did Martha mention Mary?"

"Yes. She referred to Mary as the beautiful and enchanting bastard child. Martha's daughter and Bea remained best friends until Bea died. After that, the daughter would watch Mary to provide Phebe relief."

Lillian's apparent disinterest confused me. Phebe and Daniel were married when Mary was born. I was sure she'd make the connection of Bea being Mary's mother, but she ignored it. "Funny, Martha never mentioned Mary in 1820."

"There would have been no reason to mention Mary." Lillian remained deadpan. Even after a hundred and eighty years, she was unwilling to speculate. Or she actually knew the truth.

"I found similar entries about an illegitimate baby being born in 1820 in a New Hampshire diary." I didn't identify them as Lucy George's. Lillian knew; she'd read them first. "I thought it might refer to Mary." I waited for her response.

Her gaze narrowed. "Martha attended Louisa and Richard's wedding and raved about the suitable match. All that Griswold family money!"

* * *

By lunch, we'd almost finished. Lillian had requested a lighter meal. She must have filled her hollow leg, too. We quit and slurped a delicious gazpacho soup and nibbled on hot empanadas filled with pork, corn, and carrot slivers that Alice had prepared from scratch. Afterward, I took the couch while Lillian sat stiff-backed in a stuffed chair.

"If we tackle the last pile, we should finish today." I took five and handed Lillian the rest.

By her late seventies, Martha's entries dwindled. Nothing about Mary's reinterment. She did mention Richard Griswold dying in 1849, leaving Frances to raise three children, but that was about it.

Lillian fidgeted while I read my last diary. When I closed the book, she cleared her throat and smoothed her blouse. "I have a confession."

My heart raced. Maybe this was it.

"The lawyer gave me this." She produced a key. "Remember, I said to find the key. Well, this is the other mystery. I discovered the lawyer had it all along."

"I'm guessing that you've withheld more. Wait, don't tell me. Your grandmother mentioned it in her diaries."

Lillian nodded.

I paced the room. "And you've waited until now to tell me about it."

"My promise, of course."

"You could've shown it to me yesterday."

Lillian held it out. I rolled it between two fingers before handing it back to her as she spoke. "I planned to, if Martha had mentioned it in one of her diaries."

I resisted an urge to grab Lillian and shake her. "All because of your promise." Grasping my hands behind my back, I squeeze my wrists to repress my frustration.

"Exactly. My grandmother mentioned it in her diary, so I kept it a secret. Among other things." She wagged her head as she spoke.

"Come on, tell me." I squeezed harder. My neck burned. I was about to become the dangerous one.

"You know I can't say."

Resuming my chair-to-window pacing, I stopped and gazed outside toward the house next door. Thanks to the undercover agents, it looked like a park. I turned and walked back toward the couch. All the while, Lillian sat there, smiling.

I changed my tactic and the subject, deciding to bait her using Anderson. "Sorry. I'm frustrated with all these relationships. At first, I suspected Mary loved Augustus, but I think it was Anderson she loved."

"Maybe the cigar magnate, but I wonder about the tenant."

Her evasive reply, basically dismissing Anderson, surprised me. "Which tenant?"

"Alfred Crommelin, the one Mary almost married. It was odd that he and his friend arrived at the scene in Hoboken to identify Mary's body."

"Not really. He and Phebe remained friends, so when Mary didn't return home, he volunteered to search for her." This wasn't exactly true, but once again I had Lillian talking.

"Maybe. But Crommelin also had a companion."

Where is she going with this? "As far as we know, Crommelin's companion wasn't interested in Mary. He was just accompanying him during his search."

Lillian placed the last diary on the table. "All finished our reading. What next?"

The woman was maddening. "We're done for now. Opening Frederick's envelope is our next challenge. We need two consenting relatives, assuming you agree."

"I'll agree. Let's see, a willing cousin..." She picked up her phone and dialed. I watched, listening to Lillian's conversation.

"Hello, this is Lillian." She frowned. "Yes, I do want something but...no. Let me explain. It won't cost much." Lillian looked at her phone. "She hung up."

I bit my lip. "Looks like this may take you a while. I'll go pack."

Lillian put the phone to her ear. "I'll keep trying."

I remained in the kitchen where I could overhear her.

Based on her side of the conversations, Lillian's relatives had no interest in helping.

"Yes, the meeting is in New York City. But—yes, traffic is heavy. I understand." Another refusal. Between the costs and the traffic in New York, nobody was interested. Lillian sat slumped in her chair when I returned with my bags. "Nobody cares if I read the documents. But they won't consider providing Bradley with a notarized letter."

I played along even though her act didn't fool me. "Keep trying. I'm heading home. Let me know when you find someone." She was probably calling relatives she knew wouldn't help. That is, if she was really calling anyone.

If I left now, I'd be home in time for dinner with Sam.

While I drove, I reveled in my successful confirmation that Bea was a Rogerene. It put me one step closer to identifying Mary's mother. That alone was worth the aggravation of spending time with Lillian Baxter. Not only that, but confirming Louisa had stayed at the Lohman clinic and used the ladies secretary where Frances hid the note brought me closer to identifying its original owner.

But I still couldn't link it to Mary.

Chapter Fifty-Nine

By Monday, Lillian hadn't reported any willing relatives, so I called her from my office. She answered after one ring. "Any progress finding an agreeable Mather?"

"Yes, as a matter of fact. My cousin, Rose Martin, has agreed. And Bradley found someone else." Lillian sniffed. "Ezekiel Rogers. His mother—well, we're related."

"Sounds good." Lillian's hesitancy confirmed she and Zeke weren't close.

"Bradley scheduled a meeting at Murbeck on Tuesday."

After Lillian disconnected the call, I dialed Zeke. This time, he answered. "Hey, I finally got you. I was afraid something had happened."

"Nothing bad." He cleared his throat. "A buddy asked me to join him delivering a boat to Florida. I couldn't refuse a chance to get back on the water."

"Sounds fantastic. And you're home safe."

"I am. Thanks for worrying," he chuckled. "What can I do for you?"

"I understand you've agreed to read Martha Wade's eight remaining diaries."

"I have. I figured I could help you now that we've become friends."

His warmth felt good. "I could use some help. Lillian's either indifferent or obstructive unless it benefits her."

"Cousin Rose won't be much help, either. She's a website manager or something like that. She's the guardian of the Mather genealogy site."

"I've been in touch with her." It was good to have Zeke watching my back.

"Yup. Those two old biddies have nothing else in their lives. If you met Rose, you'd know what I mean. Envision Mr. Ed with gray hair," Zeke laughed.

"The horse?" I laughed aloud.

Zeke composed himself. "Yup, don't fret. I'm on your side."

"Thanks. I'd better let you go. I've got a few more calls to make."

"Keep smiling, young lady."

Zeke's reference to Mr. Ed reminded me of someone, but I couldn't place who. I immediately called Professor Carver and explained the situation. "Lillian and two cousins have agreed to sign the consent form. That may not be enough. We need a backup plan."

"I'll provide a backup. I have a friend who's a Mather." Carver's confidence made me question why he hadn't offered Mather expertise earlier.

I disconnected and called Austin. "It's me. We read the Wade diaries."

He replied without hesitation. "Now you want the missing eight."

"Yes. What can you do?" Maybe Austin knew of a loophole.

"I assume Lillian told you about the restrictions. She was thrilled about that. Said something about protecting her and her family."

"Yes, and I called Carver. He said he'd help. Who restricted the eight diaries?"

"Lillian's father, back in 1937."

I groaned.

"Don't worry. We'll figure something out."

"Easy for you to say. I'm FBI bait and a pawn in whatever game Lillian's playing. I don't want to deal with her any longer than I have to."

* * *

Within the hour, Carver called back. "All set. My contact will schedule a trip to New York in the event of a no-show." He gave me a cell number. No name.

"Fantastic." As I took down the number, I thought about calling it to see who answered.

"I have a second party in the wings." Carver provided a second number, but still no name.

"Thanks." Though surprised, I didn't ask questions. I looked at the two phone numbers. Both had New York City area codes. I decided to respect their privacy. Instead, I called Austin back, realizing I'd forgotten to ask about the shredding.

"It's still on. Plus, I found the Griswold family records, also scheduled for shredding."

"With special restrictions, I assume." I'd come to expect the worst.

"No. We only need one signature to salvage history."

"Does Lillian know the Griswold documents exist?"

"I didn't tell her about them," he replied. "I figured you'd appreciate them more than she would. We'd like to release them to the New York Genealogical Society. Legally, we can only hold them or shred them. We're looking for a relative. It's heartbreaking to lose history due to a technicality, but I'm hamstrung. That's why I mentioned them to you."

"Call your golf buddy. Carver said his friend could save the Mather papers. I'll bet he can help with the other documents, too. The Griswolds and Mathers intermarried."

"I'm on it."

All I could hope was that Carver would find a Griswold relative before it was too late.

Chapter Sixty

On Tuesday, Lillian phoned me after she met with Austin. "I have the eight diaries to read today. Cousin Rose gets them tomorrow. Then, she'll give them to Ezekiel on Thursday."

I groaned. "You're kidding."

"I wouldn't joke. We're meeting again on Friday."

More delays. I wasn't surprised, just disappointed. "What was in the sealed envelope?"

"Nothing important. Lawyers make such a big deal of things." Lillian's voice remained flat.

She was lying. A sealed envelope had to be important. At the moment, though, I was most interested in seeing the journals. "Right. Sometimes they do. Call me when the diaries become available for me to read."

"Don't worry, I will." Lillian tittered again and hung up.

The woman wore me down. She thought she had won. But I wasn't so sure just yet, and I held out enough hope that I didn't think Lillian should be too sure yet, either.

* * *

The days dragged while I waited for the eight diaries. By Thursday, I'd lost hope for the Griswold papers. Carver hadn't reported back, with only days until the shredding. I was in the library on the couch when my phone rang. It was Austin.

"Bad news." He sounded grim.

I had a sinking suspicion before he said anything. "It's Lillian, isn't it?"

"Yes. She wants to give you redacted copies. Plus, she wants you to sign a more restrictive confidentiality agreement with consequences."

My stomach did a flip. "That's ridiculous."

"I agree, but she claims she's protecting the family name. Her usual song and dance."

"I really doubt that. It can't be that bad." I had underestimated her again.

"Actually, it's something major. All I can say is there was a coverup at the highest level."

I tugged at my sweatshirt, gritting my teeth. Screaming wouldn't help. "What are our chances of changing Lillian's mind?"

"Slim. It's doubtful we'll find two more agreeable relatives. Even if her family doesn't like her, it appears Lillian has influence."

I didn't respond. I had nothing to say.

"I've prepared the papers for you to sign tomorrow at my office at four o'clock." Bradley paused for a moment, then added, "Don't give up. She hasn't won yet."

"Right." Once we disconnected, I grabbed a blue satin pillow, covered my mouth, and screamed at the top of my lungs. Sophie jumped to attention. "Crap!" I flung the pillow as hard as I could across the room. Sophie retrieved it, shoving it onto my lap. "Life's a game, Sophie. At least, it is for Lillian."

* * *

"You look tired." Sam stood as I entered the kitchen for dinner.

"I have an appointment with Austin Bradley tomorrow to sign another confidentiality agreement. Lillian consented to me reading the remaining eight diaries under limited conditions. It could be worse. She could have refused altogether."

He headed for the door. "Wine's on the porch. Fill me in out there."

"Absolutely." A drink might relieve the crawling sensation on my scalp and arms.

Sophie flew out the kitchen door ahead of me to chase the birds off the feeders. Her predictable behavior relaxed me. I sank into my favorite chair, watching the standoff. Strategically, the dog positioned herself under the feeder. The fleeing birds chirped loudly as they landed in the treetops nearby. I brought Sam up to date while we watched her spar with a fearless cardinal. When the bird flew away, Sophie rejoined us.

Sam patted her head, then straightened up. "I'm going with you."

"You don't have to. I'll be okay."

"Rae, come on. I haven't fully forgiven myself since your last trip to New York alone."

"I'm sorry." I made a face. "You didn't escort me to Lillian's."

"True, but I knew an FBI team would be camped out next door the whole time."

"It's just a quick trip to a lawyer's office. If you go, we'll have to board Sophie."

He frowned. "I suppose. What about Caitlin or Greg?"

"They're both working. Greg's meeting a client, and Caitlin has an interview with a Granby city council member. Besides, Grace's team will be watching out for me."

Sam pressed. "We're talking about New York, not Rocky Hill. I'd say that's a much bigger challenge."

"Grace is on it. I'll be fine. I'll let you follow me on the Find My Phone app if that would make you feel better." I'd refused to let Sam track me in the past. It felt like Big Brother was watching me even though he'd assured me he wouldn't abuse the feature.

His face relaxed a little. "That works. Just a day trip to Austin's office. Nowhere else. You should be safe."

I nodded, then told Sam about Carver pursuing a lead. He'd discovered that Frances and Richard Griswold had two daughters with grandchildren still living. Sam was surprised I hadn't discovered this.

Maybe I'd jumped back in the game too soon. Sam was right, I should have caught it myself. I'd been careless. I checked the time. "I'll give Carver a call."

The professor answered immediately.

"Were you able to locate the Griswold children?" I asked.

"Yes. Frances's daughter, Louise, had grandchildren —girls."

I groaned, realizing once again that I should have handled the search myself.

Carver grunted. "It's a challenge. Names change in marriage."

"You'll find them in the public records, births, deaths,

marriage licenses—where the birth name is recorded. I'm sorry. I should have done this myself months ago."

"I'll put one of my students on it. Once they locate a relative, I'll ask my sponsor for help. He has influence and tons of contacts."

I hung up, glancing over at Sam. "He sounded confident and said the sponsor has clout."

Sam's eyes narrowed. "Let's hope so."

Chapter Sixty-One

On my way out of the house on Friday, I grabbed an unopened letter I'd received the previous day from a corporate law partner at Murbeck. It felt thick enough to hold the corporate filing documents for the Mather LifeWays Foundation I'd been hoping for, listing their officers and agents. I tucked it into my pocket to read later.

I phoned Zeke from the station while I waited for the train. "I have a bad feeling about this meeting. Bradley's going to shred everything if I don't sign the agreement before five o'clock. It feels like I'm walking into a trap."

He chuckled. "Don't worry. I'll be there. I'm already in New York."

"You're right. Not much can go wrong in a lawyer's office."

I'd barely disconnected from Zeke when my phone rang again. Claire's name displayed on the screen. "Hey. What's up?"

She burst into tears. "Emma's missing."

"Missing? What? How?" My hands began to shake.

"On Tuesday, I said she could stay at a friend's house. When she didn't come home the next day as planned, I called her friend. She didn't know anything about it." Claire began to wail again. "Emma lied to me. I checked her room to see if she'd taken clothes. She left a note saying she went to meet the guy who has the pictures."

My heart began to race. "What guy? Where?"

"I don't know." Her voice cracked. "I got a bank alert on Wednesday I never bothered to read. She's a minor, so I set an alert on her account for withdrawals exceeding a hundred dollars. She exceeded the limit twice to buy clothes, so I didn't worry too much about it. Rae, she'd emptied her bank account. Over two thousand dollars."

"Any idea where she's meeting this fellow?" A million horrible thoughts ran through my head. I couldn't share them with Claire. If I was going to help, I needed to hold myself together.

"No. The note said she borrowed her boyfriend's car and not to worry." Claire paused. "I called Grace and gave her the information about the vehicle already."

"Okay. Let Grace and her team handle it." We disconnected as I boarded the train. I tried Emma's number, hoping she'd answer. My heart skipped a beat when I received a standard message. *We're sorry, the number you have dialed has been disconnected or is no longer in service.* "Crap!"

Frantic, I tried Grace. Thankfully, she answered right away. "I called Emma's phone and it's out of service. What's happening, Grace?"

"We know. We're on it. Things are heating up."

That's one way to look at it. I knew I had to continue my part, but Grace was dangling me out there like bait on a hook. It didn't feel very good. "I'm headed to New York. Are you still covering me?"

"Keep working on the case. Don't worry. Yes, we've got you covered."

"Geez, Grace. What about Emma? I'm having trouble breathing and you're just saying you're on it. Heating up how?" I flopped into a vacant window seat on the train.

"One of my guys recognized her, but we don't have her yet."

"From the photos Claire sent?" I felt ill. "I can't believe you exposed Emma to your whole team."

"Just her face for identification." Grace's voice softened.

Her consideration for Emma stifled my anger a bit, but it didn't alleviate concerns about my own safety. My throat had tightened. I could barely speak, but I needed to know Emma's whereabouts. "Thank you. Where is she now?"

"In a car on I-95, headed north."

"Claire should be told that you've found her. She's frantic." I was fighting panic myself. It was hard to imagine what Emma's mother was going through.

"One of our agents is en route to Claire's right now. You keep pushing until we find where these guys are taking her."

I wasn't as confident about the plan as Grace was. "If you say so."

"I say so. Trust me. We've got this. Gotta go." Grace disconnected.

I leaned my head against the train window. *What have I done?* There was no turning back. I had no choice but to play it out. My stomach roiled, and it wasn't from the motion of the train.

I'd agreed to sign a confidentiality agreement. Emma was missing. Things were spiraling out of control.

And then, there was Lillian's tittering. She'd offered me a bribe to drop the case, then, as if nothing happened, she'd helped to find the diaries, which we read together. No, together was too strong a word. We'd read journals while in the same room. I swallowed the rising bile. Something was up. Keeping my enemies close didn't seem to be working out very well.

I'd barely stilled my trembling hands when my phone rang again. This time, it was Sam.

"Rae...oh God! Sophie's missing. I've looked everywhere. I can't find her!" Sam's voice cracked.

My heart stopped. "What do you mean?"

"I let her out when you left. When I realized she hadn't barked at the door, I went looking for her. She's not in the yard!" His voice had an edge of dread to it.

"I didn't leave the gate open. What about that hole under the fence?" My mind ran through every possible escape route she'd used in the past.

"The dirt in the hole hasn't been disturbed. I drove around the neighborhood. Nothing."

"Call the pound. Someone may have picked her up. Please call me when you find her."

First Emma, now Sophie. My world was collapsing from all angles.

The train ride blurred. Slipping my hand into my pocket, I realized I had the letter from Murbeck, so I opened it and read the list of Empire Auditing's executive officers.

Lillian Baxter, President, and CEO. *Ta da!*

My phone vibrated. Grace had texted. *An undercover agent has ID'd Emma among several girls moved from Rhode Island to NYC. Emma's meeting was a kidnapping.*

I texted back with shaky fingers. *Well, get her out of there!* "Damn it, Grace, she'd better be okay."

Grace didn't respond.

I checked my defenses as we approached the station. Reaching under my shirt, I felt for the bandolier holding the mini recorder and my mace corgi fob. As insurance, I planned to record Bradley explaining my rights. Then, if things went amok, I'd have documentation. I doubted I'd need mace in a lawyer's office, but somehow, I felt safer with it.

I arrived in New York with a two-hour buffer, wondering why I had left so early. I got off the subway at the Thirty-Fourth Street Hudson Yards station. On the street, I noted the location of the high rise in Hudson Yards where the Murbeck offices occupied three stories. Bradley's space was on the twenty-eighth floor.

Bella Abzug Park honoring "Battling Bella," a feminist and civil rights activist, was less than a block east. With two hours to kill, I walked toward the park, then cut south toward West Thirtieth Street. Since I was already in Hudson Yards, I'd check the progress on a building called The Shed. Sam had read an article to me, describing it as a new cultural center. Scheduled to open soon, I wanted to see how they bubble-wrapped a steel-ribbed structure.

As I crossed Eleventh Street, a panel truck edged to the curb. There was no time to process what was happening, or even run. Two men jumped out, sandwiching me between their guns.

"Scream, and you're dead," snarled one of them. He wore a baseball cap.

I was pushed into the van. "What do you want?" I demanded to know, but it was too late for answers. They covered my mouth with a rag, I felt a prick on my arm, and all went dark.

Chapter Sixty-Two

When I regained consciousness, I found myself on a couch in an ultra-modern media room and library. The outside wall held floor-to-ceiling windows and two sets of French doors onto a balcony overlooking Central Park. A familiar pair of matching Regency hall chairs flanked the doors.

Woozy, I rose and staggered toward the second-floor balcony. The House of the Redeemer was visible a few buildings to the east. *East Ninety-Fifth Street.* My watch read three forty-five. I hadn't been unconscious for long. Too dazed to think, I returned to the couch.

I must have fallen back asleep. The next thing I heard was the sound of soft voices. When I opened my eyes and attempted to sit, a cold cloth fell from my forehead. Betty White stood by one of the Regency hall chairs.

"Lillian." My voice cracked.

"Of course. Who did you think it would be, Barbra Streisand?" She turned toward the man. "Wait in the hall and have your gun ready. She might try to escape."

"Okay, lady. But you said nobody dies."

"I lied."

He grumbled something and left the room. Being alone with Lillian was no comfort. Her crazed look scared me. It had to be something I'd done or found. Otherwise, I wouldn't be here.

In another attempt to sit, the strap of my bandolier cut into my chest, reminding me of my mini recorder. Her cronies had missed my bag. Probably because it was small, like me.

"What am I going to do about you?" She stepped toward the window.

While she faced away, I fumbled to power on the digital recorder.

She lingered by the window, then turned to me. "You'll never see the diaries as long as I live. Or these." She waved yellowed documents my way.

"The O'Reilly letters." That was it! When Claire found those letters, she had elevated the stakes because Lillian learned how thorough Claire really was at her job.

"Of course. And…" I knew by the way she stared at me that something hurtful was coming next, so I braced for it. "You're guilty," she snapped. "What you did at fifteen. Now, you want to clear your conscience by exposing our family skeletons."

Her remark rattled me. I knew she meant my abortion, but what I hadn't known was that my secret had spread beyond family. "How did you find out?"

She grinned. "I have my ways."

"When did you uncover my past?" I suspected I knew, but I wanted her to say it for the recorder.

Lillian pulled a memory stick from her purse. "When you visited Lempster."

"You had someone download my files and hired thugs to

steal my laptop, didn't you? Let me guess, that's where you've stored Emma's photographs." Blood pounded in my temples.

Lillian smirked. The only way she'd have known was if she'd read the notes on my laptop. The one lifted from my car at Duck River Cemetery. My mind spun through the scenarios and halted at an obvious conclusion. "Your so-called ways include kidnapping, computer theft, and data piracy."

"You're the pirate, out to pillage our family's good name!" Her face twisted in rage.

"Come on, Lillian. What's this really about?" Fear and dread froze me to the couch.

Her true nature had surfaced. At times, I hoped I could trust her. I tried, but trust had never been in the cards, and for good reason. Lillian wasn't trustworthy. Sure, we'd read the diaries together, but she'd planned to monitor my discoveries. "What do you want from me?"

"Quit this case now!"

I stared at her.

"I'm a direct descendant of Reverend Richard Mather. I'm a respected member of the DAR." She pointed at me. "I have influence, RaeJean. Ask your husband."

Her mention of Sam sent a wave of fear and rising anger coursing through me. "Sam doesn't have anything to do with this."

"Oh yes, he most certainly does. I'm surprised you didn't get suspicious when he had to make an emergency trip to Boston with an antique chair." She laughed, motioning around her. "As you can see, I definitely don't need another one."

I glanced at the matching Regency hall chairs. A rolled-up oriental rug lay on the floor in front of them.

"I forced the first genealogist to quit the case. Now, I'm going to force you." Another burst of laughter followed.

"I trusted you." I had to slow this down. Distract her.

"Quit the baloney. You know nothing about trust. Again, ask your husband."

Her innuendo fell short. Blunted. Foiled. "Sam knows everything. You can't hold my past actions over me." I was grateful I'd finally had the courage to tell Sam about the abortion myself.

"No matter. You'll never solve this case. I've got the only solid evidence you need to prove anything." She waved the papers again.

I couldn't see where this was going. Lillian didn't care about the case. I needed to invent something else, keep her talking so I could think. "Mary trusted someone who failed her."

Lillian paced by the French doors. "Well, it wasn't me. I've kept her secret all these years." She crossed her arms. "I could have told the story, made a fortune. But I didn't."

"No, you didn't. But Mary didn't live a privileged life like yours. She struggled." I talked to distract, to think. I shifted my weight. My mace corgi fob was within reach.

"I deserve my privileges."

"Why? Your bloodline doesn't grant you the right to suppress evidence."

Lillian laughed. "One more chance to quit. Or else."

"Don't do this, Lillian." I fingered the mace dispenser hidden beneath my shirt.

She fiddled with her phone, then moved closer to show me a video. "Look."

I felt like I'd been punched in the gut. My dog lay on the rug of what looked like a hotel room, her belly rising and falling. "You have Sophie!" My voice was shrill, distraught.

Her eyes flashed with excitement. "Promise you'll quit this case, and I'll give her back."

Sick with fear, and accompanied by no brilliant alternative, I was forced to lie and let her think she'd got exactly what she wanted. "I promise, I'm done fighting with you. Please, please, return my dog!"

With a smug look, Lillian retrieved a piece of paper and a pen from the table. "Put it in writing." She called in one of her henchmen from the other room to witness it. "Now, sign it."

I did as she said to slow things down. She read my guarantee, then handed it to the witness before dismissing him again. "Now, call whoever's holding Sophie," I demanded. "Prove you've released my dog. My word is good, you know that. You have my written agreement. Show me that my dog is safe."

"I knew you'd come around to my way of thinking." Lillian made a call, instructing whoever held Sophie captive to take her home.

The lump in my throat distorted my voice. "Sam will call once she's home safe."

"He might, but we have your phone."

I felt my pocket where I'd stuffed it. It was empty.

Lillian called out the door. "I need you back in here. And bring her phone." When her henchman reappeared, she added, "I have an important phone call to make. I'll be right back." Lillian left the room.

She wasn't gone long. Within fifteen minutes, my phone rang. As Lillian handed it to me, she mimed silence. I knew she meant that I couldn't let Sam know my location.

"Hey. Is Sophie back?" I asked him in a calm voice. At least, I thought it sounded calm.

"Everything's fine. She's back. I can't figure out how she escaped, or how she got back in. You sound stressed."

"I'm okay. Like we said, Sophie must have escaped under the fence. I'll fix it when I get home."

Sam was silent as my message sank in. He whispered, "I'll call Grace," then disconnected.

"One more thing, Lillian. I know your game. Mather LifeWays. I studied their financial statements for the last fifteen years. President and CEO of Empire Auditors. Lillian, really."

She growled, strutting toward the French doors.

"You've been stealing funds from the Foundation, haven't you?"

Her face had contorted into something scary enough for a horror movie. I'd definitely hit a nerve. "I'm not a thief! I deserve that money! It's rightfully mine."

My hand closed around the corgi fob. I managed to unclip it from my purse as I pretended to struggle to stand, then fall back onto the couch.

Lillian chuckled. "You're as helpless as a kitten and not much bigger."

To be convincing, I feigned another unsuccessful attempt to stand.

She checked her watch. "Thirty minutes and Bradley will shred everything."

"He'll wait. He knows I'm coming."

"Wrong again, Short Stuff. That's the call I made. He thinks you've abandoned the case."

Confident that Austin wouldn't believe her lies, I played along. "You win, Lillian. But you can't keep me here. Sam will wonder where I am."

"Sam will wonder where I am," she mocked.

"Come on, I can't possibly do anything now." I slouched forward, feigning defeat.

Swaggering to the couch, she leaned over me. "I'll tell you what, you little—"

I raised my arm, squirting Lillian with mace, right in her cerulean blue eyes. It felt good. She screamed, fell to the floor, and dug wildly at her eyes. "Oh, God! It burns! Help me...help!"

My opportunity to escape narrowed with each passing second. Footsteps sounded from the hallway, so I staggered out the French doors onto the balcony.

Lillian screamed behind me. "Get her, before she gets away!" A man mumbled something, which only made Lillian more furious. "What do you think?" she cried. "Kill her!"

As I crept toward the edge of the balcony, I heard a noise—rapping on glass. I searched frantically for the source. Emma's face was pressed against an upstairs window. I gave her a thumbs-up, blew her a kiss, and mimed that I'd go for help. She waved back. I teared up at her bravery.

Muffled sounds from inside drifted through the open doors. Two men had joined Lillian. She continued to wail.

There was no way I could get to Emma without going back inside, but I could drop from the first-floor balcony to the street. I laid on my back and stared up at Emma's face, still visible in the window. I froze. I couldn't leave her.

Then, I evaluated my alternatives, but nothing short of a herculean effort by someone better equipped than I could possibly get by Lillian's men.

I groaned. Rolling over, I slid off the balcony, landing in a crouch on a deserted sidewalk on Ninety-Fifth Street. I ran west toward Fifth Avenue as fast as I could manage, where I hailed a cab and shouted Austin's address at the driver.

"Give me your phone," I shouted. "Please! I've got to call the police." He probably guessed by my disheveled appearance that I wasn't joking. Without hesitation, he lobbed his phone over the seat and pulled into traffic.

Grace answered quickly. "Walker."

"Grace. It's me. Lillian's got Emma. I—"

"I know, we're on it. She was spotted at Lillian's twenty minutes ago. We subpoenaed Lillian's phone records and discovered she's got friends in Rhode Island. Surveillance teams are covering both her properties, but we didn't have time to plant listening devices. The team leader followed you on foot to Fifth. Once you caught the cab, the rest of the team busted in and took everyone into custody. Emma's fine. Rattled, but fine."

"Thank God." I couldn't stop shaking.

"I'm sorry we put you in danger. My surveillance team watched Lillian's penthouse apartment for hours. All they recorded was a rug delivery."

The rug beside the chair. I knew it looked out of place. "I was in that rug, I'm sure of it. A five-by-eight Kenneth Mink. Nothing but the best for Lillian." I glanced down at the phone. I could feel the color drain from my face.

"What's the matter?" Grace asked when I grew quiet.

"My meeting at Austin's office. I'll be late."

"Meet you there."

We disconnected the call.

Chapter Sixty-Three

When the cab drew up to the Murbeck building, I leaned over the seat, returned the driver's phone, and begged, "Please don't leave until I get inside."

He nodded. "Got your back."

I rushed into the building. The wall clock by the elevator read four fifty-seven. Three minutes, and they would shred the documents.

Luckily, an elevator waited with the door open. I punched Bradley's floor number. After what felt like an eternity, I arrived at the twenty-eighth level.

Four fifty-eight.

I bolted the length of the hall toward Bradley's office. If I didn't sign by five, then chop, chop. Goodbye documents. History was lost forever.

When I burst through the office door, Zeke stood there, grinning. "Tiny and tough! I assured Bradley you'd be here. Too bad you missed it. You're too late. They're gone."

My heart sank. "No!" I cried out. "I've failed."

"Failed what?"

"To save the diaries. They've shredded them." My eyes stung.

Zeke smiled. "Not that. Relax, the diaries are fine. I meant the meeting. You missed six Mather relatives attending and having a Lillian-bashing party. I told you she's not a popular family member."

I collapsed onto the nearest leather couch, tucked in beside a water dispenser. A Kuhn print, one of his clowns, hung above a shelf of napkins and glasses. Sunlight spread across the plush burgundy rug between the couch and the cooler. Magazines were fanned across the glass-topped mahogany coffee table. My face felt numb.

"You're saying that the release is signed, and I can have the diaries. No confidentiality agreement." I wasn't sure I'd heard Zeke correctly.

"That's right." Austin emerged from his office with the diaries and a tattered box in hand. "They're all yours."

"What took you so long?" Zeke asked. "We thought you'd be here on time."

"I had to deliver a rug to Lillian." I gave him a faint smile.

Puzzled looks crossed both men's faces.

"And I called the police from the cab on the way here. The FBI are at Lillian's now." Halfway through my story, the police arrived. Close behind, Grace entered with Emma in tow.

"Aunt Rae!" Emma leaped onto the couch and pressed herself against me.

"Hey, Em," was all I could say. I pinched my thigh so I wouldn't cry.

A tall Chinese agent wearing a ballcap sauntered in behind them.

"Meet my team leader." Grace introduced the man.

I stared at him, breathing a sigh of relief. "You kept me guessing. I had no idea you were on Grace's team."

"I'm good at my job." His brow furrowed. "How'd they get you into Lillian's unseen?"

"Inside the rug," I laughed.

Emma sniffed my shirt, giggling. "You smell like a wool blanket."

The agent fought a smile. "You didn't make a lump."

Zeke wrapped his arm around Emma and me. "Now, don't go teasing this little spitfire. Size doesn't matter. She's the real deal."

"Thanks." I leaned against him, explaining to them all how Lillian had admitted to embezzlement. Then, I remembered something. "I almost forgot." I pulled the recorder from my bandolier, still hidden beneath my shirt, and turned it off. I held it out to Grace. "If you download the most recent file, you'll have Lillian's confession and my retelling of the story."

Claire stepped into the room as Grace reached for the recorder. Emma flew into her arms. They both started crying, having been separated for almost four days. Pretty soon, the whole room was in tears.

"This calls for a celebration. Lemon water for everyone!" Zeke headed toward the cooler.

"Not yet. I have one more issue. Lillian has photos of Emma that we need to find."

Grace scribbled in a notebook. "I'll call the Rocky Hill Police and have them confiscate Lillian's computer. They can check for duplicate files on other devices. The person who took them may still have copies."

I shuddered at the thought. "Have the police check for my old laptop, too. Lillian implied photos of Emma might be on it."

One of the NYPD officers in command spoke up. "We'll do that, but it's unlikely they'd post them now."

"My team can follow their electronic trail," Grace added. "We've also ID'd the two men working with Lillian. Once we finish with her phone records, we may have more suspects."

"The perpetrators have nothing to gain unless the mother's rich," an officer explained.

"We're definitely not rich," Claire replied wryly.

"Mom, can we go home now?" Emma looked around the room. "Thank you, guys."

Grace spoke first. "Take her home. We'll call if we have more questions. You have a courageous young woman there."

Claire waved as she escorted Emma out the door.

I turned to Grace. "What crimes do you think Lillian committed?"

She didn't hesitate. "If Emma's photographs traveled through Lillian's phone or on the Internet, that's a federal offense, and kidnapping is a capital crime."

I laid my head back, resting my eyes.

"You look exhausted. Go home. We can fill in the gaps later. We've got this." Grace wielded my recorder like a sword, interrupted by a beep from her phone. She scanned the text message, then announced, "New York's finest. They're at the precinct, and they've booked Lillian Baxter for kidnapping."

I smiled at Zeke as we headed for the door, my arms full of the stack of diaries and the tattered box.

He leaned toward me, whispering, "Let's go see if we can finish the puzzle you were hired to solve. With Lillian out of the way, the pieces should come together more easily."

I looked up at him. "Speaking of Lillian, what did she have on you? What's the deal about your mother?"

He winked. "Are you trustworthy?"

I linked my arm with his. "Of course."

"Mary wasn't the only bastard born to a Mather. Now, go solve this case."

Chapter Sixty-Four

When I arrived back in Wyncote late in the evening, the library lights were on. Sophie lay stretched out beside Sam's chair. I kneeled and cuddled her while she licked my face.

"She's fine," Sam promised. "They must have fed her well. She refused chicken."

I patted her round, pink tummy. "Little Miss Piggy."

I had briefed Sam by phone from New York, excluding a few details I'd share later.

"Thank God, you made it home safely." He hugged me tight, nibbling at my ear as we sat holding hands by the fireplace. "Tell me more about your latest abduction."

"The typical nightmare. Lillian told her hired thugs to kill me." I swallowed. "And she was holding Emma in an upstairs bedroom. If she was willing to kill me, she probably would have had them kill her, too."

Sam squeezed my hand. "But you're both alive, and you're okay."

"We are. In the meantime, the Feds have lined up a human trafficking sting."

"I don't see the relationship with your case."

"Coincidentally, Lillian hired syndicate guys involved in trafficking to grab Emma early on Tuesday and stash her in a motel room in Rhode Island with other young girls smuggled in from Havana. Early this morning, they moved all the girls to New York."

"Geez, that's awful. How's Emma doing?"

"She's doing fine. She's a tough kid." I touched my side where she'd pressed against me.

"Let's hope so. What about the other girls?"

"Grace turned them over to Victim Services, where they'll get the assistance and care that they need."

"That's good. And Lillian?"

"She confessed to stealing money from the Mather Life-Ways account." Still, I had a nagging feeling that her blathering about the family name and diaries was a foil. There had to be more than embezzlement.

"You'll never go wrong following the money. So, what's next?"

"Lillian's been charged with stalking and kidnapping, but fraud and blackmail—they're a different ballgame. The Foundation hired a forensic analyst to quantify their losses."

"Could be big bucks." Sam took another sip of his wine.

"Absolutely. She offered me a quarter of a million to quit the case, but I'm guessing millions were stolen. Both of her mansions are filled with antiques."

Sam shook his head. "Is the case over?"

"Not yet, but close." I still had to prove the remains belonged to Mary Rogers.

"I've heard that before." Sam sighed.

"I mean it. I have the O'Reilly papers and Claire's affidavit. The eight Wade diaries should contain what I need. Otherwise, the family wouldn't have restricted them. If they don't have what I'm looking for, my client says he'll get all the Mather papers."

My phone rang as Sam leaned in to kiss me. His eyes promised everything I wanted. Caitlin's name displayed on the screen, but I didn't pick it up. I texted her, *I'm busy right now. I'll call you back tomorrow.*

Chapter Sixty-Five

The next afternoon, I returned Caitlin's call and shared my latest New York adventure. "I have the missing Wade diaries and more."

"Geez, Rae. You've set some kind of record for being kidnapped." Caitlin forced a weak laugh. "What an ordeal."

"No kidding. Thanks to the FBI, Emma's safe." Reading the diaries had become secondary to Emma's safety. I realized that whatever I discovered in them about Mary's death might almost feel anticlimactic in the wake of everything else. Plus, Mary might not have been the woman I'd envisioned. I didn't know what to think anymore.

"What did you learn from the Wade diaries?"

I exhaled. "I haven't read them yet."

"Why not?" Caitlin asked. "What's the matter, Cub?"

"I'm not sure." The diaries remained in my tote, sitting on a box of letters Bradley had withheld from Lillian. My behavior made no sense, even to me.

Caitlin cleared her throat. "If you hold the presses, I'll join you tomorrow. We can read them together. Greg and I have tickets for a Phillies game tomorrow night. I can come early."

Sometimes, Caitlin knew me better than I knew myself. She'd correctly guessed that I was afraid of what I'd find. Her moral support would make tasks easier. "Great idea, but now I feel silly."

Caitlin laughed. "What's a big sister for?"

"Thanks for looking out for me. Sounds terrific."

After we disconnected, my unease returned. I retrieved the diaries from my bag. Why was I worried? Frances had loved Mary for a reason. I wanted to believe Mary was a good person, maybe a little ahead of her time. Tenants at Nassau Street had described her as hard working. She tolerated, or perhaps even loved, John Anderson, a man who'd used her beauty for profit. She bravely made a difficult decision that ended her life.

I picked one diary up, started to open it, then set it down again. I wasn't ready. "Not yet."

* * *

Sunday afternoon, Caitlin and I sat together in my library. The eight Wade diaries and the battered box from Frederick's office sat between us. The box hadn't been opened for decades. Cutting the rotted twine, I lifted the lid. "It's business letters and deeds from Bradley."

Sophie slept at our feet.

"Where do we begin?"

"Let's go through the loose items first. It shouldn't take long. Sort them by type—deeds, wills, business letters, and personal correspondence. We'll be less likely to miss something important." I sounded like a broken record.

Caitlin went to work on a stack. "And then by date."

I nodded, shuffling through my pile. An envelope with familiar handwriting caught my attention. "This handwriting looks identical to an entry in the funeral register Lillian sent me."

"Yes, but everyone's handwriting looked similar back then."

"True. But it's the same scripture, *Whoever welcomes this little child.*"

Caitlin stared at me.

"It's from the Bible. Luke 9:48. Williams New Testament. Published in 1937, the year of the funeral."

"And you know that, how?"

"I looked it up. I've seen it before."

She rolled her eyes. "Open the envelope, for Pete's sake."

I removed a folded document and note, choosing to unfold the document first. "It's a birth certificate for a baby named Lillian Jones. Her mother is listed as Suzanne Jones, father unknown." I reached for the note and began to read.

The Mathers, Lillian's parents, never officially adopted Lillian, but gave her their name and raised her as their own.
   ---Sarah Mather Seggerman

"No way!" Caitlin grinned.

I grabbed my laptop and signed onto the Mather website to check Lillian's birthdate. Rose had added her picture to her profile. "I'll be darned. Rose Martin's the same person who bought the chairs in Connecticut and was in the photograph that Valerie sent."

"So?" Caitlin peered over my shoulder.

"Rose is a Mather. She could be Lillian's accomplice."

"Wow, what a long face and big front teeth." Caitlin made a beaver face.

"When I asked him about her, Zeke told me to think of Mr. Ed." We both laughed. I scrolled to Lillian's page. "The baby's birthdate matches Lillian's."

"So, Lillian isn't a Mather."

"Not by birth, and the Mathers never adopted her." I retrieved my photo of the funeral register entry. "The handwriting matches. It's the same Sarah. I've told you before, past secrets have a way of seeping up from the soil. The past doesn't go away, but it can hide."

"This means Lillian isn't a legit Daughter of the American Revolution." Caitlin's sly look made me laugh.

"I'll have to research their by-laws, but it appears so unless she has a patriot on her birth mother or birth father's side."

"Wow."

"Let's see what else we find." I picked up Martha's 1835 diary, the earliest year Mary and Phebe may have lived in Manhattan. I hadn't gotten far when I discovered a strange passage about a baby. "This is odd, Caitlin. Listen to this entry Martha made."

Thank God. The baby has a home. God, give her the love and security she needs with her adoptive parents, and watch over her beautiful birth mother.

"This could be Mary's descendant that Frances alluded to in the note you found in the desk." Caitlin's eyes widened.

"Maybe. I found baby Iantha."

"So, she could have been Mary's baby."

"Maybe. But I've discovered that Mary Rogers was a common name in the 1800s. That's one reason why the mystery has remained unsolved for all these years." I was midway through 1838 when I came across a significant entry. "This is it."

Caitlin looked at me. "What is?"

Augustus attended Louisa at Ann Lohman's clinic with her first pregnancy in 1839 when she miscarried, and Mary stayed with Louisa for a week.

"So, what?"

"Nothing, really. But the time frame fits with Mary's highly publicized disappearance. She never revealed her reason for being gone from Anderson's that week in 1839."

We returned to our reading.

"Another confirmed relationship." I read Caitlin the entry.

Mary's grief after Louisa's death drove her to despair, and John Anderson abandoned her in her hour of need.

"That's the nut! John Anderson."

"It has to be. Anderson was never the same after Mary's death. Guilt haunted him. He'd used Mary to grow his business. I was pretty sure he had deep feelings for her. Not deep enough to provide her the support she needed, though."

Caitlin shook her head.

I continued on, but Martha never mentioned the Rogers women again until April 1841, when her entries reported gossip from New York. According to Martha, Mary's mother wanted financial security, and Mary's marriage to someone of means was her only hope.

"That could just be women's gossip."

"I don't think so. Mary might have wanted it to be Anderson, but he was already married. Besides, Anderson worried more about his business and status in New York society than the women in his life. I read where his first wife, Mary Eisler, was shy. She withdrew from the New York City scene. Anderson responded by badmouthing her in public, suggesting she was from an inferior class. That tells you what kind of man he was."

Caitlin closed the diary she was reading. "He'd convinced himself that the women in his life would always be around for him."

"Yes. Anderson wanted the income that Mary's presence in his shop provided. If he publicly admitted his love for her, she could no longer flirt freely with his clientele. He'd lose income, his good standing in the business community, and his wife and children."

"What an idiot. In the end, he lost them all."

"Still, maybe Mary loved him, and in defiance, she accepted advances by the law clerk and other young men— patrons of Anderson's store."

"Mary toyed with the law clerk, Alfred Crommelin. What's the line on the cork cutter?"

"It was her job to flirt with Anderson's clientele. Her acceptance of Payne's proposal baffles me. Unless it was another ploy by Mary to make Anderson jealous."

"And Augustus?"

"I bet Mary loved him, but not in a romantic way. Augustus, Louisa, Frances, and Mary were close. Louisa had photos of them hanging out together. New York was a tough city back then. They probably provided each other with the emotional support needed to survive."

Martha's diaries made me appreciate Mary's last few months. Conflicted by love and burdened by responsibility, she needed a distraction, so she entertained herself with Daniel Payne. But Payne's behavior, bar hopping the entire week until Sunday and repeating the route on Monday, drinking at each tavern along the way, suggested he was irresponsible. He may have been clever, funny, or handsome, but he wasn't remarkable enough for historians to write about him.

Martha had made an entry in April after reading a letter from Phebe.

Mary confirmed her mother's greatest fears. She would marry the cork cutter with a family already in the womb.

Caitlin stared at me. "Martha suggested that Mary was pregnant in April of 1841. But she wasn't when they found her body."

"No. Either Phebe misspoke, Mary miscarried, or she had an abortion."

"The abortion theory?" Caitlin's eyes widened. "This is more proof."

"It appears so. This could mean a bonus after all."

Chapter Sixty-Six

Monday morning, I was in our library rereading one of the Wade diaries when my phone rang.

"We did it," announced the familiar voice of Carver's anonymous sponsor.

"Did what?"

"We saved the Griswold documents. Edith, a great-granddaughter of Frances Mather, wants to preserve the documents and has agreed to let you review them."

"Outstanding."

"It's all here. Photos, diaries, letters, deeds—everything."

"Wow!" I paced around the library. "When will I receive it all?"

He cleared his throat. "In the morning."

I gave him our street address before I disconnected, even though I suspected he already had it, and went back to reading the diary. It startled me when, for the second time in the last hour, my phone rang with *Shadow Client* scrolled across the display. "I've just left Bradley's office. He had a key from Frederick's envelope he forgot to give me. Apparently, he'd given it to Lillian, but after the hullabaloo, he insisted she return it to the trust. Her lawyer didn't argue. Alice, the housekeeper, returned it."

"Does he know what it opens?"

"No. That's still a mystery."

I had handled it at Lillian's. "Describe it."

"It's old. Heck, it's easier to send a photo. I'll call you back in an hour."

I went to my office and searched the Internet while I waited for the picture, remembering the bow being three rings. I found a similar key to a jewelry box on eBay.

Sam walked in as my phone signaled an incoming text. "Your boyfriend?"

"How'd you guess?" I laughed. "No, silly. Carver's sponsor has the key."

"The one Lillian mentioned but kept."

"Yes, but we don't know what it opens."

"Let me see it." Sam examined the photo. "No idea."

I turned my laptop around. "Check out this one."

Sam studied it for a minute. "That jewelry box looks familiar. In the photo album, I saw a box like it on the table next to Louisa. It's nineteenth century Victorian, walnut with parquetry inlay."

"You're a genius." I reached for Louisa's memory book and flipped to the page Sam had mentioned. Victorian knick-knacks cluttered the table. I snapped a photo and enlarged it on my laptop, allowing me to see more details of the room. Zooming in, I spotted the box. "That's it!"

"It matches the one on eBay."

"The key must open Louisa's jewelry box. Maybe the family still has it."

Sam rolled his eyes. "You're never going to find it."

"Oh, ye of little faith." I swatted his arm.

* * *

The sponsor was punctual. He called back precisely an hour later. "Any luck?"

"I think so." I relayed our eBay findings. "My husband, Sam, noticed a jewelry box like it in Louisa's album. Maybe a family member still has it."

"I'll call my partner. She's the one who remembered Louisa's album. She'd remember a jewelry box if there is one." The sponsor didn't waste time, calling back within five minutes. "I've left her a message to call me ASAP. You'll get the documents late tomorrow morning."

"Great. Thank you." At last, things were coming together. Maybe, hopefully, I would soon be able to close the file on this case.

Chapter Sixty-Seven

An unfamiliar Lincoln Town Car loaded with boxes slid in beside Sam's Jeep at close to noon the next day. I couldn't see the driver. I shouted to Sam, "The documents are here."

Sophie and I flew down the steps. I stopped short, recognizing the man behind the steering wheel. He wasn't only a well-known journalist, but also on the list of adjunct professors at Connecticut College. "William Pence!"

He grinned. "That's me. Carver and I have been friends for years."

Sam approached the car.

"Sam," I gushed, "Meet William Pence from *The Village Gazette*."

William climbed out of the car and shook Sam's hand.

"You're Carver's sponsor. The man behind the scenes, the shadow client."

"Not in the shadows anymore," Pence chuckled. "My car's packed with historical documents for you, Ms. Hunter."

"Unbelievable." My mouth hung open as I peered into the backseat.

"It is." He grinned. "The trunk's full, too. And you'll love this. My research partner, Edith, has the jewelry box. It was in an old trunk that belonged to her mother."

"In her attic." The vision of a dusty attic full of treasures filled my mind.

"Where else?"

We hauled the boxes into the library. Pence sauntered over to the arched fireplace and ran his hand across the oak mantle. "I'd never leave this room if I lived here."

"It's my favorite." A warm feeling washed over me. It was nice to finally feel safe in a library again.

Pence's phone beeped, announcing a text message. "Damn."

"Bad news?"

"Of a sort. It seems the Rittenhouse has no available rooms."

"You were planning to stay in town tonight?"

"Yes. I scheduled an interview tomorrow when I realized how close I'd be to Philly. I always stay at the Rittenhouse, but there's a convention in town. No rooms."

I looked at Sam and arched one eyebrow, an idea brewing. He nodded. "You're welcome to stay here. We have a guest room."

"I don't want to put you out."

Sam and I replied in unison. "It's our pleasure."

"If you insist. What a fabulous location. It beats the constant rumble of city traffic."

I resisted the urge to skip lunch and dive into the boxes. After driving four hours, Pence was probably hungry. "Grab your bags, and I'll fix some sandwiches. Let's eat before we begin rummaging."

Pence retreated to his car, returning with an overnight case. "Where should I put this?"

"Up the stairs in the foyer, turn right at the top. The last room on the right at the end of the hall is our current guest room. Lunch is ready whenever you are."

After a few minutes, Pence returned downstairs. His face was slightly ashen. "I hope you don't mind. I peeked into the office upstairs. This is going to sound strange, but I could have sworn the tulip glowed on the desk. And you won't believe—I saw a blurry image of a woman."

"Really." I tried not to smile.

He nodded. "The desk strongly resembles the one I marked in Louisa's album."

"It does. And I'm ninety-nine percent sure it's the same desk."

Pence swallowed. "No way."

I smiled. Pence didn't know the half of it.

"It was probably my imagination." He rubbed his eyes.

Jingshen. I shrugged. "Maybe not. I think there might be a story there."

"Let's delve into that story once you solve the New London case. It sounds intriguing. I'll follow up after I receive your final report on the remains." Pence's eyes were partially closed. "Do you know where the desk came from?"

"Hoboken, New Jersey." I glanced at Sam. This could get weird—ghosts and all. It was time to change the subject.

Sam cleared his throat. "I'm curious, Mr. Pence, are you related to Lillian?"

"A distant relative. Lillian's name has appeared repeatedly during my research. She's the widow of a well-known businessman who had suspected ties to the mob. I interviewed her for a piece I wrote for the *Times* after her husband died. Her fixation with the DAR, flaunting her

Mather heritage, didn't ring true. Something about her pinged my reporter instincts, so I did some digging. She inherited money when her husband died, but not enough to live like Batman in Gotham. I was determined to see how she managed."

"And you connected Mary Rogers with Lillian." I hadn't spotted an obvious link.

"Yes. I've dug around in the archives of New York for years. I suspected the body in Connecticut could be Mary since she wasn't listed in New York. I'd heard rumors of the Wade diaries, but never found them. That's where you and Claire came in. I figured one of you would discover them."

"Except Claire got chased off before she could. And Lillian located them at Murbeck."

Sam put his arm around me. "Take credit. You led her to Murbeck. Lillian would never have found them without you."

"I suppose. I have Martha's diary entry. Mary *was* pregnant before she died." I paused, then asked, "Did Lillian threaten you, too?"

Pence chuckled. "No. But when Claire dropped the case unexpectedly, I wondered why. I started poking around. One thing led to another, and I found Lillian listed as President and CEO of Empire Auditors. I wondered how she managed that."

"You knew all this, and yet hired Claire and I." I stared at him. Suddenly, I felt used.

Pence's neck reddened. "Frankly, I got stuck and needed help. Plus, I couldn't deal with Lillian. I knew she'd insert herself into the case. She's a grizzly bear when it comes to protecting the Mather name."

"And all this cloak and dagger stuff? Being a shadow client?" I laughed just saying it.

Taking a deep breath, Pence continued. "The truth is my mother was a Mather. And my research partner, Edith, is my sister. It was our mother's attic she was cleaning out."

"That explains why Professor Carver agreed to help with the Griswold documents."

Sam spoke up. "How do you feel about being a Mather, knowing Mary Rogers was one?"

"Proud." He answered without hesitation.

I stepped closer to the journalist. I wanted a good view of his reaction when I told him the next tidbit. "There's one more thing you might find interesting. I found Lillian's birth certificate, and she's not a Mather. Not by birth, or by adoption."

"No way!" Pence laughed so hard, I thought he might get a hernia.

Chapter Sixty-Eight

During lunch, I choked down half of a ham sandwich, a Coke, and a handful of M&M's. Sam and Pence had piled their plates high. I fidgeted, only partially listening to their conversation. The documents had been sitting in my library for over an hour.

Sam covered my hand to stifle my nervous tapping. "Okay, now you're making *me* nervous."

"Sorry."

Pence pushed back his chair. "I'm ready, and I can see you are, too."

"I'll deal with this." Sam picked up the dishes. "Go find your answers."

I stared at the mountain of boxes. "It's difficult to decide where to start."

"Try this." Pence dangled Frederick's envelope in front of my face. "I read it. I couldn't resist."

The writing matched the scroll from the puzzle box

signed by Frances Mather Griswold. "Lillian mentioned the letter, but she said it was nothing. A list of old artifacts."

Pence shrugged. "She lied."

Sam appeared in the doorway. "Who lied?"

"Lillian." Pence shook his head, handing me the note.

"No surprise. I'll read the letter aloud, if that's okay." I looked at the two men. They both nodded.

"May 24, 1846

To Whom It May Concern:

If you have come into the possession of this letter, you have followed a problematic path cloaked in lies.

The Presbyterian side of Mary Rogers' family did not want her death to cast aspersions upon them. Consequently, they used politics and diplomacy to turn Mary into a victim. As tragic as her death was, Mary was not altogether blameless. Her unconventional lifestyle contributed to her early demise.

The Mathers had another reason for concealing the events surrounding her death. You see, Mary's father was Daniel Rogers, and her half-sister, Bea Mather, was her mother.

Five years ago, from this day, Mary confided her condition to me. We consulted with Ann Lohman, who furnished Mary with potions to initiate an early delivery. Mrs. Lohman made no guarantees, and for good reason. After consuming the herbal remedy, Mary remained with child.

At a second conference with Mrs. Lohman, Mary inquired about surgical methods to relieve the situation. Upon Mary's request, Mrs. Lohman contacted Augustus

Mather, who'd worked with her in the past. However, he was unavailable and sent an inexperienced medical student in his stead.

On July 25, 1841, Alfred Crommelin and Archibald Padley escorted Mary to Nick Moore's Tavern, owned and operated by Fredrika Loss, a known associate of Ann Lohman. In a backroom procedure at the tavern, complications arose. Upon realizing the gravity of her situation, Mary requested that Padley fetch John Anderson. He arrived just in time to watch Mary take her last few breaths. The medical student could not stop her uterine hemorrhage.

After several weeks, I requested a meeting with John Anderson, Alfred Crommelin, and Archibald Padley to give witness to the lawyer, Frederick Mather, concerning Mary's death. Her grandmother, Phebe Rogers, and Phebe's sister, Mrs. Downing, were also in attendance.

Frederick Mather informed me that he had collaborated with the men and her grandmother to cover up Mary's condition, alleging protection of Mary's virtue. In truth, they wanted to protect their family names. From there, the lie spread to influential relatives of the Mather, Wait, and Rogers sides of the family.

The horrid disposal of Mary's body lies on the conscience of the Loss brothers and their desire to avoid prosecution for involvement in an illegal act. They planted some of Mary's clothes by the river to make it look like she had been attacked and killed by ruffians.

Due to her body's condition, the police decided to inter her without consulting family. Questions regarding identity caused the police to exhume her body. Finally, the police released her remains to Phebe for a proper burial based on Mary's wishes and unconventional beliefs.

I've prayed for Mary since her death.

. . .

I write this with God as my witness,
  Frances Mather Griswold

"I can't understand why Frances would hide a note if she'd already taken steps with a letter." Pence looked puzzled.

"Insurance. The Griswold family owned the desk. I'll bet Frances intended to give the desk to Mary's descendant." I slipped the letter into its envelope. "Mary died of an abortion, and her hoity-toity family members covered it up to protect their names and maintain their status in New York society."

"Sadly, a common practice. Look at the omissions from American history textbooks. If the history isn't pleasant, leave it out." Pence stared at the floor.

"You're right. And Mary's case is no different. Poor Frances didn't judge Mary by her life choices. She loved her and didn't want her remembered as the unfortunate Cigar Girl," I said. "I detected a special bond between the female cousins when I went through Louisa's album. Mary might have confided in them, told them Phebe didn't value her as a person and that John Anderson used her beauty for his gain."

"What about Frederick?" Sam asked. "He was complicit in the coverup as well."

"Yes, but Frederick picked up Elijah's mantle and had a change of heart. Honor overrode his concern for his own name, and honor compelled him to help Frances." Frederick's honor impressed me.

"Fredrika Loss's deathbed confession was true, but nobody believed her." Sam sighed.

Based on the era, I was pretty sure I knew why. "Loss was a woman. And her association with Ann Lohman damaged her credibility."

"The letter solves your mystery of Mary's death," Sam said. "What about the remains?"

"Yes. It provides a third corroborative source. But I still don't have enough evidence to prove the remains are Mary."

"You might have it." Pence lifted a journal from a Griswold box. "Mary kept a journal."

My eyes filled as I reached for the worn, leatherbound book tied closed with a blue satin ribbon. It smelled musty but I didn't care. I clutched it to my chest. "I'll read it later. May I keep these documents for a while?"

Pence patted my arm. "Of course, as long as you like. Once the family is done with them, the New York Historical Society has agreed to preserve them."

"Thanks, Mr. Pence. These documents will keep Rae out of trouble for a while." Sam smiled. "Let's retreat to the deck and let Rae take inventory."

"Great idea," Pence replied. "She doesn't need us for that."

They spent the rest of the afternoon on the deck, but I didn't mind. I was relieved to have the documents to myself. I opened one of the boxes and inhaled the scent of history.

* * *

In the morning before leaving, Pence slid an envelope across the table. "Your last payment."

"I can't accept it until I've positively identified the body and delivered the final report."

"I'm confident you'll complete the Mather family tree and identify the remains."

Pence's smug look confused me. "Are you saying that the answer is in Mary's diary?"

"I have no idea. You'll have to read it to find out," Pence replied. "Call me once you've finished the case so we can discuss a magazine article about the desk."

"I will." I wondered about his angle for a desk story. The link to my case, its provenance, or maybe the presence of a ghost. If it was the latter, I doubted his readers would believe him. Most people didn't believe in spirits.

I, however, had become a believer. And I suspected the particular spirit in question to be either Frances or Mary.

Chapter Sixty-Nine

After Pence's visit, I poured through the material, saving Mary's journal for last. I was rummaging through the box of the deeds and wills when Sam entered the library.

He frowned. "It's strange that Lillian didn't open that box."

I shrugged. "It is, but she didn't care about solving the case. Perhaps, she feared finding the birth record that revealed her actual lineage." Sam watched me cut a string and sort the deeds from the wills. "This could be it. It's a deed record filed by Frederick." I waved a yellowed document. Unfolding the paper, I read the title on the top of the page.

"Deed of Rogerene Burying Ground
Established in 1751 by John Rogers in New London,
Connecticut
Present and future admittance to this cemetery
requires proof of the Rogers bloodline."

. . .

"It says here that Frederick secured a lot in September 1841 for the daughter of Daniel Rogers, fourth generation descendant of James, the first Rogerene. And it's described using William Peck's grave as a reference." I pumped my fist. "Yes!"

"Mary was reinterred there." Sam's eyes sparkled.

"I'll be right back." I dashed upstairs to retrieve Carver's map of the known graves. Back in the library, I rolled it out. When I located the site on the deed and placed it over Carver's map, it fell a quarter of the way to the railroad berm outside the existing cemetery. I looked at Sam. "This section of the cemetery washed away, and it matches the plot description for an unknown female. It must be Mary."

"You're sure?" He arched an eyebrow.

Sam's look deflated me. "You're right. It isn't conclusive. I'm not finished."

"Read Mary's diary. Maybe she mentioned something. You're driving me crazy."

"Relax. I'm about to." I opened the journal, turning each page while Sam paced.

He stopped in front of me. "Well? Has she said anything yet?"

"You know my methods." I fluttered my eyelashes at him. "But in this case, I'll skip to her final entry. Maybe she confessed something there."

Sam kissed my forehead. "Go ahead."

I flipped to the last page and read it aloud. My voice shook. Still, I continued.

. . .

"I love John Anderson more than anything, but I cannot have him. He belongs to someone else.

I've been foolish and careless. I carry Daniel's child. Tomorrow, I will go to Fredrika Loss's tavern in Hoboken. Augustus has arranged to have me induced for early delivery. A medical student will perform the procedure.

Phebe raised me with a firm hand since birth. While my father and sister, Bea, were alive, they provided comfort and affection. When Bea died, I thought I'd died, too. When my father died, we fell into hard times. I did what I could to help provide, and I bore a baby girl for my efforts. She's with a good family.

I dearly loved Louisa, my best friend, who left me in despair with her death, and her sister, Frances, who has tried to fill Louisa's shoes.

My decision to end the pregnancy pains me deeply, but it is my choice. At Phebe's urging, I realize that I need to wed someone of more significant means than Daniel Payne. He cannot provide adequately for me, let alone my mother. And I certainly cannot enter into a different marriage arrangement pregnant or with a bastard child. If I do not survive the procedure, I hope Phebe will lay me to rest somewhere besides this city. A place where I can rest in peace."

"That's it." Sam put his arm around me, kissing the top of my head. "Case closed. You found your three confirmable primary sources."

I shrugged.

"You did. The DNA contained both Mather and Rogers markers. Frances's letter confirms Bea was Mary's mother, Daniel was her father, and there's a deed for the

Rogerene burial ground with a letter from Frederick securing a plot after Mary died."

"And Greg's facial recognition program had several photos of Mary that received a high score. Also not conclusive, but it provides supporting evidence."

"You have Mary's journal. Mrs. Downing's statement that Mary was buried with family. The student's estimates about the physical attributes of the remains. The match to your estimate of Mary's size based on photos in Louisa's album. And all the family trees you made." Sam waved his arms as he threw out more and more evidence.

I nodded, staring down at the journal entry.

"Admit it. You nailed it."

"I can make a strong argument that the remains are Mary Rogers, but I can't definitively say it's her." I sighed. "There could have been another New London woman, a Rogerene, the same size as Mary, with Mather and Rogers parents. There are still forty-four missing graves."

I read Mary's journal entry again, wiping a tear from my cheek. I hadn't found a solid connection between John Anderson and Ann Lohman. I thought if I could prove they knew each other, I'd have a stronger case for the abortion theory. Obviously, I didn't need that now. That said, it still bothered me to leave it unanswered.

Chapter Seventy

My rule was to never accept final payment until a report was finished. For two weeks, the envelope remained unopened on the kitchen counter. When I finally mailed Pence his copy, I slit the envelope and pulled out the check.

"Sam! Sam!" I ran toward his office. We collided in the foyer, and I handed him the check for two hundred and sixty thousand dollars, along with the enclosed note.

One-upmanship on Lillian's offer. Thank you, W. Pence

Sam whistled. "What did he owe?"

"Sixty thousand, plus a hundred thousand dollar bonus."

Sam wrapped his arms around me and whispered in my ear, "You more than earned it."

I called Pence. "Done. Your report should arrive

tomorrow afternoon. But, really, I can't accept that much extra money."

"I couldn't let Lillian's offer outdo my compensation," he laughed. "I'm glad you called. We opened the jewelry box. I'm sending you something."

"You've already paid me a huge bonus. I don't need anything else."

"It's a surprise. It should arrive tomorrow."

"Our packages will probably cross in transit." I smiled. I loved presents.

* * *

An overnight Priority Mail package from Pence arrived the next day. I slipped it into my sweatshirt pocket. For some reason, I wanted to open it at my desk.

Once seated, I slit the seal. As a small box wrapped in paper dropped onto the leather blotter, the tulip flickered. My hands began to shake.

Sam walked in. "You've got Pence's surprise."

"Yup." I examined the box. "It's jewelry, based on its size and shape." Calm spread through me as I unwrapped the paper around it. The tulip pulsed.

Sam's eyes widened. "The tulip just flickered."

"I know." I took in a breath. "And the air feels dense."

"I don't feel anything." He looked toward the window. A ray of sunlight had reached my window. "Probably the sun."

"Right. The sun." I nodded as I studied the tiny box. "It's an unusual shape, and it's leather."

"Let me see."

I handed it to Sam, and he sniffed it. "It's definitely old

leather. Vegetable tanning—gives it an easy-to-identify smell. No chemicals."

"Right." Sam knew his antiques. He rotated the box, chattering with each turn. "It's nineteenth century Victorian. Cool. First octagonal one I've seen that's made of burgundy leather." He handed it back to me.

I released the tiny latch and lifted the lid. "No way!"

"I hope it's not stolen." Sam leaned in, staring at the ring.

"Oh, Lord, no. It's Louisa's ring." My heart raced. The moment I slipped it on, I knew I'd found Mary and solved her mysterious death. The tulip flickered again, more brightly this time.

Sam looked toward the window. "Afternoon sun."

Or *Jingshen*. "It always warms the desk about this time."

"Ah." Sam looked puzzled.

I held up my hand, showing off the ring to Sam. "Pretty, isn't it?"

Sam went into appraiser mode. "Late Georgian engagement ring. Probably 1830s." I removed it from my finger and handed it to him again. "Hmm. Looks like a real diamond, rose gold band, and these small stones circling it are rubies or red spinel, not sure which," he explained. "If the stones are real, it's worth around a grand." He held it out to me.

I slipped it on. "Even if the gems are fake, it's priceless to me. I'm confident the remains are Mary, now. I've solved her case."

"You had doubts yesterday."

"I said there could be other explanations, but now I know I'm right. I feel it in my gut, Sam."

He shook his head. "You solved the case. Never mind your gut."

* * *

Getting the ring and thinking about Louisa reminded me of the sister desk in Keene. I looked up the phone number for The Colony House Inn. A woman answered. "How may I help you?"

"My name is RaeJean Hunter. I stayed at your inn several months ago."

"Right. The genealogist. I wondered if you'd call about the desk."

"Do you happen to know the provenance of your Van Boskerck piece?"

"I do. I looked it up after your visit. The auction house provided me with a document when I purchased it. Someone named Richard Griswold bought the desk for his wife in 1842. It was in the Griswold house in Connecticut until 2015 when the house sold. I'll send you a copy, if you want one."

"That won't be necessary. Thank you for your help."

After disconnecting, I patted the desk. The tulip flickered, but no apparition appeared. "You not only have a twin sister, but sisters owned both of you."

I gazed at the ring. Frances kept Louisa's ring after she died. Now, I had it. No one would believe this story.

Two sisters, two desks...

Jingshen.

Chapter Seventy-One

It took a year for Lillian's case to reach the courts. Mather LifeWays filed injunctions preventing Lillian from selling assets until after the trial. Lillian posted bail within twenty-four hours of her arrest, then moved to Clifton, New York, to live on a family farm with her house-keeper, Alice.

Cousin Rose received a light sentence for assisting in the crime, posing as a client buying chairs. The judge gave her a year's probation along with a hundred hours of community service.

Pence insisted we co-author an article about the desk. We argued over the title, but in the end, we settled on *The Desk from Hoboken*. He subsequently received recognition for his insights into the early women's movement.

Since Claire found the O'Reilly papers and signed an affidavit to support my conclusions, I shared a quarter of the bonus with her. She put it into Emma's college fund. Claire and I also collaborated together on a few inheritance cases. She accepted a case working with the FBI again. I declined.

Emma planned to enter Yale in September. She asked if

Claire or I influenced the admissions board, but we assured her that Yale accepted her on merit. She said she wants to be a forensic genealogist.

Connecticut College expanded its curriculum to include a major in archeology with an endowment from the Mather Trust. Pence and his sister convinced the Mather relatives the endowment was a noble use of a minuscule portion of their inheritance. Apparently, the trust had grown to ten digits under Murbeck's management. Austin Bradley signed the check as the trust manager.

And Sam, he kept me busy with antique shows and another bedroom remodel. Time had reduced my sorrowful moments. I'd probably always deal with melancholy, but it was no longer debilitating.

When summer arrived this year, I was eager to do things. So, Sam bought four tickets to a Phillies baseball game on a Friday night in August. Caitlin called earlier to let us know she and Greg were on their way.

My phone rang. Austin Bradley's name appeared on the screen. "Hey, what's up?"

"The judge accepted a forensic accountant's estimate. Lillian embezzled over five million dollars. The defense lawyer didn't bother to cross-examine. The jury deliberated for less than an hour and found her guilty. The woman had padded her silk pillow with Foundation money for more than twenty years. I never suspected millions."

"What will happen to her?" I no longer feared Lillian.

He cleared his throat. "The prosecution asked for life at a low-security facility in Danbury, Connecticut. They argued that Lillian deserved time behind bars."

"Wow." I wasn't enamored by Lillian, yet her age played on my conscience. Jail wouldn't erase what she did. Nothing could change history.

"Her lawyer argued that at her advanced age, prison confinement would be equivalent to a death sentence."

"Especially after the life of luxury she's lived thanks to Mather LifeWays," I added.

"The judge waived prison time. Alice, the housekeeper, petitioned the court to allow Lillian to remain with her in Clifton."

I laughed. "Lillian, living on a farm!"

Austin chuckled. "Hard to imagine, isn't it?"

"Almost as bad as prison for Lillian." I laughed again. I couldn't help it.

"He also awarded Mather LifeWays the proceeds from the sale of Lillian's New York and Connecticut properties."

"That should make a nice donation. When I researched Lillian, her real estate was worth about eight million dollars."

"Not too shabby." Austin paused, then said, "It's over, but I'm sure our paths will cross again. I look forward to working with you in the future." We disconnected.

I had to get ready for the ballgame. Grabbing my Phillies baseball cap, I tucked my mop of curls up underneath.

I glanced down at Sophie. "That ought to do it." She barked and ran to the door.

On my way to join Sam, I slipped into the nursery for the first time in a month. The bunny Sam bought still sat in the Boston rocker. I lifted it to my nose. It still smelled sterile, not the sweet scent of a newborn baby. I returned it to the chair, smiling. "Maybe soon."

Sam was in the kitchen waiting for Caitlin and Greg. I wrapped my arms around him, leaning my head on his chest. We'd moved to a higher level in our relationship. Plus, we'd agreed the time was right to try for a family again.

I told him about Lillian's sentence from the state. "The FBI case against her for kidnapping is still pending."

Sam shook his head. "What a crazy old woman. I almost feel sorry for her. Almost."

A car door slammed, announcing Greg and Caitlin's arrival.

It took a year to get enough information and courage to talk to Caitlin again about our father. I took the opportunity at the ballgame to explain the multiple DNA groupings I'd uncovered using Aileen O'Leary's DNA markers. One of the family clusters included Aileen, Caitlin, and myself. When I said we could be cousins or even half-siblings, Caitlin fell silent.

"Don't you want to find Dad?"

After a pregnant pause, she answered, "Let's watch the game."

* * *

On Labor Day, Sam and I sat sipping our wine, enjoying a warm day outside before the cooler autumn days hit. The air smelled fresh, and the edges of the maple leaves held a hint of red. Within a month, our yard would be brilliant with color.

"Any new projects?" Sam asked.

"I have an inheritance case that won't take more than a few days. Nothing fascinating." The case was definitely my strawberries. I'd hardly spoken the sentence when my cell phone rang.

"Is this RaeJean Hunter of Bloodline Forensics?"

"Yes."

"This is Officer McNally with the NYPD. We've found

a elderly woman's body in Central Park." He hesitated. "She had your business card in her purse."

A shiver ran down my spine. "You're kidding."

"And the dog sitting next to her must have been hers."

The pieces fell into place. "Eli," I said without thinking.

"Who's that?" the police officer asked.

"That's the dog's name. Eli. He's a Pembroke Welsh Corgi."

"Are you a relative or friend? Do you know her name?"

"No. I only met her once while I was in the city on business."

"Do you remember anything that might help us identify her?"

"We shared a bench near Seventy-Ninth Street. She made an offhand remark about Dorothy Arnold's route the day the woman disappeared in 1910."

"Was she related to this Dorothy Arnold?"

"She didn't know her natural parents. She was adopted out of New Zealand at age four. Nothing else comes to mind. It was a short conversation." I envisioned her hobbling off with Eli. The police officer gave me a number to call if I remembered anything else.

"What was that all about?" Sam asked.

"Remember the old woman with the corgi who joined me in Central Park while you talked with Valerie? The police found her body on a park bench. She still had my business card." As I patted Sophie, a sinking feeling washed over me. "What will happen to the dog?"

"He'll be sent to the pound. If nobody claims him or adopts him, he'll be euthanized."

I looked at Sam.

* * *

A week later, I sat at my desk with two corgis at my feet.

The police had identified the woman in Central Park as Jill Hamilton, a single woman who'd lived alone since her parents died. According to her obituary, Jill's maternal grandfather had practiced law at Murbeck. Her adopted father was a descendant of Alexander Hamilton.

As I opened my laptop to begin a new case, the tulip shimmered ever so slightly.

Author's Note

My fascination with genealogy began at least forty years ago when my mother received an original copy of her family tree dating back to the American Revolution prepared by Arthur Henry Bassett in 1922. Having listened to adult conversations as a child at family gatherings, I read names familiar to me, many of which appeared in the Antebellum period. The closer I looked at the document, the more excited I got. I had ancestors who fought in the American Revolution at Concord and Lexington.

What frustrated me about my family history was the conflicting stories. I needed a way to verify the relationships. To do this, I began to study the process used by genealogists to prove their work. I learned about diaries, letters, photographs, public records, and more.

This led me to collect stories about cold cases solved using genealogical methods and DNA. On April 10, 2018, the DNA Doe Project announced that it had used this method to positively identify a twenty-one-year-old woman, previously known only as the "Buckskin Girl," who had been found strangled in Ohio in 1981. It was the first time the public learned about a cold case solved with genetic genealogy.

My file has gotten thicker and thicker as more cases have been solved. So far, the oldest case dates back to 1956 when teen lovers in Great Falls, Montana, were found murdered. A breakthrough in technology using a single sperm cell, genetic genealogy, and the cooperation of the murderer's children, provided the evidence needed.

The announcement got me thinking, if a sixty-five-year-old case could be solved, how far back was it feasible using the current technology? This led me to research disappearances and mysterious deaths going back centuries. The Mary Rogers case caught my eye. The online articles, like my ancestral information, were full of conflicting information.

Edgar Allan Poe had tried to solve the case. I went to work collecting everything I could find about Mary.

During my efforts, I found that, besides Poe and the NYPD, four other detectives had attempted to solve the mystery as well.

1. In 1904, William M. Clemens, editor and journalist, proposed that Mary and a sailor friend were robbed and murdered at Fredrika Loss's tavern, and both bodies were thrown in the river. He based his theory on the discovery of a man's body (the sailor) found downstream a few days after Mary's body was recovered.

2. In the 1920s, Samuel Worthen theorized that Mary's abortion had been paid for by John Anderson. She died, and a tall, dark abortionist threw her body in the river.

3. In 1955, Irvine Wallace suggested three
   possible killers who could have arranged for the
   fatal abortion: Crommelin, Phebe Rogers, or
   Edgar Allan Poe.
4. In 1970, Raymond Paul concluded that Daniel
   Payne murdered Mary out of anger over her
   change of heart.

Although *The Desk from Hoboken* is based on extensive research and numerous field trips to actual locations, it is a work of fiction. All the present-day characters are creatures of my imagination. The locations in the story are real places. I visited all of them to verify my facts, except O'Leary's Publik House in Jersey City, and the Big Wong restaurant, and Gran Morsi in New York City.

The research techniques RaeJean Hunter uses to solve the mystery are based on information I acquired from reading *Forensic Genealogy*, co-authored by Colleen Fitzpatrick, PhD, and Andrew Yeiser, and *The Family Tree Problem Solver* by Marsha Hoffman Rising.

The Mary Rogers mystery has fascinated mystery buffs for two centuries and has been documented in a variety of books. I read *The Mysterious Death of Mary Rogers: Sex and Culture in Nineteenth Century New York* by Amy Gilman Srebnick, *The Beautiful Cigar Girl: Mary Rogers, Edgar Allan Poe, and The Invention of Murder* by Daniel Stashower, *The Crimes of Womanhood: Defining Femininity in a Court of Law* by A. Cheree Carlson, and the short story *Marie Roget* by Edgar Allan Poe.

In addition to those resources, I mined the Internet and read dozens of articles on the topic. As well as Poe's short story, a recent creative project was inspired by the case. Planned for 2020, a Borough of Manhattan Community

College production based on Mary's story was canceled due to COVID-19. It has been recorded and is available in a 4-part podcast on their website. (https://www.bmcc.cuny.edu/mary-rogers/).

All of the historic characters in the book existed (Mathers, Rogers, Wait (Waite), Wade, Griswold, Calkins, Gee). Iantha Rogers was an infant born in New York the year Mary turned fifteen, but I was unable to find evidence she was related to Mary, although her name appeared in the U.S. Presbyterian Church register above an entry listing the baptism of Mary Rogers, an adult. Mary and her mother, Phebe, moved to New York City between 1835 and 1839. The exact time is unknown. For simplicity purposes within my book, I settled on 1835.

I believe Mary Rogers was a young woman who was ahead of her time. Hampered by the limitations forced on her by society and the quality of medical care available to women, I believe she died from an abortion at age twenty-one. Had she lived, I imagine she would have married Daniel Payne, but she probably wouldn't have been satisfied. He was poor and an addict. For those reasons, their marriage would have been challenging at best. She sought independence, a dream held by many women.

Ann Lohman clearly believed women had the right to choose, or she wouldn't have freely provided information and methods for birth control. However, she remained in a minority. Public opinion after the Mary Rogers case forced Ann to go underground. Mary's case was used as an example to pass anti-abortion laws in New York. Ann's reputation was ruined during that period. Her final act, suicide, was a strong statement to the world that she understood the current political climate but was in control of her own destiny.

All of the documents used to "solve" the case are imaginary but are of the type a forensic genealogist would use. Obviously after 180 years, any intimate relations are speculative.

In truth, I haven't solved this historic cold case. But within this book, I've attempted to reimagine and piece together what might have happened. Like Poe's Detective Dupin, I've used RaeJean Hunter to investigate the mystery.

Have I gotten any closer to solving the case than others have? In reality, the only new information I uncovered was the baptism record of Iantha and Mary Rogers, and that may be an entirely different Mary Rogers, as I discovered there were at least fourteen women with the same name living in New York City during the same time period.

I doubt that the cause of Mary's death will ever be proven unequivocally. Time has erased the evidence needed for a forensic solution. But if the collective opinions of the experts mean anything, then Mary died from an abortion gone bad.

Acknowledgments

Thanks to my agent, Dawn Dowdle of Blue Ridge Literary Agency, LLC who brought me into the fold, held my hand as she queried publishers, and found me a publisher.

Thanks to my publisher, Harbor Lane Books, LLC, and their team who have helped me get my book ready to market.

Special thanks to my husband, Brian, who read *The Desk From Hoboken* several times in various stages of completion, even though it's not his kind of story, and gave me numerous suggestion that made the story better. In the end, he gave me his highest compliment of "pretty good."

In my early writing I couldn't have completed the book without my granddaughter, Emily Young, who was both a copyeditor and beta reader. She helped me sort through research documents and was probably the only other person besides myself that read the novel a kazillion times.

The novel would never have reached this level of completion without Sarah Branham, SBE Editorial, a developmental editor who took my rough draft and turned it into something that made sense.

Thanks also to the instructors Suzanne Frank, Carmen

Goldthwaite, Kay Honeyman, Keith Goodnight, and Amanda Arista of the SMU's Writer's Path who taught me about story structure, specifically the hero's journey.

And last but not least, my team of beta readers:

Joan Arnold
Gary Christenson
Diana Crane
Peggy Freeman
Karen Ford
William Humble
Jeffrey McClanahan
Janet Richards
Tex Thompson
Melissa Toliver
Mollie TeVrucht
Meridith Young

Thanks to the many unmentioned folks who helped bring *The Desk from Hoboken* through its the many steps in a writer's journey to reach publishing, then marketing.

About the Author

ML Condike has published short stories in anthologies that include *Strange & Sweet,* (2019), *Tall Tales and Timeless Stories,* (2022), *Malice in Dallas, Metroplex Mysteries, Volume 1* (2022), and won first place in the fifteenth annual Writer's Digest Popular Fiction Awards, Mystery/Crime category (2019), and 2nd Place in the Tennessee Williams Short Story Contest, Key West Art & Historical Society (2022).

She's an associate member of Mystery Writers of America Florida Chapter, Sisters in Crime National, Sisters in Crime North Dallas (Treasurer), Granbury Writers' Bloc, and Key West Writers Guild.

As the result of her study of genealogy for her debut

novel *The Desk from Hoboken*, she researched her own family and she discovered she had a direct bloodline to a Patriot. So, most recently she has been inducted into the Daughters of the American Revolution (DAR).

Website: https://mlcondike.com

Facebook: https://www.facebook.com/marylou.condike

Facebook Author: https://www.facebook.com/mlcondike

Instagram: https://www.instagram.com/mlcondike/

LinkedIn: https://www.linkedin.com/in/mary-lou-condike-b16117187/

About the Publisher

Harbor Lane Books, LLC is a US-based independent digital publisher of commercial fiction, non-fiction, and poetry.

Connect with Harbor Lane Books on their website www. harborlanebooks.com, TikTok, Instagram, Facebook, Twitter, and Pinterest @harborlanebooks.